Lookaway, Lookaway

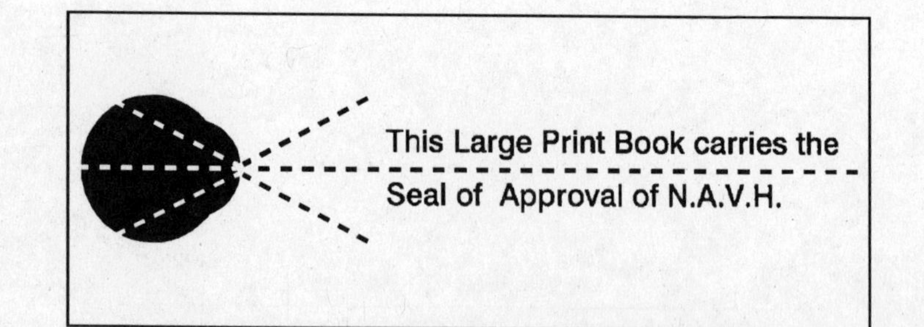
This Large Print Book carries the
Seal of Approval of N.A.V.H.

LOOKAWAY, LOOKAWAY

WILTON BARNHARDT

THORNDIKE PRESS
A part of Gale, Cengage Learning

Detroit • New York • San Francisco • New Haven, Conn • Waterville, Maine • London

Thorndike Press, a part of Gale, Cengage Learning.

Thorndike Press® Large Print Basic.
The text of this Large Print edition is unabridged.
Other aspects of the book may vary from the original edition.
Set in 16 pt. Plantin.

LIBRARY OF CONGRESS CATALOGING-IN-PUBLICATION DATA

Barnhardt, Wilton.
Lookaway, lookaway / by Wilton Barnhardt. — Large print edition.
pages ; cm. — (Thorndike Press large print basic)
ISBN 978-1-4104-6498-9 (hardcover) — ISBN 1-4104-6498-9 (hardcover) 1. Upper class—Fiction. 2. Dysfunctional families—Fiction. 3. Domestic fiction. 4. Large type books. I. Title.
PS3552.A6994L66 2013b
813'.54—dc23 2013036383

Published in 2014 by arrangement with St. Martin's Press, LLC

Printed in the United States of America
1 2 3 4 5 6 7 18 17 16 15 14

to Tom and Sandra McCormack,
children of the book

■ ■ ■ ■

Book 1
Scandal Averted

2003

■ ■ ■ ■

Jerilyn

There were only two white dresses that ever would matter, her mother said. The first of these was the Debutante Dress that Jerilyn would wear when she would take her father's arm and march across the stage in Raleigh, into the single spotlight, radiant, along with all the other debs in North Carolina.

As of last week, the suspense concerning that dress had been extinguished, when Jerilyn and her pals from Mecklenburg Country Day, Bethany and Mallory, besieged uptown formal shops to hunt down their quarry, capturing and releasing, debating, embracing, denouncing many white gowns before claiming the perfectly flattering one as their own. Jerilyn suffered an hour of agony as she prayed that her more assertive friends would not fall in love with the beautiful number on the mannequin near the cashier's station as she had. The crinkled taffeta, treated with some French-termed process, so smooth, like petting a puppy, had an internal corset, mermaid tail, subtle beading that sparkled opalescent around the slimming bodice, all blooming out upon layer upon layer of tulle, soft and dreamy. Wearing it would defy gravity; to walk into the light would be like floating in on a tulle cloud, something right out of an antebellum cotillion, which would please her father. He did his best to remain in that world before 1860: Duke Johnston, descendant of Civil War General Joseph E. Johnston.

Even though the debut was a year off, she had an impulse to take the gown with her to university, let it hang in her Chapel Hill closet so she might look in on it, stroke and adore it, have it as a beacon before her. But the gown was so wide at the bottom, and surely dorm room closets were tiny and who knows what could happen to it there, when it would be safe and sound right here at home.

The second white gown, the Bridal Gown, was thought of solemnly; it would involve years of decision-making. It was, really, a life's work. Jerilyn and her female contemporaries, having just graduated high school, had already put in reverent hours with scores of bridal magazines, begun the opinionated window-shopping, attended the society weddings like dress rehearsals for one's own event, notes mentally taken, good things memorized so they might be borrowed or varied, atrocities eschewed. The decision about that gown, mercifully, could wait some years hence.

When she'd brought up the issue of a show-stopper wedding dress with her mother, she was cautioned to whoa the horses. "You'll do something, I would hope, with your future Carolina degree," her mother reasoned. "Enjoy your independence. Work for a few years before you see which of the young men you met at Carolina seems destined for something besides his parents' basement. Or, given the atmosphere at Carolina, rehab."

Even though Jerilyn's mother was her hero — Jerene Jarvis Johnston, director of the Jarvis Trust for American Art at the Mint Museum, respected matriarch of one of Charlotte's first families — and her mother was almost, almost her best friend . . . her mother did not understand everything. Jerilyn would be very happy to find a husband quickly at Carolina and begin fomenting wedding plans no later than her senior year. She did not yearn to be part of a workplace, never failing to be somewhere for a set time in the morning, nor did she care to learn what it was to balance checkbooks and be frugal; she felt her life would be quite fine without those improving, self-revealing years of sacrifice starting at the bottom rung of something. She wanted (1) to be married in four years, (2) move soon into a beautiful home, (3) babies soon after. She longed to decorate her own new house, having her father and mother — who was an accomplished hostess without compare — over to their new home to see what she, Jerilyn, could offer as hospitality, how she could arrange a centerpiece and the Provençal floral tablecloth with the majolica place settings from Umbria she coveted at Nordstrom. See, Mom, how the tiger lily is picked up in the fleur-de-lys along the golden trim of the dinner plate and the scarlet mandala pattern on the Kashmiri linen napkins (on sale last week at Saks)?

And this desire led to Jerilyn's one upcoming act of proposed rebellion. She was going to rush a sorority. She had visited older friends at Carolina, girls content with life in the dormitory, study breaks at ten P.M., girls in sweatshirts gossiping and squealing in the hallways with bowls of microwaved popcorn, pop music blasting. Seemed nice. But it wouldn't get her where she wanted to go: before the eligible men of North Carolina, the next generation of doctors and lawyers and tycoons. Mother had forbidden sororities, because of expense and distraction, and provided lectures on how very different they had become "since her day." On some mornings, Jerilyn hoped that she might persuade her mother otherwise.

No, she quickly told herself on this particular morning — Jerilyn, get real. She would not change her mother's mind. Mrs. Johnston had never, since birth, changed her mind about anything. It had to be presented to her mother as a fait accompli. Even then, Jerilyn reflected in these last minutes in her childhood bedroom, her mother could scotch the whole enterprise, such were her powers' vast and immeasurable sweep. She'd probably call the chancellor or something, get the sorority disbanded nationally . . .

Jerilyn stood looking at the Debutante Dress hanging in her bedroom closet, along with the unwanted clothes not making the journey to Chapel Hill. She had packed three suitcases of clothes and another three boxes of accessories, the heaviest being her curling irons and blow-dryers and expensive hair care products. "You can open your own salon, sweetheart," her father said, as he packed the car. There was another suitcase — well, a small trunk — just for shoes, then her computer and stacks of school supplies . . . the BMW was full to the brim. No, the dress would not be going. She touched it a final time and respectfully shut the closet door.

She should feel more wistful and sad, shouldn't she? Here it was at long last, farewell to her childhood room, bye-bye to the stuffed animals (well, the pink panda Skip Baylor gave her for her birthday was headed to Chapel Hill, after all), bye-bye to the Justin Timberlake poster inside the closet door, her faded valentine and birthday cards taped to the vanity mirror, remnants of proms and parties, all of it girly and vaguely embarrassing. Nope, no sadness at all. She had waited and waited for this day — couldn't wait to get to Carolina and begin her life. She was the last of the four children, the "accident," no matter how they euphemized about it, a full ten years out from the other three, Bo, Annie, and Joshua. Her siblings doted on her, patted her head, thought she was a little pest or brat or doll, some entity at whom love could be directed but not quite fully human. She used to hate being the outlier youngest, but she reconciled to it. It meant being the baby, being spoiled a little.

She checked the vanity mirror one more time. Her stylist had convinced Jerilyn to cut her hair short in a nice rounded bob. Everyone loved it; they loved it so openly and insistently that she realized she must have looked quite dreadful beforehand with dull brown hair to her shoulders that never kept a shape, that fanned out and frizzed. She could grow it long but it was never shampoo-commercial long, gleaming silken tresses that coiled and released, forming waves of sheen. If she lolled her head like a model in a L'Oréal commercial, the hair moved in a piece — it was never silken tresses, it was shrubbery. So Jerilyn had given up that fond fantasy of luxurious hair, as well as a notion that she was a certain kind of beautiful. With the bob she was cute, not beautiful. Mind you, she could work with cute. Big eyes looking out from under bangs, very winning with a subtle suggestive smile, a natural shyness she intended to kill off as soon as she got to Chapel Hill, starting later this very day when her father would charmingly stall for time making small talk with her new roommate, launching into perfectly interesting but wholly irrelevant ruminations on North Carolina history, before kissing his little princess goodbye and driving back to Charlotte.

"Alma?" Jerilyn left her bedroom and called out from the upper-floor staircase. Their housekeeper was nowhere to be found. It would have been a special goodbye had Alma been there to receive it.

"Dad?" she called out. He wasn't back yet. He said he would take the BMW out to fill the gas tank for the two-hour journey ahead.

Mom wasn't fooling anybody. After breakfast she invented some small crisis at the museum, the site of her upcoming fundraiser. She hugged Jerilyn briefly and said they would talk this evening. Mom didn't do mush. Jerilyn knew that her mother was privately distressed to be losing the last of the four children; the nest was looking a little too empty that morning, so off she went to yell at the caterers. Jerilyn didn't mind. She admired her mother's complete lack of public sentimentality — she hoped to emulate it, one of these days.

So, she had the house to herself.

Jerilyn walked down the foyer steps of the two-story entrance hall, the grandest room in the house which, given her imminent departure, suddenly struck her as a feature she might well miss. The Johnston house dated from 1890, built by her great-grandfather (also Joseph Beauregard Johnston, like her father). It sat regally high on its hill on Providence Road for all to see, at the very entrance to the Myers Park neighborhood, the most monied enclave of Charlotte, North Carolina. Jerilyn had been told that the house used to be surrounded by acres of land that they had once owned but, through the decades, the property had been divided and sold for infusions of cash.

Given the neighboring piles of tacky turrets and mansard roofs, faux-antebellum columns and sentry gates bearing coats of arms, the Johnston compound appeared modest. It was part of the architect's genius — it advertised to the world an unassuming, comfortable two-story home from the outside, but it was spacious as any rambling mansion inside. Cushioned by ancient oak trees, the house sat back contentedly, hiding even its best feature, a large columned side porch, and its second best, a brick verandah and a perfectly enclosed backyard with its whisperings of a country estate: a small birdbath fountain that had not burbled since her childhood, a rose garden which needed much tending, and an arbor and trellis which needed none at all, dependably covered in wisteria or morning glories no matter the neglect. The upstairs of the house contained the six bedrooms. The downstairs had been featured once in *Southern Living* magazine: the long elegant dining room with the imitation Adam plasterwork on the ceiling, a kitchen large enough to provide hospitality to parties of a hundred or more, several beautifully realized sitting rooms — a classic American room, perfect for one of her mother's high teas; a blue French sitting room for solitude on gray afternoons, for reading and not being disturbed, avoided inexplicably by every male in the family; an off-to-the-side warren of parquet floors and custom cherrywood cabinetry that picked up a Frank Lloyd Wright flavor for the TV room and entertainment center.

The main attraction, of course, was her father's Civil War Study, which might have been directly swiped from the mid-nineteenth century. You had to take a small step down in order to enter it; Jerilyn imagined this small difference of elevation to be part of the magic spell that allowed you to leave the publicity and bustle of the rest of the house for the rarefied sense of the past. Like a carnival barker, Jerilyn had offered peeks to the neighborhood children, sometimes sneaking in illegally with her schoolmates — invariably boys — who would beg to take a closer look at the swords, dueling pistols, old maps of battle plans, engravings and parchments of the period, a cannonball. Every book on the Study's shelves was a first edition from the Civil War era (Dad kept his more modern history books upstairs in the bedroom). Prohibitions against entering, let alone touching anything, haunted all secret reconnaissance missions — and Alma, if she saw any signs of trespass, would tattle on her or any of her siblings, so all forays had to be timed for when Alma was out in the laundry room attached to the garage. Jerilyn loved to have an excuse to visit her father there amid the smell of pipe smoke, burnished leather, book mold, and the aromatic hickory wood in the fireplace; it smelled of an ever-welcoming past, of lost causes and unvanquished honor.

She heard her father's car in the driveway. So now it really was goodbye to the house. What do you know, she sniffed: one tear, after all.

■ ■ ■ ■

Nothing Could Be Finer

By Joshua Johnston

Your best introduction to Chapel Hill would be to make your way to the hill where the chapel used to be. Saunter into the Carolina Inn for a proper mint julep by the fireplace in the Crossroads Bar before going into the big overdone dining room. It looks like half a dozen plantation drawing rooms exploded in there. Chow down on an eight-course creole-Piedmont gastric blowout, before stumbling to the nearby corner of Franklin and Columbia Streets with all the bars. Try negotiating the balcony at Top of the Hill when Carolina beats Duke in basketball some Saturday night. The scene rivals something out of Ancient Rome, except with lots more vomiting.

This is, indeed, the top of the hill that had the chapel. Even before the university was established, in 1790, as the first state-funded university of the

United States,[1] locals had already given up on the local church. So it was knocked down so taverns and public houses could take their rightful place. We have our priorities here.

In 1980, *Playboy* magazine determined that the University of North Carolina at Chapel Hill led the nation in student alcoholism, followed by Ohio State and Alabama.[2] This was based on the high freshman-year flunk-out rate for which drink was to blame

Jerilyn stopped reading there and nervously began twisting her hair. She reached for her cell phone to call her brother.

"Josh. Thanks for the essay, but —"

"But nothing you can use? I mean, I wrote it when I was a senior but I don't think UNC has changed that much."

Jerilyn didn't want to sound ungrateful. "Who let you write a paper like this? It's so opinionated."

In Jerilyn's ENG 101 Rhet-Comp class all the students picked names of North Carolina towns out of a hat. She got Chapel Hill. "We're supposed to write a factual historical paper. I don't think Brandon would want us to write it like this."

"You get to call your instructor by his first

name? God, Chapel Hill. Whoa, a customer. Looking at the five-hundred-dollar silk ties, too."

"Go make a commission," she directed. Her brother with his two degrees from the University of North Carolina, for years now, working retail in an upscale men's clothing store. Jerilyn was hoping for a better future, but for the moment she was hoping, with the aid of an online encyclopedia, and by semi-plagiarizing her brother's old essay, to knock out her first comp assignment so she could be free and clear of any schoolwork by the weekend. She had to keep that totally open. You never know which of North Carolina's storied sorority houses might summon her to appear.

Jerilyn did not want to spend much more time in stately lonely-making McIver Residence Hall. Of course, her randomly assigned roommate, Becca, was really really nice. Jerilyn wondered if she'd hurt Becca's feelings when the subject of rushing sororities came up.

"Sounds sort of fun," Becca said. "Lots of free cookies, I guess. We can laugh at any of the houses that are too hoity-toity."

"Oh Becca . . . They say it's bad to go in pairs because they won't remember anything about you individually."

Jerilyn then said nothing about rush registration to Becca, so the date deadline for her to participate came and went. And what Jerilyn truly couldn't explain was that Becca was a jeans-and-T-shirt, dykey-haircut kind of girl, and sure, those kinds of casual sororities existed, but among the top powerhouse sororities, you showed up stylish and sharp . . . just not so sharp that it looked like you went to the store and bought the most expensive thing they had.

Jerilyn was recommitted as ever to Operation Sorority; her future husband was not to be found in McIver Residence Hall. But at this point in the secret plan, Jerilyn was losing sleep over her mother. Someone just saying the word "mother" caused her heart to race. The closer she got to her goal the more she feared the Wrath of Jerene (a well-established family concept). Maybe no sorority would take her, she thought darkly, and that would be that.

She liked the girls at Sigma Sigma Sigma; they had a Carrie Underwood CD playing the whole time in the background — Carrie was a TriSig made good. Jerilyn figured the social committee must have heard that CD repeat itself fifty times this week, which represented a seriousness of purpose. At Delta Delta Delta (on a repeat visit), Jerilyn politely enthused over the historical plates on display (God only knows how they famously partied without breaking the whole collection). If she got accepted there — which wasn't going to happen — she contemplated the long sophomore exile to the lesser TriDelt houses, probably three or four to a bunkroom in some lightless basement, something like where hostages were held, until one day, as a junior, as a senior, she would be summoned to the mother ship and the glorious upper rooms of the big white mansion with the wraparound porch. Bethany and Mallory, from Mecklenburg Country Day, were rushing these same houses; they were crossing their fingers that they'd all get an invitation to the monied Pi Beta Phi . . . but would one sorority accept three girls who had been to the same high school? Wouldn't some naysayer stand up at the meeting and say that they shouldn't accept a ready-made clique?

Oh dear God, she was wasting her time! What delusion, what folly! Jerilyn, get real! These elite sororities could smell her desperation, they could tell she was a party-girl fraud . . .

No, no, her best bet was to run, crawl, abase herself before her mom's house, Theta Kappa Theta, and hope for a legacy bid. She had a paper due but this was now or never! Her mind was made up . . . and this new plan had the added tactic of possibly pleasing her mother. Mother would be officially furious, of course, but she'd be a little proud too, just a tiny bit, and would probably relent and pay her dues for her. Oh God, there she was, stressing out about her mother again.

Jerilyn grabbed her handbag. She wore a sleeveless Carolina Blue linen dress, formfitting and flattering, Stuart Weitzman sandals. She would wow them at Theta Kappa Theta; she resignedly marched out to West Cameron Avenue. Soon Theta House rose into view, a brown-brick box with narrow horizontal upper windows which made the structure look like it was squinting. She glanced across the street at the legendary Sigma Kappa Nu and thought how much more grand their old mansion was, despite their torn-up front yard, repair trucks and construction cones. She saw a laughing band of girls emerge, happy, thrilled to be there . . .

Nope, Theta it is.

θKθ was a hyper-preppy sorority, retro add-a-beads and sweaters, men's dress shirts and khaki shorts for crazy casual wear, Italian wool hunter-green peacoats, pearls with little black dresses for evening events. Jerilyn breathed deeply and strode inside with false confidence for what was now the belated second visit. It looked like a furniture showroom, Jerilyn thought again, overstuffed with love seats and china cabinets full of plaques and trophies. Jerilyn was asked her name (and to spell it out) while a smiling older girl wrote it out in lovely penmanship on a peel-off name tag and gently affixed it between breast and shoulder. "Now we'll all get to know you,

Jerilyn," she chirped.

Margaret, a homeroom acquaintance from Mecklenburg Country Day, spotted her from the stairs and sped down to hug her. "I'm so excited you're here! I've talked you up to so many of our women . . . I didn't see you for the first part of rush and I thought about calling you which is dirty rushing and wrong wrong wrong, but . . . oh I know I shouldn't ask, but are you aiming for any other houses? Naughty me!"

"Well, of course, Theta's my mom's sorority, so this is my priority."

Margaret squealed and squeezed her arm.

"Though I had a good time at Alpha Delta Phi."

"Oh yeah, well, they're nice girls over there," said Margaret, powerless to berate them.

"I haven't been in Sigma Kappa Nu yet — been scared off by the mud, I guess."

"They've become the big drug-and-party sorority, you know," Margaret said with real sorrow, not able congenitally to savage anyone, even if they needed savaging. "It's sure not our style," she added.

Yep. That was the settled, empirical truth about unexciting, underdated, good-girl Jerilyn Johnston: being wild was simply not her style, not her scene. Two-beer maximum. Politeness and manners and good breeding, associating with the right people who did the right things — that was her summary, Young Ladyhood's Southern poster child, halfway to some law firm's partners' wives' charity's annual luncheon — non-alcoholic of course. She winced a bit as she sipped from her crystal punch cup; someone had put in way too much unsweetened citrus. Next thing she knew, there was a *tink-tink-tink* of a spoon against a teacup.

"If I could . . . Each even-numbered hour on the hour, we ladies at Theta Kappa Theta want to introduce ourselves to you and let you know what we're all about. Each of us, with the red name tags — you, the visitors, have the blue name tags — will be happy to tell you about life here at Cozy House. In truth, the house is named for our chapter's founder, Sarabeth Scarples Cosy, C-O-S-Y, but through the years we've just stopped fighting its being constantly misspelled and gone with Cozy House, C-O-Z-Y, because, you know . . . it IS cozy here." Hums of assents from the red-name-tagged girls. "This is a great house for you to pursue your dreams of being all that you can be. We have the highest grade point average at Carolina of any of the houses, male or female . . ." A slight pause for some of the red-name-tags to let out a mild whoop, some dry hand claps. ". . . and our sisters have gone on to so many impressive walks of life."

Jerilyn subtly abandoned the punch cup on

a windowsill, and sat on the arm of a sofa while the roll of the immortals was declaimed. The wife of the state attorney general, the assistant to the agricultural commissioner, the CEO of a Durham-based company that manufactures cruelty-free lipsticks. Plus, scads, just scads of prominent communications majors!

"But," the young woman was saying, "who really can give y'all the rundown is Mary Jean Krisp, who is our president, and oh so many more things."

Jerilyn saw, presumably, Mary Jean, with her immobile blond hair-helmet and foundation-heavy makeup, smiling to each corner of the large living room like a lighthouse beaming into every cranny of the coast. She wore a peach turtleneck whose collar nearly swallowed her chin — the old hide-the-double-chin trick, thought Jerilyn — and below that hung a small gold chain with a pendant with a gold Greek theta and a cross.

". . . during Greek Idol 2002, Mary Jean was named Most Talented Female Singer, and that's just . . . why, I'll read my durn notecard. President of the Panhellenic Council, junior Panhel delegate. The 2001 Theta Kappa Theta State Convention Delegate; 2001 National Convention Delegate, Rush Chairman, co-Chairman of the All-Greek Council, Chairman of the 2002 Homecoming Activities Committee, Director of the

Sorority Presidents' Council — I mean, I don't know how she does so much important work! — Assistant to the Student Representative on the Chancellor's Task Force on Greek Issues, an Adopt-a-Grandparent volunteer, a Big Little Sister, a volunteer at the Chapel Hill Animal Shelter, and . . . phew . . ." She playacted being winded. ". . . most importantly, the 2003 Outstanding Greek Woman for her work in the community and on campus. Here she is, Mary Jean Krisp!"

Mary Jean had been beaming to all her subjects, winking to someone she knew, rolling her eyes at some of the honors, little waves to someone special she just noticed, but now it was time to speak. After the mild applause subsided, she began.

"What does it mean to be Greek? I'll tell you what it means. It means we give a little more, work a little harder, and do a little more than our friends who favor a non-Greek lifestyle. Some people think of a sorority as a place to drink or where women go shopping together and, yes, well, we do that too!" Mild laughter. "But the real point of our being here is to raise ourselves to a higher plane. We are in a position, since we are banded together, to really really help some underprivileged people in this state — to make a difference. Girls whose mothers have made bad life choices: poverty, hopelessness, drugs. Sometimes their kids are lucky and they end up in foster care or in shelters but, even so, they must feel sometimes that nobody cares. But we at Theta Kappa Theta care, and our Little Sister program, which brings these girls out for a weekend here at Cozy House, is one of the most important things we do. I think of a little girl, a little black girl, named Tasha and . . ." Mary Jean looked away, a noble stare into the middle distance, then composed herself. ". . . I'm sorry, I just get a little emotional when I see how some girls have literally nothing in life and I think what good it does for them to see us, in school, on a positive path, with nice things to aspire to."

Jerilyn smiled at Margaret, but when Margaret looked away, she looked at her watch and mapped a path to the door. She could still stick her head in Sigma Kappa Nu by four P.M. and then get home and write her paper.

Old East, Old West, the Playmakers Theatre, and many other landmarks of campus were slave-built,[3] but there was some free-black labor as well, particularly where furniture and ornament remain (many of the original Thomas Day[4] pieces survive). In 1799 the debate club took up the proposition of "Ought slavery to be abolished in the United

States?" Starting Chapel Hill's long history of being a radical hotbed, the "yes" faction won the night.[5] But that was just a brief foray into abolitionism. UNC would not have been possible without slavery.

Chapel Hill never bought slaves outright, but they were in the business of leasing, trading and selling. All the young gentlemen at Chapel Hill were provided servants and they had to pay a fee to the university for their services that in turn went back to the slave-owners whose slaves were being loaned to UNC. You could expect $35 for your slave in a school-year contract.[6] Wealthier boys were always bringing their own personal slaves to campus, but they put a stop to that in 1845 – it cut in on UNC's slave-leasing enterprise.[7]

UNC owes its existence to something called the "escheat," which means that when someone died intestate or without a surviving heir, their property, including slaves, went to the university. UNC would auction off all the human property and thereby fund itself.[8] Funding the university with, say, a tax would likely fail before the historically cheapskate North Carolina voter, so the escheat remained in place. This is out of Kemp Battle's History of the University of North Carolina, 1776-1799, which shows how it worked:

> A free negro had a daughter, the slave of another. He [the free negro] bought her, and she then became the mother of a boy. The woman's father died without kin and intestate. His child and grandchild became the property of the university. They were ordered to be sold. This sounds hard, but it was proved to the board that they were in the lowest stage of poverty and degradation and that it would redound to their happiness to have a master. It must be remembered that slaves were considered to be as a rule in better condition than free negroes.[9]

That was probably the most-beloved president of our university soft-pedaling human trafficking for UNC's gain — and he wrote that as late as 1907.

There is no one, particularly local historians, who will say a word against this sanctified place.

Joey D had spent the morning rummaging through boxes in the basement of Zeta Pi house, even making a trip to the aluminum shed with the outdoor party items. He hadn't bothered to dress; he wore what he slept in, T-shirt and boxer shorts. Now he was attacking the boxes under the first-floor stairs. "Where's the damn slave auction stuff?" he finally yelled, within earshot of Frank.

"I think the last president threw that shit away," Frank said, hoping to discourage the search.

"How we gonna have a slave auction without the woolly wigs and the chains?"

Skip Baylor, sophomore, naturally pink faced and, when drunk or excited, an alarming lobster red, cried out, "Slave auction? Great!" Skip had heard about the slave auctions of other houses. You bid on a sorority sister, and if you won, you owned her, she had to do what you say! (At minimum, a hand job.) But it could be more exciting the other way around, when they bought you. Two or three Skank sisters making you take off your clothes and service them, and all you could say was *Yes, mistress,* and *Whatever you say, mistress.*

Indignantly hurling broken toys and props to the back of the under-the-stair space, Joey D muttered, "Spears and shields and all the African stuff, Frank. Shoe polish for the guy who goes all in."

"Listen good. We are not having a slave auction, and if we do, then we'll go with Romans and Toga Night and there'll be no racial element. That's the sort of thing that goes national, one Polaroid gets found by the local media and it's on CNN. Speaking of that. We need to all watch a video sent by the Zeta Pi alumni board, okay, Joey? Now's as good a time as any."

"I saw it last year."

"I honestly doubt that, since I got it today." Frank was determined not to be Southern-nice and passive before Joey D's mocking up-North assertiveness. Why did he come down South at all? With all the suspensions and flunkings-out from northern schools, what was he by now — twenty-four? Frank had heard about Colgate (an incident involving a blow-up sex doll and the steeple of Colgate Chapel) and then a graffiti incident at Brown (the red spray paint — ALPHAS ARE PUSSYS — did not wash off the white Vermont marble of the Hay Library evenly, and led to a sandblasting of the entire façade) and, unwelcome at the private academies, Joey D went next to Florida.

At Florida, as activities officer for the Zeta Pi chapter there, Joey D was the mastermind of Blob Night, which involved the importation of a giant parade-balloon-sized blob which was inflated alongside the pool. The object, Joey D explained, was to jump from the third-story window of the frat house and into the blob, which would propel whoever was sitting on the other side high into the air and, ostensibly, into the pool. Joey D demonstrated, sending his drunken, loose-as-a-ragdoll roommate up ten feet and down into the pool. Then Joey moved to the bounce position and another guy shot him up even higher where, in midair, he opened and chugged an entire Red Bull before hitting the water. Now that was the gold standard. Soon it became irresistible to see what would happen when Moose (320-pound rugby guy) jumped from the third story and bounced Micro (his name was Michael, but at five-two he was the smallest of the brothers). Micro sprawled upon the blob with a Red Bull in his hand, ready for launch; Moose tried to wedge himself out the window . . . what happened next varies from what you read about it online, but what was undeniable was that Moose hit the center of the blob rather than the operative side, which flung Micro the wrong direction two stories up, smack into the brick wall of the house; having broken his nose and his right pinky finger, he fell back on top of Moose, audibly breaking Moose's arm and breaking his jaw (with the still-clutched Red Bull can) . . . then they bounced together up and over the blob onto the pavement around the pool, with Moose landing wrong, breaking the arm in a second place, and Micro hitting the metal arm of a deck chair with his chin and, for all appearances, having broken his neck.

"It was like something out of a Road Runner cartoon," Joey D once explained, still amazed by the Newtonian physics of it.

Despite the groans and blood and abundant injury, no one called 911 but rather picked up and moved the boys inside to a couch until there would be a discussion about what would be done next, whether an ambulance was necessary, whether it might be best to make a discreet drop-off at an emergency room in Gainesville and quickly drive away. Which was the course of action decided upon and, later, punished by the university administration, getting the chapter on probation.

Frank might have thought Joey D had gotten the message, but later that night, over a kegger and Linkin Park blasting at high decibels until the police were called, he overheard Joey D sharing the Hell Night plans with Cory and Kevin: pledges have to walk up all the flights of stairs of Zipperhaus with a brick tied around their testicles — he read about that somewhere!

"Joey," Frank said, shadowing him, "I would appreciate being able to have a Hell Week where the imprint of our pledges' balls or spread ass cheeks are not emblazoned on my mind for eternity. Did you watch that video?"

The Zeta Pi home office annually sent out to the 126 houses around the country the same safety video, the video that warned of hazing rituals —

"Fuck all that," Joey D said. "It's time for Shelly! Shell-laaaayyyy."

The other guys were led by Skip, too drunk to enunciate but not too drunk to chant: "Shell-lay, Shell-lay, Shell-lay . . ."

Frank shook his head, so vigorously his beer spilled from the plastic cup he was holding. "Guys, I am sure Shelly is dead."

"Bullshit Shelly is dead!"

Alec chimed in: "She's in some meat aisle at Food Lion."

Alec's roommate Eric: "Yeah, when Jim graduated, that was it for Shelly. His dad wouldn't let us use her anymore."

Joey D was truly exercised. "No more Society of Ram and Ewe?" Pronounced *Rammin' You,* invariably. "Ladies, it's not Hell Week at Carolina without Shelly! We're not Zippermen without Shelly!"

The next morning, Frank rousted Joey D out of bed at ten A.M. Frank looked away as a naked Joey D with his morning erection hopped out of bed. "Eh? Say hi to Frank, Little Joey . . ." Frank by now had seen Joey D's penis more times than that of his own brother, with whom he shared a bedroom for sixteen years. More times than could be counted, he had seen Joey D grab his penis and squeeze the end so it looked like it was talking. Little Joey extolled the virtues of sexual congress with Maribelle McClintock, before bemoaning all the fags and pussies at Zeta Pi who didn't know how to conduct a Hell Week, concluding, "Hey Little Joey, big gay Frank is looking at you . . . Oh noooo, Big Joey . . . Thanks a lot, Frank, you made me lose my erection."

"I have to call the chapter and give my word that the committee watched their video. See you in the Dungeon in five, okay?"

The video, circa 1997, with dated hairstyles and goatees and one-day stubbles, was hosted by Kip Donnelly, some pretty boy who was on a three-season WB Network nighttime soap set in Orange County. Kip was a Kappa Sigma at USC and tried to be, you know, totally L.A. cool-like, talking seriously for a minute about Hell Weeks and misadventures with pledges. *So you see, guys,* he was saying, *I was a pledge once too . . .*

"The only pledge you ever made was to tongue my hole," yelled Joey D, now in his boxers, falling into a weather-beaten stuffed chair and popping a beer, 10:17 A.M. "He's got more makeup on than my alcoholic stepmom on her way to church!"

There is no initiation, said Kip, *worth risking someone's health or someone's life.*

Joey D: "I got your initiation right between my legs, Kippiepoo!"

Alcohol poisoning, Kip intoned, *is the number one Hell Week misadventure. Phi Kappa Tau at Rider University was not only ruined by criminal charges and lawsuits, but the dean of students had to face charges as well when a pledge died with .4 alcohol in his body. Many chapters get in trouble for forcing the pledges, who are not twenty-one years of age, to drink alcohol.*

"I know what you want to drink, Kippie — my steamin' cream!"

Frank: "Joey, shut up and listen, willya?"

A student at Indiana University, after drinking heavily during Hell Week, fell and fractured his skull and no one got him help for days. Kip reported that two days after being admitted to a hospital he passed into an irreversible coma and was taken off life support.

"Awww, Kip, Kip, look how sad you are: one less rod for you to suck!"

There have been alcohol-poisoning pledge-related hospitalizations in the last few years at the University of Illinois, Ohio State, the Univer-

sity of Nebraska. In between Kip's narrative, faded high school–era photos of the lost boys dissolved on and off the screen. Pledgemaster Joey D looked to the ceiling while the others on the pledge committee looked at Joey D; as each tragic occurrence was related, they checked to see if any of it registered. At Kip's own Kappa Sigma at USC, a pledge choking to death on the raw meat he was forced to eat. A frat at Stetson University shocking pledges with electrical devices. An Ohio State frat feeding their pledges nothing but salty snacks for days, locking them in a dark closet with nothing but plastic cups so they could collect their own urine if they were thirsty . . .

"That's freakin' brilliant," Joey D marveled.

"We're not doing anything remotely scatological this year," Frank announced. And since Joey D looked puzzled by the word, Frank clarified: "Nothing to do with piss or shit."

Grayson: "Or naked guys, or guys in wet underwear. That's just gay."

Skip: "No vomiting. We just have to clean it up."

Joey D stood up. He'd seen enough of the "anti-frat propaganda." He crushed the beer can, belched loudly and flung the can behind the TV set.

Later he pulled his fellow pledge committee members aside, Skip and Justin. There was a way to bring Shelly back from the dead.

■ ■ ■ ■

Lightning struck. The planets must have moved into single file. Surely all the zodiacal signs scurried into their right moons — or however that stuff worked. After Pref Night, Jerilyn had two matches: Theta Kappa Theta and, stupefyingly, Sigma Kappa Nu!

"Oh my God," screamed Becca as the slow opening of the bid envelope took place in the dorm room, Jerilyn scarcely able to complete the physical act with her shaking hands. "I mean, that's the wild one, right? Drugs, booze, and boys!"

"Well, my mom was in Theta . . ." But this little pretense of weighing her options was too exhausting to finish. Of course she would move heaven and earth to make herself agreeable to Sigma Kappa Nu. Phone calls to Bethany and Mallory revealed they were making their peace with their second and third choices, having to separate, not getting interest from the same house. They screamed in delight for her when she told them: "My God, Jerilyn Johnston is a Skank!" (Well, that's what even they called themselves at ΣKN, tongue in cheek.)

She knew the night would be a glorious celebration, and so, dead tired, dragged out from a week of death-by-shmoozing, she lay down for an afternoon nap. She skipped

ENG 101 yet again. But what a coup! She had only wanted to see inside Sigma Kappa Nu when she crossed the street from Theta. She was thinking of it like a Farewell Tour: here, Jerilyn, is where the future rich and powerful frolic, here is the place you'll never be . . . She stood before the ΣKN chapter house, three stories with a grand columned porch, azaleas and two giant magnolias, all menaced by a muddy construction project, the dug-up yard, and a terrible sewage smell.

"Don't run away!" It was Layla Throckmorton from Mecklenburg Country Day. Despite a long painful acquaintance, Jerilyn was still a little surprised super-popular Layla remembered her. "Hoo, I know it smells like manure every-damn-where. This work was supposed to be finished the first of August." Layla was threading a careful path on flagstones through red-clay mud to reach her. "I'm on the New Members Committee," she said, breathless. "Long story short — we all are this close to probation if we don't get our GPA up. And then I was looking out the front door and I saw you and I went, hold everything, maybe we can get our hands on Jerilyn Johnston, brainiac!"

Jerilyn had thought it was wrong, back in high school. Layla, a confident senior to her terrified junior, expected Jerilyn to just hand it over, their homework, last night's chemistry or social studies take-home. Jerilyn had castigated herself for how weak she was to let her cheat, someone who had it all, really, who was smart enough to study but didn't, just rode around in rich boys' sports cars and always dressed in casual designer-labeled clothes, oh and she always smelled so nice.

"Aw, I'm not that smart," Jerilyn said, "I just work twice as hard as the smart ones. At least in a house like Sigma Kappa Nu, you know at the end of all that work there is some serious playtime."

Layla gave Jerilyn a hand up to the porch, then looked at her intently. "I see our reputation precedes us. And Jeri, I just love the short hair!"

Jerilyn was led past the columned portico and inside toward the thumping bass of a hip-hop song. It was lovely inside . . . a little battered, but rich wood paneling in the front downstairs rooms, solid dark wood furniture upholstered in strong earthen colors, pastel hallways to living quarters and the kitchen . . . and then a step through a brief sheltered walkway between buildings to the dining hall, where the girls were gathered.

Jerilyn had floated light-headed through the whole process. She relived it all, every conversation, every successful attempt at wit . . . how had she done it? Adrenaline, poise, a lifetime of practice for just such an occasion: she had charmed and smiled, performed her light girlish laugh which had been declared attractive, and she cleverly managed to strew hints of her old-family connections. Jerilyn Jarvis Johnston, yes, a Johnston of Charlotte, some tenth cousin once removed of Joseph E. Johnston, the Civil War hero.

"Well," Jerilyn sang, "he surrendered North Carolina and the whole of the South to Mr. Sherman, officially sealing the Southern defeat, so less said about that the better!"

(Cue her infectious laugh.) Yes, daughter of Duke Johnston, the city councilman in Charlotte, Republican, for about six years, back in the 1980s. There was a baby photo of her being held aloft by her father at a victory rally; there were red campaign buttons and an autographed picture of Daddy standing beside President Reagan. And then there was her Uncle Gaston, Gaston Jarvis! He was even more famous, the bestselling author of *March Into a Southern Dawn,* all those Civil War romance and battle series that everyone reads. "Though," she added, "I've never finished one of them yet!" occasioning good-natured laughter.

"I've read all of them!" cried a gorgeous blonde named Tiffany. "You tell your uncle I should play Cordelia in the movie versions! I sometimes put the books down and give her speeches to my mirror — I am *so* obsessed!"

Squeals, some hugs, more laughter.

Jerilyn: "I'm hoping, since he's a gazillionaire, he'll kick in big for my debut next year."

Oh she'd done it. She'd dropped every clue of class and privilege and money, and made it seem like they pulled it out of her. It was, without compare, the greatest sustained social performance of her whole life. Of course, Layla would expect Jerilyn to do everyone's homework and get Layla's sorry lazy butt across the graduation line. Layla was a user, but Jerilyn was rolling up her sleeves and getting ready to use Sigma Kappa Nu as well.

She would turn the page on decorum-blighted Jerilyn Johnston. She knew that the PG-13 summer-movie sorority stereotype of the wild, hot girls, barely contained in clothes for all the suds and water that came their way, and the male-model-hot fraternity stud, beer in one hand, cell phone in the other, hooking up with the girls like a harem — she knew all that was a cartoon image of sorority life, but it was precisely the movie stereotype she was curious about; she now wanted to immerse herself in this too shallow pool. And if a frat brother was a cad, two-timing her with another sister, if there was face-slapping and tears and throwing herself into his frat brother roommate's arms . . . wasn't that all Life? Excitement, drama, action? For once, someone should say, *That Jerilyn Johnston! Back at Carolina, she was a wild one!* And everyone knows these frat boys eventually knuckle under, pass the bar, say yes to being in their dad's law firm, partner in eight years. God, it was all going according to plan!

Her chance to be Wild Jerilyn Johnston came up fast:

"Here's the thing, okay?" Layla had pulled Jerilyn aside after the pinning ceremony. "How life was back at MCD was one thing. How we live our adult lives here is another. I mean, you're gonna find out anyway about the cocaine, so I wanted to feel you out on the topic."

Jerilyn looked especially blank.

"Oh come upstairs, I'll show you."

Layla led Jerilyn to her room where two older girls awaited, Brittanie and Taylorr.

"Girls," said Layla, "this is my old friend from our private school I was telling you about, Jerilyn Johnston."

Jerilyn smiled and looked at what the girls were looking at, a table with a baggie of white powder, and a few lines of coke arranged on the polished cherry tabletop.

"You cannot keep the weight off without this, Jerilyn," Brittanie said with authority.

Taylorr: "Nope, won't happen."

Brittanie: "Look, it's not addictive, but it will spike that metabolism and let you have that extra ice-cream cone. The day I leave Sigma, I'll never touch it again."

"Me neither. Because by that time, I'll be engaged to future-governor-of-the-state Kevin Flaherty — or that's the big goddam master plan!" Taylorr added, shrieking with laughter.

Jerilyn cleared her throat. "I'm not sure if I . . ."

Layla put her arm around her. "Now Jeri, you don't have to do it, a lot of the girls don't —"

Taylorr coughed a disbelieving laugh.

"Tay-lerrrr," said Layla, exhaling a huff, shaking her head. "Okay, everyone does it, just not every night. Doesn't matter one way or the other, but you cannot *talk* about it. Your mom knows my mom. It just cannot get out into the Charlotte gossip universe. And you know Skip Baylor, right?"

"We went to the prom together."

"Oh that's right. Well, he's our source — he and that Benjy guy at Zeta Pi, with the white-boy dreadlocks." She rolled her eyes.

"Well, I'm not a gossip or a tattletale, Layla. You know that."

"I didn't say you were! But you see how you have to be so friggin' discreet."

Taylorr was snorting her line, followed by Brittanie.

Layla smiled down at Jerilyn. "You've done it before, haven't you?"

"Uh, well . . ." She'd smoked pot once, to no effect, no pills or coke or meth or anything else. Jerilyn had only been drunk a few times in her life, one of those times thanks to Skip Baylor at the prom. She once took a second codeine pill too close to the first pill, after her wisdom teeth were pulled — that was really something. "I'm more a booze and pills kinda girl," she announced.

The girls laughed. "Don't worry," said Brittanie, "we got plenty of that, too!"

"If I thought," Layla said, almost whispering, "that you weren't cool with this, and that you might tell someone, some family member, and it would work its way back to my mom, well . . . well, I couldn't see offering you a place here at Sigma, much as we're dear friends."

"Layla! Please, I would never tell my mom anything and I assume, no matter what I get up to, you would never, you would never tell my —"

"Hell no, of course not," she said. Jerilyn's readable terror of being thought untrustworthy prompted Layla to add, "Oh calm down. Skip said we had to take you, and though we never take orders from Zeta Pi . . ."

"If Skip and Benjy are happy," Taylorr chanted, "then we're happy!"

Layla was now kneeling before the table to take her line. She vacuumed the whole of it up her nose, pressed a nostril with a finger and waited a moment, a smile spreading on her face. "Aw that's good stuff," she murmured. Then she looked up at Jerilyn. The fourth line was cut for her.

Jerilyn bent down to the table. If she was

too goody-two-shoes to do it, then there were three blackballs right here in this room, Skip or no Skip. She sniffed too vigorously and it all went up her nostril in a clump. Then she was aware she was giggling too much as she stood, then sat, then sprawled on Layla's settee. "It is good stuff," she said to be agreeable.

And it was good stuff. Her heart raced a bit as she sat back on the bed but within moments she was giddy, uncontainable, a little breathless. She was going to be Sigma Kappa Nu, people! She belonged to the coolest party sorority on campus! And secondly, the issue of boys and figuring out ways to meet them, talk to them, attract them — that seemed about ninety percent solved. Tonight, a new life would begin on that front. Mom could just put those expectations of Jerilyn the Career Girl on the shelf with Annie being a society matron and Joshua marrying and having children and Bo being a lawyer and politician like Daddy. Her siblings broke free to do their own thing — why should she alone march to the family orders?

"You feeling all right, Jeri?" Layla checked on her.

"Why yes!" she said too eagerly, to everyone's amusement.

"Mellow out and enjoy," Taylorr advised, inhaling another line. These girls would show her how to live, Jerilyn decided. And do it in a size four, and at 110 pounds . . . Suddenly she had the inspiration that it was at last time to call her mother with this new assertiveness — this woman who stood in the way of so many pleasures and normal college experiences that awaited her. She had to deal with Mom sometime anyway. She popped off the bed and walked down the stairs to the little garden in back of Skankhouse.

And suddenly she was on her cell phone with her mother.

". . . I suppose, Mom, I wanted to let you know, not so much as asking permission but as a courtesy, information, information that may interest you —"

"Jerilyn, honey, what on earth are you talking about?"

"I have decided to be in a sorority, Mom. Sigma Kappa Nu. It's just who I am."

There was a pause.

"I know, Mom, like, you said it wasn't a good idea but I'm an adult now and I can make my own decisions concerning these things and I know it goes against your general principle that I should not have one bit of fun up here in Carolina where no one would talk to me if I just was a plain old student and —"

"My land, child, how much coffee did you drink today?"

Jerilyn realized how fast she was talking so she stopped, then couldn't remember what her thread of argument was.

"There is no money for this sort of thing, Jeriflower," her mother said calmly. "It's thousands of extra dollars. Dues, parties, trips to Tijuana or wherever the kids go for spring break these days. And then you have to have new clothes all the time, the most expensive this or that, or the girls will think you're poor. Well, we are poor, Jerilyn. We can cover it up well enough in Charlotte but our finances are very stretched."

"Well, whose fault is that?" Jerilyn exploded. "Why haven't you made Dad go back to work?"

Another pause. Somewhere, far back, there was a depth charge from the remotest areas of the brain saying nooooo that should not have been spoken, dial it back . . . what was her mother now saying?

"I very much do not appreciate you speaking of these matters so vulgarly. And should your father take up his law practice again, I assure you that it will be for reasons other than your wanting to waste thousands a semester inebriating yourself and abandoning your studies at Chapel Hill."

"You got to be in a sorority but I don't — that's how it works, I see. I rushed your house, Kappa Theta Kappa, by the way —"

"Theta Kappa Theta."

"That's what I said, and I told them my mom was an alumna, but . . . but they didn't invite me back," she lied. "Do you know what I accomplished here? Do you know how many rich girls from good families are in Sigma Kappa Nu — some of your friends' daughters like Layla Throckmorton and Corrine Hutchinson who is the president —"

"Stop talking so fast, Jeri; you're breaking up. The Sigma Kappa girls had morals that would shame a Babylonian in my day, and I suspect little has changed there. Their mothers were wild as hyenas, too. Maybe if you'd let me know you were attempting Theta, I could have made a phone call."

Jerilyn, in a crunching flash of self-doubt, thought of how she had kicked Theta to the curb, how she most assuredly would have been given a bid and a rubber-stamp vote for admission, whereas here . . . some of their pledges will be judged not good enough after the pledge period. Sigma Kappa Nu was famous for that, actually. Maybe they were discussing her inadequacy, up in Layla's room right now. And when it comes out she doesn't have the money to hang with the others, Jerilyn imagined the mock sympathy in Corrine's we'll-have-to-let-you-go speech.

"Sell one of the paintings!" Jerilyn cried out, the thought just finding itself on her tongue.

Another pause. "Sell off the family's legacy — your legacy — so you can get drunk at a sorority every weekend?"

"Skip Baylor is in the brother frat . . . what's it gonna seem like if I drop out because we have no money? It'll be all over Charlotte that you and Daddy couldn't afford to keep their daughter in a sorority." In her mother's renewed silence, Jerilyn hoped she had at last hit paydirt.

"Well, then it shall happily make its way around Charlotte that I thought turning you into an alcoholic and being a plaything of rich drunk boys, and watching your grades go down the pan, was not acceptable to me and your father and we would not pay for it."

"Okay then, like, as I said, I'm just letting you know what the case is, Mother, and I'm not so much asking permission. It's going to happen — they're voting in two weeks. I'll find a way to pay for it."

"I have no objection to your paying for it."

Wait . . . suddenly Brittanie and Taylorr, looking panicked, waving their arms, were in the garden with her, mouthing, *Who are you talking to?*

Jerilyn mouthed back, *My mom.*

Both girls' eyes filled with horror. *Get off! Hang up hang up!* they pantomimed.

Oh yes, she'd better hang up. But her mother was saying something: ". . . and do you remember the trouble we went to, sweetheart, for the SAT? The prep classes and the private tutor, that nice Mr. Catherwood, and how you took the test three times? You can do anything you want to academically, Jerilyn, but like your mother, you have to work for it and study; you have to put the time in. And we both know running around in a sorority and racking up a huge credit card debt and going to Tijuana —"

"It's Cancún, Mother — nobody goes to Tijuana."

"None of that is going to get you a good degree."

Her future ΣKN sisters were doing elaborate unvoiced screaming: *Get off the phone!!*

"Oh goodbye," she said, flustered, clicking the red button and hanging up on her mother for the first time in her life.

Brittanie and Taylorr were an immediate chorus: YOU NEVER call anyone on coke! God, she called her mother! Both girls were soon in hysterical laughter. Brittanie had to lower herself to the ground she was laughing so hard — her mom! Jerilyn called her mom! It would go down in legend: the girl who did her first line and immediately called her mother to fight! Soon Jerilyn was hysterically laughing too. Oh it felt good to laugh; it was like laughter took over every cell and flowed through her. And her mother would, of course, come around and help her achieve this dream. Already, in the few afternoons with these wonderful, fabulous girls, she had known the most joyful moments of her young life!

Jerilyn had heard that at most every other house, once you were on track toward being a new member (no one says "pledge" anymore), you were as good as in, barring catastrophe. But not Sigma Kappa Nu. Commonly, a few fell by the wayside. Already, in this year's group of thirty-six girls, a girl named Katrina had been caught out lying about her background, fabulating membership in Raleigh's Carolina Country Club. Like that couldn't be checked easily.

And then there was Cathyanne. She saw it with her own eyes. Cathyanne, who was sweet as can be, first had announced that she didn't judge about the drugs but they weren't for her. Strike one. Then at the Big Little Dinner (where Big sisters sat with new Little sisters), Cathyanne ate two desserts. Cathyanne wasn't fat but she was buxom and she'd worn this sleeveless top and had, okay, some flesh on the upper arms but she was shapely and fun and good-natured, and after Cathyanne left for the backyard with some of the sisters, Jerilyn saw Brittanie turn to some other girls and put a finger to her lips and blow out her cheeks, and then do the thumbs-down sign! She was too fat . . . or maybe was likely to be fat down the road. This was the sorority, after all, that got scornful national attention back in the early 1990s for making pledges stand on stools in the front yard, dressed in skimpy underwear, and marking them up with black Magic Markers, circling the "problem areas" during pledge period, prescribing weight loss or liposuction. Dear Cathyanne — she was so sweet!

And so here, right in the middle of pledge period, Jerilyn's sister Annie was in town to visit her. And Annie, gargantuan Annie, almost 250 pounds and heading toward 300! She had said she'd never seen the inside of a sorority house before — maybe she'd have to have a "look-see." Jerilyn had to stop this in its tracks! THAT'S your sister? Does your family all get fat? And then Brittanie would put her finger to her lips and do the blown-out-cheek thing and they'd all shake their heads and blackball Jerilyn when the time came . . .

Maybe she and her sister could go somewhere completely unfashionable and uncool where no ΣKN had ever set foot: the Sunshine Café (where old ladies and ancient townies went for lunch). As Jerilyn strolled down Franklin Street, shopping bags clutched to her side, purchases from her new credit card with a way-too-small limit, she was overcome with shame and repented of her disloyalty. For much of her life, she had craved Annie's attention and approval; their twelve-year age difference had only recently not seemed so unbridgeable. She brightened when she saw her older sister lodged in the backmost table; with a wave she sidled her way past the other Sunshine habitués, lifting her shopping boxes high.

"So Jerry, this is your favorite place?" They were not a kissy-huggy family.

"Haven't been in Chapel Hill long enough to know where my favorite is yet! I picked based on geography." Jerilyn could see that Annie, who could barely hear above the din sitting two feet from her, found this venue annoying. Jerilyn scooted her chair so she could see the door in the event any Sigma Kappa Nus ventured into the Sunshine by accident.

"What's good here?" Annie flipped the menu over for the desserts.

"Oh I've eaten."

Annie glanced over the top of the menu. "It's eleven twenty-five. Nobody's eaten yet."

Jerilyn patted one of her department store bags. "Trying to fit into a little number here for the parties. Cross your fingers."

"A sorority, huh? Can't say I'm pulling for you there."

"I know you're not pro-Greek, believe me. I promise not to go on and on about it." Jerilyn knew the price of the lunch would include at least one rant about fraternity-sorority racism, classism, the underlying social inadequacy apparent in people who needed ready-made sisters culled from a bunch of money-worshipping strangers, et cetera. But Annie held off. She ordered a tuna melt and fries, and could they bring a little cup of mayonnaise with the fries, please?

Jerilyn asked, "How's Chuck?"

Annie was blank for a moment. "Great. Hurricanes are good for business. Nature keeps knocking the houses down and Chuck keeps rebuilding. God-awful eyesores, too, up and down the Outer Banks."

Jerilyn knew it was tricky asking after her husband, although she wasn't quite sure why. Annie never wore a wedding ring. Annie retained her last name, Annie Johnston, even though "Annie Arbuthnot" would have been way cool. Annie never volunteered anything about Chuck. Maybe they had a very open, wide-open kind of marriage, or . . . well, Jerilyn had lots of theories, including that the marriage was Annie's third mistake in a row and divorce was imminent. Over the last few years Annie would descend upon Charlotte for family occasions without Chuck, making excuses for his not being there, always trapped by some construction project down on the coast.

And then a silence. The tuna melt arrived and Annie devoured it all with amazing speed. Jerilyn stole a fry. What to say next? Truth be told, there wasn't much of a real sisterly track record here. Jerilyn reflected that this was, after all, a first undiluted meeting for the two sisters, Annie and Jerilyn Johnston, no filtering parents, no accompanying brothers.

"How's your end of the business?" Jerilyn asked.

"Boom times. Commissions galore but the real money will be when I buy some of these undervalued homes and fix them up. I'll be a landlord capitalist businesswoman — some adjectives you never thought you'd hear in front of my name."

Silence again. She and Annie would never be friends had they not been in the same family. Jerilyn was clothes and hair and girlie stuff, she was pop radio and watching the tween shows on the Disney Channel even though she had long aged out of the target audience, she loved fashion mags and the Harry Potter books were about the only novels she had ever finished, she had few political ideas whatsoever, while Annie . . . well, Jerilyn couldn't begin to imagine what Annie listened to on her iPod (lots of foreign women singers, howling in African or Slavic languages) or if she even watched any TV; there were all manner of save-the-earth blogs that Annie was always linking her by e-mail. Annie was in perpetual war with Mom and Dad, while Jerilyn, until recently, had done her best to obey and please, usually with tangible rewards. And men. There was the real Grand Canyon. By the age of thirty, Annie had been married and annulled, married and divorced, and now was married again to laconic macho-man Chuck Arbuthnot, who seemed the mismatch of the century. Jerilyn had limited experience in any sexual direction, not counting some pants-off touching and experimenting with Skip Baylor at his family's Lake Norman house last summer.

"You know," Jerilyn began, brightening. "You ought to let me take you shopping sometime."

"Jeri, there's not one thing in the overpriced boutiques you patronize that would fit around my arm."

"Well now, if you're going to take people into luxury homes all afternoon with your real estate license you can't look like . . ."

Annie smiled, patting her belly, her sweatshirt and stretch jeans. "This is my casual wear. I fix up for clients."

"Yeah, but I mean dressed to the nines, dressed to impress."

"My God, Mom did a great job on you."

"No, c'mon, you know you have to have some sharp business suits and things that feel loose and good on you. Expensive things to prove to your clients you've gotten rich off your brilliant ability to place people in homes. And admit it, you don't have a lick of taste where clothes are concerned, and I do." It was the most courageous assertion she'd ever made to Annie.

Annie squinted at her suspiciously, before the smile returned. "Hm. In the interest of financial success and independence, I'll take a rain check on . . . that Armageddon. Me in a clothing store."

"I'll hold you to it."

"Clothes sure look good on you," Annie said, eyeing Jerilyn sip her ice water with a lemon wedge. "You're a cheap date, sis. Promise me you're not going to be bulimic like every sorority bimbo in town."

"I would never —"

"Oh yes you would, don't bullshit your big sister. Let's face it. The Johnston women come in two varieties. Matronly: me and Aunt Dillie and Grandma. Thin and stately: you and Mom. I believe you're not sticking your finger down your throat only because I've never seen you or Mom give the least thought to what you ate. In fact, I can barely remember ever seeing Mom eat. She stirs stuff around on the plate and lets the waiter take it away. She's an alien life-form with no normal human desires."

What would Annie do without Mom to rail against, Jerilyn thought. "Speaking of Mom."

"Yes?"

"So far there's been no thaw about her helping me pay for the sorority dues. I hate that she pretends we're poor."

Annie met her gaze quite seriously. "You

may not have gotten the memo, but as a family we really are flat broke." Annie cocked her head, giving this small rebellion the benefit of her lifetime of military wisdom. "I'd try to work around her and go to Dad. He might sell off a Civil War pistol or something. Then, failing that, hit up Uncle Gaston."

"To be honest, I'm scared of him."

"Tell him there'll be lots of drinking and partying and Mom doesn't approve. He'll probably send up a Brink's truck right away."

Jerilyn watched Annie brace herself on the table and push up from the chair. Once on her feet, Annie was active and so dynamic that her weight didn't register, but in the transitions, getting up from the table, compacting herself into the car, Jerilyn often found some distant object to focus upon. What a success this lunch had been, after all! They had actually started something here, something to build upon. Jerilyn gathered up her shopping bags and felt like she might float back to McIver Hall . . . when at the front, just where Annie was heading to pay the bill, was that . . . were they . . . My God, three green T-shirts blazoned with ΣKN? How could . . . oh yes, they do no-fat yogurt smoothies to go, very dietetic. She should have seen that coming!

"I've got to use the restroom!" she blurted and set her shopping bags back down on the table. She hid in the bathroom stall for another ten minutes until, surely, that smoothie had been made and purchased and the Sigma Kappa Nu girls were all out window-shopping on Franklin. She sat there long enough that she heard the women's room door open and close several times, once with Annie leaning in: "Jeri, are you all right in there?"

"I'm fine, really!"

"You're not abusing laxatives, are you?"

"Annie, ssssh! I'm fine. Time of the month."

Annie pleaded that she had to get going back to the coast, but she'd paid the bill and she promised to come again, real soon. She brought Jerilyn's shopping bags and set them inside the door of the ladies' room. And Jerilyn felt terrible about the expedient goodbye, but Annie being gone was a relief and if the Sunshine Café was full of Sigma Kappa Nus, it didn't matter now.

Justin drove his Lexus convertible back to Durham and pretty-pleased his mom into lending him her Suburban van for one night. Then he swung by Zeta Pi to pick up Skip and Joey D for the mission to Raleigh, twenty miles away by interstate.

"Shouldn't we put down newspapers or something?" Skip asked.

Justin, amazingly, hadn't considered this pitfall when borrowing his mom's prize possession. "Oh yeah, we need like a tarp, in the event she shits all over the place."

Joey D overruled them all: "Home Depot's closed. My cousin, the poor bastard, is waiting for us. If there's a mess we'll clean it the-fuck up."

Justin knew that meant that he alone would clean it up.

"Why is he a poor bastard?" Skip followed.

Joey D checked his watch, and sank back exhausted into his seat. "Because he goes to NC State, that's why. NC State is thirty thousand farmhands who wanted to attain the . . . the heights of Chapel Hill but had to settle for Cow College U instead. I can already smell the stink. You can major in Manure Science at State, you know."

Skip yawned. "I have a hot cousin in the Design School at State."

Joey D: "Poor her, having nothing but Dungeons and Dragons losers to date! When she brings back someone named Rajeev or Abdul for Christmas dinner, remember I told you so."

Justin sometimes secretly wished he had gone to NC State or Appalachian State. "Joey, Zeta Pi has a chapter at State —"

"They don't do Greek at State! They don't understand what the Greek lifestyle is all about — they're too busy losing at all the major sports and shoveling manure from one half of the campus to the other. Da only party is a Tar Heel party, or maybe you should transfer down to Zeta 'Cow Pi' and play Tony Hawk 3 with Rajeev and Abdul every Saturday night, while the hottest got-it-goin'-on, sorostitute shawtys in the South work my joystick in the BJ Room! Do you think there's a Blow Job Room anywhere on State? Hell no, 'cause no one's ever had a blow job or sex of ANY KIND at State. Oh I dunno, maybe some cow or pig starts nuzzling another animal's crotch — but that's as close as it fuckin' gets!"

Silence for a minute before the contrarian Skip offered, "The pot is better at State, and cheaper. All those horticulture students. Hydroponic stuff, grown in the dorms."

Tonight Sigma Kappa Nu was visiting those hellcat Zippermen, the Zeta Pis. Yes, it was Hell Week over there and the pledges would be enduring some unspeakable stunt. Jerilyn heard that last year at Zeta Pi, the boys had to parade naked through the party in something called "the Elephant Walk." One guy reached between the legs of the guy in front and grabbed his penis, and with the other hand put a finger up his behind. Then they had to walk in a chain like that around the outside of the house, through all the rooms — with all the sisters providing shrieking commentary and trashtalk — and then up the stairs. If anyone lost their grip, the whole group had to start over! That was their grand finale of Hell Week. Jerilyn hoped they wouldn't do anything like that; she would be embarrassed for them. She tried to imagine Skip Baylor, her slightly stiff prom date, doing that and she couldn't . . . yet he pledged last year, so he must have.

And the older girls were cooking up something involving nudity, no doubt, for the Sigma pledges too. The Tri-Delts had done a nude run through the library (with all the frats tipped off, in order to line the parade route and make catcalls) so the Sigmas had to top that.

Jerilyn was shy but she had resigned herself to public nudity — it came with the territory with pledge stunts, and she didn't think she looked so bad. She just wanted to make sure it wasn't videotaped, and of course, wouldn't you know, that was the very nature of what was being talked about.

The pledge director, Marlie, laid out a potential plan: "It's called SororitySleaze.com. They pay ten thousand dollars — ten K — for amateur girl-on-girl action. If we made and sent in, say, three videos and they accepted them, that would be thirty thousand dollars! That would get the whole house to Ocho Rios, right?"

There was affirmative squealing — oh my God — Jamaica!

"Uh, aren't you worried," one pledge asked timidly, "that my — your dad or brothers will see these things?"

"Ten thousand dollars — you're not listening. All the new pledges just have to do it! You're out if you don't help us get this cash! In these scenes, everyone sits around a dorm room or the sorority living room and everyone's bored and horny . . ."

Parker: "Just like real life!"

"Yeah, and so someone says they're, like, so horny they could do a girl and the other girls go oooh gross, but then one by one they start kissing, then playing truth or dare . . ."

Kidge: "They should have seen my junior-high slumber parties. They'd be writing me a check for ten million."

"Shit, why do the pledges get to have all the fun?" said Brittanie, leaning in too close to Marlie, flicking her tongue as if she might commence girl-on-girl action right here.

Jerilyn remembered some materials they handed out at the registration for rush; it clearly stated that if any of the initiation activities made you uncomfortable or violated your sense of right and wrong, then you were to tell the house president about it, and if you didn't get satisfaction, then you could approach someone on the Pan-Hellenic Council, but if you went that far to rat them out, surely it would compromise your being accepted. Jerilyn exhaled heavily: get real, she told herself, you'd be finished . . . or they might have to let you in, but never include you in things, never really befriend you.

She would have a private word with Corinne, their chapter president.

Joey D's many-times-removed cousin Ryan met them at the Sheep Research Center and hopped into the back of the van, directing them to a parking place near the animal pens. Ryan was a thickset country boy, dark gold frizzy hair stuffed under a farmer's cap; he scratched continually at his goatee, smoothing the beard to a point. Ryan led Joey D, Skip, and Justin to a low-lying brick building with classrooms on the first floor, and animal pens in the basement.

"Hold it," Ryan said on the stairs, fairly certain any involvement with his cousin was trouble. "We'll go in the stall, you can take your pictures, and then we got to go."

Skip said, "Yeah, we really appreciate it."

Justin tried to assure Ryan that they weren't going to do anything weird with the sheep, just a photo.

Ryan: "I don't need or want to know what you're doing — I can imagine."

Joey D: "Oh yeah, cuz? Just what is it you can imagine?"

"Some frat boy shit. You pretending to screw the sheep or something for some dumb initiation."

Joey D was getting hot, but he couldn't

blow the arrangement this close to completion.

"Heck," Ryan went on, "I'd do the sheep before some of y'all's sorority girls. Probably far fewer venereal diseases."

"Just let us see the sheep," Joey D said, barely audible.

Ryan used his key to open the basement door between the stairway and the sheep pens. There was a clean hallway with twelve sheep pens in a row against one wall. Third one down was Ryan's pen; a clipboard chart was hung on a hook showing feedings and shearings. A removable cardstock label declared this was the pen of FURBALL.

Ryan: "Now take your picture and then get gone. We're already breaking a hundred rules being here."

Joey D now saw the difficulty of escaping with Furball. "Uh, could you give us some privacy?"

Ryan stared at them. "You really gonna screw my sheep?"

Skip Baylor cleared his throat. "It's supposed to be an embarrassing photo. Like you said, a fraternity initiation stunt. You know, our mascot at Carolina is Rameses, a big, um, sheep."

Ryan mumbled, "Your mascot is a horned Dorset, this is a polled Dorset. Does that matter?"

"Sheep's a fucking sheep," said Joey D. "No

offense."

Ryan frowned, then turned and walked to the stairwell . . . before turning back. "But none of y'all are pledges. So who exactly is being initiated?"

Joey D smiled. "Skip here. He was sick last year when he pledged so we don't want anybody missing out on the sheep-photo fun."

Ryan frowned again. "Furball is my — and about five other people's — senior project, Joseph. Nothing better happen to her or I can promise you a righteous shitstorm of biblical retribution. Can't y'all just drink each other's piss or spank each other in wet underwear or the usual stuff?"

Skip and Justin hunkered down, waiting for the explosive Joey D response, but their Northern brother remained all smiles. "If you just give us ten minutes or so, Ryan. C'mon Skip, down with the pants . . ."

Ryan crossed his arms. Skip, smiling weakly, began to undo his belt.

"What?" Joey D asked his cousin. "You wanna see him in his underwear?"

Ryan narrowed his eyes to a squint then left them to it. "I'll be back in ten minutes," he mumbled. "Try not to give my sheep genital herpes."

After Ryan was out of earshot, Skip whispered, "We're never going to get her out of here —"

"We'll take her out that door. Grab her by the collar." Joey D headed to the emergency exit, which promised loud fire alarms if opened.

Justin pushed and Skip pulled on the collar, but Furball wasn't budging.

Joey D told Justin to run back to the parking lot and bring the van around to the emergency door; if he sees Ryan tell him, Joey said, "that you need some fresh air."

Skip had an idea. He got a handful of the green feed pellets from the pen's trough and tried to lure Furball toward the emergency door. Furball happily ate what was held out to her. "It tickles," Skip giggled, as Furball grazed from his palm. "I wish you could get a picture of this! Joey, look! She's eating from my hand!"

"Yeah, it's an Animal Planet moment right there — look, I'm all teary."

Joey D's cell phone rang; it was Ryan. "Y'all about done with your unnatural acts?"

"Two more pictures, thanks!" Joey D sang out, while thrusting his middle finger at the phone.

"I don't wanna be washing y'all's bodily fluids out of the wool tomorrow."

"Hey Ryan, fuck you, you know? I ask for a simple favor, cousin to cousin —"

"Yeah, like that simple favor I asked for, that I come over to Chapel Hill for one little party? And you told me — what was it? —

the girls would smell the barnyard on me."

"Hey, cuz, that's true, isn't it?" He hung up on Ryan.

There was the honk of the Suburban from outside. Furball started bleating, barely allowing herself to be dragged, trotters skittering on the smooth industrial floor. They came to the emergency door with its dire red warnings. Joey with one hand banged the emergency exit panel and held Furball's collar tight with the other. *Whoop-whoop-whoop-whoop . . .* Now that's a really loud alarm, Skip thought.

"All right," Joey D cried out, wrestling with the back half of the animal, "you bag of sheepshit, you're coming to a party in Chapel Hill, okay? That's a good girl . . ."

Justin jumped down from the driver's seat to help, his mom's van idling in position with its tailgate down, ready for loading. "I scraped the exhaust pipe," he whined, rubbing the scratch with a licked finger. "I backed it up over the curb onto the sidewalk here — oh shit, you can really see this scrape. What is my mom gonna say?"

Joey D screamed in profanities violent and volcanic that Justin and Skip should participate more helpfully in getting the sheep into the back of the van.

Ryan arrived in time to see the emergency door ajar to the outside; he staggered back to the pen . . . no Furball. He ran through the emergency door in time to observe the van, tires spinning in the grass, pull away, divotting up mud, and speeding directly into a metal pole atop which was a purple martin birdhouse. The pole swayed and the birdhouse came loose and landed with a smash onto the windshield, shattering both objects . . . The van then backed up quickly, straight into the fenced outdoor daytime enclosure, putting out a taillight, before speeding away . . . but not back toward the highway but rather deeper into the meadow, bouncing out of sight with a spiraling-free hubcap catching a gleam from the streetlight before the van disappeared.

Ryan squeezed his cell phone . . . then hesitated.

He had let them in the building, he had let them in the sheep pens. He would surely get in trouble with the rest of them if he called the campus police. He called his cousin's cell, but Joey D didn't pick up so Ryan left a message:

"Of course, I'm gonna beat your smug-Carolina-bastard face in. That goes without saying. My friends and I will be at your gay-boy frat house in an hour and I want my sheep back."

Jerilyn nervously tailed along behind Corinne, the president, hoping to speak to her alone. It was eight P.M. and they were due to arrive at the Zipperhaus around nine. Corinne was in high makeup, formfitting designer jeans and a floppy silken top with a plunging neckline that would have revealed all, had she bent forward. Corinne explained that this was the first full-on party of the year and it was a tradition the Sigma Kappa Nus would be in super-slut mode, flash a little bosom, laugh, flirt, and then get out "at maximum tease," right as the boys were panting and desperate. "This is the time for you new girls to show your wares," Corinne chirped. "If they want you, then we want you!"

Some of the older sisters were chiding the pledges on looking like Library Science majors. Jerilyn figured she didn't have one dress in her entire closet that was right for this sort of gathering. She settled for her tightest jeans — not so much tight in a designer way as they were outgrown from high school — and a midriff-baring top . . . But anyway, she had to talk to Corinne. She thought she finally had her alone when there was a knock at the door.

"God, what now?" Corinne said.

One of the workmen who had been digging up the front yard throughout the day was standing on the Sigmahouse porch.

"Yes?" Corinne hissed, as the older man in the blue workman's clothes towered before her. "If you're trying to get a free peek at all the girls, fella, I'll call your boss and have a few words."

"I am my boss," said the man, "and we can talk about the plumbing situation here or inside."

Corinne pursed her lips and stepped out. Jerilyn stood in the doorway, sort of curious. Now the smell of sewage was everywhere. "I'm gagging," Corinne said, her neck pulsing. "God, how could you guys do this to us? We're trying to convince thirty young ladies to call this house home and every day they have to walk through this torn-up front yard and the smell of septic tanks and shit everywhere! I thought this was going to be done two weeks ago!"

"Miss, you need everything replaced," the man said somberly.

"Oh what a fucking shakedown. You dig everything up and now we have to pay big money to get our yard back to normal."

"I'm telling you what every plumber in town would tell you. You have got blockages in three pipes and the septic is not breaking down the waste matter."

"For God's sake, just fix it, fix it already!"

"You have to . . ." The man, who could be anybody's grandfather, looked concerned, perhaps for the plumbing, not so much for the girls. "You have to . . . You have to chew your food, miss. Get the girls to digest their food. You can't just swallow it for a little while and throw it up into the toilet. It —"

"Look, we'll do in our toilets whatever we want to do in our toilets — they're our toilets!"

"Just telling you what the problem is, miss."

"Fix it, whatever the bill is, then give it to me, and I promise you, Mister . . . Mister Old Plumber Guy, that the Greeks in Chapel Hill will boycott you and I will see to it that you will never have another bit of business from any sorority in this town."

Corinne stormed away, pushing past Jerilyn.

The man returned to his van and Jerilyn stood out on the porch for a moment and gazed across the street to Thetahouse, having some kind of do tonight. A small limousine pulled up in front and six men and six women got out, all dressed in formal wear, beautiful. Jerilyn watched a man in a dinner jacket put an arm around the lower back of his date, and escort her lovingly up the walk. Jerilyn was already feeling chilly in her skintight jeans and bikini top.

Layla appeared beside her on the porch. "They think they can see my tits through this top but they can't . . . see?" Layla was exhibiting herself under the porchlight. Her gauzy Kleenex-thin skirt barely made it over her privates. She had Carolina Blue pumps that added three inches to her height. "Want to feel good?" she asked, and Jerilyn understood there was more coke to be sniffed on some surface somewhere inside.

"I like feeling good," she said, following her friend.

Five of the pledges, wearing only a jockstrap, were marched into the television room, all dark except for the TV, tuned to a static channel and muted.

Cory and Kevin bade them stand at attention against the wall. The boy christened Smegma (their pledge names were written on their foreheads in permanent marker) was shivering. "The Pledgemaster will be here shortly," Cory said gravely.

Kevin added, "You must do as he says or you'll never be a Zipperman."

The pledge christened Scrotum mumbled, "Better not be any gay stuff . . ." There were frats that filmed their hazing rituals — unending hours of nudity and homoerotic dares and things inserted places — and then sold the videos to hazehim.com — again, for a bit of spring break money.

"You'll do whatever the Pledgemaster demands!" Cory barked.

There was noise and the sound of, maybe, a chair being overturned, some muffled cursing . . . Then Skip was present, holding one end of a dog leash, lingering in the shadows. Kevin and Cory stood on either side of the doorway, affecting dire solemnity. Joey D slowly, as if marching in a funeral cortege, stepped into the TV room with his long black robe with its Death cowl, a costume rented and never returned for a Halloween some years ago.

"Within the brotherhood of Zeta Pi," Joey D intoned, "there is a more ancient and secret society going back to the days of the fraternity's founding in Tulane in the 1800s, when French aristocrats, uh, you know, down in Louisiana where they're French — French aristocrats laid out the initiation rites that we practice today and have practiced through the centuries. A society with a special name and coat of arms and, um, the seal of Côte d'Agneau . . ."

Scrotum was sniggering, trying to hide it.

"Something funny there?" Joey squinted to read the name on the sweaty forehead. "Scrotum. Something strike you as amusing?"

"No, sir."

"Assistant Pledgemaster Baylor!" Joey D called out, surprising Skip who wasn't aware he had a title. "Bring forward Shelly."

The pledges exchanged anxious glances.

Joey D explained that the University of North Carolina has a mascot ram and Zeta Pi has Shelly, a ewe, hence the Society of Ram and Ewe. Skip pulled the sheep into the room, its four legs rigid and stationary, its hooves sliding evenly over the linoleum. Shelly, née Furball, having shed itself in the back of Justin's mom's van of every fluid and solid a sheep could manufacture, was remarkably passive after its being fed a ground-up Valium in a bowl of water. It stared at them unblinking and the pledges could have been forgiven for wondering if Shelly was stuffed.

"Blindfold these gaylords," Joey D continued, as Kevin and Cory obeyed. "Everyone has, in the Zeta Pi archives, an incriminating photo which is your passage into the Society of Ram and Ewe." Joey D, who had taken a Valium himself, after a six-pack and two Red Bulls, was having trouble focusing. He had thought of making everyone bestialize the sheep or having green feed pellets eaten by the sheep from their buttcrack but Skip reminded him that a simple nude photo, with the sheep tactically placed to cover the genitals, was traditional and incriminating enough. If anyone ever betrayed the Society of Ram and Ewe, this picture would then haunt them for eternity.

Scrotum cleared his throat and announced his jockstrap was not coming off, he was going into pre-Law and might run for office one day and he was not interested in this photo being sold to *The National Enquirer* and then shown on CNN.

"Assistant Pledgemasters!" Joey D screamed, not used to being defied. "Take Scrotum away and begin the ceremony of . . . of depledgerization!" Scrotum was shuffled away, mumbling, "You can't throw me out. My dad paid for the building of this house."

And then two others said they also did not want a picture with Shelly. "Okay, you pieces of shit, there's the door! You see it? You walk out that door and . . . you walk out and there will never — don't you go and think that — there will be another . . ."

They were walking out the door.

"Does nobody," screamed Joey D, "wish to be part of the fraternity's most sacred obligation, the Society of Ram and Ewe?"

"Sir yes sir!"

"Drop that jockstrap, Smegma!"

"Sir yes sir!"

"You wanna be a Zipperman, don't you?"

Skip was laughing and he could barely hold the camera.

"Sir yes sir!"

Now Joey D noticed, too, that the pledge was completely aroused.

The party upstairs was in full tilt. At least two hundred people spilling out on porches, verandahs, in the back by the pool, crammed into every room, with music loud enough to shake the foundations of the whole edifice.

At first Jerilyn was a little shocked to see the pledges running around in jockstraps with matted hair and other caked-on indignities, but then she got used to it. Layla had shared a line of cocaine and, eased by several beers, she was, as promised, feeling good about everything, as her eyes followed two strapping pledges' bare rear ends down the hall to the kitchen where other Zetas and Sigmas were filling a giant industrial-sized trashcan with every liquor known to man — cheap vodka, cheap gin, cheap tequila, 7UP, Hawaiian Punch, box wine. A frat guy, bellowing some rock-song chorus, held aloft an emptying bottle of Everclear over the trashcan while the girls brayed in mock-horror, *Oh no you didn't!* Cortney dunked her cup beneath the surface to fill it, then sampled. "Ellch. Needs something sweet," she called out, as someone went looking for where she had set down the discount-brand triple sec she had brought.

"Jerilyn!" It was Skip, with his trademark drunken-red face. "I was hoping you'd be here. You know, I told Corinne and Layla, hey, if Jerilyn isn't going to be a Skank, then I may have to change fraternities."

"Thank you so much."

"We'll figure out some way you can pay me back," he said. Then suddenly he was tongue-kissing her. She pulled back.

"Caught me off guard," she said, trying to make a joke of it. She looked at the floor, and by the time she looked up, Skip was off down the main hall of Zipperhaus, towel-whipping the buttocks of some passing pledges.

Back in the kitchen, the trashcan had nearly

brimmed thanks to what some guy promised was a gallon of moonshine.

Overheard, from two of the Sigmas:

"My dad can get rid of all of that upper-arm fat," Georgina said, volunteering her father's plastic surgery practice for a Sigma Kappa Nu discount. "Not to mention up your cup size."

"Puh-leeease tell me," Cortney said, "that your own dad didn't do your boob job."

Georgina straightened her posture and let the kitchen admire her newly titanic prominence. "You better believe he did them — so they'd be done right. It's all like working with meat to him; he doesn't think about these as boobs."

Boy, that was another thing Jerilyn did not get in the least. Some girls bragged about their surgery; some hid it and got whispered about ("I heard she had two nose jobs . . ."). Some girls said they loved to make out with girls and were so popular and funny and beloved; yet one girl, Amanda, whose name was nearly always sneered, hit on another girl while drunk at a party and she was whispered about as some kind of creepy dyke. And then the frat brothers and sex. What on earth were the rules there?

Taylorr bragged about having oral sex with all but two of the Zeta Pis her third year at Carolina; in fact, she said they were renaming the BJ Room after her when she graduated. This set off a contest of sorts about who had come in second, who had been through the most guys, Lew, Richard, Andy, Joey D, and Frank — no one had Frank, he was still in mourning for some girlfriend that dumped him, but two or three of the really slutty-popular sisters were determined to get him in a threeway. And yet, while all that was acceptable and breakfast-bar gossip, Jerilyn heard girls talk at dinner about Sara who was with two guys in a ménage à trois and what a slut she was, how she had "a problem." The rule, Jerilyn decided, was this: the popular ringleading girls could do or say or screw anything and it was all right.

Jerilyn always listened to see if Skip's name was mentioned as a frequent conquest, but so far no.

"Jermaine!" called out Britannie. Jerilyn corrected her about the name. "Aw honey, I got close! You be our taste-tester."

A plastic cup was dunked into the mire and something opaque and brown was forced into her hand. Jerilyn took a tiny sip from her cup, and almost retched at the strength. "It's a little like drinking mouthwash," she reported.

As the mixmasters tinkered some more, Jerilyn slipped away to the pantry where no one was standing. She felt she was getting sad again; the cocaine was slowly wearing off, the brightness and tingle was becoming intermittent.

"You don't like it?" some guy said.

"Hm, oh it's all right," she said, lifting the cup. "Not exactly delicious."

"Yeah, I'm more of a beer person," the tall boy said, almost apologetically.

"Me too, but I couldn't get near the fridge."

"Tell you what. I'll get us both one." He flashed a shy smile and she smiled back. God, he was a cute one! Didn't sound like he was from the South. Some trace of the cocaine reignited within her; she felt her heart pick up.

"Here we go," he said a moment later, handing her a beer. The boy took the trash-can cocktail from her and dumped it into an already dead potted plant. "I'm Joseph, but the guys call me Joey D."

"Jerilyn, you can call me Jeri."

Just then a shirtless young man walked down the hall — a pledge, she figured, given the wet and matted hair, though he had put on a pair of jeans. Joey D and all the guys erupted into "Baaaaaa baaaaaa!" as he walked by. He angrily gave them the finger and everybody laughed.

Then there was a crash in the next room, some raised male voices, a door slamming, another crash . . .

Joey D muttered something under his breath and bounded upstairs, away from the action in the kitchen.

Jerilyn stuck her head around the corner:

some guy had another guy — Justin, right? — pinned to the wall, while he sputtered, "Look, man, she just ran off — I couldn't help it!"

Then the new guy hit Justin squarely in the face, then once in the stomach, which bent him over double. Another young man in a red windbreaker kicked Justin once he was down on the ground. Lot of screaming. What woman were they fighting over? Two Zipper-men came to Justin's aid . . . and soon had smashed noses, too. Then one of the Sigma Kappa sisters ran in to do the screaming-stop thing . . .

"I saw your sheep! It was out by the pool, I just saw it!"

The three interlopers stopped using Justin as a punching bag and backed toward the door. By the time Corey and Kevin got to the kitchen, a gathering mob of Zeta Pis was ready to avenge Justin's pummeling. The man in the red windbreaker and his friend then took the full trashcan of alcohol and tipped it. To deafening shrieks, the fifty gallons of hard liquor and fruit juice flooded the kitchen, flowed into the carpet of the hallway, out the door, soaking people's shoes.

"You're gonna die for that!" yelled one Zipperman.

But now the guy in the red windbreaker held an old-fashioned cigarette lighter, which he opened and sparked the flame. Jerilyn hopped up on a chair. "Stay right there or we'll see if this all is flammable," he said calmly.

Everyone stood where he was.

The young man and his friends escaped out the back door.

The fumes of the spilled alcohol, the weed smoke, and her little bit of athletic activity made Jerilyn feel sick. She decided she would go out the front door, avoiding the mess, and get some fresh air . . . maybe just wander back to McIver, although Corinne said there were rooms back at Sigmahouse set aside for crashing and composing oneself. She wanted to dispose of the rest of her beer; she looked for another garbage pail only to see the stack of paper cups reeking of the trashcan cocktail, plates and saucers piled high with cigarettes ground into congealed dollops of chip-dip . . . and her nausea renewed itself.

She made it outside to the front curb where the Zeta Pi sidewalk met the street and sat down a yard away from another party refugee.

"I may hurl in the next minute," Jerilyn said in the stranger's direction. "I'm apologizing in advance."

"Whatever," he said, barely audible.

"You all right?"

He turned toward her. It was the boy everyone was making baaaa noises at. "I guess. Not sure if they're gonna vote me in."

"I wonder if the Sigma Kappa Nus are having second thoughts about me, too. I can't really hang with the professional partiers."

"You wanna lie down?"

He held out his hand and she wobbled to her feet, and then they were walking back into the Zipperhaus, past the foyer, toward the stairs . . . Jerilyn thought of the woman in the cool green formal wear, the man in the formal suit with his hand at her lower back walking toward Thetahouse, the way she looked up at him, the way he smiled back at her . . .

"Watch that," he said, steering her away from a puddle of vomit with a high concentration of Cheetos. She looked around the strangely quiet Zipperhaus, now a war zone of party debris, alcohol stink, Doritos ground into the rug, the hallway to the soaked kitchen and sodden carpets. Some guys were going in and out of a small room across from the stairs where the lights were off; female laughter emanated from within. She saw Skip Baylor come from the bathroom heading to the little room; he looked up and did a double take seeing Jerilyn ascend the frat house stairs with . . . what was his name again? Well, fine. It's not like Skip and she are a couple. Skip clearly is playing the field, so why shouldn't she?

And then suddenly they were in a dark room with two single beds — one for each of us, she thought. But as she lay down he snuggled up beside her. He slid his hands around her waist and buried his head in the crook of her shoulder. To slow him down she reminded him, "I still could throw up, remember."

He didn't say anything. "You just tell the Skanks I'm not some gay weirdo who wants to screw a sheep. These guys are . . . it's so fucking unfair . . ." He punched at their mattress once with a clenched fist.

Then he was kissing her. He tasted of beer and she imagined she did too. He was very insistent, a little rough but . . . but he kissed better than Skip who always gave her a tongue bath. Then he was undoing his jeans, and guiding her hand between his legs.

Someone opened the door and light from the hall poured in; Jerilyn instinctively hid her head in the pillow. "Uh . . . okay. Next time use your own room, all right?" said the voice, before leaving and pulling the door shut.

Then he rolled on top of her. He kissed her some more and she felt the pressure of his erection through her clothes. Okay, well, this was all right if it progressed no further . . . She was certainly willing to do things with her hands, like she'd done with Skip, so she reached for him down there and he took her hands in his own hands, which was sweet, and . . . wait, he pinned them back behind her head as he straddled her. He was inside her. Was her underwear off? When did that happen?

"Wait," she cried. "Stop. Hey stop —"

And then one hand was over her mouth. She tried to bite it but that just got the hand pressed further, harder into her mouth. So she tried to kick and writhe and break free . . . but he was already doing the thing she didn't want him to do.

Gaston

Gaston Jarvis, condemned to Plunkett, North Carolina, and its literati, beyond the reach of mercy or redemption, would offer himself to the sun. He pressed the button to lower the driver's-side window and positioned his face. Indian summer, seventy-something degrees, sky an autumn blue, not really warm . . . cool, in fact, when a hint of a breeze made itself known, but still the sun could sear, could revive the spirit, could keep the dwindling flame of his humanity guttering a moment longer. It was like in France, this weather. Cool brisk days yet a warm sun.

Well, that's what he thought he remembered about Paris sunshine. It had been rainy, cold and damp most of the time, hadn't it? American writers were supposed to go to Paris and write. That's what he'd done in the late 1970s, once upon a time, when he was one notch above poor and had published his first, justly praised debut, *The Rapeseed Field.* Then his second novel was published, the one he wrote in Paris, the ponderous pretentious artsy-fartsy bullshit Paris Novel (*Reunions of the Tomb,* taken from an inscription on the tomb of Abelard and Héloïse in the Père-Lachaise cemetery . . . oooh that was some High Art). Then, thanks to Book Number Three and his heroine Cordelia Florabloom, he landed again in Paris with beaucoup cash in pocket to debauch himself, eat richly and drink copious amounts of wine. Then the writing fell away and it was just the debauch. Still, he was working within a time-honored American tradition, you had to admit.

He checked his watch. A half hour more until this godawful reading. Thanks for nothing, Norma.

He closed his eyes again. It had been easy to sustain his personality traits in Paris. Love of excess, immoderation, petulance. He was especially good at petulance. He didn't go back for his father's funeral. He hadn't lifted a finger to help his mother, nor had spoken to her since — what? — a decade, at least. And it was easy to manage his social life in Paris, too. Every slight, every nuance of denigration or indifference had been repaid many times over by his cutting people off, not doing fledgling writers the literary favors that he had promised them, dropping hostesses cold . . . and Paris egged him on *à juste parfait.*

Then came the summer in 1978, when he was about to purchase a top-floor garret in the scuzzy *vingtième* to make his Paris-escape permanent. "Not the Twentieth!" his friends shrieked in horror, judging that *arrondissement* slightly less barbarous than Mogadishu. Gaston was already building his American roué legend; he joked that he would buy a grave in nearby Père-Lachaise, where he strolled almost daily, leave it open and just drunkenly stumble into the hole when the time came. As the centuries rolled he'd burrow a bony finger over to Colette and cop a feel. An attic room on the rue Stendhal — how was that street name not a talisman? Yep, the purchase papers were drawn up, the former apartment packed, the change-of-address cards were ready to mail . . . when the most appalling homesickness came over him.

Homesick. The word for once literally true, sick, unable to eat or sleep well, sick for thinking of shabby little North Carolina, all the while bar- and café-hopping along Haussmann's monumental boulevards. He longed instead to be driving on the tar-patched macadam of N.C. Highway 49, speeding from Charlotte to Durham, still an undergraduate racing back to campus in his rattletrap used car, the red earth of the roadside embankments, the surprise views of the ancient Uwharrie Mountains, that upland ridge connected to no other, smack in the middle of the state for no logical geological reason, dense green woods crowded with deer, roadside vegetable stands with hand-painted signs, red painted scrawl on a white-washed board, that last chance in September for a taste of the Sandhills peaches . . . He longed not to speak his fatally flawed French anymore or pretend interest in incomprehensible films or junkpile art or crackpot European politics. Americans are servile before Paris; they creep about it feeling unworthy of it, not good enough for it. He had done that, cringing and worrying about what wait-people, concierges, cleaning ladies thought of his French.

And Gaston, the lone wolf, the recluse, even missed some people back home . . . yes, mustn't let that get out! Not so much the people he had dropped or written off, the three agents, the earnest editors whom he put through hell, but his two sisters, Jerene and Dillard, pains-in-the-ass that they were, and he missed his friend Duke. Duke most of all. He had tried to write off Duke, banish him from the good life that Duke himself had introduced Gaston Jarvis to, many years ago at university. Gaston prided himself on how successful he had become on Duke's terms

— wealth, good clothes, fine wines, specialty tobaccos, how he moved easily between countries and grand hotels . . . but that was just money, wasn't it? The whole planet opens its mouth wide for American money; it was nothing personal. Europe didn't really love him. And North Carolina claimed him but he hadn't valued that at all, not until that summer in 1978 when he was homesick for the first time in his life, a nostalgia like a terminal illness, aching, unrequited nostalgia for being a young writer just starting out, for Duke and him sitting up until the dawn, sorting out the world and its problems, under the eaves in the attic room of Arcadia.

So autumn of 1978, he returned. Things back to normal, all irritants and indignities at a low volume, humming beneath the surface, for the most part . . . Dillard, long abandoned by her husband, was semi-functional then, though letting her boy Christopher run wild — we see how that ended up. Jerene and Duke had made a happy home. It never ceased to strike him as odd how their progeny rallied round him at family occasions and called him "Uncle Gaston"; it always sounded strange to his ears, aged him a few decades. He hated kids. Although he had mentioned all the brood in his most recent will, giving them each $20,000 when he kicked the bucket. See? Uncle Gaston loved you, he just didn't want to see or deal with you or get to know you in the least. Beauregard, a bright fellow, going to Duke University as he had done, then going to seminary at Davidson, peddling that Christ-in-the-sky claptrap to the yokels across the Union County line (beyond the pale) in Stallings, N.C. The two young ones, Joshua, that little fruitcake, and Jerilyn, who is her mother's clone with less smarts and personality. And Annie — she was the smartest, come to think of it, but willful and self-ruinous. He chuckled — wonder what side of the family she got that from?

Seven minutes to the reading. Norma set these things up for him. Gaston wasn't quite sure how this old friend whom he had broken with innumerable times kept crawling back to insert herself into his life. She was the number dialed when he couldn't get a cab and was too drunk to drive. She was the pocket picked — admittedly years ago — when debts and canceled credit cards left him without money for breakfast. When he complained of his publishing house's apathy in setting up readings, it was Norma, super-spinster, to the rescue, setting up small but well-attended events all across the South. He owed her a great amount for her services, her keeping his life on the rails, but the payment she wished for, marriage, a permanent association — heck, she'd be fine with affection and being seen in public together, being identified as a quasi-couple — that he would not give her. He felt his cell phone vibrate. And that would be Norma. Reminding him that in five minutes he had to give a reading. Just in case he wasn't at the bookstore but had detoured to a bar. Which would have been the better idea . . .

But I'm a creature of the old manners, the old courtesies, Gaston assured himself, as he opened his eyes and took in his surroundings. Another once down-at-heels mill town subsumed into the Charlotte metastasizing sprawl — McMansions, six-lane parkways through deforested fields where they had yet to build the development that justified the highway, identical strip malls, Panera Bread, Old Navy, Bed Bath & Beyond, Pottery Barn, P. F. Chang's, arrayed in characterless malls, a poor man's Florida with brick sidewalks and pastel awnings. Amid the bourgeois boom was the Antiquarian's Bookshelf in Plunkett, North Carolina, a little family-run independent store that hung on. And Gaston Jarvis was here to read from his new work, move some product, press the mottled and antiquated flesh of his antiquated readership of the Antiquarian's Bookshelf. He leaned toward the glove compartment — even this activity at his weight was a reddening strain — where he found his flask and retrieved it, sipped from it.

I'm too nice, saying yes to everything, he thought. He always yearned to be a curmudgeon, aimed for it, a Sheridan Whiteside whose rudenesses and insults to his loyal following could become the stuff of literary anecdotes told for a century on the order of Faulkner's snapping at his annoying offspring, *No one remembers Shakespeare's daughter,* or H. L. Mencken inscribing hotel-room Bibles with *With compliments from the author.*

Gaston watched a van pull up before the bookstore, in the handicapped spot. Out came the enfeebled and disabled, a lady in canary yellow with two sticks, a human scarecrow with a cane . . . and here come the motorized chairs out of the back. The old folks' home emptying itself, backing up the boxcar, shooing the livestock down the chute. Behold the kind of babes and groupies he can expect — Ethel and Hortensia and Letitia, all scrambling over one another with their walkers to get to the front row so they can hear properly. Gaston sipped from his flask, taking stock: the halt and lame, the elderly, white white white, varied only by the degree of palsy or blueing in the hair.

Gaston noticed two black women in their twenties, perhaps, walking out of the store with coffees to go. Staff, he figured. No, of course they would leave before he read. Indeed, they probably demanded not to work on the night Gaston Jarvis was coming to read; these young women, probably students at UNC Charlotte, they might act up, might have to say something to the old white man peddling his slave-times romances. It was as if he were wrapped in the Confederate battle flag. Why should anyone colored care one little bit what Gaston Jarvis had to say for himself? Back before his Civil War shtick, Gaston Jarvis was briefly the toast of New York after his wondrous literary debut. He had sat on a panel at 92nd Street Y with William Styron and gotten himself invited back to Roxbury, Connecticut, where (fellow Duke graduate) Styron lived and where James Baldwin was visiting. Bill and Jimmy — joking with him, enjoying his wit and youth . . . it was like an apostolic succession, writers who made their mark before thirty anointing another gifted young writer, entwining the laurel, the apollonian crown to place upon his head . . .

What would Baldwin, if he were alive, say about him now?

It hardly mattered, he well knew, that he tried to depict the horrors of slavery here and there, highlighted the white Southerner — and there were such people historically — who thought slavery a great wrong. North Carolina had to be dragged into the Civil War; that's why Sherman didn't ravage the state, knowing there had always been sympathies against the Rebellion. Indeed, once, in the third of his Civil War titles, *To Bleed Upon This Sacred Earth,* his editor insisted that Gaston not be "so hard on the whites," cut out a harangue or two. Did he not understand that his one hundred percent white readership didn't want to read about whites being lower than snakes for four hundred pages? He sipped from the flask. Just a few cuts, but no more, Gaston said at the time. Gaston imagined the editor suited himself once the final manuscript was in his hands; Gaston had never read the final draft. Boy, that was an activity that didn't pay — reading your own published work. Taking down an old title from the shelf and giving it a leisurely self-loathing peruse.

The young black girls were waiting for their rides, smoking cigarettes, conspiratorial over something, laughing. I am less than nothing to them. And now here comes . . .

"Merciful Christ," Gaston muttered aloud.

To the door stiffly walked a middle-aged man, with his white beard trimmed like Robert E. Lee, in full CSA military regalia, a dress uniform, undoubtedly researched to the final pin and button, probably a friend of Duke's. (How Duke Johnston had fallen so far into the whole Civil War reenactment cult, he wasn't sure.) Are they going to let General Lee bring that sword in the store? Turn him away, Gaston urged in his thoughts . . . but that old clown was not going to be turned away. He will be seated right down in front (next to Ethel and Letitia and Hortensia) so I can meet his worshipful gaze while I read about Jackson's dying words at Chancellorsville. And he will buy three copies, too. Gaston craned around in his seat to see if the black girls had seen Robert E. Lee, but they were gone.

He sipped again — not really a sip, a good long draw. I'm going to do it one of these days, he swore to himself: for eight books he had followed the travails of Cordelia Florabloom. She had become his most popular inescapable character, slipping through enemy lines to help the Rebels, dodging Union enormities, searching always for her betrothed whose whereabouts were unknown since the Battle of the Wilderness . . . I'm going to make her a Union camp follower in the next book. Have her service Sherman! *Oh general sir, I would so consider it my honor to receive you into my hindmost quarters . . . If you would but only kindly instruct those newly freed, strapping black bucks over there to come join us —*

There was a knock at his passenger's-side window which jolted him into a near coronary.

"Well, hello there!"

Two blue-hairs. Gaston pushed the electronic button that lowered the window.

"Why, Mr. Jarvis," said the taller, uglier of the crones, "whatever are you doing with yourself out here in the parking lot? Come on inside!"

"Let me just tell you . . ." This was the short impossibly pale lady with the livid red lipstick that suggested she had just supped upon a fresh animal kill: ". . . let me say that I just love to pieces the new book! You get better and better each time out. You mustn't let one fool thing happen to Cordelia in the future now. I think I would just perish myself!"

Renewed incentive, Gaston thought. "Aren't you ladies lovely to say so. I'll be in momentarily."

"You're not nervous, are you? Why, Gertie, I think he's got a little stage fright!"

"Maybe he does, aw, maybe he does. Just let me say that it's so good of you to trouble with us out here in the wilds, Mr. Jarvis!"

They waved bye-bye and toddled inside.

And the phone vibrated again — Norma. "Yes, you old cow — I'm going in already!" he said aloud to the unanswered phone. Norma must have been called by the bookstore owner inside wondering if Mr. Jarvis was on track for the big event. He popped open the car door, still not really moving. All right, showtime. He tucked his flask in the breast pocket of his sports coat. Of course, he will do the reading. You see, that's what no one understands, he thought, scrambling, launching his bulk to his feet from the too-low sports car. I'm a creature of the old niceties, the old Southern graciousness. I'll be sweet to every one of those hyenas in there, because though raised amid violence and brutality, I have embraced the old manners, the old courtesies.

Too much a pussycat for my own good!

Norma must have an atomic clock instead of a heart; Gaston had never seen a rival to her punctuality. The doorbell rang at 10:30 A.M. exactly. He was up but not dressed, having made his way, hungover, to the shower. It was a luxurious, multi-nozzle chamber with too many controls, where he could sit on a tiled bench within, being bombarded with mists and sprays of three different densities . . . and he had nodded off in there, while being wizened to a prune.

For decades people drove down Wendover Road and wondered about the vast overgrown vacant lot so near to downtown, so close to Myers Park, and wondered what indifferent owner had let this piece of prime real estate go fallow. Then suddenly a three-story mansion went up; a ten-foot wall accompanied it, cutting off the familiar view, frustrating the curious. There was relief when everyone learned that it was famed local author Gaston Jarvis who had commissioned the forbidding, Gothic-looking mansion with turrets and towers, dark brick and narrow thick-glassed windows one might have found in a Northern European church, some place of worship punitive and severe. The Jarvis place was a point of pride for a marginal neighborhood that now could say it was coming up, despite decaying evidence to the contrary. Gaston planted more trees, imported a giant boulder or two, then let the grass grow wild, all the better to insulate himself from the rest of Charlotte. Mustn't have the fans getting at him. Though a fanatical fan would have been hard-pressed to find Gaston Jarvis at his house; he barely used it. There was a trail from bedroom to bathroom to kitchen, and the other twenty rooms were left to themselves, décor that had dated itself many eras over, furniture unsat upon, books never taken down from shelves, and a living room blank except for a chair, a table and a telephone on it.

Gaston answered the front door on the third go-round of Norma's buzzing, in his bathrobe.

"It's Tuesday," she sang out.

"Norma," he said, bowing his head, and then also addressing his amanuensis, the impossibly old Mrs. Meacham, prim, frowning at his bathrobe, whom he still did not call by her first name. "Ma'am," he aimed in her direction. "Come inside, the coffeemaker has been on for some time."

Gaston and his guests all settled in the kitchen. Mrs. Meacham had been a court reporter, a stenographer who typed up law offices' notes after hours, a great adept. Nearly fifteen years ago Norma procured her services so Gaston did not have to hammer out his own first drafts but could dictate them. Mrs. Meacham would take everything down, no matter how scattered, then produce a word-processing document for Gaston to edit on his computer. For a few books, Gaston had dictated privately into a tape recorder, slurring, drunk, and Mrs. Meacham threatened to quit, saying the tapes were indecipherable and the sounds of drunkenness an immoral thing to countenance. Since then, Norma insisted that all dictation be done live. Furthermore, Norma would be in attendance and prompt Gaston until he was "up to speed," though why she should care at all if another Cordelia book came out was a mystery.

"I thought I might kill off Cordelia in this book," he announced, after a first sip of strong coffee. "A fatal slip into a pigpen, drowning in the slops."

"You'll do no such thing," said Norma.

Norma was the keeper of the flame, the pre-editor, the proofreader . . . hell, she might even be co-writing these damn things, Gaston had occasion to think. He rambled and spoke of historical occurrences, made a mishmash of battles and what state's regiment crossed what river, only to be vanquished or victorious under Colonel Whatsisname . . . somehow it all got straightened out, polished up, turned into another bestseller. Oh no one, not critics, not even the hardcore fans, thought these last books were as good as the earlier ones, but neither publisher nor reading public stopped demanding them. Gaston's earlier Civil War productions dated from an era when Gaston thought he was working toward something serious, actually thought he was adding to an important body of work.

Gaston had made a study of Confederate heroines. He was aware of the mid-nineteenth-century popularity of doggerel like John Dagnall's *Daisy Swain: The Flower of Shenandoah,* in which a purer-than-snow heroine searches through the mud and mire of prison camps for her truelove. There were plenty of real-life models. It's not standard knowledge concerning the Civil War but the Union was harsh beyond belief when they found women ferrying goods and necessities to their imprisoned fiancés and husbands; they were tried as smugglers, the gifts were seen as contraband in the service of the Rebellion, and many a fine lady was tossed into the clink for long sentences, $1,000 fines (a sum far exceeding yearly incomes), and not all survived the disease and degradation of prison life. Gaston had been struck by

Memphis's L. G. Pickett, who wore several layers of clothes to reach her only brother and his Negro boy attendant, to provide them both clothing for the winter. She was convicted for smuggling, wrote an elegant and persuasive letter that survives, but was nonetheless sentenced to six months in prison. There was Emma Latimer, who as a teenage girl pulled down a Union flag in 1865, and was charged with treason, ninety days in jail and a $300 fine, which was two years' soldiers' pay. A higher-up Northern general overturned the sentence, chiding the prosecutors: "Their first battle for the flag was with a thoughtless schoolgirl."

There was something literary in all this, Gaston thought, so he had his heroine, Cordelia Florabloom (he got that preposterous last name off a tombstone in Edenton, N.C., and had come to regret the choice mightily), take down a Union banner in Yankee-occupied Wilmington, then fall afoul of General Benjamin Butler, the scourge of North Carolina's Outer Banks, who captured Fort Hatteras and Fort Clark before imperiously serving in New Orleans, where he earned worldwide opprobrium for his Order Number 28. That directive inflamed editorial pages around the nation and Europe, in that: any woman who did not return the normal courtesies of the Northern occupiers would be treated and dealt with as a common prostitute. "Spoons Butler" they called him for stealing the silver when he went to dine at Southern houses. Butler, while in North Carolina, had put a man to death in 1862 for taking down a Union flag — he was the perfect villain for Southerners, the perfect martinet to send young Cordelia to a dank Union prison.

March Into a Southern Dawn was not a bad book. Cordelia has much time to think over the lost cause of the South — the "Old Fatuity," Henry James called it — the doomed conscription of her father, brothers and truelove, her own lamb-innocent upbringing shielded from the sordor of war and slavery's ugliness, sequestered from masculine mischief. It made money and even won some plaudits. Gaston wiped his brow . . . he should have stopped there, or maybe at three, a trilogy — who could blame him for a moneymaking trilogy? *This Chivalrous Hour* was the second in the series and even by then, the New York critical press was beginning to turn; the reviews were derisive. It sold fabulously and that should have been reward enough, but the slipping away of his literary reputation was a wound of pride that could only be assuaged with drink. And it was through a monsoon of drink that he indifferently churned out the third in the series, *To Bleed Upon This Sacred Earth.* Then the fourth. And the fifth.

His series was up to Book Number Eight, two decades from the first one, a span four times the length of the War Between the States itself. Indeed, even he could not stretch out the series much longer. Right now, he had lots to work with. The rapacities of the March to the Sea, the burning towns, the destroyed plantations, the avenging freed slaves telling the Union bummers where the silver was buried and the family heirlooms hidden, the last savageries inflicted on the Union troops and, especially, black troops by the ever-more-hopeless ragtag Southern forces. Sometimes the Northern boys would let the freed slaves beat their masters for a lark . . . all good stuff for a writer. But if the books were well into Sherman's campaign in the Carolinas, then it meant that the war had a few weeks to go. Yes, he could have Cordelia face the horrors of the occupation and Reconstruction, but his heart wasn't in that at all. Besides, he knew what he wanted to write next. And it wouldn't be with these harridans in the room with him, either. He would write it by his own hand, go back to Paris, if he had to —

Norma's cell phone burst into music. She took the call, so it had to be important, meaning some penny-ante appearance in some independent bookstore, moments before they declared bankruptcy, started firing the staff, boarding up the windows . . . "Oh I see," she was saying. Then profuse apologies, a gentle parting of ways, then Norma turned to him: "Did you have words with the editor at the *Queen City Times*?"

Nothing enraged him more than those literary pieces in *Our State* magazine or the Sunday sections of the *Charlotte Observer,* "Ten Writers Who Matter" or "Twenty Voices of North Carolina," in which they rounded up the usual publicity sponges and took late-light soft-focus photos of them in their oh-so-quaint studies, their "caves of making," where they crafted their Suhthrin' masterpieces. And was he ever among them? You see the limits of Norma's meddling right here! Was she able to get these local rags to interview him, publicize his books, even mention him? The most recent insult was in the slick, mysteriously funded *Queen City Times,* the kind of area attractions/current happenings magazine known to a thousand executive hotel rooms, and their "Voices of Charlotte" ten-page spread. For God's sake, there was not one living, breathing local writer who sold one hundredth of what he'd sold!

"Giordano is a good acquaintance of mine," she explained, "and I thought it would do well to flatter him rather than annoy him. I've been cultivating him."

"With your own special grade of manure," he grumbled. Norma had called the magazine and proposed a time for the article's author to talk to Gaston Jarvis, who surely would be included in "Voices of Charlotte." She was told on her first attempt that there was no interest, plenty had been written through the years on Mr. Jarvis. Then Norma called her acquaintance Giordano, attempt number two, and tried to work around the first editor and received initial encouragement . . . only for the first editor to leave a message that Mr. Jarvis would not be included, but thank you very much for your "inexhaustible" interest in the *Queen City Times.*

Gaston had spent last week investigating the purchase price of the *Queen City Times.* He would buy it, sack everyone, and . . . no, that act would most certainly end up as a poisonous anecdote, told deliciously by his enemies, a snarky column in *Vanity Fair.* He should have left it alone, moved along — hell, his books were reviewed in *People,* in women's magazines with millions of subscribers . . . but to be disrespected by the nothingness that was the *Queen City Times*! He couldn't let it go. Drunk, home so late from the country club that it was morning and during business hours, Gaston last Friday called the *Queen City Times,* affecting a higher, younger voice.

He mentioned "his employer" Gaston Jarvis would be traveling on a European tour quite soon and if he was an intended profile subject, then they had better schedule a time for a photo and a sit-down, which Mr. Jarvis would be more than happy to do . . . hm, what's that?

He wasn't among the Voices of Charlotte?

They did understand, didn't they, that Mr. Jarvis still lived in Charlotte and had eight bestsellers under his belt, translated indeed into sixteen languages and . . . oh, may I ask who is being profiled if not Mr. Jarvis?

Forrest Wrightway? Yes, he was born in Charlotte and proceeded not to spend one full year of his life in this town but . . . oh yes, of course, how could he not be included, someone of his stature and inestimable seminal importance. Oh I do hope there's no scheduling conflict — that you fellows can schedule a time when he isn't on WUNC, the PBS affiliate-monopoly, sitting by the fireplace being folksy and homespun, spinning off his bucolic spew in order to better market — what are we up to now? — three down-home folksy books set nowhere near Charlotte, set nowhere near Planet Earth for all the reality about life in the sticks that . . .

Oh and who else? Christine Flaherty Bain. Who the hell is . . . Oh, I see, a memoir out from the local press your rag has been pushing for the last two years, Kings Mountain Press, publisher of cookbooks and novelty books about How to Speak Suhthrin' with the gummy granny chasing a bear (pardon me, *bar*) out of her vegetable patch, waving a skillet high about her head, requesting the varmint to git and skedaddle. Why, they're doing fiction now! Oh Ms. Flaherty Bain's work is a memoir about growing up and having had an actual mother, an old sweet kind knowing wise Southern mother and a fine old homeplace which is — you don't say! — not around anymore. Well, we must have one more of those deathless books, yes indeed, Mason jars and puttin' up peaches and front porches and butter churns and that certain special painful summer where young Christine went a few miles down the road and then how she came back a few miles down the road. Lordy yes, those Mama-books by women with three names just fly from the shelves, bought by other women with three sacrosanct names . . . If only we could find a lady writer of a certain age with *four* names — then we'd really have something, wouldn't we? Maybe if Mr. Jarvis used his middle name, perhaps you could . . .

And who else? Shequanda Nketo Harris's *Aint No Love Thang.* Up from the Dillehay Courts housing projects to confront her sexual identity. A black lesbian memoir . . . ah yes, how vital and unique! There hasn't been a black lesbian novel of self-discovery published this whole month! Perhaps this discerning new press should consider hunting for a black woman who toys with the idea of heterosexuality since none of them seems to ever write books. About time, yes, for some affirmative action for the straight black females. Maybe she can check with her Ancestors about what that man-woman experience was like, hm? I am insinuating nothing of the sort, I just . . . No, no — now no hanging up before you tell me who else is a Titan among the Olympians of Southern Fiction, who else resides on your Charlottean Parnassus, the western slopes of our own Crowder Mountain, come down to walk among us mere mortals at the B. Dalton's at the Eastwood Mall?

"I don't think it's useful," Norma was saying, apparently having been reproving Gaston for some time now, "to burn bridges."

"I'm going to hire someone to burn the *Queen City Times* down to the ground, just you watch," he added. "I've driven by their offices a few times. One can of kerosene would do it —"

"You mustn't drive by! They'll report you to the police!"

Here they were again, functioning like an old married couple, in his own kitchen no less. He wanted no claim or obligation to restrict him in any way, no expectation of his time, no imagined commitment to even trifling regularities — he did not even wish to have to be courteous or make explanations for why he wasn't courteous. He treated Norma badly, he supposed, but that had only acted as Super Glue to bind them ever closer. She could not be persecuted away or crushed in spirit. He'd have to take out a hitman's contract to be free of her — a twofer, get her while she's having lunch with Giordano near the *Queen City Times.* He could move out of Charlotte, for New York, for Paris again . . . but that wasn't going to happen. He hated that she'd made herself his indispensable parasite. He was the rotting log, Norma was the garishly hued lichen . . .

"Cordelia was about to go to the garden," said Norma, now trying to nudge him back to work.

"Cordelia wandered into the gardens," Gaston dictated, hurting behind his eyeballs, pinching the bridge of his nose. He was past the one-hour mark, way past his usual endurance. "Somehow, though the house had been torched by Sherman's men, leaving two leaning, charred chimneys at either end, the winds had kept the fire from the Dunsmuirs' splendid garden, with its domed gazebo. Of all the things — sorry, Mrs. Meacham, quote, Of all the things to remain standing, unquote, thought Cordelia, the gazebo where Wilkerson had first declared his love for her had survived the general devastation visited upon Orangeburg. Maybe it was a sign, she prayed, that Wilkerson too was among the living . . . Ladies, that is enough," he added in a different voice. "I am done for the day."

Norma beamed. "It was a good day, Gaston. I'm proud of you!"

Gaston stumbled back to the coffeemaker, now brewing its third pot. "You condescend to me like a child who has gone caca in the potty for the first time. Although, admittedly, the child of my simile and Gaston Jarvis do seem to be producing the same item."

"Oh really. Your metaphors and similes lately are all about excrement. Honestly, I think this book will be the best yet. Now some business. Do you want to do the Asheville Book Festival?"

Norma was insensible to his opening a kitchen drawer filled with airline miniature liquor bottles. He opened two Chivas Regals into his new cup of coffee. "Speaking of excrement, will Forrest Wrightway be there? Will I have to sit on a panel beside him?"

"I'm sure he will be there, since he lives in Asheville. I take it the answer is no. How about the Public Library Book Fair in Goldsboro?"

"Is there never anything from a university? Did you . . ."

Norma did that thing she did, a quick intake and release of a breath that signaled effort and disappointment. "Yes, I called a number of university reading series, but they have other bookings this season."

How long had it been since a university English department had wanted him as a guest lecturer? Backaways, for sure. The academic and literary types don't have much truck with Mr. Jarvis these days. Mind you, when they have a state literary festival or some fund-raiser to raise lucre for the library, who do they call to fill the tent? It's either me or Anne Rice or Pat Conroy with a line around the block while the Algonquin and Farrar, Straus & Giroux, and Grove and Vintage and Holt and Norton authors, the MFA-program parasites, *les artistes,* who couldn't sell five thousand books collectively, cluster and lurk and complain to each other at the cocktail parties, make a meal out of the hors d'oeuvres like starving undergraduates, brag about who endured the least attended event, wear their obscurity proudly — always ready to be assured, on cue, in rotation, that *The New York Times* or *The Washington Post* or some momentarily venerated blog said just-wonnnnnderful things about their last title. How they all cling to each other in the literati life raft, what a comfort they are to each other —

"Yes or no to Goldsboro?" Norma prompted.

Gaston was in that brotherhood once, after the first two underselling books; that was him thirty-some years ago, clustered with the Real Writers at such functions, envying the money of the Shit Writers, wondering how they managed to write schlock so poorly and earn so much money. Now not a one of the literati would deign to come over and talk to old Gaston Jarvis — Gaston Jarvis who would embrace them and praise their (nearly invisible) masterpieces! Gaston Jarvis who understood their plight! No, they leave him to his crowded corner fending off the blue-hairs and the neo-Confederates and the tyrannical book club presidents encountered only when his books come out, who pick and choose titles for some little library system in some trailer-filled red-clay goatpen of a county, who expect to be treated like Marie, Queen of Romania, paid court to, given obeisance . . . *ah ah ah, Mr. Jarvis, you wouldn't want us to not select your novel as the Cow-pat County, Georgia, Book of the Summer!* You arteeestes ever wonder with whose profits the Germans (who run all of American publishing) pay for your little literary exercises? It takes a Gaston Jarvis or two to pay for your little writing hobby, your linguistic *divertissements,* to underwrite your little post-divorce, post-modern, post-plot-and-character twaddlings excerpted in some online gazette read by three people associated with some lefty Massachusetts rag that serves as a slurry pond for all the Fine Fine Writing cranked out from the medicine-off-the-back-of-the-wagon snake-oil MFA mills throughout the Northeast . . .

"No, fuck Goldsboro!" he said.

Mrs. Meacham shook her head. When he started becoming a "sewer mouth" it was time for Norma to take her home.

And time for Gaston to head to Charlottetowne.

To repeat, Gaston Jarvis had a respectable mini-chateau northeast of Myers Park, but no one who knew him ever expected to find him there. Phalanxes of maids and grocery delivery boys came and went but Gaston would have gotten just as much use out of a hotel room out on I-85. No, his real headquarters was the Charlottetowne Country Club. The Nineteenth Hole was his royal court, where the cream of Charlotte society passed through after rounds of golf, some lingering, some pointing him out to out-of-town guests, hoping to hear Gaston Jarvis — "our local writer and wit!" — say something evil, gossip savagely, hold forth. (Gaston briefly entertained a campaign to get the prettifying *e* off the end of "Charlottetowne," but that was a battle as doomed as the Southern cause itself . . .)

Charlottetowne's main building, wherein resided the Nineteenth Hole, was known as the "Big House" and many of the club's devotees earnestly reported to visitors that it was antebellum. Which was nonsense. In slave times, who would have need of a country club? Every white man's home was a country club. Set back from the modern pool and tennis and golfing facilities, gyms and clubhouses, spas and steam rooms, stood the four-story, blindingly white, symmetrically square plantation house, eight thick columns on each side, enclosing a wide verandah on the first story and a balconied porch on the second, all mounted by a cupola and a widow's walk. It could be a movie set. There had been numerous approaches from production companies, petitioning to use the house as a pre–Civil War setting, a ready-made Tara, with its ground-floor ballroom that spilled through twelve-foot French doorways to the verandah, its sweeping marble staircases to private function rooms in the second story, its gilded bedchambers on the third floor for overnight stays (to be rented by equity-holding, first-family members for their out-of-town guests during high-society weddings).

It was an ingenious fraud, built in the 1920s to appear much older in that time of Klan-besotted neo-chivalry and high romanticism about Civil War glories. Still, it was a grand place, a worthy second home, Gaston Jarvis often thought, enclosed with tall pines and ancient oaks, ringed by an array of azaleas — flame, orange, magenta, white — at its base, with young magnolias tactically beckoning at the right angles of the Big House, wafting the evening air with sweetness . . . as he stumbled nightly to the parking lot where scrupulous bartenders, withholding his keys, had rung for a taxi or for "Miz Norma" to come pick him up and drive him back home.

Gaston heartily endorsed the club's snobbery. Charlottetowne Country Club was the city's most exclusive, discriminating, judgmental, double- and triple-screened enclave. The club you had to be born into. Only a member could get you in (and then only for a non-equity, "residential" membership, precarious, liable to be snatched away for any infraction), and these all-powerful trustees had to be of the first families of Charlotte, some wealthy before the Civil War, most wealthy as a result of the War, many wealthy in the ruined South's aftermath, when Charlotte's elite cashed in royally on the last intact supplies of cotton.

Gaston could not have dreamed, ordinarily, of gaining admittance to such a patriciate bastion, but his college roommate and brother-in-law, Duke Johnston, vouched for him. The trustees were worried: mightn't he be a writer who could one day embarrass the club with a racy or a too liberal book? But Duke stood his ground. Now that Gaston was a millionaire and their one-man Algonquin Roundtable, the trustees were delighted with their earlier gamble. Indeed, club members were likely to think that he *was* an equity, come to them from an ancient Charlotte family; people would be surprised to learn that he was merely a resident member. Gaston was a fearful snob. Every time certain elements in the club contemplated a loosening of the membership requirements or thought how nice it would be to host a PGA or LPGA event — which would bring unwonted attention to the club's exclusive membership policies — Gaston was loudly in the forefront of these discussions, no, no, never! Perhaps there was some fleeting prestige in having Jack Nicklaus and Tom Watson traipse through on the Senior Tour, but there was truly more refinement in being able to resist such calls to the public spotlight. Besides, Gaston thought, anything that made the Nineteenth Hole any more overrun was a bad thing.

"Afternoon, Mr. Jarvis."

Gaston's eyes adjusted to the Hole's comparative dimness. It was Dexter. All the bartenders were black, similar in age and appearance (fifties, close-cropped graying hair, a neatly pressed uniform in the club colors) and Gaston took a moment to identify his bartender in the gloom, a nearly windowless cavern of dark wood, stacked bottles on shelves, muted table lamps on round wooden tables, alcoves and booths and places for quiet conversation.

He was determined not to make this agreeable perch one more location he had besmirched with bad behavior. Gaston had almost blown it a few times. Sharing gossip with a small group, where inevitably his calumny got back to its victim. He had to dedicate his sixth installment (*The Cannon's Silence*) to Belle Bennette to get out of the doghouse a few years back. So he had learned his lesson on intra-club gossip or supremely clever remarks concerning ladies' hats, horrendous fashion choices, hair of unnatural hues or heights. But it was on just one such Dictation Day (every second Tuesday), a day like today, that he had lost his temper with Norma in a public scene, still whispered about.

A crowd would gather because they liked to hear Norma banter with Gaston. Gaston liked it when Norma was his foil, urging charity and patience, as he savaged and laid waste — it often was quite a public performance. Of course, Norma had her hobbyhorses, the topics she could not fail to warm to, every few Tuesdays.

"I come from a long line of spinsters," she would say with that soft proud smile.

And Gaston would parry. "And how, pray tell, do these virgin maidens spawn successive generations of virgin maidens?"

"Oh somebody or other breaks down and accepts a troth, and produces mostly useless daughters, good for nothing but schoolteachers, such as myself, and librarians. Of course, you gentlemen realize the whole of Southern culture and society would crumble without its underpinning of spinsters. There's not a church I have ever heard of that does not entirely depend upon the service, the cooking, the efforts of the unmarried or widowed older women. I daresay some of you gentlemen have been taught by spinsters."

Many hands were raised, many gray heads nodded. Harker Ballimer reminded the group that in Mississippi, when he was young, only spinsters could be teachers and when they married they resigned their place in the school.

"Oh yes," Norma said, "down east here in North Carolina, also, until after World War Two, at least. It was a vocation, it was nothing less than taking the veil, to be a teacher. I was taught by women who were known simply as Miss Campbell or Miss Gwinnett, if she were the eldest sister, though usually oldest sisters felt a duty to marry to jump-start the marriage-ability of the sisters waiting in line behind her. You see how intractable my spinsterhood is, that I managed even as eldest and first in line not to be entrapped! But more often, it was Miss Mary Lee or Miss Evelyn or Miss Elizabeth."

"Seems a bit familiar," a transplanted Northerner pointed out.

"They were not eldest daughters and therefore the use of 'Miss' and the first name was entirely proper. And you underestimate the power of 'Miss' in those days, the awe and respect that honorific could wield. These women were fearsome tyrants of their subject and their curriculum. The principals were mere functionaries who shuffled papers and came and went; it was the Miss Mary Lees and Miss Elizabeths who ran the schools with an iron will. And there was no need to complain to your parents about being struck with Miss Mary Lee's ruler or humiliated by Miss Elizabeth making you stand for a barrage of questions until your not having read the assignment was abundantly clear . . . because your parents likely endured the same torments under the same women — and still feared them!"

She loved to invoke the noble sisterhood of teachers, but one night a month ago, Gaston grew impatient with her routine and decided to romanticize the fraternity of writers, in mild opposition:

"I'll give you a brutal occupation," he began, warming to his audience of after-dinner drinkers. "It rarely leaves a man unmarked," he said, before finishing off his bourbon, setting the glass down with a loud enough clunk that the bartender turned and was signaled with a head nod to refill it. "Robert Penn Warren, my old pal James Dickey — good Lord, Faulkner was in the bottle half the time."

"Hmm," Norma said. He could tell she didn't approve of the premise.

"I remember after *The Rapeseed Field,* when I went to Connecticut to stay at Bill Styron's and Jimmy Baldwin was there. Now there were two men who could put it away. Styron could drink. O. Henry lived in the bottle, too — Thomas Wolfe a manic-depressive and drinker — that's just the North Carolina contingent. Writing well didn't make them very happy, it appeared. Look at Tennessee Williams. Look at Capote. We didn't care for each other, true enough . . ." Gaston was once at a publishing party in 1978 featuring a mobbed Truman Capote occupying the far side of the hotel ballroom, but that proximity would do in his cavalcade of name-dropping anecdotes. "But Truman ended up spectacularly unhappy. The most treacherous profession, don't you think?" He dramatically took a sip and looked at his enthralled audience. "Southern writer."

Norma held off for a moment, then let the counter-argument flow: "Well. Harper Lee and Eudora Welty didn't end up all miserable. Katherine Anne Porter, Zora Neale Hurston, though God knows, she had every cause to drink. Flannery O'Connor was sick, but not spiritually miserable. Let's see . . . Alison Lurie and Annie Dillard and the Ellens, Ellen Douglas, Ellen Glasgow. Toni Morrison, Valerie Martin — has she ever written one bad thing? — and Anne Tyler, Gail Godwin was in North Carolina for a while, wasn't she? Jill McCorkle, Bobbie Anne Mason, Elizabeth Cox —"

"Your point being?"

"All these women seem to be able to whip up lots and lots of wonderful books without careening into the bottle or beating their children or publicly disgracing themselves."

Among their laughing listeners, one older woman shouted, "She's got you there, Gaston!"

"Norma," asked one man in a seersucker sports coat, "to what do you attribute the fact that the Southern women writers are well behaved and the men less so?"

"Typical Southern male behavior. Lots of nonsense and noise and drama. I suppose we owe the Civil War to this strain of male self-dramatizing preposterousness. Wait — Carson McCullers. Wrote her first novel right here in Charlotte. She messed up her personal life in spectacular fashion."

"Yes," said Gaston, with his eyes narrowed to slits. "She kept taking up with homosexuals and wife-beaters, as I recall. Devoting her life to men who had no intention of loving her back." He enunciated with surgical precision: "No future in that, hm?"

He didn't look at her as he said it. Nor did he look at his embarrassed listeners who could barely imagine the lighthearted topic had ended with the plunge of such a dagger. He didn't want to meet any eyes, so he looked into his drink. He heard her gather her things and leave. And he let her do it, no running after her. He hated to think of that now. Not so much the cruelty to Norma — she was begging for it. She knew better than to ruin one of his great literary musings . . . but the publicity of it, fighting like a real couple might in public.

It wasn't like he did nothing for Norma. After each Dictation Day, Gaston rewarded his muse and life-manager with a dinner at Charlottetowne. She, too, was a resident member, vouched for by Duke Johnston, and fees paid for by Gaston. These nights out were her motivation, he supposed, for all the selfless hours of toil on his behalf. To be arm in arm with the celebrated Gaston Jarvis, a long candlelit dinner (with the impeccable service the CCC was known for, black middle-aged men and women in pressed white suits, some who had been there for decades, discreet, laconic, always at the ready, no request too much trouble). While Gaston had been here drinking all afternoon, Norma had been to the beauty parlor (where "the girls" requested every gossipy detail of these Tuesday dinners), before treating herself to a spa or salon or some alchemy to take a few years off. By evening she would look lovely in a dark conservative floor-length dress as she made a grand entrance into the Charlottetowne dining room and he stood at the table to greet her . . . how the heads would turn, how people would smile to be in the room with them. *Why did they never marry?* they must speculate. Some of them theorize that Gaston Jarvis must be homosexual. *He never got over his affection for his college roommate, Duke Johnston,* they would whisper.

Good guess, but wrong.

Yes, and speaking of Duke Johnston, his brother-in-law, he had put a foot wrong there, too, in the Nineteenth Hole for all to see. God, these public slipups were more and more frequent. Once again, he had a small coterie of Charlotte's rich and powerful hanging on his words. He was up off his stool, sloshing his bourbon around, animated in his depiction of bitterness.

"I *love* bitter people," he was saying. "No better conversationalists in the world than bitter people. We have it all wrong in this country." He mocked some Polyanna somewhere: "Now now, *mustn't be bitter!* That's the refrain. It's un-American to be bitter. We're the land of pick yourself up and try try again."

Norma was back to her usual role of feeding him straight lines. "Oh Gaston, please. What on earth could you possibly be bitter about? You write bestsellers!"

"I can't think of a more fertile soil for bitterness. The paltriness of American success."

"Bitterness," Norma insisted, "is *not* a very attractive trait when you're successful, Gaston."

"My darling," he answered, warming to his Oscar Wilde mode, "it takes true success to make for true bitterness. How important is the bitterness of the failure? It is an easy bitterness, hm? Simple to achieve, almost effortless. No money, no recognition — the resulting negative feelings are . . . child's play." His country club barroom audience was chuckling. "No, the real art is to succeed and find it all wanting, find it insufficient for petty and small reasons. To sour on a successful life . . . speaking of that, Benjamin, another bourbon sour, please." More laughter. "This club is full of CEOs and rich entrepreneurs and the first families of Charlotte, and yet I bet there are subterranean chambers beyond chambers, fathomless caves unknown to man, of bitterness and smoldering disappointments. Lateral promotions so close to the top. Investments gone wrong —"

"With the Dow mired in the seven thousands, that would be most of us, Gaston!" cried one jolly red-faced man in a yachtman's blazer while everyone laughed.

"Marriage to the wrong spouse," Gaston continued his crisp adumbration. "Social slights. Children turning out to be layabouts."

"Lord, that's true," said a white-haired

queen bee known as Mrs. T., a woman who lived at the club as much as Gaston. "You have been reading my diaries!"

Another heavyset patron: "Not just the children, Mr. Jarvis — the grandchildren!"

Much laughter. A lively widow held her martini aloft: "Anyone here have grandchildren that aren't spoiled completely rotten and incapable of working a day's honest labor in their lives?"

Widespread agreement. The gentleman in the blazer, through laughter, cried out, "Three grandchildren, all propped before the TV or their video games every waking hour — and every one of them obese!"

"I would bet my brother-in-law Duke Johnston would be at the head of that line, if he ever had a moment's self-reflection," Gaston began, while he heard audible gasps and oooohs. Oh his hangers-on had been waiting for this one. "Duke had it all, family, money, he was a city councilman, before that a football hero and a scholar . . . and what's it come to? He was expected to be our governor by now, if he hadn't run out of steam." One or two women smiled guiltily, another put her hand to her mouth. "Hope the money doesn't run out on my old friend. I would hate to have to call a meeting of the equity members for us to decide his status . . ."

Suddenly, it appeared, his sister Jerene —

Jerene who was never here at this hour, who *never* stepped into the Nineteenth Hole! — was hovering. "You should go home, Gaston," she said calmly, but the worse for its being calm. "Everyone in the club knows what you were saying isn't the least bit true."

His assembled admirers had wincing expressions of uh-oh, and turned away to whisper among themselves, leaving the siblings to talk privately at the bar. Norma instinctively moved to sit at the richest of the tables; thanks to her, soon everyone there was laughing again.

Jerene stepped closer, still staring him down, speaking quietly now: "They built this place around Joseph Johnston, Duke's grandfather. They were equity members, and your membership here, I apparently have to remind you, was due to Duke's own kindness —"

"Yes yes, of course that's how it is." He swallowed the words, grinding his hands together as if that could snuff out this whole conversation.

Jerene wasn't done. Duke, she reminded him, took him under his aristocratic wing at Duke University, introduced him to important people, befriended a young man of promise, a young man who became an ungrateful old man —

"All right, Jerene, I stand corrected."

She then seated herself on the barstool next

to him, smoothing her soft rose-colored silk dress. She always dressed like she was going to a wedding as mother of the bride where a conservative couture had been approved; her appearance often put him in mind of one of those severe Puritan portraits, high collars, erect carriage. Probably a first for her, sitting on a barstool in this much derided den of imbecility. "I don't know when you started hating my husband, Gaston," she said so no one could hear but them. "Your former best friend — probably one of the only real friends you have left in the world. I can see your contempt every time you raise your eyebrows and talk down to him like he's . . . like he's one of your annoying, senile fans you go on about. My land, Duke does not deserve that. And he lets you mistreat him because he loves you."

It had been years since Gaston had apologized for anything, and his first impulse was to lash back. "Duke doesn't provide for you or your family. I don't find much to admire in that."

"And you're worried that I will come with my hat in hand to you?"

"I didn't say that —"

"I am sure rather than objecting to my begging at your door, you would like it very much. You could lord it over Duke. Tell all your acolytes here in the Nineteenth Hole what a freeloader he is, the great Duke

Johnston who all of Charlotte loves. How he would be nothing if it weren't for the even greater Gaston Jarvis."

Gaston threw back the icy remains of his bourbon, then set the glass down with a loud enough clunk to cue Dexter that he needed another.

"You may," Jerene continued, "have already rehearsed that monologue, which I'm sure will feature your trademark wit and acid. Well, let me tell you, little brother, things would not be so tight around the Johnston household if we weren't . . ." She paused as the inscrutable bartender set a new glass down quickly. ". . . if we weren't taking on the lion's share of the bill for Lattamore Acres. Poor Dillard, she can afford her share less well than we can."

On this subject, Gaston could come to fiery focus. "That solution is the simplest. Let her wander downtown like a bag lady. Throw Her Highness out of the palace."

"The simplest solution is for you to contribute your third like a decent human being. You would be doing it for us, not for her. An even more decent thing, since I observe you have millions of dollars, is to pick up the whole tab which would be as nothing for you. It would come to less than the bar bill in here, I suspect."

"Not a dime for her, now or ever." He smiled, taking a sip and actually savoring the bourbon for a change. "Not for that witch."

"You would have us move her into one of our homes? I understand your ill feelings toward her, but toward us? What have we ever done to you that you would wish that fate on your sisters?"

He looked steadily ahead at the mirror behind the bar. He enjoyed playing this scene with the very same dialogue with both his sisters, every few months. "Turn *Maman* out in the goddam street." He reached for the peanut bowl. "I will not lift a finger. She can have an old age as fine as the childhood she gave us. I wouldn't have thought you had any mercy for Mother, after what she let Daddy do to all of us."

Jerene stood from the barstool, straightening out her skirt, gathering her thoughts. She leaned into his ear and said, "And it doesn't bother you to have the whole of this club, many of whom knew our parents in society, know that you are this Scrooge-like with your own mother?"

Gaston stopped popping peanuts as all that remained in the bowl was peanut dust. He leaned in another direction to nab the bowl of pretzels. "People put up with a lot from writers as successful as I am. It's a free pass for bad behavior — trust me on this. Invitations will continue to pile up in my mailbox. Jerry darling, I've had everything said about me that can be said. I've heard I'm addicted to pills, that I'm an alcoholic, that I have a steady habit of prostitutes coming in and out at all hours. That other people write my books and I put my name on 'em." He laughed, crunching a pretzel. "I am beyond the reach of scandal. So *Maman* shall not see one dime of my considerable fortune. You think I'm joking about the women's shelter. Tell her to consider euthanasia. I'll mix the hemlock."

Jerene, who didn't speak passionately or ever show emotion — not since she was a girl — turned to go. "Just for my working information," she asked, "if Duke and I have to declare bankruptcy, publicly, and with no shortage of embarrassment, would you help us then? Not Duke, but *me,* your sister who would find a bankruptcy and public ruin *very* distressing."

"Jerene, I would write you a check for a hundred thousand dollars tonight but I know as I am sitting here you will spend it to keep our mother living like a dowager empress at Lattamore Acres and I will not let my money go to that enterprise." He popped a pretzel into his mouth. "You could, you know, always sell one of those paintings of yours." He had said it lightly but he felt the temperature lower as he said it.

Jerene's place in society was amplified by managing the Jarvis Trust for American Art, an entire room in the Mint Museum devoted to American landscapes that were, by obscure methods, piled up by their ancestors. Jerene was the dictator of a little ladies-who-lunch, time-on-their-hands circle of society good old girls, most of them chosen for their sycophancy, who called themselves "trustees" and met monthly to compare shopping, children, to get tipsy at lunchtime, and play at being fund-raisers for the purchase of new art. That would be intolerable to Jerene, Gaston knew, if Duke ran out of money and she had to start selling off the precious family art pile! The Jarvis Room at the Mint . . . well, it might have to be called something else if the paintings passed into someone else's hands. Maybe he could buy it up and the sacred room could be the *Gaston* Jarvis Room and it could be the *Gaston* Jarvis Trust for American Art . . . had a nice ring to it . . . Nah, screw Art. He didn't care about it that much. Frederick Church, George Inness, bunch of haystacks and cows in fields, gleaners and hay wains, blah blah blah — like Savonarola, throw 'em on the bonfire. He turned to Jerene . . .

But she had gone. Well. That wasn't a nice way to leavc it. He'd make it up to her on some other occasion.

Alcohol was supposed to depress, to relax . . . but it only made Gaston more awake as night wore on. He'd fall into the bed tired enough but in a few hours he was wide awake again. No book or television show could interest him then. God knows, he had no intention of writing on the latest Cordelia Florabloom installment. But he might, in this inconsolable time of night, in just such a mood, work on a literary project long dreamt of, long threatened.

He rolled to the edge of his grand king bed and bounced his portly frame into an upright position. He padded into his slippers, found a bathrobe hanging in the bathroom, and shuffled across the hallway to a nearly unfurnished room. But there was a small desk and a laptop, which he now opened up.

So far there had only been notes, lines, musings, fragments. Somewhere amid all his things there was a box of student papers and notebooks, back from his days at Duke University, where some notes toward this literary comeback resided, youthful notions sketched out decades years ago. God only knew what immature dreck he'd written as a teenage undergraduate. But that youthful writing, whatever its faults, was before the rot set in, when he wrote from his soul, when he was insensible to the market and wouldn't know a royalty statement from a bubble-gum wrapper. When the one reader he wished to show things to was Duke Johnston.

Duke Johnston at Duke University. "Duke" Johnston, the legend. The name was Joseph

Johnston but over four years this handsome, smart, athletic student had become "Duke," the embodiment of all that was dashing and prestigious about the university. One heard of Duke Johnston witticisms, Duke Johnston parties, Duke Johnston's romantic exploits, although he steadily remained unattached, driving the sorority girls into frenzies. Duke Johnston, who had principled opposition to the Vietnam War — mostly about its strategy, and not so much about the need to fight Communism — but nonetheless would answer his country's call and would enlist in the Officer Corps after finishing up his degree in 1966. Because Gaston arrived at Duke University in 1967, he got to hear, endlessly, religiously, of Duke Johnston's athletic exploits and his most famous misfortune.

Duke was the handsome, easy-in-his-skin quarterback, his blond hair holding the late Saturday sun at Wallace Wade Stadium as he sat on the sidelines waiting for his chance at glory. He would take the field and they would chant his nickname, *Duke, Duke, Duke,* and he would oblige the crowd by a dazzling feat, an impossible threading of the needle, a completed pass the length of the field with every opponent bearing down on him. Duke University had slumped at football in recent years, though it had been the conference champion as recently as 1962; South Carolina (still then in the Atlantic Coast Conference),

NC State and Clemson were the football powerhouses. But with the advent of Duke Johnston, who at his best could score against anyone, the pent-up years of university football frustration broke forth like dam waters, he was praised, loved, adored, worshipped. But in a game against Maryland, he took a terrible sack, going down hard, hitting his neck on another player's knee while another player fell upon him with his full weight. His neck was thought to be broken; he was carried off the field immobile. That night, the local radio stations reported, he sank into a coma.

Such quiet on Duke campus — it was as if President Kennedy had been re-assassinated. Students, professors, alumni walked with heads down, everyone in dark contemplation, in premature mourning, barely muttering to one another, prayerful and hoping this young good-natured boy, this emissary from the sun, was not paralyzed. The *Durham Herald* proclaimed a week later: FOOTBALL HERO RECOVERING. Young Johnston was not paralyzed, but this most certainly ended his gridiron days, and his much publicized dreams of going to officer's school at West Point, joining the Vietnam War effort. In interviews that reported how close he had come to paralysis, how long his recovery would be, how he would be afflicted with vertigo and should walk with a cane, Joseph

Beauregard "Duke" Johnston, son of Major Bo Johnston, a hero of World War II, descendant of Confederate General Joseph E. Johnston, defender of the Carolinas against the savageries of Sherman's army, let it be known that the loss of football was truly nothing to him, but the inability to serve his country as his ancestors had before him . . . alas, that was the end of a passionately held dream.

Of course, the local Democrats hoped to recruit Duke for office, there and then on the spot — and the head of the Republican Club paid him a hospital visit as well. Duke Johnston, showing up to candidate debates with his limp and his cane, handily became student body president. He got to go to Washington to shake hands with former Vice President Nixon (a Duke alum), he lunched with the governor and asked Senator Sam Erwin, who had come to Durham for a lecture, to attend one of his famous barbecues at Arcadia House — and Senator Sam said yes! What a college career, what greatness was portended . . . and now, in Duke Johnston's first year at law school (Duke University forbade him from heading up north to Harvard or Yale, gave him every fellowship, threw at him every prize and scholarship not nailed down), insignificant wretch Gaston Jarvis had an invitation to a house party at the next-to-campus mansion known as Arcadia, was going to meet this philosopher king and his legendary coterie of smart, gifted young men and the gifted ladies who adored such men.

Gaston Jr. hated his father Gaston Sr., but he had to give his old man credit for allowing him to keep up appearances at Duke University. Gaston Jarvis Sr. had always been a bit sensitive about the provenance of his own law degree, so after a lifetime of belittling his son, he nonetheless was willing to pay for a Duke University education, so as better to allow a confusion, a sense that maybe son followed father to his ol' alma mater, a few backslaps in the club, a bit of "Yes, just like the old man!" when asked how his son was getting on at Duke. Nor did he wish his son to show up as some rube with one Sunday suit.

A lifetime of parsimony was instantly corrected by Gaston's new wardrobe. Gaston was put through a round of exacting measuring and fittings at Tate-Brown in uptown Charlotte (back in the days when such stores existed in uptown), and three suits, two blazers, a score of shirts and slacks, were the result. "I won't have those Yankee blue bloods looking down their Semitic noses at a Jarvis," said his father, who had a talent for mingling any positive development with something hateful.

The only time his father set foot on Duke

campus was to see Gaston off, see what kind of room he had been assigned, wonder whether he should raise hell on behalf of his son. He didn't want his son associating with the hippies or war protestors or radical professors (Duke had its share of all). It went without saying that drugs were forbidden, but it would be good, his father said, to learn how to drink. Men drank, and would always drink — drink to make deals, drink after golf, drink to charm women, and these four years could be a time to practice and refine that skill. Gaston Jarvis Sr. suggested he only date women from good backgrounds, find a nice coed at Duke, leave the town hussies alone. He speculated loudly, surely within earshot of the other boys and boys' parents moving into the dorm rooms, that there was many a tramp in town that would like to latch on to a future lawyer or banker. "Screw 'em if you have to, but don't get caught in a pregnancy scam." Those hours of unpacking were among the longest of Gaston Jr.'s life. His new life would begin, as if out of a chrysalis, the second his father returned to his brand-new Lincoln Continental, which Gaston believed was also bought just for the drive up to Durham, lest anyone form any meager notion of Jarvis patrimony.

Gaston could have portrayed himself as another privileged Southern kid at Duke; he could have joined a fraternity and played a sport, been rowdy, drank and caroused through his money and goaded his father to send more, which — now that the measure of his father's love of appearances had been taken — would likely have been sent, no matter the misbehavior. But Gaston already was in his habit of silent observation, hypercarefulness in social affairs. He longed to make true friends, escape into rooms filled with worthy people, go home with someone else's son for Christmas and Thanksgiving, erase steadily and resolutely his own unhappy family. His mother, suddenly sentimental about his departure, pressed some family photos in nice frames into his luggage, but upon reaching his assigned room in Craven Hall, he confined them to a bottom desk drawer. His sisters looked pretty and some of the fellows might well ask as to their marital status or whether dates were possible, and that thread would lead back to his family.

His mother, now without any of her children in the house, probably guilty for all the violence she oversaw or pretended not to see, wrote him flowery letters of affection — he read one or two. After a month, he began to toss them into the trash unopened; she was writing them more for her own boredom and to cast herself as martyr and hero, and he never answered a one. After a year, the letters stopped. Gaston fantasized about being able to sell a story of being an orphan on a trust fund . . . he never risked this fiction, but he dwelled on it at night.

But Arcadia! *Et in Arcadia ego . . .* Gaston could even now remember the precise details of how he, a lowly freshman, had been admitted into Arcadia, the heart of the university's social world. It must have been Henry, his hallmate back in Craven Hall. "Oh you've got to meet Johnston, and the whole group at Arcadia," Henry said, brandishing a bottle of single-malt scotch. You could not buy such a treasure in nearly dry North Carolina at that time, but Henry had taken it from his own father's stash, some overstocked beach-cottage pantry on Long Island. "I think this is Duke's favorite," said Henry, showing Gaston the staid Balvenie label.

"Should I bring a bottle, too?" Gaston asked.

"Oh they won't care," his friend said of the Arcadian revelers, all but taking him by the hand and running across campus, by the grand cathedral-like bell tower (that would make you think Duke University was immemorially old rather than a faux–Ivy League creation of tobacco money in the 1930s), through the autumn woods along Alexander Street to the many-eaved Victorian house from which a joyous Louis Armstrong record was playing.

"Well done, Henry," said Duke, holding the Balvenie whiskey to the window, letting the golden liquid catch the afternoon light. "You boys will join me in a wee dram?"

Henry said yes, and Gaston, like some kind of mute, stray dog, followed the men into the heart of Arcadia, past the packed rooms of celebrants, past the young pipe-smoking profs and dashiki-clad black students, debutantes and jocks and one young man perched on a sofa arm wearing eye makeup!

Duke waited until Gaston had tried the Balvenie. "Suitable?"

Gaston nodded, and managed to bring out, "Quite nice." There was a half-second pause where Gaston felt the need to keep talking, make a mark on the moment. "More of a bourbon man, myself."

"Really?" said Duke. "Oh thank God — me too. My peers here would have us drowning in scotch. What's your favorite?"

Gaston had maybe sampled bourbon no more than three times in his life; the truth was it was always bourbon on his father's breath when the beatings and abuses were in the offing. Somehow, across the miles, he saw the label on the bottles his father had left out. "Well, Maker's Mark and Wild Turkey of course, but at the house we . . . my father, a lawyer, he has a special thing sent from Lexington, something called Dunlap's Hundred —"

"Oh yes, I know it!" Duke smiled and transformed the entire room, giving off light.

"It's impossible to get. I have just a bit of it, upstairs."

"I'll be happy to bring you a bottle," Gaston said, awfully pleased with himself. His determination not to have a father had failed — indeed, his father had made for his sole social victory, but he could live with it, in the approving gaze of Duke Johnston.

"You will find yourself on the permanent invitation list, I think. Heavens, a million apologies, I don't know your name yet."

"Gaston Jarvis."

They shook hands and Duke did not let go, pulling him along toward the door. "Duke Johnston," he reported, in that Southern baritone that could not have been more soothing and rich had he drunk all the whiskey in Scotland and smoked all of North Carolina's cigarettes. "Come upstairs."

Duke's own attic bedroom under the eaves was tidy, with law books and dictionaries, pictures of family, a saber over a long-closed-off fireplace, and two Civil War–era pistols in a display box, propped on the mantel. Gaston thought how disgraceful his own ill-kept room was back in Craven Hall. Duke must never see it.

Duke opened a closet door and, rather than clothes, there were ten constructed shelves, an array of bottles, scotch, gin, vodka, bourbons, old dusty-labeled wines, ports, sherries, libation for all occasions. There was a clinking and tinkling of bottles colliding as he rummaged, before producing a bottle of Dunlap's Hundred with about two shots' worth of honey-brown liquid left in the bottle.

There was a young woman there who had been Miss North Carolina her junior year, had gone to Atlantic City to compete for Miss America. There were football buddies demanding Duke come down to the front lawn and referee a game of touch football, directing and officiating with his glass-knobbed walking stick, now a campus trademark. There were two female exchange students from France who looked as if they had walked in from a Paris runway; they took over the turntable and played a Françoise Hardy LP and sang along to the lyrics while the rest of the party's males looked on adoringly and the females sulked. All of these and more, interrupting Gaston and Duke, begging Duke to come downstairs and join the party, to bestow a small unit of attention on them . . . and yet that night, Duke sat drinking with Gaston, for some reason finding in his young acquaintance someone he could trust and confide in.

And from there on, Gaston's social accomplishment at Duke was secure; he was a regular at Arcadia. He joined the newspaper and the college literary magazine. His witty reviews, his editorials, all popular, all noticed — but he only wrote them to shine reflected glory on Duke, to win Duke's praise. He loved Duke. He would drop anything, if Duke (always so busy with law school and exams and social calendars) called. Life was only where Duke existed and noticed, and what he disparaged or thought boring, Gaston thought worthless, too. Duke dated quite a lot, beautiful women, smart women, odd and talented women — he liked female company but not for very long, it seemed. Gaston would get a call in his dorm: "The girls are gone, and not a soul 'round here to have a drink with, wouldn't you know." And it wouldn't have mattered if Gaston had an exam the next day or was attempting a date himself late that evening, it would all be flung aside in order to garner precious audience up in Duke's room, to sample some new miraculous brew brought forth from the cupboard.

The friendship with Duke had faded, Gaston thought, sitting in his empty room with his laptop, but he had kept faith with the drinking. What had soured their friendship? As far as Duke was concerned, Gaston was still a friend. It was all Gaston's doing, the deterioration between them. Was it that he resented Duke for marrying his sister? Was he supposed to choose a lifetime of solitary drinking with Gaston over marriage and children with Jerene? Duke had once pulled him close and said, charmingly, with an intimate catch in his voice, "Marrying your sister sets us up nicely, Gaston," he said. "We don't have to do without our talks and our nightcaps — I'll always be close by. Thank God, you had a lovely sister or two — I'd have had to marry *you* otherwise." Yes, it was said to be charming, but he meant it at some level.

So what went wrong? That was a question fit for a rainy September night, his laptop's cursor blinking, waiting for him to do something. No, he did not mind Duke marrying Jerene. It was very strange, of course, weird to think of Duke screwing his sister. Jerene had been with that boor Beckleford Baylor, heir to a sock fortune. Then Jerene had dated Duke's housemate Darnell McKay, who went on to be a rich tax lawyer . . . and then Duke — the one out of the three who had squandered rather than made a fortune. No, that was not the source of the resentment.

Gaston could always replay in his mind the night, two months into their friendship, when it was two in the morning and they had been at it, discussing *Flags in the Dust* and *Absalom, Absalom!,* the peculiar burdens of sons from great families or, at least, from families with fathers who had pretensions of greatness, military greatness, Southern greatness, wealth and a family name with status, when Duke looked squarely at him and asked outright: "You hate your father, don't you?"

Gaston had talked with Duke about everything but this.

"I know you do. You don't have to say it. I know because I hate mine, too."

Major Bo Johnston, decorated hero of Patton's African campaigns, then Sicily, then mainland Italy, the vanguard of every Veteran's Day parade for twenty years.

"My father was traumatized by the war," Duke pressed on. "It exposed him to terrible things — I can only imagine. There was nowhere to put that anger, that violence when he came home, so he let us have it . . ." Duke shot back the rest of the bourbon in his glass. ". . . his sons, me and my brother Carry. It would have made an absurd documentary film, had it been filmed. This little angry man, five-nine, maybe 180 pounds, gone to seed in fact, unathletic, unsteady on his feet, whaling upon his oversized boys. Carrington's six-five, I'm six-three. We just let him do it. Put our heads down into the pillow and let him satisfy himself with his belt, like we owed it to him. In some twisted way, maybe we did owe it to him. All that we were, all that we had, was because of him."

Gaston's heart was in his throat. He had survived to this point with only his family knowing what went on, and even that was a silent acknowledgment with his sisters, briefly held eye contact, sighs, a shake of the head when the house fell quiet again.

"I'm presuming, of course," Duke said, having refilled his glass with Dunlap's Hundred. "But I recognized it in you early on. That you know, more or less, what I'm talking about."

In time, Gaston, months later, would speak candidly about his abusive alcoholic father, as Gaston became his own person, gaining fame as a writer, as an Arcadia regular; slowly without any epiphany or joyous single moment, Gaston Jarvis Sr. began to seem powerless, dismissable, a failed life, a sad life, a failed sad life that wasn't even original or damned in some special way but just the common mean old drunk way.

But that shared endurance of fathers only bound them closer! No, why had Gaston sabotaged their friendship, why had he ruined what was so necessary once upon a time . . .

"Lookaway, Dixieland," Gaston said out loud.

Lookaway, Dixieland. The book. They had been talking about it for at least a year, planning it out, arguing over the plot points.

"I prefer *Lookaway, Lookaway,*" said Duke. They had been raiding the lyrics of "Dixie" hoping to drop the perfect title. Gaston loved these sessions, up late until three or four, running out for more ice for the bourbon, or lying on Duke's famous leather sofa — a relic of the Divinity School, put out to trash, hauled by four men to Duke's room.

"That scans better," said Gaston. "But it

needs 'Dixieland' in the title."

It was almost *their* book; Duke's passion for it often seemed to exceed Gaston's own. Faulkner, Duke declared, had masterfully written about the post-Reconstruction South — there was no need to ever visit any of that again, for a white writer, at any rate. But what of the way we live now? But Gaston imagined setting a book before, during and after the Civil War, which had always been a historical fascination.

"Why not write a contemporary book?" Duke asked, perhaps weighed down by his illustrious ancestors, weary of all things Civil War.

"What's interesting about the New South?" Gaston insisted. "Nothing. The New South sinking into the monoculture of the United States, deracinated. No, it needs the grandeur of the earlier era."

While Duke mused as to the grand overarching idea of the book, Gaston knew it had to be about a Southern family. They would start from nothing, rise to great heights, then lose it all . . . the essential Irish-inherited doomedness of the South. Fortunes were always temporary below the Mason-Dixon because they were based on commodities. Families rich because of hemp, of tar, of cotton —

"Of gold," Duke reminded Gaston. North Carolina had boasted the nation's first gold rush; Charlotte owed its pre-War population spike to gold.

"Yes, gold or whatever. If the whims of the market didn't finish off the great families, then there was the Civil War, and if a family had survived that, then they were bust due to holding Confederate money, and after that, Northern predations during Reconstruction and countless panics."

Duke egged them both on. "Yet through it all such a sense of . . . of honor and family survival, all of it so precarious."

"One scandal could ruin a family's name." And that scandal always arrived fatefully, inexorably. Gaston's plan would be to have a book divided into smaller books, like a Walter Scott or Anthony Trollope epic, as a great family fights to hold its fortune for a final generation before the collapse and ruin. Book One: Scandal Averted. Book Two: Scandal Regained . . .

"They must not simply rise and fall," Duke had said. "They have to embody the central conundrum of the South."

"You mean, race?"

"There's something fatal from what the slave trade fostered, a kind of barbarism side by side with the civility."

Southerners. Such literate, civilized folk, such charm and cleverness and passion for living, such genuine interest in people, all people, high and low, white and black, and yet how often it had come to, came to, was still coming to vicious incomprehension, usually over race but other things too — religion, class, money. How often the lowest elements had burst out of the shadows and hollers, guns and torches blazing, galloping past the educated and tolerant as nightriders, how often the despicable had run riot over the better Christian ideals . . . how often cities had burned, people had been strung up in trees, atrocities had been permitted to occur and then, in the seeking of justice for those outrages, how slippery justice had proven, how delayed its triumph. Oh you expect such easily obtained violence in the Balkans or among Asian or African tribal peoples centuries-deep in blood feuds, but how was there such brutality and wickedness in this place of church and good intention, a place of immense friendliness and charity and fondness for the rituals of family and socializing, amid the nation's best cooking and best music . . . how could one place contain the other place?

Gaston had published a shelf of books now yet he had never felt more like a writer than on those nights in Duke's room, dreaming of what was to come, what he would yet write, bourbon in his glass, a Lucky Strike consuming itself in the ashtray. Of course, his first breakthrough short story, published at twenty-two, was in *The New Yorker,* "A

Brother's Warning," a sentimental but beautifully written piece, two brothers, one ready to ship out to Vietnam. Gaston took a larger than usual gulp of bourbon — if he were honest, the brother in the story was none other than Duke, and the story a projection of what it would have been to lose him to the Vietnam War meat grinder, if not for his football accident. Then came a story accepted by *The Atlantic,* "In the Pines, In the Pines," taking a cue from the Leadbelly song which always was a late-night favorite on Duke's turntable. That story was pure Southern gothic, woods and backwoods types, a town with too many secrets . . . maybe if James Dickey's *Deliverance* movie hadn't come out that year, he would never have gotten such an accidentally derivative piece published.

But 1972 was also the first novel, *The Rapeseed Field,* which was hailed as a short, brutal masterpiece. It was, in fact, a short story that got carried away to novella length and thankfully Alfred A. Knopf knew how to puff the thing out to an elegant 210 pages. As the too obvious title implied, there was a rape of a servant girl at the hands of a villainous patriarch. Gaston lifted his glass in a pretend toast to his father: they didn't have a servant girl but if they had, his father might likely have done it. The villain was an homage to his father, featuring blistering, abusive quotes his family could privately recognize as their father's repartee. The other characters gang up on Dad and kill him in secret, bury him in the yellow field of rapeseed beyond the homeplace. Gaston took another swig as if to wash the title from his mind — way too obvious, the whole book immature, too grotesque, too hysterical . . . yet, the critics saw promise, declared it a permanent addition to the canon of Southern Lit.

"When are you going to do it?" Duke persisted in saying, each time they'd meet in the years after Duke University, then rarer with Duke Johnston in his law practice. "When are we getting *Lookaway, Dixieland*?"

Gaston Jarvis began the book a thousand times. Gaston rented an antique attic room in eighteenth-century Hillsborough, in a colonial-era house falling down around its old-maid proprietress, writing most days and driving into Durham most nights . . . Yes, when indeed?

That was it, wasn't it? That was why he had grown to despise his friend. Gaston looked at Duke and saw a washout, someone who fumbled away many chances for a great role in life's pageant. And when the world looked at Gaston, everyone saw a success . . . except Duke. Duke looked at him and thought that they were partners in failed promise. To Duke — though he would never say it or remind him of it — Gaston was the writer who failed to write his masterpiece, who whored out his talent, who never wrote *Lookaway, Dixieland.*

Right now! Right here with the blank computer page before him, like Canute ordering the tides, the dark waters could be forced back, the novel could still rise!

Instead, Gaston sighed and clicked on MY PICTURES, and up popped a folder marked GIRLS, and he clicked on that and looked at some racy photos of Lucinda, a lovely ample black woman, of Maria, a saucy dark-skinned Latina, of Cherie, a thin smooth brown woman with sensuous eyes . . . he clicked on Cherie. He got to his feet and returned with the remote telephone. Cherie's number was on speed dial.

"It's a little late, isn't it, sugar?"

Gaston sat back down. "I thought you never slept."

"I'm always awake for you, big daddy. You always know when I feel like getting hot and wet . . ." She breathed heavily into the phone.

"You think you can get a cab?" There was a pause. "Of course, I understand with the hour and all, you would be compensated at our special rate."

"Wasn't even thinkin' about that, sugar. I was thinking about my big ol' daddy, and, ooh, I hope you're saving it all up for your Cherie." Since Gaston didn't respond, she wrapped up the call: "Be there in about forty minutes. Don't you fall asleep on me now."

“That will not happen,” he said, hanging up.

Dad was wrong. Wrong about advising against the tramps and hookers. These were the women who understood men best. They had perfected the one act for which women were irreplaceable — they had distilled it, refined it, unencumbered the sex act with an agendum. These were the women who didn’t gouge or cling or manipulate. And money made it all possible, easy, clinical. He looked at Cherie’s picture, those seductive big brown eyes, one more time and felt the early electric stirrings of arousal. Then he closed all the computer files, leaving the blank document called LOOKAWAY, DIXIELAND for last, and closed his laptop gently.

And why was September in North Carolina getting to be worse than August in recent years? The merciless summer sun was in no hurry to depart.

Gaston drove into the Charlottetowne Country Club parking lot, and was annoyed to find it full. Some ladies’ luncheon garbage going on, some do-gooding nonsense . . . every single place filled in the near lot. So he drove to the overflow lot and looked at the prospect of a several-hundred-yard walk in the ninety-six-degree sun, eighty-some percent humidity, just pure mid-Carolina hell. His linen suit would be soaked by the time he made it to the air-conditioning. He decided to do the much-forbidden remedy of cutting across the eighteenth green to the Nineteenth Hole. There were signs proscribing this activity to save the lawnsmen from having continually to repair the trace of the popular cut-through.

"Well, lookee there," called out a voice, when he was halfway to the clubhouse door. "Is that Gaston Jarvis on a putting green?"

Gaston turned to see Bob Boatwright, attired in his usual pink shirt and plaid golf pants and a jaunty golf cap with a pom-pom to make his presentation even more clownlike.

Bob's friend broke in: "Now Bob, you promised to introduce me . . ."

"Indeed I did!"

Bob Boatwright, Gaston understood, was among the wealthiest people in this club, entirely off real estate development. Bob had figured that Charlotte was going to be a boomtown long before the NBA franchise and the NFL stadium, before Wachovia and Bank of America grew into top-five banking behemoths, before trucking and warehousing gave way to high-tech and money managing, and he bought up prime properties in the urban wards accordingly — bought 'em for a song. He developed the northern reaches of South Carolina, which offered lower taxes and an effortless commute to Charlotte across the state line. He developed that mud-wallow of a lake called Lake Norman in the 1970s — formerly middle-class and cozy, old men in bassboats — to an upscale destination until everybody who was anybody had a home and a powerboat on it. He bought up land in the poor-black northwest and the poor-white southeast and built affordable condos and, next to that, upscale gated communities, and no matter where he built people bought. Jesus Christ, what a Midas touch.

"Still happy at that semi-abandoned lot of yours, Gaston? Wouldn't let me talk you into a little lakefront property befitting yo' station in life?"

"I like being close to the club," Gaston said, feeling the sweat bead on his forehead, ready to flow into a number of unattractive streams. "Makes for fewer DUIs."

They all laughed. The swarthy man showed the whole of his upper teeth and gums as he chuckled, a snarling dog before an attack. Another man, fat, in puke-green plaid golf pants, Charlie Brownbee, Gaston thought his name was, leaned forward as if to catch their collective scent.

"We may have to have a word with your brother-in-law," Boatwright added, coming down from his laugh. "We're interested in the Fort Mill shore of the Catawba, down near the old trestle. Looks like it's light industrial, Duke Power and their power lines own a wide strip, and then there's a big ol' beautiful chunk all zoned away for historical preservation. And Duke Johnston's name is all over the trust."

How acidly deprecating should I be, wondered Gaston for a second. He liked to rain abuse on his brother-in-law's Civil War preservation and re-enactment mania . . . but he didn't care for these moneymen either. "My brother-in-law imagines there was a skirmish of historical importance along that riverbank," Gaston said, taking a middle avenue. "Perhaps a musket ball fell in the vicinity, though I rather doubt it. Stoneman's Raiders and all that."

The men looked at him blankly.

"Nonetheless," continued Gaston, "my brother-in-law and some Civil War obsessives are going to make it a memorial park, honoring the zeroes of brave men who fought alongside the U.S. 21 Bypass."

"So it's not whatcha call historical?" asked the loud New Yorker in the ugly plaid puffed-out golf trousers. "The designation could be overturned?"

Gaston was struck by the nakedness of the greed, a stupefaction that anything or anyone would get ever so slightly in the way of their making another mountain of money. Plowing up the clay, turning the river brown, cutting down the old growth. Screw 'em, Gaston thought.

"Stoneman's Raiders did burn the bridge there," Gaston said, wiping his brow, wet throughout his torso now. "A few shots were fired, in point of fact. That was about it for Charlotte in the Civil War but you know how folks are about the Civil War, and what little visible Charlotte history there is. I'm afraid you fellows may be out of luck."

"Aw now," said Boatwright, "I betcha there's a way. Maybe we should sit down with Duke and see if he'd be interested in a property there, let him participate. Could be some real gain in it for him."

Gaston reflected how Duke of all individuals was the least moved by money and practicalities. He had never capitalized on being a city councilman, never scooped up the appropriate graft. "Be my guest," Gaston said, thirsting for the clubhouse and the liquid bounty awaiting within.

"You might put in a word," said Charlie Brownbee with the ridiculous pants.

"Yeah," said swarthy teeth-and-gums, "I hear he might need the money."

Boatwright blanched at this tactless comment. That was clearly something Boatwright told in secret to his partners, shared at some strategy session. Gaston could imagine the PowerPoint presentation: Obstacles to Success, with Duke Johnston's affable face popping up as a slide. *But we hear he's run through the family money,* someone in charge of market research would pipe in. As much as Gaston wanted to deliver a savage response to this vulgarian who would lightly bring up his brother-in-law and sister's financial standing, Gaston also felt bad, really bad, about his ugliness with Jerene in the Nineteenth Hole a few months back. What would be the harm of putting Duke in the way of these shysters? Maybe Duke would make a little money, keep his sister Jerene in pearls and matronly fashion.

"I assure you," Gaston said, "Duke has plenty of money tucked away, hence his life as a Civil War bon vivant. You are not likely to persuade him to do anything for money." He paused briefly, they were all ears. "That's the difference down here, my Northern friend, between Old Money and vulgar, crass, showy, greedy New Money which would jump at any opportunity for a sweetheart deal." He enjoyed his perfectly pleasant tone, looking right at the man with the snarling dog teeth. "If you think a man such as Duke Johnston will spring at the sign of a few dollars like a trained seal lurching for a fish, then you don't know Duke Johnston. If your little development honored the site in some way . . ."

Boatwright broke in, "Yes, well that's an added value to the property, that we could preserve the integrity of the Civil War site.

We would be open to that sort of development — indeed, it might help sell the units. I think Duke might well be the perfect person to help with design and planning." Boatwright talked on, having surmised the situation perfectly, as well as Gaston's contempt for his partners. Gaston felt he could see Boatwright's wheels turning: *Yes, take meeting with Duke, don't bring my partners, talk Civil War claptrap, sacred ground, how only Duke Johnston could guide us . . .*

"Bob," Gaston said, aiming himself toward the clubhouse, "I am melting like the Witch of the West. I'll see what I can do."

Gaston's suit was indistinguishable from a towel after a shower, and when he plunged through the double French doors of the clubhouse, and felt its arctic air-conditioning, he wondered if he would faint. Keeping himself aloft by a steadying hand on the bar, he found his way to the next-to-last seat, his seat, his sentry post, at the end of the Nineteenth Hole. Dexter saw him enter and had his bourbon (an especially generous pour for drink number one) waiting for him in the chilled silver julep cup, surrounded by a high-thread-count cotton square with the club blazon embroidered upon it.

"Got the silver out today," Gaston exhaled, near collapse from the change of temperature.

"Founder's Day is this weekend."

“Yes it is.” Gaston wrapped the smooth silver tankard in his hand, protected from the chill burn by the napkin square. Oh bourbon does taste its best in chilled silver — what so much of the world does not know. And Charlottetowne keeps alive this nicety . . . the old ways, the old manners. Should have told Bob Boatwright and those Yankee carpetbaggers where to go fuck themselves, but that’s my central downfall right there. Should have buried Norma and Mrs. Meacham and my war criminal of a mother in a trench down by the Catawba River, too. I’m too accommodating, a creature of the old courtesies. Too nice for your own good, Gaston — he lectured himself between divine sips — too nice for your own good.

Jerene

On a Sunday late morning, the Mint wasn't open to the public but the lights were on and a janitor and a few administrative staff were in early. Jerene Johnston dressed for church, but then decided to skip it and drive to the Mint. She knocked on the main door until someone waved to her through the glass; moments later Jerene could see that it was Miss Maylee, an ancient docent, who toddled over to the front door with a string of heavy keys to let her inside. "You're certainly here early, Mrs. Johnston," she sang.

"I know that Lynne and the catering people have everything well in hand," said Jerene. "I'm just being a Nervous Nellie."

The Mint Museum of Charlotte was different from other museums because it was not conceived as a museum. It was a columned, porticoed neo-classical U.S. mint building from 1836 turned renegade Confederate mint, printing out all that Confederate scrip that would bankrupt the region, with a turn as a Confederate hospital, then a once-grand building you could rent space in — Thomas Edison worked on his lightbulb in a rented space here (or was that apocrypha?) — then finally it was pressed into service as an art museum. This was a museum organized not by period or school, but by rich benefactors' hoardings. One walked through the various high-ceilinged rooms, as Jerene was doing now, looking above the grand doorways to see the gold-plated names of donors' families — the Rankin Room, the Crosland Room, Belk, Dowd, Harris — some names among the pinnacle of Charlotte society, some names no one had heard of until the embossment of the golden name above the doorway.

Jerene could home in like a pigeon on the Jarvis Room, walk through the other galleries of art without looking up, turn left once, right twice, and then raise her head in time to see the family name shining above the door. She never tired of surveying the room itself, the holdings of the Jarvis Trust for American Art, five big and ten miniature paintings of varying value by American nineteenth-century artists studied by art history students, plus a few engravings and watercolors, too.

The ghostly Miss Maylee had materialized behind her to see if there was anything she could do. "Antoine Blanche," she added, with an approving smile.

"Getting Antoine was a coup, wasn't it?"

Charlotte's hottest semi-celebrity chef was debuting a run of his fall hors d'oeuvres tonight, and that would bring Charlotte out even if a hurricane materialized. At 8:30 P.M. tonight Jerene Jarvis Johnston's brainchild, the Mint by Gaslight, would commence. Patrons, friends, dilettantes and donors, for a hundred dollars a ticket, would be given little gas lamps and allowed to wander around the many rooms, casting romantic shadows, all fueled by an open bar that rivaled any high-society event of the season. Jerene had imported the two best bartenders from the Charlottetowne Country Club . . . well, Gaston, her brother, had assured her they were the best and he would know. Antoine Blanche from the packed-nightly Carte Blanche in the Marriott Uptown would cook, then mingle; it didn't hurt that he was a handsome Frenchman who shamelessly played up his accent. The six trustees of the Jarvis Trust for American Art, all contemporaries of Jerene, handpicked for their sociability, wealth, pliancy, would be in attendance too. These ladies had contributed the necessary money to the foundation (tax write-off!) for catering and cocktails.

Every year it was a mob scene and the invitations were much sought after but Jerene knew the whims of these sorts of events. She would announce the date months in advance, then pray the date held up, unmenaced by tornado warnings, civil disturbances, unforeseen NASCAR events or a Panthers Sunday-night game, hastily announced concerts of pop stars — she spent weeks divining the best possible Sunday evening — before the new fall TV season and the NFL heated up in earnest. She was not about to have *The Simpsons* trump the Mint by Gaslight.

Charlotteans came just for the liquor and the snacks, of course, oblivious to the greater purposes of raising money to purchase art. The Jarvis Trust had to give a slice of the ticket price to the Mint Museum itself, but at least $75 out of that $100 ticket went to the Jarvis Trust, multiplied by . . . what was this year's body count? At least two-hundred-ten RSVPs, so they'd be 15K in the clear. Ideally, every year she would gladhand and swan about the room, someone would chime on a glass, she would briefly greet everyone by microphone in the Jarvis Room, a little banter, a few shout-outs to the most important people in the room (to let the unimportant people know they were swimming in rich waters) and then she might unveil another print or take the cloth off a newly purchased miniature to polite applause. This would be followed by obsequies to the many people who made it possible, the people gathered here tonight, the core of culture in Charlotte right here in this room, art lovers, heroic, dependable. After her brief but memorable speechifying, the event was then on the downhill side: some carried their lanterns around the shadowy rooms of the second floor, other people took it as a cue to mow through the contents of the hors d'oeuvre trays, suck down the last of the free booze, then stumble into taxis or risk a Breathalyzer stop, all the while thinking, *That Jerene Johnston can throw a mighty fine party,* and well, at least they had "supported the Mint."

But Jerene knew it wasn't about the Mint, which did quite well on grants and gifts and legacies, it was all about supporting *her* legacy, her legend.

The Jarvis Trust for American Art was the ticket into Charlotte society for the Jarvis women, in perpetuity. The core of this collection had been purchased by her great-great-grandfather who indulged his wife's fondness for art. Jerene had seen the Jarvis homeplace site down near Waxhaw, North Carolina, a stone's throw from the state line with South Carolina, now just a bit of dirt and weeds between two shambling, still-standing chimneys. It hardly seemed that anything confined between those two chimneys could ever have been a grand enough house for the Jasper Cropsey, the Thomas Cole and the David Johnson, let alone any other sort of finery, but the story went that her great-great-grandmother Adeline was from Wilmington, North Carolina, a woman from an old grand colonial family (the Bells), who found the hinterlands of Waxhaw intolerable. So, her great-great-grandfather Hermann Jarvis indulged whatever decorating whims would content her. He took her to Charleston to buy European furniture, to Baltimore to buy American landscapes. Hermann Jarvis and his brothers Wilhelm and Otto. People often assumed the Jarvises were Scottish, because Jerene and her immediate family went to Presbyterian churches, but Jarvis was a German name and her people came in with the original Germans who settled Mecklenburg County and named the central market town after the English king's German bride, Queen Charlotte, hoping to gain royal favor.

In the years following the Civil War, such rural outposts as Waxhaw were subject to raids by bandits, bummers, ragtag groups of ex-Union or ex-Rebel or newly armed black soldiers who felt deprived of spoils and rapine. The family story — known to most of Charlotte, since Jerene regularly told it most years at Mint by Gaslight — was that a group of Northern bummers arrived on Adeline Bell's doorstep when Hermann was away in town, and after hiding the paintings behind the upright piano, she then loaded her husband's shotgun.

Ya cain't shoot all of us, miss, said one of the brigands.

Yep, but I'll get one, maybe two of you and,

since you opened your mouth, you're first, she said back.

The men backed off with a laugh, helped themselves to well water, raided the vegetable garden and carried off a goat for that night's stew, and let her be. And that's how, Jerene would say, indeed Jerene would say again this very night, how Cole's *Cabin by the Lake* and George Inness's *Approaching Storm,* Cropsey's *Bear Mountain* and Frederick Church's *A Catskill Sunset* reside with all of us today, "safe from the torch or the carpet-bagger, safe in our care." It was always an applause line.

It may have seemed to Charlotte that the Jarvis Trust was equally venerable as the family but that was a misapprehension Jerene never corrected; it was a recent notion. Her grandmother began using the art collection for social purposes back in the 1950s, reigning over a small, select, sporadic punch-and-cookies reception at the Myers Park Country Club, the details of which were obscure (despite some intensive detective work by Jerene who wanted to backdate her family's efforts). Jerene's mother, Jeannette Jarvis, later supervised the annual reception and enlarged the guest list to nab not only high society but the run-of-the-mill rich who came with the growth in banking in Charlotte's boom times, and who, like cats scratching to be let in, were more than eager to plunk down money to be in the same room with the Belks and the Rankins and Mayor Gantt and board members from First Union and Bank of America. But Jeannette Jarvis had been erratic as a hostess. Some years her fund-raising event flourished, others it fizzled, with Jeannette not realizing you put it all in the well-paid caterer's hands. Jerene remembered vividly her mother running around, fraying to a frazzle, in the hours leading up to her smallish event.

No, it had been Jerene who had launched this annual event into the stratosphere. She had made it a lasting legacy for any of her daughters and granddaughters who would host the Mint by Gaslight for generations to come.

"Mother, please," Annie had said when her mother projected that Annie might one day preside over the event, "it doesn't even make sense. Who wants to see art in bad light? And they're oil lamps, not gaslights. And what if someone drops a lamp and burns the place down?"

(The lamps were faux-oil lamps, with an opaque glass, running on batteries and a small lightbulb.)

The line of succession would be skipping over her eldest daughter, Annie, who consistently threatened to sell off the art and give the proceeds to charity. As for her younger, Jerilyn, Jerene had not seen the titanium will necessary to pull off this kind of social performance, to dominate a room, to host and chat and pour and soothe, but maybe that would come. She never considered passing the trust along to Bo or Joshua — this wasn't, in her mind, intended to be a male legacy. Men, for their part, had no need of a contrived social event to place themselves at the forefront of things. She did wish her own daughters had some appreciation of just what it was she intended to pass on. She would settle for mild, diffident interest! Annie would not be here tonight — just as well, in the event Congresswoman Myrick was around for Annie to buttonhole about her right-wing voting record. Jerilyn had already called this morning and left a message that Jerene had not listened to — likely she was apologizing for not being able to make it down from Chapel Hill, swept up in sorority nonsense.

Her oldest son, Bo, and his wife, Kate, would be there dependably. Jerene hoped to offer Kate — cultureless but good-hearted Kate — a seat on the Jarvis Trust on the principle of keeping it all in the family.

Her youngest son, Joshua, and his friend Dorrie would come too. Joshua loved to mingle in a crowd and Dorrie was an Art History major and could actually talk with authority about the art on the walls. Of course, there would be the predictable prying questions: are Joshua and Dorrie going to be married? You never see one without the other! Not that she isn't just lovely, but . . . but are you and Duke all right with having a black daughter-in-law? Jerene was a little bit exhausted already, and the event was still ten hours away.

And, more exhausting yet, her mother would be in attendance. Alas. Bo and Katie would pick up Mrs. Jarvis from Lattamore Acres. All night long, she would malinger in a wheelchair being pushed about, fishing for praise, taking credit for the evening as if Jerene were some sad figurehead propped up in her place, and eliciting sympathy for whatever illness, real or imagined, she was afflicted this year. Jerene would prefer not having her mother attend because that meant Gaston, who had such a following among Charlotte's elite for his gossipy bonhomie, would *not* attend, since he and their mother could not be in the same room anymore "over my or her dead body, preferably hers." Jerene would spend a percentage of tonight's small talk explaining why Gaston didn't come this year; some of the women would bring books for him to sign hoping that they would run into him at this party.

Jerene would also have to lavishly thank her mother for all her work bringing the Jarvis Trust to this pinnacle. Many of the elderly women without whom any cultural fundraiser (or Charlotte society itself) couldn't function, sanctified Jeannette Jarvis, had paid court to her for years. Jerene would attribute vision and wisdom to her mother and there would be a round of applause wherein Jeannette would take a bow from her wheelchair (which she didn't ever use to convey herself around Lattamore Acres, mind you!), inflating like a balloon with adulation, bringing a trembling hand with a handkerchief to her eye as if she were unexpectedly moved by all this honor due her . . . Oh my land, thought Jerene, unable to dwell on that tableau a moment longer.

Aside from Yankee bummers and family indifference, threats to the Jarvis collection competed on all sides: Dr. Misra, the high-voiced, Indian-accented new curator who never glimpsed her but that he tried to interest her in the tax benefits of simply offering up the gems in her collection to the Mint as a permanent gift. There was an equally persistent Lester Fontine, a representative of Sotheby's, who wanted her to sell the Church for a Northern collector who was a completist . . . and it wasn't as if the Johnston family couldn't use the money. And then there was the new uptown Mint, proposed for 2010, in seven years, a world-class museum space built by some post-modern architect of note, right in the heart of Charlotte, to be organized like a proper big-city museum, she imagined, with the collections mingled and her family name consigned to a little notecard beside the painting. Well, maybe that obliteration would or wouldn't happen on schedule. In the here and now, the Mint by Gaslight would reign as the gold standard of Charlotte artmongering.

"I don't think there's a thing for me to do," Jerene said aloud.

"I don't think there is," Miss Maylee said agreeably.

"I used to be so nervous before these things that I could never eat lunch, but I think this year I could eat an entire buffet line." She made a final unnecessary check or two, called the caterers for an update, thanked the docent again, then decided to join Duke at the Charlottetowne Country Club, where the famous Sunday spread would just have begun to be laid out.

"It's like," Charlie Brownbee faltered, "what is it called? That film we went to go see . . ."

"Don't ask me!" screamed Dollie. She turned directly to Jerene. "You get me in a movie theater and I fall asleep like that! I haven't seen a film in years!"

"Aw, that's not true, baby doll. What about that *Lord of the Rings* film?"

"The second time we saw it, I mostly stayed awake, that's right. But the first time I slept like a baby. Same with the symphony! Something about a dark theater and I'm snoring away! Isn't that how it is, Charlie?"

Jerene let Dollie monopolize, marching toward the social front lines with a personality based on proudly cherished incapacities: "I couldn't make heads or tails reading that *Da Vinci Code* — put me right to sleep!" And "I haven't cooked since we hired Letisha and Charlie's not exactly begging for me to go back in the kitchen, are you, honey?" And "I won't go on a plane!" And why she will never be caught dead doing committee work again because she did some for the Ladies of Charlottetowne annual fund drive and she helped sponsor a luncheon for a ticket price from which some portion went to charity, and when Lurleen Hemsdale Parker said she couldn't make the luncheon and wanted her money back, Dollie said she couldn't have it because everything went to charity anyway and Lurleen Hemsdale Parker wanted to make a federal case out of it.

". . . and I said, you'll get it for $39.95, including shipping and handling!" This apparently constituted a joke and Dollie threw her head back cackling at her own line. Jerene smiled politely. Dollie regained her breath long enough to interrupt Charlie, who was talking easement politics with Duke. "Charlie, Charlie —"

Charlie: "So Riverview is planning to offer homes on the Rock Hill side of the Catawba for two hundred fifty thousand — can you believe it?"

Dollie: "Did you hear what I said, Charlie? I was saying what I told Lurleen Parker —"

Charlie: ". . . cutting down that old growth, for a bunch of middle-class condos?"

Dollie: "Did you hear, Charlie, what I said to Lurleen Parker?"

Charlie: "What's that, baby doll?"

Dollie: "I said I'd give her luncheon ticket back for $39.95 for handling."

Charlie: "Yeah, you told me before."

Dollie: "That wasn't it . . ." She turned to Jerene. "What did I say?"

Jerene managed to bring it out. "Shipping and handling."

"That's it! $39.95, including shipping and handling!" And then she cackled again.

"You'll excuse me?" Jerene said, standing up, looking beyond the elegant Club dining room toward the restrooms; she bowed toward the Brownbees and Bob Boatwright before glancing at her husband, observing the panic in his eyes, not wanting to be abandoned. Once out of sight, Jerene veered into the Nineteenth Hole for a little hiding out, and a check of her cell phone messages. Thank goodness — no emergency flares from the caterer. Jerilyn had called twice more. Before she called her daughter back, she squinted to the end of the bar . . . where her brother was already drinking, 11:45 on a Sunday morning. He raised his glass as if to toast her.

She walked over to offer the thanks she should have offered a few weeks back, if she hadn't still been miffed. "You might as well forward your mail to this place, Gaston."

"They'll make a brass monument out of it one of these days, the stool whereupon the great Southern author lowered and raised his ample posterior. I saw you in the dining room being royally entertained by Bob Boatwright and Dollie and Charlie. My, what a *salon des artistes* you gather about yourself."

"I need a sip of that," she said, stealing the glass from his hand and taking a necessary swallow.

"I'd be happy to buy you one."

"The idiotic Dollie Brownbee notwithstanding, I suppose I should thank you for putting Duke in the way of a business deal. Of course, my land, the sums I'm overhearing are in no way possible for us."

Gaston had a mouth full of peanuts which, in his habit, he popped into his mouth one at a time. "Umm . . . I don't think they want money . . . They want permission to develop down by Duke's piece of sacred earth."

"I'm not sure why they need Duke to do anything." She reached for Gaston's tumbler, but he was too quick and snatched it back.

"Let me buy you one. And the devil you say about sweet Dollie Brownbee, the belle of Forest City."

"I'd say Forest City is in even sorrier shape than I thought, if that's the standard for belledom."

"Oh, come on. I would have thought you were impervious to stupid women, as many committees as you serve on — all those gaggling biddies in your artsy trust you'll be mingling with this very night. Ten minutes in a room with those women and I would hang myself by my necktie from the sturdiest-looking lighting fixture. Most women as they get older empty themselves out and get even stupider. Shopping, grandchildren, very little else to talk about —"

"Don't let Norma hear you talk like that." Politely, a glass of ice water was set down half an arm's length away from Jerene. And while she appreciated the subtlety of the bartender's observations (that she wanted a drink of something), it also meant every word they exchanged was being heard and taken note of. She leaned closer to whisper, "Speaking of women you are fond of abusing."

"If Jarvis *mère* is in attendance tonight, I will not be — you know my policy."

Jerene's phone rang again. It was Jerilyn.

"I'll castigate you later," she said, drifting back from her brother to take the call privately.

"Mom."

A mother knows from one syllable something is wrong. Jerene spotted a remote table near the window, out of public hearing. Jerilyn was babbling, there were false starts, and an attempt at empty small talk, before Jerene cut her off, "Now Jerilyn, you're going to have to tell me exactly what is wrong."

Her daughter was vague, but confirmed certain things had transpired.

"Did some boy do something to you?"

Silence.

"One of those frat boys talk you into something you wish you hadn't done?"

More silence, maybe a stifled sob.

"Did you let him?" She listened. "Did you tell him no? But what? Did you have your clothes off? If you're rolling around on top of each other naked, Jerilyn, you cannot stop a boy from doing what boys —"

Jerilyn imparted more muddled information.

Jerene momentarily remembered from her own Theta Kappa Theta days a blur of faces — or maybe the same face — but differing physiognomies, boys with beer guts, or short and compact, tall and gangly, vodka breath and aftershave, all with eight sets of hands, moving and taking possession of body parts through her ball gowns and knit sweaters, a legion of onslaught furiously repulsed at the vaginal redoubts. "Are you saying he . . ." They would have to work up to the word *rape.* ". . . are you saying he forced you?"

More nonsense.

"Jeriflower, he either did or he didn't. I'm coming down. Yes, that's right, it *is* the night of my thing, but that's not important." It was a two-three-hour drive to Chapel Hill, two-three back . . . plenty of time. "My land, *yes,* I'm coming down and we'll sort this business out. But you have to stay put. No showers, no changing clothes. Try not to engage in any more *orgies* until I get there."

Her baby girl was in bad shape.

"And no tears. We have to think and act with great precision about these kind of things." Jerene and Duke had taken different cars to Charlottetowne, and Duke's Mercedes was the nicer of the two. She decided Duke would figure out that she had taken it, and she got into the Mercedes. It might come in handy.

Her daughter was not back at her dorm but now at the sorority house where she went to cry herself to sleep and pass out after the unfortunate encounter. Sensing she was fragile, and possibly aware of what happened, the girls had let Jerilyn lie down in Tylerlea Bumgardner's big room upstairs. Jerene wondered just what gossip had spread and how far.

It was Sunday so parking was free on the street. Jerilyn pulled the Mercedes to the curb and gathered up her purse. She gave a wistful look to her former home, Thetahouse, then proceeded to step across the flagstones, past the construction toward Sigma Kappa Nu's porch. She was aware she looked like a minor British Royal Family member, moving importantly in a conservatively cut Chanel mauve pastel with a perfectly matching Prada clutch. Jerene approached a wide-open front door and was only asked once who she was and if she could be helped ("I think Jerilyn is upstairs . . . that is a gorgeous purse, Mrs. Johnston!"), but she had the run of the house if she wished. There was noise from the backyard, lots of whooping and hollering; she glimpsed a few Sigma Kappa Nus, all in ratty sweatshirts and gym pants. Jerene permitted herself a small tour, the dining salon, the main living area and their beaten-down barely presentable furniture, the smell of beer, perfume, Febreze carpet cleaner . . .

Jerilyn was asleep when her mother knocked on the door. Jerilyn let her in and then returned to lie on a bunk bed, curled up in several blankets with Tylerlea's teddy bear within reach. Her mother leaned against the desk, preferring to stand for the most unpleasant part of their discussion.

"Jerilyn, darling. The worst thing in life is feeling like you have no control over things. I try to avoid those situations at all costs. It's like my committee work." Jerene breathed, knowing she was stalling for time. "I'd rather be president and run the whole show, even if it takes a year off my life, or do nothing at all, but I can't abide being somewhere in between where I don't have any power yet am supposed to do things for everyone to look at and judge."

Jerilyn just stared at her mother, waiting to hear something that applied to her situation.

"You have to make a decision today. And it's one of those decisions that you have to live with your whole life. A job you can quit, a boyfriend you can break up with. Even a marriage you can get out of, as your sister has amply demonstrated, though we don't approve of that sort of thing. Almost anything can be undone, but some things *cannot* be undone once committed to. They can merely be decided upon. And you have to make such a decision — a decision which will *absolutely* conclude the matter in question. Do you understand?"

Jerilyn did not understand, but gave up a nod as if she did.

"Either you accuse this boy of a crime . . ." The word *rape* still need not be said, for once released into the air, Jerene sensed, it might have a life of its own. ". . . and have him arrested and put on trial, for which you will have to single-handedly take the stand and convict him — starting right now by our going to the police and filing a report and having a doctor examine you . . . intimately. Or, you chalk this up to a misunderstanding and never think about it again."

Jerilyn mumbled, "But couldn't we — couldn't I —"

"Darling, those are the only options. Prosecute this boy and spend the next few years, and few trials, I suspect, since he'll appeal and all that, devoting yourself to punishing him for what he did last night or call it a learning experience and never, ever mention it to anyone."

With her daughter thinking it over, Jerene gently paced the room, to the window and back. "If," Jerene began again, "you wish to take this boy to court and put him in jail, your father and I will support you. We will spend whatever it takes on lawyers, and it will take a lot, Jeriflower, a whole pile of money, since I suspect his parents are well off, that could be better spent sending you to Europe or buying clothes for a job interview — you name it. What does this boy's father do, by the way?"

"I don't know."

Jerene, her back to Jerilyn, stopped pacing. "Darling, in the future, you may not invite to a bed any young man about whom you do not know his father's profession, his eventual means, his status in this world. That is a one-way ticket to the mobile-home park. These are most important details. I did not . . ." Jerene now stood by the window, looking down on the spectacle in the backyard. Young sorority girls in cutoff jeans and tube tops washing cars for charity, lathered up, wet, receiving the hoots and catcalls of the university boys, who were bringing their sports cars, their Audis and Saabs and father's Lexuses down the side lane to wait in line to offer up their dollars for a car wash and a nudie show, with these girls, like the harlots of the Old Testament, splaying themselves on the automotive idols, all but mounting the hood ornaments . . . "I did not," she continued, a little absently, "approve of your being here, spending this sort of money and wasting time. I did not want you to drop anchor in a place like this but now that you are here you must promise me to cast an eye for only the best, most wonderful men of good family and, yes, fortune if you can find it."

Jerilyn said, "Mama, all the other girls —"

"Many of the girls here are whores. Their mothers were probably trash, too, whatever their pedigree. You can direct the men who can't behave themselves to those girls who'll spread their legs gladly. It hardly matters what they do, it only matters what you do."

Jerilyn's one gasp of rebellion: "I pledged Sigma Kappa Nu because I, for once, wanted to have a little fun."

"Jeriflower, let me clarify your mission here at the University of North Carolina. You're at Carolina to pick up facility with some subject so you can work until you get married. Learn to do something you enjoy for a little while then retire to a nice home with a nice husband and have some nice children. There are many fine men to attach yourself to. Marry a future surgeon, a lawyer, at least. Trade your good looks and good name for an even better life than we have, darling. So *your* daughter can do as she pleases."

"Why can't I do as I please?"

"Because you are *my* daughter." Jerene pulled the curtains closed, as a duel with the garden hose broke out, shrill squeals and hard nipples through cotton tops for all to see. She turned to Jerilyn, offering her daughter a more loving countenance. In a few hours, three or four at the most, this whole episode would be behind them. Jerene said gently, "You will not get pregnant here, you may not be the girl everyone whispers about having had an abortion. You may not be the sorority tramp —"

"Mama, I wouldn't!"

"Last night, apparently, you were well on the way. Now what's it going to be? Shall we go to the police and let them insert some kind of kit into you, collect some . . . some sample or will we wrap this up here and now?"

Jerilyn wasn't sad anymore, just exhausted, defeated. "I'm not going to sit through some trial and have some lawyer call me names."

"That's very sensible. But what about part two?"

"Whadya mean, part two?"

"I mean, are we agreed that this is finished *right here and now,* that you are not going to dwell on this? You cannot decide not to press charges and then gossip around creation that you were assaulted — that will have consequences, and not just for the boy. You must decide that it never happened."

"Never happened."

"I have no intention, Jerilyn, of paying for ten years of therapy as you *relive* and relive it, and — oh whatever you see on *Oprah* these days from people who can't buck up and move on. There'll be no hating yourself and turning to drink and pills . . ."

"Oh, Mama."

". . . and falling apart over what is really a small thing like this kind . . . this kind of miscalculation."

"You don't want me to even *think* about what happened?"

"I most certainly do not. Unless it stops you from doing something equally foolish in the future."

"All right."

"Repeat after me," Jerene said, raising her hand as if administering an oath. Jerilyn raised her hand warily as her mother pronounced, "I am a Jarvis woman."

"I'm a Jarvis woman."

"There will be much in life that will not go our way."

Jerilyn rolled her eyes, but said it.

"But we will make our choices clearly and never look back."

Jerilyn dutifully repeated that as well.

"And this misadventure is now officially behind me."

"And this misadventure, Mama, is now officially behind me."

Jerene now sat on the bedside and put her arm around her daughter. "Now don't you feel a little better? It's *done,* and now you can move on. I might have thought a hundred times about whether I should have married your father. He should have married a Civil War cannon, I think."

Jerilyn smiled again, then chuckled, the first laughter since the assault.

"But I made up my mind not to be one of those unhappy women. One of those women who is always second-guessing herself, trade up, do better, outthink, overthink — there's no future in it. He's who I married. I was there at the altar, I could have said no, but I said yes, and that's the end of it. You cannot go through life regretting or second-guessing everything."

"No, Mama."

"You can control what you do from here on out, so let's dwell on that, Jeriflower." Jerene kissed her daughter's cheek. "Oh your hair smells nice. It must've cost the earth whatever you put in it."

"It's just old bargain shampoo, Mama."

Jerene retrieved the purse she had laid on the desktop. Jerilyn had two hundred-dollar bills pressed into her hand. "Well, no bargain goods for this pretty eligible young woman, with her debut coming up just around the corner. You buy the best thing there is for my best little angel, hm?" Another kiss, and a tighter hug. "Now who was this boy?"

Jerilyn faltered. "What does it matter? I thought it was behind us."

"No, you're putting it behind *you,* darling. It is not quite over for your mother. His parents shall be made aware of their son's behavior —"

"Oh Mama, no."

"I will have his name."

This could have waited until another day, a late afternoon without Jerene's Mint by Gaslight scheduled to begin in five hours, but the boy in question hailed from Durham, and the parents' address was easily found with the help of a service station map. In any event, Jerene reflected that in another hour, three at most, this would all be behind them and then she could focus on her little speech tonight. A nice two-hour drive back home where she could rehearse and practice — just perfect.

Jerene pulled up into the driveway, 683 Grosvenor Lane, in an upscale neighborhood near the Southpoint Mall, not a mile from the interstate. Not a fine old district of columned houses and edenic vegetation, but something newer, something not there ten years ago. Jerene had seen more vulgar mansions — the inside would tell the tale. It wasn't polite to just drop in. Manners, even in a crisis. Though yards from their front door, she called the MacArthurs' number.

"My name is Jerene Johnston and I am parked in your driveway," she began when Mrs. MacArthur answered. "I am sorry to disturb you on a Sunday but there is something we must urgently discuss concerning our children, my daughter Jerilyn, and your son Luke."

Moments later, Jerene was met at the door. Mrs. MacArthur was in her early forties, lovely, an oval face with large brown eyes and a small mouth that played successfully at a smile even in repose. Still dressed from church, perhaps. Custom designer, a small shop in town . . .

"I take it this is not a happy call," Belinda MacArthur said graciously, the right note of concern in her voice.

"Do you already know what this is about?" Jerene asked.

Belinda paused. "No," she said simply. "I'll get some coffee."

She does too know, thought Jerene. The woman has given away the game already.

Their little darling has been in trouble with girls before. Jerene entered the foyer, seeing a golf bag and clubs leaned against a dark wood table; perhaps Mr. MacArthur was bound for the golf course . . . Louis Vuitton bags with a pouch for a mobile phone, Jerene noted, and a bouquet of gleaming silver-headed Nike clubs within.

"Welcome, welcome," boomed Lucas J. MacArthur Sr., a bearish man, much older than his wife, dressed in high-end leisure wear. Sixty-something. Belinda must be the second wife; a first wife is probably eating him alive with alimony. Good. Perhaps daddy can't keep it in his pants any more than sonny can, in which case he is practiced in the art of paying to make trouble go away. "What can we do for you?" Mr. MacArthur purred, directing Jerene into the living room.

"I'm afraid it is a most unpleasant business," she said, meeting his gaze without a flinch.

"We should wait until Belinda brings in the coffee. She'd like to hear."

Jerene faintly smiled. All right, who was the power in this family, who had the name to protect? Who was more scared of scandal? Jerene assessed the living room. Acceptable taste but nothing very fine. The glass-fronted cabinets were Thomasville, not antique, all newish. A Persian rug of no great antiquity or distinction, maybe not even Middle Eastern, baubles, odds and ends, small statuary (possibly from Pier 1), oil reproductions of the English countryside, a fox-and-hounds lithograph over the fireplace, not a trace of originality. The first wife is probably in the good home, Jerene figured; this one had to be moved into quickly and filled hurriedly, so as not to look empty. There was the sound of a coffeemaker whirring from the kitchen. Sailing magazines — they must have a boat. The door slowly opened, revealing a three-second glimpse of the kitchen: French copper cookware hanging from hooks, a pasta maker, granite countertops, Illy, Le Creuset, Miele . . . Belinda's domain, so he has spared no expense in pleasing her. Belinda approached with the tray and coffee things. China cups and saucers, not just any old mugs from the kitchen, no instant coffee blasted in a microwave. Belinda wanted her to see they were refined people, too.

Belinda poured well, placing the cup on the saucer and not spilling a drop as she poured with her left hand; the saucer and cup were extended with balletic grace. Jerene upped her assessment: he married the college-era sorority girl for Wife Number One, then he married society for Wife Number Two, once he made partner. He didn't just marry his secretary. Position and reputation are important to him.

"I suppose, then, we might as well have it

all," said Lucas, leaning forward.

"My daughter — and there is no easy way to put this — tells me that she was assaulted by your son. It happened in a bedroom, in the Zeta Pi house. There had been a wild party — 'Hell Week' they call it — with the boys violently intoxicated beforehand. My daughter had lain down in a bed, not feeling well, when Luke . . ." Jerene paused for effect, terrifying her listeners that she might cry or break down. "She had her clothes on, when he . . . I know you can't possibly want to hear this about your son."

Belinda was all empathy: "We're so sorry that . . ." But she trailed off as Lucas shot her a look. Ah, the woman must never play cards for money, thought Jerene.

"Honeybun," Lucas said to his wife, "will it be all right if Mrs. Johnston and I have a little talk, privately."

She nodded, relieved, and left the room, pulling the double doors closed behind her.

Lucas folded his hands on his belly and leaned back in his chair sagely. "She's not Luke's real mother — his stepmother."

Jerene accepted this with a slight nod.

"I don't think, Mrs. Johnston, my son is capable of . . . of assaulting your daughter. It's not in his nature —"

"My Jerilyn has not showered. Or washed her torn clothes. She has not gone to the police yet, or the doctor's."

He was utterly attentive.

Jerene decided to wade in a little deeper. "Jerilyn, though she was upset, put a brave face on it and went down to breakfast with the other Sigma girls and brought up his name. It would seem Luke already has a reputation of sorts."

Lucas stared at Jerene and Jerene, chin high, stared back, expertly holding her saucer and sipping from her coffee cup without breaking his stare. "Perhaps you should call your son and ask about his side of the story."

"I will do just that." Yet he didn't move.

"We have a name in Charlotte, Mr. MacArthur. My husband was a Republican city councilman; despite the commonness of the Johnston last name, we are prominent and . . ." Another tactical pause. ". . . and I assure you, I would no more make something like this up, or bring this sort of attention to my child and family, than I would shoot the president."

She sensed him sizing her up, the clothes, the hair, the bearing. Lucas MacArthur reached for the remote phone on a nearby end table. He speed-dialed his son. His son was still asleep. "Get him up," Lucas growled to a roommate. Finally, his son came on and his father asked if he knew Jerilyn Johnston from Sigma Kappa Nu.

"Uh-huh," mumbled Mr. MacArthur. "Never heard of her?"

He looked at Jerene, whose expression was stone.

"Son, this is important. Were you with her last night?" He listened. "Who were you with?" A pause. "What was her name?" Lucas closed his eyes for a full two seconds. "So you do know her."

But Jerene was not prepared for what happened next: Lucas mumbled a few yesses, an "Oh really?" then hung up on his son, in the middle of what seemed a long explanation, and flung the phone into the bricks above the fireplace, smashing it. Jerene jumped in her chair, wondering what this moment of rage would lead to . . . but that gesture was the whole of the storm. Jerene sensed he had been here before, another mother in his living room, another girl with a court case, another incident. Jerene returned to granite ineluctability. In another half hour, forty minutes maybe, she would be in her Mercedes on her way to see if the caterers had obeyed her about the narrow-stem cocktail glasses, all of this over.

"What do you intend to do?" he asked.

"We're both parents," she said, softening. "I want a trial no more than you want a trial. You will hire someone to destroy my Jerilyn and my husband will most assuredly call in the A-team from his former law firm to destroy your son. The question is what are you prepared to do?"

Lucas seemed to have shrunk in size. "What am I prepared . . ." he repeated timidly.

"What are you prepared to do to make this right?"

"You mean, you need money —"

"We hardly *need* money. However, if my daughter is pregnant, it will be most unfortunate. I will not have her reputation ruined, her chances for a good marriage obliterated. Her brother is a prominent minister in Charlotte," she said piously. "We do not believe in abortion. We are active in family values politics." Jerene briefly flashed on her telling both daughters that she would go through the kitchen drawers and find sufficient implements to perform a five-minute abortion at home if her daughters dared get knocked up in high school. Moving along. ". . . we would have to construct an elaborate scenario by which my daughter studied overseas and was out of sight for the term of her pregnancy. We would have to delay her debut. She would be showing by this winter, so it would mean a semester out of school."

Lucas shifted in his chair; his eyes showed something akin to relief. A price was going to be named, after all. Jerene could see the weight lift off him as she spoke. Money, he was thinking — she will go away and sweep it under the carpet for a check — a check he could write easily!

She sipped her coffee, to make him wait a

little longer. "Switzerland for foreign language study, Paris for art history — none of that is cheap. I do not intend to have her sleeping with backpackers in train stations. Good hotels, hostels for young women run by the Josephine Sisters." Jerene had just seen a PBS special on the Josephine order two nights before.

Lucas nodded eagerly. "That could well be ten thousand —"

"Twenty thousand, so far, I should think. Sorority dues, tuition, all of her studies interrupted, while she's in hiding, like a fugitive. She's not bright enough for this sort of disruption; I envision having to hire a tutor. Doctors, obstetricians, of course she should have the finest health care. And I do not need to tell you about the counseling ahead, her sense of guilt and shame, the pain of giving up a child." She drew a difficult breath and this time it was not playacted.

"But we don't know," he said gingerly, "if she *is* pregnant."

Jerene stared at him icily. She set the saucer down and stood. "If you would like to take a wait-and-see approach, I will drive back to Chapel Hill and accompany my daughter to the police, like I should have done when I first heard —"

"Oh please wait."

She gathered up her purse. "I thought we could come to an understanding, being people of a certain station with much to lose from this type of awfulness —"

"If twenty thousand is acceptable —"

"Thirty thousand, Mr. MacArthur."

He was wiping his brow with his sleeve, beginning to breathe more shallowly. "And the extra ten thousand, Mrs. Johnston, is for what?"

"Because your son raped my daughter last night."

They proceeded — Jerene reflected that it could fairly be said that Lucas MacArthur staggered — to his dark-paneled study. Medical books, encyclopediae, fine leather volumes of literature probably never once opened. Certificates from the University of Alabama medical school in Birmingham. More magazines, a wall of plaques: Duke Cardiology, Duke Clinical Research Institute, some award from the Frederick R. Cobb non-invasive something or other she couldn't read fast enough. He was a heart surgeon. She should have asked for a hundred thousand dollars. With one quadruple bypass, he will get this money back, Jerene thought. Thanks be to God he wasn't a lawyer, or he might have fought her.

"I could wire-transfer the money —"

"Three checks for ten thousand dollars each. One made out to my husband, Joseph B. Johnston; one to me, Jerene J. Johnston; one to Jerilyn Johnston. That will be her money for Europe. No federal curiosity on checks below ten thousand; that should keep us all out of tax trouble with the IRS."

The checks were written (Dr. MacArthur had excellent penmanship, a lovely signature). They were slid into a cream stationery envelope and Jerene placed it without looking into her purse, as if it were nothing.

"I do not know what else to say, Mrs. Johnston."

"Not the first time with Luke Jr., I take it."

Lucas looked at his desk, shaking his head no.

"One day, Lucas, it will not be a woman of good standing who comes to visit. It will be someone from down east or the milltowns, some father and a shotgun with a pickup truck in your driveway and they will not be satisfied with what is fair. They will be after everything you own and will care nothing for the importance of appearances."

"I can't tell you," he said, finding his breath, "how glad I am, given the horror of it all, that it was you, Mrs. Johnston, and not someone who might have . . ."

"Taken advantage."

"Yes."

Her brother Gaston was right about N.C. Highway 49. He had told her how he had been homesick for this backdoor Triangle-to-Charlotte route when he was isolated in Paris. With only four hours to spare before her

Mint by Gaslight, she indulgently decided against the crowded interstate, and saw that she remembered, somehow, the cut-through down N.C. 87 out of Chapel Hill to U.S. 64 and the two-lane wilderness N.C. 49, a route that the Jarvis family always insisted was a shortcut, true or not.

As a student, she had always taken the bus to Chapel Hill; how refreshing it had been that once to be in Gaston's old junk heap of a car, windows down, North Carolina still underpopulated and defiantly verdant. How charmingly pompous Gaston had been, narrating the drive, preparing her for rapturous visions: a collapsing old house worthy of a Faulkner novel, a tasteless compound of brightly painted trailers, a rich landowner's folly complete with moat around a modest castellated home, county-seat towns like Pittsboro with old court buildings in central squares of old white cement, patched with tar, little awninged and alcoved shops ringing the courthouse square, unchanged since 1930. And then the Uwharrie Mountains, which were, she supposed, hills since nothing a mere fifteen-hundred-, sixteen-hundred-feet were technically mountains.

Yes, Gaston had narrated the journey, never suspecting that she had been down this road one fateful time before, in 1966. She could not then tell Gaston, nor did she ever tell him that she and their sister, Dillard, had made a heartbreaking commute along this road to Halliford House, a home for unwed mothers run by Miss Grace, an elderly black woman, and her sisters, far from the notice of Charlotte society, unlikely to attract the least bit of white interest.

Her cell phone vibrated. The caterer. She smiled with relief. A few unpleasant hours, a little concerted effort and determination to will life back into proper shape, and now we can all go back to what we were supposed to be doing. In Asheboro, in Chapel Hill, in Charlotte, she had always unfailingly done what had to be done, while so many among her family and friends never did.

"Hello, Lynne," she said to the chief caterer. "Antoine has arrived? Good, good. And the long-stemmed glasses . . . Marvelous. You're one of the few people . . ." Suddenly she felt a sob well up, unable to stop it. ". . . one of the few people I can really count on."

Book 2
Scandal Regained

2007–2008

ANNIE

Annie was named Jeannette Jerene Johnston. Jeannette after her grandmother and Jerene after her mother, who, Annie reflected, was still looking to unload a century-plus of JJJ-initialed silver-service thingamajigs, tea towels, tonglets, olive spears, relish trays, gold-plated napkin holders, an attic full of aristocratic and pseudo-aristocratic junk. Her little sister Jerilyn had the triple-J initials too, like some kind of high-society cattle brand, Annie once announced.

After an elementary-school misfire with "Jeannie," Annie told the teachers when she started at the Mecklenburg Country Day School that at home "she was called Annette" (which could be carved, arguably, out of Jeannette), and preferred "Annie." Happily, she could count on her mother to take no interest whatsoever in her schooling, so half a year had come and gone before the Christmas pageant program gave her away to her family.

"And just what was wrong with 'Jeannie'?"

"Like *I Dream of Jeannie* on TV? Everyone wants me to blink and make things disappear. Tara Brindley has a pony named Jeannie."

Having tasted victory, Annie sought out all opportunities for rebellion. She joined a group of other ten-year-old girls who wanted to play soccer on the boys' team. That made the *Charlotte Observer* as a cutesy item, with her mother naturally horrified to see the family name in the paper in that context. There was the issue of her grades. She willfully flunked and underperformed in most of her classes, yet everyone knew that Annie Johnston was the smartest girl in the school. The fall of 1988, a hapless student had been found in the vicinity of a badly hidden bag of marijuana, and in the ensuing witch hunt, even though Annie was not involved, she revved up a group of students who signed a petition that they would *all* choose to be suspended if the original innocent bystander was to be unjustly suspended. That too made the Charlotte newspaper.

"What kind of school," her mother cried out at dinner, "is so unconnected with the local powers that be, that every time something untoward happens it ends up in the morning paper? I swear, you don't read about the Charlotte Country Day kids in the paper — ever! — and they're all drug addicts and drunk drivers. From the best families, too!"

Sunday was a weekly battle that Annie

relished. She not only wanted to skip church, she wanted to elucidate other family members in the folly of their going. While others arrived at the breakfast table dressed for service, Annie would waltz down late, waving around a Blockbuster Video bag. "While you're listening to the shaman drone on and on, I'll be here enjoying the Sunday paper, my orange juice, and a Preston Sturges comedy."

There was a short-lived attempt to coerce church attendance by grounding her or withholding privileges of some kind but Annie declared she would simply stand right up in church, interrupt the sermon anytime she felt something ignorant, fatuous, or demonstrably hypocritical was being preached with questions like: *If we're so full of brotherly feeling, why aren't there any black people in our gated community of a church?* Or: *In imitation of Jesus, I think we should have an outreach to the men's shelter not four miles from here. I will draw up the flyers and arrange for transportation. Any Christian objections?* Her mother and father believed she would do it, too, so she got to stay home . . . which began the chorus of "Why does *sheee* get to stay home and *weee* have to go?" from Joshua and Jerilyn.

"Because one child bound for the Fiery Pit is enough," Jerene would say, through a last sip of coffee.

"Won't you come, sweetheart?" her father cajoled.

"Mother," Annie asked, "if we lived out in the country and the only church was some clapboard old-timey thing without one single society member in attendance, you would never go. Why can't you admit it's entirely social? The central aisle of Sedgewood Presbyterian is like a fashion-show catwalk for you."

"Everyone to the car now," Jerene concluded, marshaling the family through the front door.

"Have fun going *ooga-booga-booga* before your long-dead island god!" called Annie from the couch.

Annie's punishment, such as it was, was to be denied the buffet spread at the Charlottetowne Country Club. Oh she had a tractate prepared on the racist perfidies and bourgeois elitist sins of the CCC, and she never accompanied her family without making sure they understood the political implications of each bite of hoppin' john and every shameful delectation of the famous Charlottetown Bread Pudding (featured in *Southern Living* and *Gourmet* magazines) . . . yet there was no denying the Club laid on a fabulous spread: haunches of Scottish Angus beef, slabs of prime rib, a superbly smoked and sugared ham done specially by some ancient farmer in his barnwood curing house, just for the Club, since forever, every Southern vegetable cooked intelligently (as opposed to the hamhock-bath favored by most Southern institutions), a salad bar green and blooming as any outdoor garden, a trove of canonical larded-up Southern dessert pies, cakes, puddings and custards . . . yes, Lord Jesus, Annie did miss that perk. Truth be told, the whole Johnston clan all thought of the excesses of the Club as a just and godly reward for two hours of public piety at Sedgewood Prez.

Annie valued unpredictability above all else, so there would be the Sunday morning surprise when Annie would appear dressed in her churchgoing best — with some tiny thing askew, a black corsage, an anarchist button affixed to a lapel — sitting at the breakfast table waiting for them. "It's just to get to the Club, you understand," she said. "I might get a bite in before we're surrounded by your shameless neo-Confederate sycophants."

"Hm. And you'll be quiet in church?"

"I will be the model of Christian womanhood." A long screed on what comprised Christian womanhood occupied the drive to Sedgewood Presbyterian, concluding with, "Let's see if we can find a man to marry me off to who will demand my complete obedience and subjugation — maybe even beat me."

"We'd all like it very much if you found

that man," her father mumbled.

Annie would cast aside whatever weight concerns haunted her preceding week of salad-ridden lunches and diet-milkshake dinners, for two and three runs through the buffet line. After lunch, when they were all near comatose, her father's Civil War re-enactment cronies would descend and sit at their big round table in the corner. Annie berated her father for his cadre of Civil War devotees but, in reality, she loved to see these old codgers pay court to her father, who, nursing an after-Sunday-dinner scotch, relaxed and easy, simply glowed with quiet authority and charisma.

"The bravest thing Lincoln did," her father was saying, "was not freeing the slaves or reinforcing Fort Sumter —"

"And starting the Civil War singlehandedly," said Benjamin Badger, whose ancestor fought with the South Carolina Third in defense of Charleston.

"It was firing General McClellan," her father continued. McClellan was a real showboat, a highly popular general with the troops, despite never winning anything. Lincoln was warned that the Northern Army, 120,000 strong, would turn on Washington and depose Lincoln in a coup if he sacked their beloved general. And when McClellan was sacked there were men who offered to undertake that coup — there were maybe members of Lincoln's own cabinet who would have quietly supported it. "McClellan was a Southern Democrat. He would have signed a peace with the Confederacy and there would have been no five-year war, no Reconstruction, no breaking of the South."

Lionel Haslett cleared his throat approvingly; he wore his snow-white beard in flowing nineteenth-century fashion, all the better to portray his many-times-removed ancestor, General Jubal Early. He and Mrs. Haslett would move into their RV and do the circuit of battle re-creations each autumn.

Annie broke in: "But the CSA would have been nearly alone in being a modern democracy with slaves. We'd have ended up like South Africa with some miserable apartheid; we'd have all died in the eventual uprisings and race wars."

Mr. Haslett clearly thought it charming that Duke's daughter had troubled herself to have an opinion. "Oh I think the South would have solved the slave problem on its own."

"No we wouldn't have. We'd still have them." She bent forward to whisper. "We *still do* have them, except they're wage slaves, like the black kitchen workers in here. And the Mexican busboys, paid a fraction of what they should be paid —"

"Annie, sweetheart," said her father, raising a gentle hand. "Let's try to enjoy our Sunday now."

The white supremacist country club, the inequalities of black and white life in the South, the disgrace of being descended from a Civil War general — these topics were perennials, and Duke and Jerene let her carry on and fume, talk herself hoarse in the car, but there was a more serious showdown of wills ahead: Annie's debut.

A debut had been dangled before Annie with promises of cash, jewelry, heirlooms, trips abroad . . . other times it was shaken at her like a stick, an obligation that in no way could be undone. "You can dye your hair lavender purple-pink for all I care," declared Jerene Johnston, "but you shall be in attendance, looking like a young lady, when your father escorts you to the center spotlight at the Raleigh Convention Center."

All the threats merely bolstered Annie's resolve. When she was sixteen she regularly floated ideas about not debuting, surely other girls didn't have to do this claptrap, what nonsense, what a throwback — why don't we have black people in slave attire carry us in on litters?

"The debut of a young woman," her mother interjected, "is not merely a Southern thing, it is a centuries-honored cultural practice that goes back to England when women were presented to the king or queen at St. James' Palace, if you read your Jane Austen. It says you have arrived in society; you are ready to receive the attentions of a young man."

Annie, fuchsia hair, two unauthorized pierced ears with massive hoops, curled up in the backseat, making eye contact with her mother through the central rearview, huffed. Annie's eyes were defiant, her mother's cold steel. "Mother, I would faint dead away if you had actually read one word of Jane Austen. I've never seen you as much as hold a book in your hand. Besides, I already receive *attentions* from men. I don't need this high-society bullshit to turn up someone to screw."

"I have no doubt you receive all the attention you can handle in tops like the one you've chosen to wear today."

Annie was already thirty pounds overweight, but it was youthful buoyant weight and lots of it was in her breasts which she displayed in tank tops, low-cut blouses. Her cleavage was the subject of repeated dress code violations (warnings from the assistant headmaster, calls to home) but Annie had managed to dodge suspension for this offense by carefully arranging and buttoning and shifting her uniform when called for. She saw herself like one of those bare-breasted figureheads on old schooners, dividing the sea of students during class changes, bounding down the hallways with a big loud personality commensurate with the biggest boobs in the school.

"I have no intention of marrying," Annie presently brought out, "until I'm thirty, if I ever marry at all. And if I do marry, I won't marry one of the Mecklenburg Country Day boys who's going to end up like Daddy's friends, wearing checkered golf pants and yellow sports coats, breathing booze-breath on everyone at eleven A.M. at some lily-white-people's country club." Failing to elicit a response, she added, "Maybe I'll live openly as a lesbian."

"You spend way too much time on the phone with boys for me to buy that, young lady. *Every* young woman does this, Annie," Mrs. Johnston said, rejoining the battle. "My land, I debuted at the height of the 1960s with all kinds of hippie-dippie nonsense and love-in debuts and flower-power debuts, but by God, whatever the noise and fuss, when it came time, those girls took their fathers' arms and marched like generations of women before them, because it is not about 'wanting' to do it. It is about duty to the generations before and after."

"Whoa lady, take a Valium — good God. Well, that convinced me: no way I'm going to do it. Save your money."

"You are doing it for your grandmother and for me, and for all your extended family, all of the aunts and great-aunts who will be there and will write a check and give bountiful gifts. Maybe I can appeal to your greed."

" 'Every young woman' does this? The women in the women's shelters downtown? Did Alma get a debut?"

Alma, their housekeeper. "You know what I mean."

"Oh yes I surely do. And I'm sure I'll give every cent of my debut *blood* money away to some women's shelter. What do I care what all these great-aunts think? You say the most hateful things about them — why should any one of us kowtow to those dried-up old hags? And they all made *terrible* marriages, far as I can see. You want me married to Uncle Lloyd? Aunt Dillie had a debut and she married, in your oh-so-Christian words, 'white trash' anyway, didn't she? You're living in one more Southern fantasyland, Mother."

At that, Mrs. Johnston pulled the Mercedes over to the emergency-lane shoulder of Independence Boulevard, stopped the car, and turned around in her seat. "You think a debut and all this society stuff is bullshit," she began. Annie certainly was surprised to hear her mother say it, *booolshit,* with her melodic cadences. "Well, I agree with you. You want to be a rock 'n roller or some kind of revolutionary? I have news for you: there's bullshit in those worlds too. In every walk of life, there are senseless rules, payoffs and shakedowns, quirks, unjust rituals . . . Ask your little friends in their rock band about the people who put on the shows and — what do they call them? — the people who deal with the finances. You want to go work in a women's shelter and give away all your debutante money? Go see what kind of dreadful politics and chicanery reigns in those charitable organizations. I've heard you say you wanted to be a historian. Do I have to tell you what academic politics are like? I know from my involvement in years and years of committee work that the *booolshit* you are too good for is lying thick on the ground in all aspects of life."

Annie hated to concede any point to her mother, so she sat silently.

"Now Society," Jerene Johnston continued, "is just as silly, but the debut is a time-honored way that good families have come up with to *increase the odds* of their decent young women marrying decent young men and not living in a shotgun shack, working two jobs, having been left by two or three good-for-nothing husbands, with a pickup truckload of screaming babies with full diapers."

"Oh, please."

"You have never listened to me for a second, Jeannette Johnston — not one full second on the clock! But I'm going to tell you something and it may take you until you're forty to know I'm right about it. Class matters."

"Jesus Christ!"

"You can be quite happy with some European foreigner or even someone from another race if they're *from your class.* But marry beneath it —"

Annie exploded: "Class does not matter in America anymore! Are we back to Jane Austen again? I'd die if I were married to some frat boy asshole living in some big tacky Myers Park mansion made to look like something in Tudor England, watching Guatemalans clean up after me all day. It makes me sick."

Annie remembered her mother's familiar expression, used with all her children, but particularly her. A squinty countenance that showed all effort had been in vain, all arguments wasted breath, a look that said, *You have ceased to become sufficiently human for me to talk to, so I'm done.* Mrs. Johnston turned around in the seat and started the car, merged into traffic, concluding by saying, as much to herself, "I invite you not to live your entire life with the singular purpose of spiting your mother."

Husband Number One. Vinicius Costa, the Brazilian pretty boy who wanted to gain American citizenship. That one was annulled.

Husband Number Two. Destin Winchell, married semi-facetiously for a gym membership and free use of a weight-loss clinic. Duration four years.

Husband Number Three. Chuck Arbuthnot, who loved her to death. Working class, a builder of beach homes, lifelong denizen of work sites and construction projects, happy to give her her independence, liked her big and beautiful, was the most regular and energetic lover since her college high-watermark (Michael), was in every way the ideal partner . . . except for the lack of shared real estate when it came to the life of the mind. Oh Chuck was plenty smart, street-smart, real-life smart, money smart — which Annie very much appreciated, somebody had to be — but there was never the option to talk books or aesthetics or philosophers or a deeper politics or what made a latex-splashed painting in the Bechtler Museum of Modern Art brilliant. He was open to it, happily gave an opinion or two a try, but he was not raised to care about this stuff. He could fake it for a while to please Annie, and he would do anything to please her, but it wasn't in him. Doomed because of class, Annie thought years hence with pellucid, exquisite clarity.

Happy now, Mom?

How did it ever make sense to her to undertake a visa marriage to a guy from Salvador, Brazil? Sometimes Annie would reflect on her college days and wonder if all of it really happened — the debut as well as the two-month marriage. All things, she inwardly cursed, took their cue from that damn debut, that one expedient surrender.

Unbiased reflection, however, would reveal that she had been suffering self-created setbacks as long ago as high school. In her senior year, Annie ran up against a first unpleasant reality: she didn't get into the out-of-state A-list schools she had hoped to. Annie applied to various good schools, sending out her spotty transcript (As and Fs) that had to be explained away by a cover letter, and a killer near-perfect SAT score. Her appeal was: *Look guys, I'm outrageously smart but I couldn't endure all the horse dung of the elite private school they made me go to. So when I was interested I showed up and made As in classes, and when it was bullshit taught by asshole teachers, I cut all the classes.* She had had two instructors at Mecklenburg Country Day who wrote for her glowing recommendation letters about what a genius she was . . . but had they really done that? Mightn't they have said she was bright but spoiled, terminally immature? As an adult, Annie was fairly sure that's the sort of thing they probably did write.

And then to Harvard and Yale and Chicago and Stanford she let it rip in the cover letter about "bastions of privilege" and "white patriarchal superstructures" and they sent her polite form letters saying she need not storm those bastions. She thought her 1560 on the SAT would act as a talisman, a charmed magical shield against what must have appeared to them an academic record positively deafening with alarm bells. Having been rejected everywhere but the University of North Carolina at Chapel Hill, and the more artsy, less self-idolizing University of North Carolina at Greensboro, she decided on Greensboro. Many of the Mecklenburg jock-and-airhead crowd, the ones she and her clique dubbed *Les Intolérables,* would be at Chapel Hill, rushing the sororities and fraternities, putting together floats for homecoming, rah-rah-rahing for that goddam basketball team that was the center of all life and conversation across the state — screw all that. It briefly appealed, being a Tar Heel who didn't root for the Tar Heels . . . oh, but the exhaustion of that social stance wearied her in advance. No, Greensboro was a smaller pond and she could be a bigger fish, perhaps.

Uncle Gaston approved. "Greensboro, huh? I suppose the *nouveaux riches* have to live somewhere and show off their Rolexes in strip clubs."

"Strip clubs, huh? I think I see how I might make a little money between terms!"

Once Annie got ensconced at Greensboro, she faced a rocky social transition. She had always been an alpha female, always the leader of the private-school pack; her girlfriends tended to be girls who didn't threaten her and laughed at her witty putdowns of others. It was harder to find such a tribe of followers at university. Junior and senior year of high school she had been a big deal in school plays, so she threw herself at college theater.

She auditioned for *The Merry Wives of Windsor,* looking every bit the part of the bawd Mistress Quickly at eighteen years of age. They trussed and girdled her up — in a "merry widow," in fact — and she was all Elizabethan cleavage. She was audible to the back row and, throughout her college years, when a big voice or a big woman was called for (Martha in *Who's Afraid of Virginia Woolf?,* Josie in *Moon for the Misbegotten*) she was every director's go-to girl. The bohemian UNC-G world put her in touch with lots of cute, dim, possibly gay actors and nerdy weak-willed young men who were powerless against her tractor beam, who were pulled into her bedroom without much to say about it.

But she was working that trickiest of territories: being a big girl who acted like she didn't mind being big, who let it all hang out and flounced, bounced, shimmied and shook it as an asset. R&B music told her she was big and beautiful but a number of her overt passes, to handsome preppy boys she *really* wanted, had been gently, ever so tenderly, set aside because the guys didn't "feel that way" about her, guys who would be on some string-bean blond anorectic's arm by the end of term. She didn't get it: who wanted to see ribs and pelvic bones sticking out? Go get a boy, if that's what you want! Of course, there were a slew of reasons a young man would steer clear of Annie Johnston romantically, but in her mind it was always the weight, and it usually was the weight.

And then came Michael Oxamander. Annie's college-era great love. Tall, freckled, with dark red-brown hair in his chin stubble and, as she learned, all over his body in considerable amounts. Michael (never Mike) was a Sociology major, wore an earring, sandals, kept his hair a little long in front, necessitating a trademark head toss which cleared his vision. Thanks to the earring, her teenage brother Joshua, who visited UNC-G any weekend she let him, wondered if Michael was gay. Josh was annoying that way — everyone was gay. Just because a man dressed in pressed khakis or wore certain colognes or groomed himself deliberately, he had to be gay. Well, there was some slight cause to wonder; Annie had met him on a swingers-bisexual-anything-goes 1-900 telephone line, known for quick no-strings-attached hookups. Annie had tried it with a woman a time or two. (Hey, it was UNC-G where it was uncool not to experiment, where one had to cull oneself from the herd of bucolics the first week.) And though she and Michael threatened to stage orgies, mutually lusted after other women, contemplated threesomes with any cute man or woman in the cafeteria, they remained intensely fascinated with one another.

Annie's sex pattern had gone unaltered since freshman year: she found someone willing, who liked an ample bosom and wide hips, she pinned him to the bed and proceeded through a routine of things that she liked to do while her willing servant obliged. Michael put up with that once and then flipped her to the mat like a wrestler and said, "Now we're going to do what I want to do," and took charge. Michael convinced her that if control had to be ceded somewhere, the bedroom was the place to do it. If she had been squeamish about any of the varieties or positions of sex acts, Michael cured it; he made sure her entire body was put to use, one big erogenous zone.

His libido was like one of those regularly erupting Yellowstone geysers — there was a morning session before the shower, sometimes a lunchtime canoodle, then at night, regular as the eleven o'clock news, they were at it again. And when you get a libido like that, you can bet there will be other outlets for it, and he was never a liar, told her up front: "I can see moving in with you but there's not going to be one hundred percent fidelity. I wish I could do it but it's not the way I work. And you can have the same openness if there's someone else you have to be with." Again, intellectually, that appealed to Annie: it was modern, it was worldly and sophisticated, a conversation European couples, no doubt, had every morning over croissants, and, appealingly, it was something her mother would be horrified at . . . but she was actually intensely bothered by it, deep down. Was there a thinner, more athletic girl out there somewhere? A blond raptor making a bony venture into her territory?

"What we have is central to my life," he said once in bed, entangled in sheets and arms, when she had dared to broach the monogamy question. "You're my number one. But you know my nature. If something presents itself . . ."

"You can't possibly imagine summoning up the willpower to say no."

"Why should I say no? To anything? Why should you? We're young, life's short —"

"I agree, I agree," she said to forestall the familiar rote.

"You think there's a Mean Old Man in the Sky looking down keeping track across the vastness of space with what we do with our genitals in our microsecond flash of human existence?"

"No, no, I'm an atheist, like you. Charter member."

"So you're bothered we're not a Hallmark card? Only I get to touch this . . ." He demonstrated by tickling below the waist. ". . . and only you get to touch this?" He directed her hand between his legs, which soon became the catalyst for round two of the night's lovemaking.

And when he broke up with her, it was sudden, unexplained, pretty much the way she thought it would play out. She had several rough weeks about it, glimpsing him during class changes. Twenty thousand students used UNC-G campus but she never failed to spot Michael between buildings, outside of dorms, at the Tate Street vortex of bars and bistros.

"That kind of guy," her roommate Gillian said, "you only lease anyway. Be glad you had it while you had it."

As a break from mourning, she excelled at history, became known and liked by her professors. She also saw herself, like her father, one day, whiskey glass in hand, holding forth knowledgeably before a table of admiring listeners. And she had majored in History, particularly the Civil War era, to better refute her father who was put on this earth for her to refute.

She had this idea for a senior project: researching the family past and seeing if she could find descendants of the Johnston family slaves. There certainly were plenty of black people named Johnston around this state.

"I think it's a terrible idea," said her mother. "How will you possibly approach these people? 'Pardon me, my ancestor used to own your ancestor. How do you feel about that?' "

"It could be a touching moment, connecting people back to their descendants who rose up from slavery. I envision some profound discussions."

"I envision some black people hanging up on you."

The real glory of majoring in History, of course, was more time at the dinner table, back in Charlotte on a weekend, tangling with her father. She had to admit he knew his Civil War history, and so did Uncle Gaston, though his version was more florid, a retail history of high drama rather than facts. Her father could be vague on politics, the Law (which he somehow, absentminded and diffident as he was, practiced once upon a time), fuzzy on when his children's birthdays were or what they were majoring in at college, but he became incandescent on the subject of Chancellorsville, Shiloh, the Battle for Fort Macon, and anything to do with their esteemed ancestor General Joseph E. Johnston:

Duke Johnston pushed the salt shaker, the pepper shaker, the butter knife, his coffee cup, all to represent the play of battle. Three twisted napkins represented the Shenandoah River.

"Now," said Duke, fondly aware that Joshua

and Annie were indulging him without any true interest, "the river had many fords and they had to be guarded. Our ancestor, General Johnston, did all the fighting, far as I could tell. General Beauregard was wed to this false notion that Paterson and the Yankees would attack from the right, but of course Johnston was correct, and commanded all the fighting on the left flank. We had Ewell at Union Mills . . ." The pepper mill was slid toward the napkins. "Jones at McLean's Ford, Longstreet at Blackburn's Ford . . ." The salt shaker and coffee cup were scooted into place. "And of course Colonel P. S. Cocke guarded Ball's Ford."

"There was a Colonel Pisscock?" Annie shrieked.

"No, darling: P. S. Cocke," Duke enunciated.

"I thought he said Pierced Cock," Joshua whispered.

"Cocke at Ball's Ford?" Annie asked delightedly.

Joshua put on an exaggerated Southern accent: "Whah, yes, Miss Johnston, Cocke valiantly made his stand at Ball's — erect before the men. Who else but Cocke to defend Ball's? Does not historuh still praise the glories of Cocke and Ball's Ford?"

Annie: "Cocke could be depended on, sir, to attack the rear!"

Duke smiled, breathing, "Now really, you two."

Joshua: "The Northern aggressors hoped to go straight for Ball's, but first they had to contend with Cocke!"

From somewhere high in the house, impossibly, their mother sang: "That's *quite* enough!"

This doubled their hysteria, both Joshua and Annie eventually becoming short of breath from laughing. Her father, her dear aging father, was hiding a smile, too.

So, at the end of freshman year, the issue of the debut resurfaced but her fight had drained away. Annie had earlier imagined she might be on a full ride at Stanford, which would have provided an easy excuse for not coming home to participate . . . but instead she was still in-state, waitressing in a greasy spoon on Spring Garden Street, poor as a field mouse at UNC-G. Frankly, free-spending Annie could use some cash, some jewels, some plate and gilt, lucre, rapine, to be handed down, and the good opinion of Grandmother Jeannette Jarvis (her namesake!), with recurring cancer, on her way to a retirement home to finish out her years, who was always musing pointedly about her will . . .

She didn't tell her middle-class friends about debuting; it might as well have been a satanic black mass for all she acknowledged it. Once, when back in Charlotte over a pre-debut weekend, she ran into old Mecklenburg Country Day acolytes Tara Brindley and Lesha Bridgewater, slumming at the Gourmet Gardens in the Eastland Mall, and they all floated the notion of bailing out on it, what nonsense, what bullshit . . . but in the end her would-be conspirators awkwardly shrugged, said they were knuckling under, there'd be lots of cool presents and gifts, and recited "You know my nana, it would break her heart" type excuses.

So in the end Annie did it, too.

Of course, her mother made sure everyone who cared about these things knew Annie was participating, which resulted in a major materialistic haul. Annie couldn't believe the loot! Good Lord, who knew the Johnstons and Jarvises had this kind of mammon tucked away? And she did, quietly, without any complaint, write thank-you notes in a single Sunday morning while everyone was at church so she wouldn't be observed performing this graciousness.

But it was every bit the hell she knew it would be, every bit the farce. There was the dull-as-if-designed-to-be drive to Raleigh imprisoned in a limo with Mom, Dad, Jerilyn, Josh, and Grandmother Jarvis. (Aunt Dillard, who ponied up an array of Wedgwood urns, gravy boats, tureens and chafing dishes, was suffering from her fibromyalgia and excused herself from festivities.) There was an interminable fancy dinner with extended family at Second Empire, and then a retreat to a hotel room for the dressing and fixing up. This was the female-only time, the investiture, where one generation of matriarchs injected the poison into the next generation.

Her little sister Jerilyn looked on in envy. After dinner Grandmother Jarvis looked like death warmed over and begged to go lie down. Josh and her father were banished to the limo. Jerene was calm despite knowing her rebellious daughter could storm out at any minute — and I just might, Annie thought at the time. But no . . . not with this much female authority and Nietzschean superwoman Will in the room. The collective conformist mass of all the Southern matriarchy, of all the debutantes current and former, made for an inescapable gravity; no mere girl could make a run for it without being pulled back powerlessly into the high-society singularity, now strengthening itself at the Raleigh Convention Center, sucking in all known objects, buildings, trees, moons . . .

Before the limo was to take them over to the Convention Center, Annie's great-aunts fussed and hovered in the Capital Sheraton hotel room, circling like sharp-billed birds of carrion. Aunt Gert had brought a small sewing kit. This was her thing, to tsk-tsk about the gown and go to work on it — she had done this for her three daughters and every other Johnston girl "back before the War of Northern Aggression." This allowed her a chance to condemn the excessive cleavage display and tsk-tsk about Annie's weight. "Certainly the largest Johnston girl we've ever seen," she mumbled with pins in her mouth, adding under her breath so Jerene wouldn't hear: "Must be the Jarvis blood."

Aunt Mamie Mae had a terrible overbite to which she drew attention by the most lurid orange-red lipstick: "Ooh honey, you've let yourself get so fat! That's for *after* the marriage, isn't it, Elaine? You take yourself out of the running, if you let yourself get too big. All those skinny little bitches —"

"Coarseness," said Aunt Gert.

"Skinny little snakes-in-the-grass from jumped-up no-account families who were living up North twenty years ago selling metal *scrap* or some such — they'll steal your beau faster'n a New York taxicab! Now *I'm* three dress sizes too big, I'll admit it, but Dennis doesn't double-dare trade me in for Miss North Carolina because I'd take him to the cleaners and hang him out to dry next to my size-eight bloomers on a *very* public clothesline." She threw her head back for the inimitable cackle. "Oh goodness, he's up to so much financial shenanigans, I figure, he won't want his books gone into very closely — and that goes for what they're doing in Charlotte at Bank of America too, from what I hear. And Jerene, I've heard Duke is throwing in his cards with Bob Boatwright and those Northern Jews come down to carpetbag us all over again."

"I think Mr. Yerevanian is Armenian, not Jewish," Jerene reported.

Annie's mother made sure her exposure to her husband's aunt was limited to the bare social minimum, but you'd never know it from her practiced easy smile. Annie realized she was just one of maybe four humans (her father, Aunt Dillie, Josh, the housekeeper Alma) who could tell her mother-being-charming from her mother-being-contemptuous, so implacable were her manners. Jerene continued, "We are brushing against the world of real estate, it would seem. Duke is helping with the easements, doing some legal work, south of Lake Wylie for another big development."

"Charlotte's grown so big, I suppose they'll be building houses on stilts over Lake Norman 'fore too much longer. Lord, I thought Duke was *maniacal* that they don't build anything near that precious bit of land where two people fired their guns and missed in eighteen sixty whatever-it-was. I think he talked me out of a few thousand for the committee to preserve that sacred patch of kudzu — what's he call it? — the Tussle in the Mud?"

"The Skirmish at the Trestle," Jerene supplied.

"The Skirmish at the Trestle. With the pestle in the castle and the chalice in the palace! Oooh I am dating myself, aren't I?"

Aunt Elaine, another of Duke's aunts and the most severe, bestirred herself. "When are you going to make that husband of yours," she aimed at Jerene, "get back to his legal practice? It isn't natural for a man with his gifts to spend all of his time piling up Civil War bric-a-brac and going out to the schools to talk to first-graders about cannons and the like. I thought he would be the state governor by now."

Aunt Mamie Mae: "Oh, I think it's charming, Elaine. He's like a nineteenth-century Southern man of leisure. All he needs is the pickaninnies fetching him his julep —"

"Vulgarity," policed Aunt Gert.

"— fetching him his mint julep as he sits on the front porch!"

Annie was about to the walking-out point. She glanced at her mother, who glanced back impassively, yet her eyes seemed to confirm that this would be ending quite soon.

"Please," Annie fumed. "Pickaninnies? There are — somehow — a few black debutantes in this pageant. Are you going to talk like that in front of them?"

"Well, of course I wouldn't. I was being colorful referring to olden times, and how the blacks got in this pageant I will never know! Don't they have their own debutante ball these days?"

Jerene brought out that there were white men from old, established families who had married African-American women or who adopted black children and those daughters were among the debutantes tonight, and yes, there was a North Carolina black debutante organization, though nothing like Atlanta, Charleston or Savannah —

"You'd think they'd want to go march in that ball and not this one in Raleigh. I cannot abide Raleigh! I get on that beltline and I'm like some ball on a roulette wheel: I'll go round and round and round, never knowing *where* to get off or be able to get over to the rightmost lane to exit. It's a wonder I'm not still on the darn thing, going round and round and round. Of course, Dennis wouldn't drive me." Aunt Mamie Mae successfully had changed the racial subject, and no one objected to it.

Annie decided she had become like one of those Virgin Mary statues in Latin countries festooned with drapings, bejeweled capes, flowers, relics, that was then lifted up and processed through the street for worship and veneration. She would try to turn off her mind for a few hours and then hope it rebooted when this despicable enterprise was over.

"I'm proud of you for behaving," said her mother on the way to the Convention Center, in the privacy of the limo.

"For not throttling Aunt Mamie Mae?"

"I would have helped you cover up that crime."

"Oh now," said her father, "Mame's not so bad. Whatever the old girls were doing in the hotel room, my daughter looks smashing."

Smashing, thought Annie. Like Godzilla through Tokyo, taking out buildings and antenna towers with her wide ass and big boobs, in a blindingly white froufrou ball gown you could spot from the space shuttle.

In the sharp spotlight of the Raleigh Convention Center, she took her father's arm and marched; she would always remember how ghastly the spotlight made her father look, one million years old, and that cold gust of his mortality further enforced her good behavior that night. Parry and thrust with her father as she did at the dinner table, she would never humiliate him publicly and, clearly, she had learned this evening, there were those in the family who thought him a layabout, a shirker, and whereas she could find fault with her folks as much as she liked, she found it intolerable that the great-aunts felt entitled to any opinion at all. That was the problem with Southern family gatherings: you came away *judged,* as to weight, as to economic progress, as to who was making good marriages, getting good promotions. And the most horrible old venomous shrews with wretched mislived lives were doing the judging too — that hardly seemed right.

There were photos of the affair, mostly destroyed when Annie could get her hands on them. Not because of any political protest, but because she truly looked stuffed into her Dupioni silk sausage casing. The photographer was the shortest man alive — all her photos were shot from miles below, she was all double chins and lit like a late-night TV horror-movie host. She was, without rival, the biggest girl at the debut, surrounded by insect-thin blondes (precious *few* of them natural . . . oh God, now she was getting catty like the rest of the women, too!), tanning-bed browned, lacquered and made up with a beauty pageant sheen, perfect teeth, some — it was rumored — with breast implants, gotten when teenagers. And she heard the whispers, the comments, saw deflected glances (as if looking upon the fat girl was contagious for one's own weight), she radioed in on the female-intuition frequency, sensing hypercritical girltalk and ruthlessness. Oh well. Looks like they'll get first crack at the boys wearing checkered golf pants and yellow sports coats, breathing booze-breath on everyone at eleven A.M. at some lily-white-people's country club . . .

After the intolerable debut, there were

several intolerable weddings of her friends.

Millicent Tilley had been Annie's partner in unruly rebellion at Mecklenburg Country Day and, from all reports, doubled down on outrageous behavior once she got to Mary Washington. She, too, caught Annie's attention at their debut, widening her eyes, mouthing *When will this shit be over?* as the older women herded and wrangled the girls into the correct presentation order backstage. But come wedding time, you might have thought her wedding was Charles-and-Diana Redux for all its ostentation, its cast of thousands.

"I want you to be the Girl at the Book," Millie asked her.

"Does that have anything to do with off-track betting?"

"No, dumb-dumb. You get to greet all the people when they enter the sanctuary and have them sign my register so I know who showed up for my special special day."

"Do I have to buy some organdy melon chiffon-fringed gown to be the Girl at the Book?"

"I've already picked it out!"

In the early stages of this wedding, Millie could be ironic about it, make flip jokes, but as the date approached she was almost as frantic as her mother, barking out orders, losing her temper at underlings and caterers, making her bridesmaids cry. This spectacle made Annie despair for women in the South, and by extension, throughout the world, this succession of high priestesses, generation upon generation, presiding with violent solemnity over foolish female fripperies like they were the serious business of human sacrifice.

"We're going to put sherbet in *this*?" Millie screamed at one point in the planning. "Merciful God, I would not expect my DOG to lap out of a . . . an on-sale-at-Pet-Smart bowl like this!" Then a cereal bowl went frisbeeing against the wall, shattering.

It's as if, thought Annie, some wicked masculine committee in charge of Life had known the women would worry their pretty little heads over all this rigmarole and thereby leave the running of the big important world to the men, who would look upon all the flounces and frills, tears and hysteria, with a knowing wink, a nudge in the side, *Told you that'd keep 'em occupied.*

It was also an education sitting next to her mother throughout Millie's ceremony. After her role as Girl at the Book was finished, Annie joined her mom and Jerilyn in the church pew. The music was lavish — a string quartet. There had also been Millicent's Mary Washington roommate who majored in music, vocalizing something or other, flat and mediocre. Annie tried to catch eight-year-old Jerilyn's eye to laugh about it, but Annie saw her little sister was enthralled by the spectacle like it was a deeply moving theater play. Then, to a processional Annie thought she recognized off a Kenny G. album, entered the bridesmaids and ushers.

"Oh lookee there," her mother whispered, as one peach-magenta chiffonized bridesmaid holding a flower basket strode by. "She has the stems facing the wrong way."

Annie turned around to see that all the girls carrying baskets had the stem end of the flowers facing the guests on their side of the aisle, rather than the flower heads.

Good God, Mrs. Johnston whispered, the best man and the groom had the *same* boutonniere . . . and look, they have the same ties as the lowly ushers — was there a Men's Wearhouse special on ties, eight for the price of six? Here came the mother of the bride, fifty if she was a day, in a gown with ample display of bosom in front and back in back. ("Mutton dressed as lamb," Jerene purred.) A five-year-old urchin smugged his way down the aisle littering the way with rose petals, with his twin brother behind as train bearer. The train of the bride was risibly long and kept escaping the hands of the fumbling five-year-old, who looked overstuffed in an excess of sateen and lace trim, a courtier mini-uniform that Gainsborough would have rejected as too much. He had kid gloves which could find no purchase on the satin train, so he kept dropping it and running after it, which everyone, even Annie, found adorable.

"That's cute, you have to admit —"

"It's appalling," corrected her mother. Jerene pointed out that his shoes were black while he was in white. The program listed five maids of honor, when only one should have had that designation. No mention of the auxiliary Girl at the Book, Annie noticed.

"At least two of them, including her sister," Jerene said quietly, "are married so they are hardly *maids* of honor."

"What are they supposed to be called?"

Matrons of honor. The photographer they had hired AND the videographer were blatant nuisances, all but inserting themselves between bride and groom for the shot. "Scarcely comprehensible," breathed Mrs. Johnston, though she was nearly swaying with pleasure. At last, after a tendentious homily that was twenty minutes of moralizing about the state of modern marriage, the preacher pronounced them man and wife and the happy couple kissed fully on the mouth — "How nice," Annie's mother noted, "to get a preview of the intimacies of the bridal suite." Then the wedded couple accompanied each other up the aisle, followed by the maid of honor still clutching the bride's bouquet. "No no, darling, pass it to a matron of honor for safekeeping," urged Mrs. Johnston, under her breath. "Oh look, she's going to actually take the arm of the best man for the exit. Maybe they can do-si-do up the aisle, like a square dance in a barn."

"How many of these stupid little rules do you know, Mother? Is this your game at weddings? Counting the infractions?"

Mrs. Johnston smiled, barely. "I've counted at least twenty breaches of tradition, and today's lapses in good taste are . . . oh my land, without number, without number."

Jerilyn broke in to say she thought it was the most beautiful wedding she had ever seen.

"I can make sure yours, Jeriflower, is better by a long shot," Mrs. Johnston said, gathering her gloves — her mother was still wearing gloves then! in 1993! — ready now to turn her attention to the enormities of the subsequent reception.

"What about *my* wedding?" asked Annie.

"I fully expect you to be married upon a mule in a national park, presided over by a hippie shaman in a cloud of incense smoke." That made Jerilyn laugh. Jerilyn would be the perfect lifeless doll when she grew up, Annie thought, for her mother to play wedding dress-up with.

"Well, Jerilyn," Annie said, "I will NOT be the Girl at the Book at your wedding, so don't even ask."

"Who says you'll get to be in my wedding?"

At the reception (where Annie lost count of the continually mounting atrocities adumbrated by her mother), she got to see her old Mecklenburg Country Day associates, and clearly her reign as alpha female had passed. Rather than shriek with delight in seeing her or pull her into a corner to recall mishaps and follies of the debut they all had shared, they seemed to look at her — was it her imagination? — with a kind of pity, a reserve. Was it the fat thing? The goth-black hair which she, nonetheless, had styled neatly for the wedding? Was it her ludicrous bridesmaid dress that only emphasized the upper arms and paunchy stomach? Before coming to Millicent's wedding, she had dreaded seeing these throwbacks to her private-school past, but when she saw them and they held her at some polite, smiling remove, she felt oddly crushed. They all had dates, trial husbands-to-be, all handsome and promising, particularly where starting salaries were concerned. *Poor Annie,* she could hear them thinking, *all strange and hanging out with UNC-G weirdos and fat, fatter than last time, fatter than anyone we know on earth . . .*

It was Annie's nature not to be coerced or obligated to do one fool thing she didn't want to do, including dieting. She wasn't a binge-eater, she wasn't one of those women who when things turned stressful ate a carton of ice cream; she ate healthfully but plentifully, and every bit of it found its way to boobs, upper arms, thighs, hips. She did tell her UNC-G roommate Gillian about the humiliation of the bridesmaid dress and the still-top-secret debutante ordeal, about her being the biggest deb in North Carolina history, and her vile old racist aunts.

"Well," said Gillian, "speaking of race. Why not go out with a black guy? I hear a lot of black men like, you know, plus-sized women."

That was a really good question. And Annie wasn't sure what the answer was. She had fantasized about driving a black boy like a parade float through some stuffy family occasion, maybe some sacrosanct old-biddy thing where her high-society grandmother was holding court like Queen Victoria. *Aunt Mamie Mae, I'd like to you meet Jeyrohn.* Annie was the least prejudiced white person she knew! She was a round-the-clock racism police with others, as a matter of fact. It wasn't that she didn't find black guys attractive — Jesus, you were blind if you didn't think some of those hip-hop guys or athletes or movie stars weren't hotter than fire. But that wasn't her fantasy, her romantic template.

Gillian kept being helpful, more devoted to Annie's couplings than to her own nonexistent dating life. "My cousin Janey is pretty, you know, plus-sized, and she goes out with this Puerto Rican boy who is *totally* fine."

Yeah, didn't that sound like Annie? She could join the Hispanic Student Association or something, and go trawling. Better yet — how about the Mexican boys who were, apparently, the whole of the university grounds crew these days? Get someone who barely spoke English and drag him to campus parties and, yes, take him home to Jerene. *Mom, this is Pedro and I love him.* Why was she stuck on handsome, somewhat jocky, potential frat boys who'd probably turn out to be future Republicans? It teased at the edge of her consciousness, the reason, just out of reach. The taint of Mecklenburg Country Day School perhaps, early imprinting. It was the challenge, perhaps. To harangue them away from their bourgeois comforts and attitudes, to detach them from their expected blond airhead escorts, to give them their political and spiritual makeover. She didn't want boyfriends, so much as she wanted converts.

As if to test the Latin theory, Vinicius Costa arrived at UNC-G Annie's junior year. There were surely better-looking Brazilian boys (photos make him look like an oily white boy with a Jheri curl) but he made up for crooked teeth and lingering acne by such animation, such loud and expressively accented English that he had a cult female following in no time. He tried to get parts in the theater, where Annie got her first look at him, but the accent was too distracting (and no plays featuring accents were on the boards), so he often was used as eye candy, the hunky centurion standing beside Brutus in *Julius Caesar,* the guy-waiting-with-a-suitcase in *Bus Stop,* all parts with no lines. He was one of those young men who never as much as glanced at a piece of gym equipment or contemplated exercise but somehow retained, on a diet of espresso, cigarettes and what was available in the Brown Building vending machines, a body ready for the cover of *Men's Fitness.*

And he liked the big girls. First, he was smitten with Rolonda, a large black singer imported from NC A & T across town to play Effie in *Dreamgirls,* and then after a few other misfires (and plenty of underpublicized direct hits), he turned his liquid brown eyes on Annie. "How did you get so good in the dramatic arts, Annie Johnston?" All of Vinicius's conversation starters seemed like lines from some teach-yourself-English series of cassette tapes that were fifty years of out sync with how people talked. But what did it matter? *The zramateek artz . . . Uhnnie Jhohnz-tone . . .* The Brazilian ability to insert a *z* or soft *j* sound into most words was aphrodisiacal.

So she married him. Yep, married — as in justice of the peace, as in I now pronounce you. Marriage was a sham, a rube's game, a dead end for women, some patriarchal antiquated holdover, right? But that meant, on the other hand, it was also so unimportant and trifling, that it hardly mattered if you married for a political purpose, i.e., to get Vinicius into the country. You could say it was cosmic payback for the forced-march debut she had just suffered. Let the catty Stepford Wives from Mecklenburg Country Day get a load of this! Vinicius wanted to stay in America (where even the Catholic girls would put out, unlike back home), where everyone made fortunes, where (given his vast theatrical experience) he would be a big star on telenovelas filmed in Miami, where he wouldn't have to go back and work as a manager in his father's small factory in Salvador that made those horizontal electric signs affixed to the front of buses that announce destinations and OUT OF SERVICE.

Everything about this scandalous plan appealed: it would horrify both sets of parents, and it made her the emissary of radical shock and surprise, a business she had been out of for too long. And she was rescuing someone from the third world! Very soon, Annie learned that most third-world people in American universities paying out-of-country American tuition with plenty of disposable income tended to be ruling-class wealthy and not up from the favelas. Details, details — her international rescue mission was undeterred. Ha, how she relished the phone call to her mother.

"You've done what now?" Jerene said, not sure if this was mere rhetoric from her daughter.

"Yes, we made it official at Greensboro City Hall."

"Can he support you?"

"Actually, I suspect he can."

"Good, because from here on out, your tuition will be your husband's affair, and your rent, expenses. I wish you both every happiness. Your father will be very pleased that — what was his name again?"

"Vinicius." *Vuh-neet-see-ooze . . .* those delicious *z* sounds again.

"Vinicius. We'll expect you for Sunday dinner. We have to meet our new son-in-law."

Oh Jerene Johnston knew, knew somehow even during the phone call, that this was a folly, a marriage that wouldn't count as a marriage, a mishap headed for annulment. Annie, throughout her later life, never had a sense of humor about this, never really would forgive her mother for her blithe performance, her smug foreknowledge of what would happen. A month into wedded bliss (during which Annie did not break the news to Vinicius that he would soon be picking up their mutual tab), Senhora Costa arrived in Greensboro. Mrs. Costa proved to be Brazil's answer to Mrs. Johnston. A round, tanned face with her features (eyebrows, cheek rouge, lipstick) drawn on, her hennaed hair pulled back so severely that it may have constituted a kind of face-lift, a lime-green linen suit and a silk floral blouse which on anyone else might have seemed warm and summery but on Mrs. Costa was suggestive of Amazonian assault.

Mrs. Costa greeted Annie, not impolitely, but then never looked at her again. She sat with her son, who began their discussion defiant, petulant, agitated, raising his voice, while she sat with the bottled water Annie offered her, calm, serious. Soon Vinicius was weakening. Annie couldn't understand the Portuguese but she sensed in the senhora's measured listing of . . . what? Incentives, bribes for him to come home? Reasons this marriage could not endure? . . . that he had seen the logic of it. Saw how his family money was cut off from him, saw how Annie would not be especially welcome back in Salvador (where the town's most eligible young women still hoped he might yet alight on them), saw how his mother could fix it all, if only he would just accompany her to the courthouse.

Mrs. Costa had only appeared, Annie pieced together in retrospect, once a lawyer had been contracted and the paperwork and court appointments were put in place. The Costas didn't mess around — they had a top Raleigh divorce and annulment specialist sweep in and declare that "there was a want of understanding" on the part of Vinicius, who was too foreign and naïve to understand what Annie had roped him into. Well, it was either that or paying a doctor to say Vinicius was impotent, and that sure wasn't the case. Had the Costas contacted her parents? Had Duke Johnston set up the Raleigh attorney, an old buddy from law school days, to argue the one (barely) defensible line before a judge who was also one of the North Carolina cabal of courthouse good old boys who all played golf and drank scotch together, who all knew each other from Duke and Carolina, who made stuff like this go away for good families? How vast was the conspiracy to undo what she had done? It was striking that she was never yelled at or told what trouble she had caused. Her mother and father proceeded as if this were a nuisance, as if there were some file in a drawer waiting for when she did something precisely like this, some set of phone numbers, instructions, directives. In her most paranoid fantasy, she imagined her mother and Vinicius's mother meeting for a brief victory champagne, some balcony in Rio de Janeiro enshrouded by palms, her mother (through an interpreter) congratulating her partner on a job well done, some archsecret conclave worthy of divas on a prime-time soap as the champagne glasses clinked.

Annie's friends at UNC-G knew about the annulment and, a month beyond it, Annie herself felt foolish and ridiculous. She took twenty-three credits that spring so she could graduate and get out of town; no theater roles, no weekend partying, no sitting in the quad where friends and acquaintances could get at her, just hermitage and lying low. In this vulnerable, sullen time, Destin made his move.

Now Destin Winchell was back to Annie's former pre-Michael UNC-G template. He was totally passive in most things, and Annie reasserted herself in the bedroom, calling all the shots. Whereas Michael provided spectacular fireworks in bed but never seemed more distant than in those moments after, during cuddling, talking of his independence, Destin was pleasant enough in bed, though often hard to inspire, never initiating things on his own, happy to be led, and it was afterward, during the cuddling and talking that he made Annie feel secure.

Upon graduation Destin took a lucrative job in graphic design at a firm in northern Virginia and they tried it long distance for a while. Annie, not liking or holding any of the part-time jobs she had acquired after graduation, sauntered back to her childhood bedroom in Charlotte for a "just temporary" transition at home to recharge and then she would be moving on to graduate school or an interim library job in no time. Instead, she deteriorated, stagnated, slept until noon, rented videos by the score and watched movies until dawn, pretended to send out resumes, pretended to go to interviews . . .

The old Balkan battle lines began to reemerge: church, bourgeois values, Republican trickle-down economics, the shamefulness of pride in a Civil War ancestor, she heard herself mouthing the same arguments made when she was a teenager, not able to shut off the faucet. It may have seemed that Annie Johnston wished to do battle in all environments in all settings, but what really mattered to her was the white house high on the bend on Providence Road, her theater of war the dining room table, confronting her mother and father — who were so complacent and wrong, wrong about everything, in such need of her corrective instruction.

The foolish marriage followed by this obvious depression had her parents worried about her general mental health, so they resisted pitching her to the curb. Her mother wondered why she shouldn't stay on for graduate school in Greensboro. Don't they have a master's program in something, she encouraged, *anything at all?* It took a sharp comment from Alma to prompt her next move.

Annie had invaded the laundry room (Alma's highly regulated province) and strewn clothes to be folded and pressed or washed a second time, an explosion of clothes and bags. Having spread out her devastation, Annie then answered a phone call from Destin, lay on her bed and talked for an hour, then got distracted with something on television, only to return to find that Alma grouchily had cleaned, folded, organized the entire pile.

"Oh. I was going to do that," Annie said meekly.

"You know, of all the children," Alma said, frowning, "I woulda figured you would be the one to get the furthrest 'way from home, the way you go on. Figured you'd be off in Paris France or California, causing big trouble out there or someplace, but no ma'am . . ." Alma bent over with a creak to pick up a final piece of Annie's underwear that had escaped the laundry basket. "Twenty-three years old, back living off your mama and daddy . . . Never gonna leave home looks like."

Since she'd returned to Charlotte, Annie had put on a great deal more weight, no longer walking all over a college campus. She understood that she was headed toward being one of those really big women, expanding past 250 pounds.

So Destin, who had never ceased worshipping her, continually proposed their moving in together in northern Virginia. She held him off because she liked but didn't love him, and then one day she said yes. Yes, because she missed affection but also because it would break up her slow sinking into oblivion. Annie started work as a research librarian and file clerk at a real estate office managed by Destin's sister, who kept nudging and nagging, *When you two lovebirds gonna tie the knot?* The whole family must have gotten the memo; Destin must really have loved her, she figured, to coordinate such a propaganda effort.

So she thought about it. His design company had great health care, lots of preventive stuff, they'd subsidize gym memberships, they'd pay for the weight loss clinic at Inova Fairfax. Well, you had to be a *spouse* of an employee to enjoy that benefit. So, Annie shrugged, let's do Marriage Number Two. It wasn't as if she'd changed her mind about the vestigial and empty institution that was husband-and-wife, but she couldn't quite man the barricades as before given her Vinicius debacle, so why not?

She lost forty pounds in the twelve-week program. Two years later, Destin started a thing with a heavyset girl at the graphic design studio. She drove by his office to get a look at her one time. If you marry for enrollment in a weight-loss program, she coldly lectured herself, this is what you can expect. Two years after that, there were divorce papers to sign and she hid out for a while in Greensboro, away from a family that must have decided she was doomed at matrimony, when they weren't worried about her psychological state. Or her health. By the time of the divorce she had gained the forty pounds back and had added thirty more. She had high blood pressure and was pronounced pre-diabetic.

Segregation was created, planned, masterminded. Charlotte after the Civil War was a well-integrated city. There had always been black areas and white areas but Uptown was scrambled, black freedman next to white merchant next to just-emancipated black next to prosperous white a block away from a black shantytown. Black and white mingled on the streets and sidewalks, black and white shopped at the same stores and depots and markets, black and white went to the same churches as they had done in slave times (blacks in the balconies, the whites downstairs in the pews).

Annie was mastering the lay of the land in Charlotte real estate, and she hoped to be a one-woman integration squad, happy to lecture family and friends about what she learned of the wickedly constructed segregation scheme. It took a slew of Jim Crow laws, a few rigged elections, many evictions, many falsely friendly "urban betterment" projects, and a whole lot of racism to get this city divided, blacks in one swath (west and north), whites on the other (south). It was the same in most Southern cities, too. The

North had already perfected the ghetto, so they were no role model either.

History major Annie Johnston forgot most of the Civil War battles and she let her future thesis of Johnston slave genealogies fade from her mind, but what she never forgot was Professor Hickman's Southern Urban History, a course she'd only signed up for because it was at eleven-thirty and she had no intention of taking the more popular classes that asked for an earlier wake-up time. That course provided a stop-the-presses headline: the natural ally of Southern blacks, in voting and in social progress, back in the 1880s, were the *rural white folk,* the poor farmers. Annie, to believe it, had to read that chapter a second time — the farmers, the rural clodhoppers and shitkickers of North Carolina, were the leading progressive edge in politics?

Yes, because Charlotte oligarchs made the small family farm impossible. A poor farmer could expect his cows or sheep to graze all over the community commons, but once the powerful whites got Fence Laws passed, the poorer farmers and their animals were confined to a small patch of often worthless earth. Farmers bought feed and fertilizer and farm equipment at exorbitant rates from Uptown Charlotte merchants (and their small town franchises) who, when the mounting debts were being paid too slowly, rammed through the Lien Law. *Forty percent* of family farmers lost their homes in North Carolina in the decades after the Civil War, many lost to Charlotte-based city merchants when they could not pay their bills, which amassed land in a very few hands. Poorer whites became sharecroppers, much like the freed blacks, on land they had owned for generations.

So farmers, black and white, joined Grange societies that declared just what prices they would pay collectively and merchants, grumblingly, had to take it or leave it. At the same time, the poor millworkers on eighty cents a day also were speaking of collective bargaining, unions. And all these groups voted Republican, the party of Lincoln, to the Democrat Southern white power structure's endless, fulminating, vitriolic chagrin. If the oligarchs were going to get around democracy, they were going to have to group the offending black voters into discrete voting districts. From 1890 to 1920, a high-watermark of neo-Confederate self-mythology and hyper-racism, most Southern cities rearranged themselves, ghettoizing the blacks, walling off the whites, and trying to keep those progressive union-loving, Grange-loving, civil rights–loving poor folk bunched up in their own underrepresented side of town.

And even that didn't fix things. Annie's Exhibit A, anytime anyone floated the notion that North Carolina “wasn’t as bad” as the rest of the South, was Wilmington, North Carolina, and its election of 1898, in which the poor folk/black folk alliance put progressive Republicans in office . . . upon which result the whites rioted, burning down the black business district, and lynching African-Americans, a hundred dead, while the Democrats seized power in the only municipal coup d’état in American history. President McKinley said and did nothing about it — not even Republican partisanship could be appealed to. Encouraged by the ease of overthrowing local democracy, the Democrats in North Carolina embraced naked white supremacy, while all the major papers trumpeted imagined crimes against white ladies with the catchphrase “Negro Domination.” The bulk of the most onerous racist laws came in this time, along with Governor Charles Aycock, who Annie noted had many things still named after him in the state, including a boulevard running through Greensboro and the big auditorium on UNC-G campus, despite his supremacist administration that openly ran and won on promises of “black disenfranchisement.”

Well now. Annie Johnston was going to strike her blow for undoing centuries of white mischief by redirecting her real estate business to the needs of black folk, Mexican legal immigrants, poor white people. If she had her way, there wouldn't be an unintegrated neighborhood left in Charlotte.

Real estate had changed Annie's trajectory. It was how she met Husband Number Three, Chuck. It was the only proper job she had ever had, working in Destin's sister's real estate office. Thanks to some night classes at Guilford Technical Community College, she got a real estate license and found herself, in 2001, struggling to move houses in the Greensboro market, working with Coldwell Banker. This office had a number of clients in foreclosure who had to unload their beach houses down on the Outer Banks. Typical of that drab office, none of the dullards she worked with wanted a free trip to the beach to assess four oceanfront cottages, meet a builder named Chuck Arbuthnot who would give them some estimates for upgrading the properties so they could re-sell quickly . . . so Annie volunteered, learning she could stay in any of the beach houses while all these assessments were being worked up.

Chuck was already at work on some kitchen cabinets when she drove to the cluster of homes in Waves, N.C., a break of private houses and small stores in a gap of the Cape Hatteras National Seashore. He got up from under a sink and stood there with his tool belt, plaid shirt, worn but tight jeans, and Annie felt a tingle. He was bald with a moustache, and there were men who were bald from becoming middle-aged in a softening desk job, and men who were bald early because of a surfeit of testosterone in their body and Annie knew in Chuck's case it was the latter.

"Well, hello there," he said in a baritone that could rattle the windowpanes, confirming the testosterone theory. He washed his hands in the now-working sink in order to shake her hand. Considerate. They toured the four properties and bantered and she learned quite a bit. He believed in support-group recoveries. Had been going to AA meetings for ten years which was as long as he had been dry. He had a sponsor who was helping him quit smoking . . . well, actually he quit smoking only to take up Skoal, a scourge of many a construction site, but he hadn't had a chew this calendar year, but he did have to call his quitting-coach now and then. And then there was Weight Watchers.

"Excuse me? You're fit as a fiddle!"

"My ex-wife used to drag me along and I think it's helpful. No smoking, no drinking, so I been eating everything in sight. Besides, ma'am, it's not a bad place to —"

"Meet women," she filled in the blank, smiling.

"Women of the sort I find attractive, yes."

And there it was. They went to a loud, crowded seafood place and paid too much for barely eaten dinners, then he drove her to the one property where the heat had been turned on and he felt he'd better come upstairs to see if the thermostat was functioning, and that led to the bedroom, and Annie greeted this development as long overdue.

After they flipped those four properties, he proposed that she come down to Nags Head and get out of slow-as-mud Greensboro where the market had stalled. Everyone wanted beach property! It was like selling ice-cream sundaes for a nickel. He'd fix them up, she'd find a buyer. And for a marvelous, fantastical year, she thought she'd solved all of life's problems. The salt air killed some of her constant appetite, and she was never more active, so she lost some weight — not all of it, of course: Chuck was careful to tell her when she was looking "a little gaunt." They made money. The sex remained wonderful. Maybe Chuck was a bit of a fetishist, maybe it was the ample proportions more than Annie proper that he lusted for — heck, he really had only brushed the surface of who she was — but don't mess up success, she'd lecture herself.

Annie, the onetime socialist firebrand, discovered she liked making money. She seemed to be the only one in her immediate family who could actually do it. But some of her youthful ideals kept gnawing at her. Putting privileged rich people (Raleigh's weatherman for Channel 17, a center for the Carolina

Hurricanes) into high-end beach homes wasn't exactly waving the flag of World Revolution.

In 2006, Zack, her high-flying banking liaison chum from Coldwell Banker, called her from Charlotte and convinced her they were in a unique era for helping middle- and low-income families into home ownership. The banks, Freddie, Fannie, Clinton then Bush, were pushing wheelbarrows of money in their direction for sub-primes . . . but he needed a front woman who could identify the up-and-coming home buyer, a seller who was at ease with immigrants, black folk, naturalized Mexicans, people moving up from rentals and, heck, shacks and trailer parks. Was she in or not in?

"I'm gonna be spending more time in Charlotte," she said, lying next to Chuck in bed, some instantly materializing Hatteras storm beating at the windows.

"Can't say I'm glad to hear that," said Chuck.

Once she got her first families into homes in the north and east of Charlotte, word spread and relatives and friends of previous clients made their way to her. By 2007, she had placed over two hundred families in homes — some weeks closing as many as four separate deals. But she lacked one thing the big real estate mavens in town boasted of, and she decided to do something about it.

She commanded Joshua come visit her in her small strip-mall Charlotte headquarters — and bring his friend Dorrie Jourdain.

Annie could see the quizzical looks, the combination of fear and fascination as Joshua and his sidekick Dorrie stuck their heads around the potted palm and took in her cubicle. Piles of papers, leads, documents, contracts, everything in perilously leaning stacks obeying a filing system she alone understood.

"Hey you guys," Annie said, closing a series of computer windows. "Thanks for coming."

"So what is this big revelation?" her brother asked.

"You'll see, but you have to take a little ride with me first," she said, pushing out of the chair and straightening her skirt. She reached for a coat rack from which hung her suit jacket.

"I've got a biggish favor to ask you, Dorrie, but I'll wait until you're trapped with me in my van."

In the parking lot was Annie's red BMW, looking just-washed-and-waxed, and her work van with the decal of the Constable & Johnston Realtors on the side.

"Who's Ms. Constable?" Dorrie asked, after the unseen partner. "Or is it Mr. Constable?"

"Mr. Constable," said Annie. Joshua knew the story but he let his sister tell it. "Pete Constable, thirty years in the business, helped

Charlotte grow into one of the most profitable real estate markets in the country — you can trust Pete and Annie with your real estate needs." After a dramatic pause. "There is no Pete Constable. I made him up, so it wasn't some ditzy woman in charge of your real estate needs. People with real estate needs prefer that there's an old masculine hand on the rudder." When you called Constable & Johnston you got a male automated voice asking you to press "1" for Pete Constable, "2" for Annie Johnston. Anyone who called Pete, got their call returned by Annie begging pardon for Pete being swamped or on vacation.

Joshua was about to hop in the front, when Annie directed him to the backseat; the passenger seat was reserved for Dorrie. Dorrie mumbled, "Not sure what you want with me, since I have no real estate needs."

"Oh everyone has real estate needs."

The Brookshire Freeway left the funky-fashionable Fourth Ward, the sharp skyscrapered skyline rising up behind, impressive to Charlotteans every time they gazed upon it, taller, vaster, more big-city than the last time they looked, sixty-story Bank of America, fifty-four-story Duke Energy, forty-two-story One First Union Center, a score of thirty-story-plus buildings, forty more skyscrapers in the construction phase, amazing to those who grew up with the old 1960s buildings the tallest things in town.

West of I-77, the freeway moved with remarkable quickness into an old but run-down northwest Charlotte neighborhood, liquor stores, twenty-four-hour check cashing and bail bondsmen. Charlotte was a Southern exception; usually the west side of town was the white half, but in Charlotte, the Westside ("the Wild Wild West") was black. Annie U-turned the van around to go back the direction they came . . . and there it was.

"Holy crap," said Joshua, while Dorrie clapped her hands approvingly.

Annie's first billboard. There was a very air-brushed and flattering photo of Annie holding a clipboard with what looked like Southern plantation columns behind her.

CONSTABLE & JOHNSTON

Let us get you into your next home!

1-800-555-7835

Generous terms of credit — Welcome
Fannie Mae & Freddie Mac!

Hablamos Español!

Josh asked his sister, "Since when do you speak Spanish?"

"Eh, I can get by. I call in a bilingual agent

I used to work with at Allen Tate if I get a phone message in Spanish, cut him in on the deal."

Dorrie: "That's a real glamour shot."

"I know you both think it's cheesy as hell but that's how it's done. I look better than Candy Kinney, that ol' tramp. She's got her billboards up all over South Charlotte."

"See if you can have as many," Joshua chided, "as Berma Bigglefield." She was a bail bondsman whose billboards were everywhere.

"Yeah," said Dorrie, "I hope it's not a bad thing to point out but this broke-flat tumbledown neighborhood doesn't have many potential clients in the home-buying market."

"*Au contraire*. This is the big feeder road for African-American commuters out from the developments around Paw Creek and Peachtree, Beattie's Ford. That's my niche market: emerging middle class and some lower income, people who've rented all their life but have good jobs, jobs but no equity. What I was going to ask you, Dorrie, was to think through your friends, your church —"

"I don't really go to church anymore. All black folk don't spend all Sunday morning in church, you know." She waved her hands like they held tambourines. "Shoutin' and gettin' washed in the blood of the lamb — praise Jesus!"

"I didn't think there was anyone who didn't

go to church, white or black, around this camp meeting masquerading as a major American city. Anyway, think through the cousins, the relatives, the family friends, if they'd had trouble in the past with banks and Realtors, if they're in a mood to move up —"

Joshua jumped in with the theme from the TV show *The Jeffersons,* about movin' on up.

Annie smiled serenely. "Mock all you want. I am not embarrassed to ask my friends and family to send me clients! You'd have thought Dubya would have shut down the easy-loan program at Fannie Mae but the Republicans like the sub-primes, too. Everybody's making money and everybody's getting a dream house and the Charlotte market is as hot as they come! Number three in the whole nation! They cannot *build* downtown units in the First and Third Wards fast enough."

Dorrie began, "If you have a business card, I —"

Annie was already pressing a business card — twenty of them — into Dorrie's hand. It had the same soft-focus sultry photo as the billboard, and a variety of phone numbers, including a cell anyone could call anytime. "Go out among the people, out into the world unto all nations," Annie said.

Josh wondered, "Why not help millionaires trade up in Myers Park and make some real commission money, sis? And then give me some of it."

"I hate those people," she said. "Money can take care of itself. I'm trying to do the Lord's work here and get normal people into homes so they can see how the other half lives, the half with credit and equity and a tax code that has bent over backward to make sure they never suffer any disruption in the flow of their prosperity. Landlords have it made. I didn't know how much until I became one."

Annie was doing the thing that any self-respecting real estate agent eventually did. Though a small fortune could be made on commissions in a hot market like Charlotte, a *vast* fortune could be made buying the homes yourself in an up-and-coming neighborhood, paying someone like Chuck to renovate them, and then showing, selling the homes, and pocketing the profit. Such a feeling of wheeling and dealing, such a high from signing the papers. Annie put down $24,000 on a $120,000 home in a marginal downtown neighborhood — enough to avoid the mortgage default insurance, then she would negotiate another mortgage with Zack at Allen Tate Realtors, spend another $10,000 to make the kitchen and bathrooms look nice — nothing too dramatic, no marble tops or gas stoves, just enough to look clean and functional. She and Tony (her renovator, he and his bunch of Mexicans) found a deal on used Kenmore stoves — they bought twenty at bulk and had them in their own basements and in a hundred-square-foot storage unit on Tryon. Wood floors, drywall, new carpet on stairs . . . Annie loved the shopping, the bulk buys at Lowe's and Home Depot, the smell of new paint and repairs, the bustle inside a home when the Mexicans who — good God — could do anything, absolutely anything to a house you wanted done overnight, under cost. What a world she had found herself in! And every little bit of those costs were business costs, ready to be written off against profits . . . which were continually sewn back into new buys and new turnovers. Annie didn't pay a cent of taxes last year! Her accountant Bob told her how much to spend and how much to write off to balance it all out perfectly.

Bob, balding and graying, with some shitty substandard CPA certificate from some East Backwater community-college-type place, but he had surpassed the Ivy League MBAs she knew from high school, both in fortune and showy possessions. Bob knew how to dress; he knew the effect of a pressed blazer and tight starched shirt. Not much in the face, chin a little weak, but he had powerful legs straining against those creased pants — oh, he could show a woman what for.

Zack at the loan office, also balding, but very fit due to a Soloflex in one of the empty offices at his Allen Tate suite. When the phones weren't ringing or his eyes weren't crossed from mortgage documents, he did a few cycles on the Soloflex which resulted in upper arms and abs to shame a gym instructor. And he had been an English major before he went into mortgages — it was just about Love the one time she was making idle conversation and pointing out that not only was Allen Tate the name of the ubiquitous Realtor in Charlotte, but there was also a poet named that, and Zack looked ceilingward and began, *"Row after row with strict impunity / The headstones yield their names to the element . . ."* Tate's "Ode to the Confederate Dead." Shame about Zack having a wife.

And of course, Tony her contractor, just like her husband, Chuck, working-class hunky Southern male, beard stubble and a moustache, NASCAR T-shirt and country music blaring from the truck. *Hell yeah,* she would do him and he was edging closer to letting her. All she'd have to do is show up late to a renovation site after he sent the Mexicans home . . . and, while we're on the subject, some of those *chihuahuaenses,* those vaqueros turned construction workers, she wouldn't mind some fiesta time with those muchachos either — and those big brown eyes never failed to scan Annie from head to toe, aficionados of a plus-size woman, reminding her of the pure carnal oblivion that was Vinicius so many years ago.

Men! A world of working men, men sanding drywall, men installing stoves, men cutting tiles for the kitchen floor, men moving money, men drawing up papers, leaning in close with their sweat and cologne and arms and chests. All that maleness orbiting around her like she was the sun! They got up in the morning to work on her projects, to do her bidding.

Michael Oxamander, though. Suppose he's out there somewhere, needing to find a home? She did wonder what he was up to. That was the one guy she kept thinking about, the one she didn't and couldn't rope in. Nowadays she could hold him. She was canny enough to keep him coming back. Perhaps. She'd give Myspace the once-over, try to find him on various social networks, Google him . . . He was off the grid. Maybe he would be Husband Number Four. Would he be proud of all that she accomplished? Or would he find her degraded by money, crass and commercial?

"Thanks for the cards," Dorrie said, committing them to her handbag. "Guess I'll be seeing all y'all Johnstons at the big wedding."

Jerilyn's wedding was at the Johnston house, which Annie took at first to mean that her family was finally broke . . . but that was before she saw the booty and swag assembled for the big day. No, it was at the house, Annie realized, so Jerene's control could be utter and inexorable.

The Johnston homeplace had never been more beautiful; worn furniture was reupholstered, the out-of-date lighting fixtures were replaced, new carpet, new paint on the walls; and their yellowing backyard lawn, in the six months preceding the big day, was transformed into a flowering garden, aisles of tulips and irises, fringes marked by azalea and camellias, all blooming on cue for the June event. The caterers, under the direction of Alma and Jerene, outdid themselves.

There was a sweepstakesworthy tableau of gifts arrayed in the living room, a buffet of the ages in the garden, open bar in the kitchen area, a ziggurat of a cake aswirl in artisan frosting-flowers, and — here was a Jerene touch — there were varieties of chairs, divans, love seats, ottomans in all rooms of the house and corners of the yard so people could really be comfortable and not worry about flimsy rented folding chairs sinking into the grass or not supporting their weight. The weather, probably also secured by Jerene in a soul-leasing diabolical deal, was flawless.

Their brother Bo, aka Reverend Johnston of Stallings Presbyterian, performed the ceremony and the effect of his faltering a little, his voice wavering, as he stated the vows for his little baby sister got everyone dabbing their eyes. Skip looked like his usual shell-shocked, just-sobered-up self. Liddibelle Baylor, Skip's mom and a longtime family friend, bawled through the whole ceremony, before, during, after, and would have kept on had Mom not slipped her a Valium. And Jerilyn was radiant. Annie told someone, without bitterness, just stating a fact, that "you could see who got the good looks" in this generation.

Annie made herself useful, talking to Aunt Dillard who was having one of her "bad days," with her fibromyalgia; she also enjoyed talking politics with her sister-in-law Kate, Bo's wife. At last, there was at least one other person nearly as liberal as she was in the family! Annie suspected Kate was on a kind of probation with Jerene, since Kate was, unforgivably, country as a turnip, twangy and loud-laughing from Fayetteville, North Carolina, but you could see why Bo married her — she was sunlight, kindness, goodness, endless energy. (In fact, she was surprised her staid brother had the good sense to marry someone like that.)

The party at the house wound down around six and two hours later, in the Westin Hotel ballroom, the young people and a few guests in their middle years who were game, met for dancing (with Charlotte's hottest DJ) and more drinking before the happy couple slipped up to the deluxe honeymoon chamber. This later "second" party purposefully skimmed off the oldsters, the aunts and uncles, as well as Reverend Bo and Kate, making it an exclusive blowout for Jerilyn and her sorority sisters and Skip and his fraternity brothers. Dorrie and Josh changed into their clubbing clothes and tore up the dance floor, while Duke and Jerene collapsed back at home, clinging to two strong tumblers of bourbon, their great work accomplished. Annie sat alone at a dark table in the Westin ballroom; this was *so* not her crowd. She got off her feet for a dance with the groom.

"Better treat my sister good," she said.

"I've learned this about Johnston women," he said, out of breath from his energetic champagne-fueled dance moves. "You better not cross 'em, and you better not tell 'em no."

"Such wisdom in one so young."

And yet men had told Annie no with some regularity in her life.

"You're still here!" Jerilyn said, falling into the chair next to her, wedding dress still starchy and crackling.

"What time is it?" Annie scanned the wall for a clock. "Shouldn't you be en route to the Honeymoon Suite?"

"Skip wants to make sure the Zipper — uh, the Zeta Pis all get into cabs instead of drive."

"I got to hand it to Mom," Annie admitted. "That was the best functioning, most beautiful wedding imaginable. Jerene Johnston can deliver the goods."

Jerilyn nearly teared up. "It was beautiful, wasn't it? I'll never be Mom, though, no matter how hard I work at it."

"Hey, go upstairs and start having some children with Skip and in twenty years' time, and a lot more practice, you'll be better than Mom, when it comes time to micromanage *your* daughter's wedding."

"Did it make you a little sad, Annie, to . . ." Jerilyn thought better of the question; it showed in her face.

"What?"

"I mean, not to have had a big house wedding with the full deluxe Mom treatment."

"Actually, I'd have died with this much attention, everyone whispering about how fat the bride was. No, I'm glad they never did this kind of thing for me so they could spend twice as much on you. You, Jerry, are the perfect, beautiful bride. You are worthy of such a beautiful wedding."

Annie never said nice things so it had much more force than the last hundred well-wishers who had told Jerilyn how beautiful she was on this special day. Jerilyn let a tear escape. "I'm glad I got to do it at home. Mom said she wanted it to be the last thing people remember about the house."

Annie smiled because she didn't understand what Jerilyn meant. Why would it be the last thing . . . "Are Mom and Dad thinking of selling our house?"

Jerilyn looked a little startled. Had she said something not intended for Annie's ears? "Um, I don't know. I mean, Mom and Dad, now that we're all older and out of the house, are, I think, going to sell it one day."

That was as a blow. Sell Great-grandfather Joseph Johnston's hundred-plus-year-old mansion on the hill, the house they built Myers Park around? Of course, Annie would put a stop to it. Maybe she would buy it from them, through an anonymous third party, and make a show of giving it back to them. Maybe she would move into it herself. Then it suddenly made sense. Of course they would sell it. How else would her parents live with her father not working? The thought of her childhood home being sold . . . "Any idea when they might sell it?" Annie asked lightly, so as not to scare Jerilyn off the topic.

"I guess when that housing development is finished. You know, the one near the trestle that Dad is working on with those investors. They're going to move into a unit there. Can I ask you a question?"

Visiting Mom and Dad at some gated community, lily-white golfing condo, just over the South Carolina state line — just great.

"Annie, do you really *like* sex?"

Annie nearly knocked over her mixed drink. "Sex. Well, yes I really do like it. It will surprise most of your sorority sisters over yonder to learn that there is a taste for big girls out there and some of those admiring men are mighty adept in the sack."

"You've always been popular, big or small," she said, reaching across the litter of wedding party favors and ruins of snack plates, and patting Annie's hand. "I *don't* much like it," she went on, clearly tipsy.

"Uh-oh. Maybe you shouldn't have married Skip if, um —"

"Oh it's better with him than anyone. We go so far back, known each other for so long that . . . anyway, it seems more natural with Skip. But still. Not crazy about it."

Poor girl. Nothing but Carolina frat boys flailing away on her, after gallons of Rolling Rock. "Sex is like coffee. People are lying to say they like it at first, but in time, it grows on you —"

Then suddenly Skip and two frat brothers swept down on Jerilyn who was lifted from her chair and was carried squealing to the dance floor for the DJ's long-awaited playing of EMF's "Unbelievable," some kind of Zeta Pi unofficial anthem.

Annie decided to make a discreet exit. By way of the bathroom.

While she was in there, a new crew of sorority sisters took up positions at the mirror, all high-gloss Southern girls in their twenties, fat-free, thin-waisted, beautiful swan necks and glimmering expensive salon hair. They were tired, drunk, exhausted, danced-out good-time girls but they still looked amazing, if somewhat artificial. Annie stared at herself critically. I'm just ten or so years older than these party girls, she thought, but my face sags like a forty-year-old; I will have this double chin accompanying me to the grave. Annie had a good man, a man's man, a macho Marlboro NASCAR-loving, work-boot-wearing, construction-worker stud of a man, while these bitches went home to the frat boys they lassooed at Carolina (wearing checkered golf pants and yellow sports coats, breathing booze-breath on everyone at the country club by eleven A.M.), and she had it all over them. But funny how having a first-rate fellow waiting for her down on the Banks didn't make these self-assessments optional, or any kinder.

She opened her clutch and found her lipstick. She thought about Michael from college who hadn't been heard from or seen in fifteen years. She looked forward to this week's meetings with Bob, Zack, Tony, and Jim, each encounter moving her a little closer to an exciting affair. Nope, Annie — Jeannette Jerene Johnston Costa Winchell Arbuthnot — was not so good at marriage. Not good in the least.

Bo

He assumed, some future day, he would be good with his own children (if he and Kate had some) but he wasn't good with other people's children. When he picked up infants at the church nursery, they began screaming until a woman — any woman, apparently — took the child away from Reverend Johnston. Toddlers and teenagers, pretty much the same response. Must be the preacher's collar, which he had taken to not wearing. He was already (reportedly) too serious, too stiff, and the dour preacherman uniform made it worse. His wife Kate connected with newborns in an instant, had them gurgling and smiling. Kate who swore she didn't even want children, naturally, a natural.

Another group of people he did badly with: older white men. He couldn't talk sports or stock cars, what Rush or Fox News said, Republican rants and ravings; they sensed some insufficient masculine gene in him, something soft and left-leaning. Kate could charm some of the old men, but the elders in their church were professionally mean, vinegar in their blood, quarrelers, grumblers, conspirators, assassins . . .

Older white women he did well with. Bo was a true Southern boy that way — always polite, respectful, listening patiently to endless twaddle and tedium, gardening and Circle gossip, catalogues of bodily ailments, explicated photos of grandchildren.

Another group Bo was ashamed to admit he was clumsy with: African-Americans. He felt white-guilty around them. There were very few black students at Mecklenburg Country Day (not even for the imagined boon to the sports teams), few blacks in his hall at Duke University. Durham was a mostly black city, yet the citizens beyond the granite walls might as well, for all Bo interacted with them, have been living behind the Iron Curtain. No blacks in his seminary class at Davidson College, no blacks in his church congregation.

When out shopping or dining in Charlotte, he saw how integrated Charlotte had become: sports-bar gangs of thirty-something men watching the Panthers lose, black, white, Latin, mixed-race, the Sikh guy in the turban, the Asian guy with the Southern accent, friends from work or school or some softball league. He envied them. Being natural around black people required there being some black people to practice on, run into, socialize with, and his world had denied him this. There was the cleaning staff at the church. As with Alma, the domestic he grew up with, he was a little suspicious of all that smiling and politeness, all those *yes, Reverend*s. He felt quietly judged by black people, even the nice ones, and furthermore, given the history of the South, he thought they were entitled. Now Katie — good Lord, she was at ease with everyone!

Maybe if he had been more socially adept he would never have landed them at Stallings Presbyterian. The Charlotte Presbytery was dominated by Zephora Hainey, one of those charismatic black ladies of the Oprah template, buxom, alert, clairvoyant when dealing with people, gathering your thoughts for you before you knew what your thoughts were. In his mind, she was ten feet tall, but in reality he was a head taller than she was, Zephora, this incarnation of womanly Christian goodness.

"That Stallings church needs to be bulldozed under the sod, and the earth needs to be salted," she said without pretense, before a bit of black preachin' from Job: "The rabble *rise,* they cast up against me their *waaaays* of destruction."

"Why doesn't the presbytery just shut it down?"

"Now Reverend Johnston," she said, taking

his arm, leading him into the garden of the Presbyterian church office, trimmed hedges of yellowing holly in an ivy patch, markedly unambitious. "We're in the business of helping and saving Presbyterian churches, not boarding them up. And if you look at our numbers, there are plenty of churches being boarded up without the presbytery going down there with our own hammer and nails. I don't have to tell you how the mainline denominations are fading away in this country, along with quilt-making and darning socks."

Stallings Presbyterian was short a preacher and, as in all Presbyterian churches, the congregation would decide on their own hiring, but Dr. Hainey had put his name in play, made a visit or two to some of the more reasonable ladies on the search committee and, as she knew he would, he became their leading candidate. But oh dear God, Bo thought, Stallings, N.C., and that beleaguered church . . .

Stallings was a rural satellite of Charlotte, right over the Mecklenburg County line, for whatever tax relief and social difference that afforded. There were still big swaths of farmland through its unaccountably serpentine town limits. Stallings in the 1970s became a middle-class suburb — ranch houses with lawns, young married folk fixing up farmhouses, storefront day cares and corner groceries, still more trees than asphalt. Then came the gated communities, the golf course, the built-overnight shopping center with the trendy food store. Carnivorous Charlotte kept growing toward Union County, panting down Stallings's neck with a poorer mix, mobile-home parks, Hispanic enclaves with *tiendas* and check-cashing services with signs in Spanish. In the midst of all this change and upgrade was a core of rural, conservative whites who had a last redoubt in Stallings Presbyterian Church.

Bo would privately tell trusted friends that Christianity in Charlotte possessed the aesthetics of the monster truck show at the Coliseum. Home of the mega-church, the auditorium churches with ten thousand–plus congregations, their endless splitting and walkouts and cabals and firings and lawsuits. The TV ministries, harkening back to native son Billy Graham and the altar call, Heritage Village and its religion-friendly amusement park (six million visitors a year!), the enjoyable rise and fall of Praise the Lord Club "evangelebrities," Jim and Tammy Faye Bakker. Bo smiled remembering that, as children, after they got home from church they raced to tune in the Bakkers' first TV effort, *The Jim and Tammy Show,* an evangelical puppet show out of Pat Robertson's TV mill of mediocrity, on . . . was it Channel 9? Bo and Annie would roll on the floor howling at the original songs screeched out by Tammy Faye, the pig puppet made out of a shampoo bottle, all urging the boys and girls on to Jesus!

"Are you children on the floor in your Sunday clothes?" their mother would cry, once discovered. "What in God's name are you watching? Oh not these people again!"

Do you ever suppose even one human came to confess Jesus Christ as his or her Lord and Savior because of the pig puppet and Tammy Faye's atonal warble? Bo wondered if that soul was one more soul than *he* had led to Christ.

"So you'll go down into Babylon for me?" Zephora was saying. "You have a sober manner, which will appeal to the conservatives, but you are progressive and loving at heart, which will become known to the more liberal element and make them happy."

"I'm not sure even God," said Bo, half-smiling, "could make Stallings Presbyterian 'happy.' I'll settle for civil."

The 1990s saw a wave of mainline church discontent. Presbyterians, Methodists, Lutherans, all the Protestant denominations began losing trade to the big mega-churches with their razzle-dazzle TV broadcasts, more showbiz and holiday pageants, dynamic preachers with altar calls. Well, that wasn't how Presbyterians did things anyway, but Stallings Prez started to feel stodgy to itself, and many of the congregation wanted a more active, charismatic faith.

And then Dr. Frankling, the grand old veteran minister, a year from retirement, became born-again. Oh he thought he had been born-again earlier, but that was a dry intellectual decision, not transcendence, not God's own grace descending upon him and bowling him over. And everything changed after that. Services were more charismatic and Dr. Frankling burst into tongues when he got excited in the pulpit. Sick people were now brought to the aisles for a laying on of hands. His sermons revolved around gifts of the spirit, and a small group of men and women met with him at his house, and word drifted back that things were transpiring. Fits and seizures, transports, all-night prayer sessions in which John and Marla Rheinhart claimed to see Jesus in the room. And then one heard about the time that Satan himself tried to interrupt the proceedings and Dr. Frankling, on way too little sleep, had them running around his house stopping drains and faucets — because that's how Satan would enter — shoving towels under cracks of doorways, taping the windows shut. You would have thought when they all came to their senses the next morning that would have occasioned some reflection but it didn't. And after the elders and deacons (some of whom were in this faction) talked it out, they decided that Dr. Frankling maybe better retire a year early and remain a great friend and congregant of the church. But he took it as an insult and left for True Vine Pentecostal where gifts of the spirit were encouraged. His last letter to the elders had been forwarded to the Presbytery and Dr. Hainey kept it in her files. So Bo got to read it.

You poor dead Presbyterians, he wrote them. *God has come calling and you will not answer; you have closed your hearts to the true revelation. You imagine yourselves shielded against His power with your purses and wallets, your small affordable charities, which avail you of nothing. I must go where I can preach Christ Jesus, active, enflaming, alive in the hearts of believers, not just on Sunday for a few diverting hours before the auto race or NFL game.* And it went on like that, and he decamped to True Vine and some members of the church went with him, including two deacons.

So that was Part One of the schism; Part Two was when the synod decided, after these Baptist antics, that an old-line interim minister was just what Stallings needed.

"Brother Bo, that was before my time of service here," Zephora said, her lips pursed. "I would never have sent Fire 'n' Brimstone Brenner to Stallings, no sir."

Dr. Brenner was some of that ol'-time religion, John Knox back from the grave. His sermons were strong, forceful, absolutely not up for discussion in any way, shape, or form because he was right, and he was insuperably right because he had God and Scripture on his side. Then it came out that the effeminate organist (who everyone thought was a closeted gay man with a bad silver toupee) was having a thing with a married soprano. Aside from the improbable visual of lovely Mrs. Hinton having an affair with Mr. Todd, there was a sense that something had to be said or done. The old unexcitable faction (who had not liked the speaking in tongues of Dr. Frankling) felt the adulterous couple should be informed that the congregation knew their secret, told to quit it, told to get counseling. The elders were determined that "in all things love," that a Christian, gentle solution might be found to patch up her marriage and return things to normal.

But Dr. Brenner had other plans and one Sunday called them out before the *entire* late-service congregation, which, of course, may have been in keeping with practices in the early church (as were sackcloth and ashes), but it had the effect of a stoning. He declared that they renounce each other and their sin on the spot, or leave the church never to return. They left. The organist sued for breach of contract, since there was no morals clause in his contract, as in the minister's and choir director's contracts. Half the congregation thought Dr. Brenner was wrong to do it; a quarter thought he was wrong to do it publicly but was right otherwise; and a quarter saw Dr. Brenner as the righteous branch that would spring forth to execute justice and righteousness in the land.

And then Stallings Prez started fighting over every little thing. Some younger members in the congregation wanted newer music as long as they were hiring a new organist. Synthesizers, guitars, miked singing — something the other churches were doing (well, the ones on TV), not that dreary old dirgey classical music all the time. They fought about who got to teach Sunday school. Lucille Gerster had given the kids nightmares with all her talk of hell to the second graders, but to remove her would mean World War III. (She had been in the tongues-speaking camp, and was still seething over Dr. Frankling's exile.) The church fought over their decade-long support of the Five Churches Soup Kitchen — didn't it seem they were paying the lion's share? And besides, is it really Christian to let these broken men get dependent on these handouts? And then one Sunday when Dr. Brenner asked if there were any concerns or requests for prayers in the congregation, Hedda and Leroy Hargett stood up and said that two blocks from their house, there was a Planned Parenthood family center going up and the staff would be counseling, if not actually performing, abortions there.

The church, on this one, could not agree to disagree: this was baby-murder right in their midst. Each controversy took its toll and people too liberal for the Neanderthal element in the church and people too conservative for this socialist bleeding-heart outpost began to find other congregations. The ones who stayed behind weren't going anywhere. They were committed to the fight for the life and soul of Stallings Presbyterian. But Bo had longed for service, and this was truly service. To save a schismatic, polarized church which had lost its Christian fellowship.

"And don't forget," concluded Zephora Hainey. "You've got another secret weapon."

Bo quickly self-scanned his known and unknown qualities.

"Kate," Zephora said, before he guessed something embarrassing. "Everyone likes Kate, and most anyone with any sense will love her."

And that prediction, Bo had much time to reflect, proved that even the great Zephora Hainey could be wrong and underestimate the malice of Stallings Presbyterian. His wife had her fans but she was as much a target for their fractured, malcontent church as he was. No, honestly, she was more so because she had never once, never once, thought to withhold her opinion on anything.

"You got yourself a Hillary Clinton there," old Jim Harker kept telling him, feeling Bo needed to hear it every week after service, pointedly not shaking hands at the door, not touching the minister as if he were a leper. Oh nothing was worse than having a Hillary Clinton as a wife. "What do you propose I do, Jim?" Bo unwisely asked him one week, when he was just testy enough to challenge the old coot. "Chain her up in the basement, put a gag in her mouth?"

"Women should be silent in the churches. They are not allowed to speak, says Corinthians," he answered back without looking.

Kate thought there was nothing lower than a politician. But Bo really felt for them, understood them. Like a presidential candidate, everything Bo ever said, every stray absent comment, every mild loss of temper, every aside to a trusted congregant, was *known,* passed around, pored over, analyzed by the whole church — and often wildly misquoted and misinterpreted, too. "A church this rich," he once said at a planning session, "has to make an answer to God why it is spending so much money on retreats and playground equipment when there are people in need of food within two miles of this church across the city line in Charlotte." That spread around the church winning him shaken heads, disgusted comments, a there-they-go-again look. "You wanna go preach at a black church, be my guest," said Hettie Bessemer, one of his chief detractors.

To want to feed the poor as Jesus commanded, to Hettie meant "wanting to do something for the blacks and Mexicans," which meant you had no business at a white church, particularly a white church which threw a set amount of money to a consortium of churches' charities which no doubt, surely, ended up doing some good for all those blacks who insist on being poor and undereducated and living in bad neighborhoods.

And if the all-white congregation wasn't an emblem of something amiss in the church, the fierce, unthinking, blind homosexual-hatred was dazzling, breathtaking in its breadth and completeness. As Katie noted, "It's not like there's any shortage of old gay bachelors, lesbian spinsters, and gay kids galore in that church."

"Yes," Bo said, "but some of them are old homosexuals who denied themselves all their lives, and they figure if they could fight off the demon and go through life without a single moment of sexual fulfillment then these kids can, too."

Bo and Kate knew about the kids. They came to talk about being gay, or thinking they were gay, or knowing they were gay having done something, something shameful, something with an adult in the church, a time or two. Bo saw the glory of Christ's taking a stick and writing the sins before the condemners among the people who would execute the woman taken in adultery. He wished at times he could borrow Jesus's gift, to show this congregation to itself, what lists of damnable offenses he could sketch out in front of some of the pious. No wonder so much of the Bible centers around inconvenient prophets or begrudging emissaries speaking truth to power, revealing the sins of the ones who would throw the stones — and no wonder they're driven mad by it all.

Which reminded Bo of the second thing the minister has in common with the politician, that nothing surrounding his life was secret.

"I know you got a gay under your roof, Reverend," said Ray Crutchfeld, even patting him aggressively on the shoulder, poor thing, to have *a gay* in your own family — imagine! "But that don't permit you to go all soft on the Bible now, do it? Sin is sin, remember that."

Bo's heart skipped a beat. Crutchfield couldn't know about . . . No, it had to be Joshua who he meant. Katie, when she was in the Peace Corps in Honduras, working in a remote village with one other woman, did have a loving and committed lesbian affair with her coworker. Once back in the States, the other woman reverted to heterosexuality, indeed, seemed to shun and resent Kate for their affair. Kate had hoped to launch an inner-city women's shelter with this woman, but that was long ago, and there was no way Ray could find any of that out. No, Bo supposed that Joshua's being gay was somehow public knowledge.

"You have some nerve speaking to me this way, Ray," he said quietly. The impertinence of being told "sin is sin," from Ray Crutchfeld of all people, on his third wife. *Christ said of marriage what God has brought together let no man put asunder, so we know what he thinks of divorce but he doesn't say a word about homosexuality, Ray, so little it concerns him* — But of course he didn't say that. "Sin is sin, Ray," Bo said, after faltering a moment. "And we're all sinners, with God finding no one sinner worse than another, but loving us all anyway and extending redemption through Christ Jesus. You believe that, don't you?"

"Well, yes —"

"Are you in the judgment business, Ray? Jesus doesn't say one thing about gays but I can give you a dozen quotes about judging and condemning and presuming to speak for God. Are you gonna be one of those with judgment and condemnation in your heart or will you have Christ's love in your heart?"

Ray met his gaze without a blink. "Ain't no fags in heaven, Reverend. And you and I both know that."

Bo knew that this exchange would be replayed and wrongly interpreted throughout the church, too. More evidence for the Katie-is-a-lesbian rumor (maybe she and Hillary Clinton . . .), more demerits which would lead inevitably to them leaving this church, being asked to leave at some meeting of the elders, some whispered-about humiliation that the whole church would know and support before it would be presented to him and Kate as an irreversible fait accompli.

Babies, teenagers, old white men, black people. But there was one more subset of humans that the Reverend Beauregard Johnston did not and could not particularly come to terms with: his own family.

His decision to be a minister was not exactly embraced. He could see it in his mother's eyes, a pall, a loss of some kind, a small distinguished settling for a lesser calling than law, business, politics. His father was always warmly supportive but even here too there was an effort behind his soft smile. "I'm sure you'll be the best minister you can be," he said, clasping his son's shoulder. God, almost any profession might be substituted in that statement ("I'm sure you'll be the best street juggler that you can be . . ."); it reeked of disappointment.

Did they think he took up the vocation lightly, as a lark, something to major in at Duke University, like Geography? He was sitting in the beautiful Duke Chapel, feeling tired but not despairing, not broken in some way, although the prospect of law school did not enliven him. And suddenly there was this bright light. He looked around in a panic to see its source, but it was all around him and nowhere else and this strange calm then suffused him, this immense peace and resolution welled up that made him wonder if his heart had stopped and that this were, unexpectedly, his death. If this were death, he remembered thinking, then let it come; he had no fear. And then a voice: *You are mine. You have always been mine.* And then gradually the gloom of the chapel returned and he was breathless, again looking around him for some source of it all. Okay, if he had been weeping or on the ropes, suicidal or despairing about life, yes, you might have thought it was a trick of the mind. But it was a Tuesday, for Christ's sake! He staggered from the chapel, into the daylight, deciding to think about it later, even deciding to ignore it . . . but he couldn't, and didn't. And soon he knew, after a bit more prayer, what was expected of him.

Annie was savage. "You can't possibly really want to peddle that claptrap about the Mean Old Man in the Sky, who created this world fifteen billion years ago so we could evolve over the last million, so that a percentage of the planet could know Jesus Christ for the last two thousand years as our personal savior and know that our every wayward orgasm and lustful thought is being tabulated by His Father who is prepared to send His imperfect children to a Hell which will last for fifteen times fifteen times fifteen billion years to the zillionth power because . . . He loves us."

"Please Annie, just save it." She had cornered him at a Sunday dinner and was stalking him as he walked steadily to his car and eventual escape.

"Here's the thing, big brother. You're gonna wake up in a few years and not believe it yourself, but by then you'll be stuck, flogging these myths and fairy tales to all the pathetic death-fearing childlike people who long to have their bigotries in common so they can go through the pearly gates while the others go to the fiery lake. You're going to resent them for needing *you* to believe it, for needing your complicity in the scam."

"It's not a scam."

"Good, then don't take a salary. Let God find a way to provide for you."

"I'm not ashamed to say I believe in something."

"No, it is I who believe in *things,* material things, corporeal demonstrable empirical *things,* and many ideals — art, clean politics, a generous social state, hatred of war. I am full to the brim with beliefs. You are the one hiding behind some two-millennia-old road show that has only recently stopped burning witches and wiping out Jews and leading crusades and inquisitions. And believe me, if the North Carolina rednecks you'll be preaching to had their way, there'd be inquisitions all over again. Having failed to keep their slaves and the black men from dating the white women in the name of Jesus, they've turned their attention to hounding knocked-up teenagers and persecuting suicide-prone gay kids. And the Moslems of course — there's an old chestnut. Do you think you're anointed, called by God to keep company with yokels?"

"Goodbye Annie," he said. And to annoy her, "I'll pray for you."

"Like George W. Bush, put by God into the White House for his Christian goodness and ready to enact God's divine plan for civilian death in Iraq and Afghanistan. And the big U.S. blank-check plan for Israel too, I guess, since the Jews are scheduled to be converted by the Second Coming of Jeeeezus before too much longer."

"I'm leaving."

"It's just typical of you — the whole thing."

He stopped walking toward his car. "What's typical? Being a minister is the very last thing one might have thought I would do." Bo Johnston, valedictorian, scholarship to Duke University, following in his father's footsteps, law school applications at one time in the mail, maybe an elected office as his father attained.

He would never forget that look Annie had perfected: of simultaneous disgust and barely contained laughter. "Oh Bo, I grew up with you. You cleaned up the abandoned lot with your troop of Webelos — it was in the paper. You made Eagle Scout — call the *Observer.* You wrote some dumb essay about how much you loved being an American and you won some VFW-sponsored fellowship, which got you in the paper. All our life you needed attention and approval. You got to Mecklenburg Country Day, you ran for class president and won. You played lacrosse and had to be team captain, too. You go to Duke and then find the Lord and you just can't say, 'Ah well, religion will shape and focus my life.' Nope. You've got to be religious *in front* of everyone, you need the grandstand of the pulpit. No one can be your minister, you have to be everyone else's minister, in control, dishing out God where everyone can see you doing it. Have you ever done anything that you didn't try to get some kind of public adulation for? If you did something wonderful, like work quietly at men's shelters or go abroad with the Red Cross, but you didn't get an article written about you, would you self-destruct? Would it be worth your while to do good without the cameras running?"

He had replayed that speech a number of

times and he knew what he should have said. That being a minister was precisely the humbling that his overachieving, Duke grad, law-school-bound self needed. Ministry was a thousand small humiliations and failings a day as you could do nothing better for people than simply hold their hand, or pray for them, or spout bromides in the face of life's real tragedies. There were sermons that fell flat. There were reachings-out to the lost souls that were rejected, community projects that fell apart, moments of leadership that proved faint and insufficient to the crisis. Hours at old folks' homes and in hospitals and with tragic teenagers, abandoned wives, broken men, and the legions, legions vast and innumerable, of the lonely-in-life . . . so much imperfect service at their behest and none of it, Annie, none of it, known to anyone but God.

A Johnston family Christmas tradition was goose for Christmas Dinner. Everyone wanted goose hot from the oven, bits of seared fatty skin and velvety dark breast or wing . . . but no one had ever wanted goose the next day. Goose casserole, chipped goose à la king, goose surprise, all inevitably scraped into the trash bag under the sink. So an edict went out unto all the family from Caesar — er, Jerene — that for Christmas 2007 there shalt be no leftovers. The refrigerator would evince no signs of there ever having been a 7,000-calorie-per-person Christmas feed of goose, an auxiliary glazed ham, five vegetables, a congealed salad, trays of pickles and chutneys and condiments, black pumpernickel rolls (irresistible, and a recipe passed down from the German Jarvis ancestors), and too many lard-enriched pies, chocolate chess, mincemeat, German chocolate-coconut, cheeses, petits fours, everything but the Roman slave holding a basin to throw everything up into. There was a bottle of champagne to begin the meal but after that temperance ruled. *We're not going to drink our way through the holidays,* was Jerene Johnston's edict on that.

"Hm, tell that," Kate noted to her husband, "to your Uncle Gaston."

It used to be Annie was the sole advocate for wine throughout the meal, Presbyterian continence be damned, but in recent years Jerilyn and Skip Baylor, now newlyweds, were equally devoted to the cause (Skip would bring a flask, so they had been cheating); Joshua and Dorrie seemed to be mildly inebriated already when they arrived, and they, too, had joined the chorus for wine throughout the meal. Bo wondered aloud to his mother if maybe this year they should accompany at least the goose with red wine, if only for health reasons —

"Beauregard, we end up fighting and saying

horrible things to each other most years without aid of wine," she said. "I fear what would become of us fueled by demon alcohol."

Last year there were so many leftovers, a gallon of brown-sugared yams, a barely touched cauldron of collard greens, halves of uneaten pies, so this year Bo and Kate were bringing a variety of Tupperware containers to take away all the leftovers for the Five Churches Soup Kitchen. Bo carried an ice chest from the garage and met Kate in the driveway who was carrying a cardboard box filled with empty Tupperware bowls and lids, run through the dishwasher that morning, likely none of them matching up.

Bo noticed that his wife had chosen to wear a man's red dress shirt and dark denims — perfect for the soup kitchen and the menial labor to come, but terrible for the impression it would make on Bo's mother. He could have said *Are you wearing that to Jerene Johnston's house?* And she might have gone inside and changed but . . . why should she change? Kate had a pageboy haircut, honey brown going gray, and her usual costume was tomboy wear, always had been. For church she had a sleeveless black frock which was just formal enough, but at most church functions, she wore a Duke sweatshirt and jeans. The youth group loves her; they barely detect an age difference. There is the fantasy fueled by afternoon women's TV shows that if you fancy someone up, do a makeover, find the right dress and personal style, they can be a fashion knockout. Not Kate. He had seen her fixed up, makeup and beauty-parlor hair, a lovely dress from one of the better stores, and she always looked like the fourteen-year-old tomboy forced into her Sunday clothes. But still, not to make an effort . . . It would be entered in Jerene's silently compiled list of grievances.

"We don't have to go, you know," Kate said, a few miles from the Johnston residence.

"We have to."

"We have the perfect excuse. We're ministering to the homeless, helping them know the love of Christ on the weekend before his birthday. *When you give a luncheon or a dinner, do not invite your friends or your brothers or your relatives in case they may invite you in return, and you would be repaid. But when you give a banquet, invite the poor, the crippled, the lame, and the blind. And you will be blessed, because they cannot repay you* —"

"You want to use Jesus to hide behind?"

"Minister's — and minister's wife's — prerogative."

They would take the Stalling Presbyterian Church van. Last year they picked up Joshua and Dorrie, then swung by for Aunt Dillard, then went by Bo's grandmother, Mrs. Jarvis.

This year was a Gaston year so Mrs. Jarvis would be staying put in the Lattamore Acres Retirement Community, by mutual consent. As they drove to the house, he wondered why no one this year wanted a ride. Kate knew: "After last year's donnybrook, everybody's driving their own cars so they can *escape.*"

Bo sighed. "I asked Mom to sit us down near Uncle Gaston and Norma and Dad. Annie will be up on Mom's end."

"Last year I had Annie on one side of me reviewing Richard Dawkins's atheism book, point by point, and Jerilyn on the other side of me, sitting there like a lump. Oh good God, we're first," Kate muttered as they rounded the hilltop curve of Providence Road. As Bo turned for the driveway, she cried, "Park in the street! Park in the street!"

"All right, all right."

"You went to Duke and Davidson and you aren't smart enough . . ." She was smiling now. ". . . not smart enough to keep us from getting blocked in the driveway?"

"And here's Annie," he noted.

Annie's unmistakable fire-engine-red BMW cruised up the hill of Providence, and she turned at speed into the driveway, the brakes squealing to a stop.

"Wonder what that car costs," Kate muttered, preparing to carry their box of Tupperware inside.

"She must be doing well. Guess I went into

the wrong line of work."

She kissed his cheek. "You deal in *spiritual* real estate."

It took a moment for Annie to raise her bulk out of her car, but once up on her feet, with her blouse and skirt smoothed down, she just about matched her billboards. Her hair was lustrous, Annie's brown was lightening a shade with each trip to the salon — blonder than he'd ever seen it, which was amazing given all her teenage rants against blondes and their innate evils.

"Her face is different," whispered Kate, before calling out hello. "Hello, Annie! You look great. You've . . . lost weight, maybe?"

Annie came over to carry one of their Tupperware stacks. She started right in on Bo: "You don't look much like Dad or Mom. You're five inches taller than the rest of us, right? Do you think there's a chance we're adopted? I don't look like either of them."

"Dad and I are both six-three," he said. "And you look like Grandma."

"Ow, thanks for that — she's a gargoyle."

"When she was younger. You have the same eyes."

"I've heard of families where they adopt and then before they can discuss it with the kids, the mom gets pregnant so they end up with adopted and nonadopted kids, so they don't want one group to feel they're different so they don't say anything."

"I have a church of a thousand congregants, probably two thousand when you count non-regular attenders, and I've heard of every social situation in the world and I've never heard of that." Bo got the ice chest from the back of the van with a groan. "This is the second time you've floated this theory. Why don't you want to be related by blood to our family?"

"That question doesn't explain itself?"

Skip and Jerilyn arrived next. Skip, Bo thought, was his usual party-boy collegiate self, coming at Reverend Johnston with a series of hip-hop handshakes that Bo had no clue how to respond to. "Are you my new sister-in-law, Kate?" he asked Bo's wife. "Or is it just the sister of my wife that's my sister-in-law?"

"We're all brothers and sisters in Christ," Annie said, a foretaste of the religious ridicule ahead.

Christmas Dinner à la Jerene Jarvis Johnston was elaborate and Bo was never unimpressed when he entered the dining room and saw his childhood dinner table expanded to its maximum, transformed to something out of a home décor magazine. Christmas china at each place setting (not to be eaten on, those plates would be substituted with other fine china when the meal started coming out in stages), polished silver cutlery, crystal glasses for iced tea and a champagne flute, a central array of pine boughs, holly with red berries (grown in the backyard), red and green Christmas ornaments arranged tastefully up and down the table, between six silver candlesticks, all candles lit, the smell of goose roasting, and something with cinnamon, Alma and Jerene taking pies out of the oven to cool, and something maternal and homey, bread baking . . .

"Don't get any ideas," Kate whispered to Bo, "that I'm taking this over one day." Kate was a functional cook, made a few things well, but she had had a childhood utterly devoid of womanly training, graces, niceties. He knew his wife felt vaguely guilty wallowing in this hospitality, this gilded bower she had married into. "What expense," she sighed.

"Gone to, let me remind you, because my mom working on this meal for a solid week is her way of saying she loves us."

She found her husband's hand. "Among other things."

Aside from the long table, there was an antique server from which the diners would help themselves to the first course, which was buffet style. Chafing dishes of sausages in croissant dough, warm copper pans with stuffed mushrooms, German meatballs, soft cheese straws, plates of dates and sweetmeats, red and green miniature heirloom tomatoes piled in a mound like cannonballs, red-skin peanuts and peeled pistachios (red and green!), rind pickles, dilled cornichons, bread-and-butter pickle slices, marinated turnips and radishes (from the Middle Eastern store), spring onion and celery sprigs for dipping into Alma's famous pimento cheese (yes, with green and red pepper flecks) — talk about your Proustian memories. Bo nearly hugged himself; how many familiar beloved tastes were assembled here from childhood.

Everyone heard the familiar noise of a car in the drive. First, Aunt Dillard was through the door looking festive (a knit sweater starring a sequined Santa Claus with his arm around a fuzzy-woolly Snowman) but afflicted in her person. Gaston had brought her and he was getting something from the trunk, while Dillard made the twenty-yard, slightly inclined commute from the driveway.

"Oh Lordy," she said, panting. "Can't do your Mount Everest anymore."

Jerene rushed to deposit her sister in a plush armchair in the living room.

"I can get you aspirin, Tylenol, Advil . . ."

"Next Christmas, if I come, if I'm still alive —"

"Hush!"

"I'll arrange to come especially early and be dropped two inches from the door. No, Jerene, save your medicine cabinet, I'm already medicated to a fare-thee-well. But I will hold out for some of what Gaston is bringing."

"Oh dear, he's not bringing wine, is he?"

A cheer went up from Annie, Jerilyn and Skip, with a quiet *Hear, hear* from a traitorous Mr. Johnston. Bo and Kate looked at each other with relief. Then Gaston lumbered through the door, carrying a cloth bottle bag that held nine bottles, arranged like a tic-tac-toe with separators to keep the bottles from clinking. "Now, Jerry," he said, heaving the contraband onto a table in the foyer, "this includes two 1996 Meursault-Genevrières, three 2000 Lafite-Rothschilds, Sauternes for the dessert course. I will not live long enough to finish off my cellar so we're going to start drinking it down right here."

Jerene sighed. "Such morbidity today."

"When my heart gives out and I am airlifted to Duke Medical they will remove a brick of your goose fat from my aorta. It's your Christmas dinner, Jerry, that edges me nearer the grave, otherwise I'd be the picture of sobriety and virtuous — aha, is that the fabulous Alma?"

Alma was setting down a plate of pickles on the buffet table. Once the goose was out of the oven and initially carved, she would take a share of her morning's cooking back to her own household for Christmas dinner with her own family. This had been the pattern as long as anyone remembered. "Merry Christmas, Mr. Jarvis."

"You're looking especially alluring today, Alma. I have millions of dollars. Let's run away together to my mansion where you can cook and I can have a nice drink while I watch you cook."

"Still married, quite happily, Mr. Jarvis." Bo could never tell whether she enjoyed Gaston's banter (or anyone's banter) or not. Bo assumed she and his mother had gotten along so well these many decades because they shared a similar lack of humor and steeliness of purpose.

"Well then, my love, I'll settle for a corkscrew. If there is such an enlightened gadget in this house of temperance and abnegation. Jerene, old girl, you look like a schoolmarm, all pruned up and pursed and ready to hand out conduct demerits. A little wine won't hurt anything. Not even you."

Bo watched his mother, frowning, accept defeat. She said, "Just so it's known that I'm not driving downtown to rescue any of you when you get arrested for your DUIs." His father was up in a flash at the china cabinet which held the crystal wineglasses, distributing a glass per place setting.

Gaston took the corkscrew from a wordless Alma, who dodged Gaston's wayward hand reaching for her apron sash. "If by dessert, this family hasn't drunk this supply, then I'm fleeing from this annual farce to find more worthy companionship."

Jerene asked, "Speaking of that, where's Miss Norma?"

"We're on parole from each other. She's become a nag about my finishing this horrendous book. Thought I deserved a break from her caterwauling."

Jerene's expression was grim as she collected the place setting for Norma and, with Alma, shifted the places down the table.

Bo, with a smile, asked, "If you hate to write your books, Uncle Gaston, why do it? You've made a fortune several times over. You've earned a retirement."

"Alas, Cordelia Florabloom has neither found her fiancé in the Union prisons nor has she met a tragic fate, so my readership doesn't consider the series over. Norma actively forbids my letting her be gang-raped by Union bummers . . ."

Dillard from her chair: "Gaston, please."

"Someone take my ailing sister a restorative glass of Bordeaux," he went on, pouring from the Rothschild. "You sure, Dillie, this won't interfere with all your many, *many* medications?"

"I'm in enough pain now that I truly don't care."

Kate went into the living room, clutching two glasses of red, to sit down beside Aunt Dillard and show concern. Bo should have been first to that chore, but he was strangely less tolerant of his aunt than he would have been of one of his congregation, where there were old ladies aplenty with mystery complaints and publicly established maladies. A firestorm of bitter invective awaited the doubters — doctors, nurses, physicians' assistants, specialists, and now family and friends, all doubting their condition, all incapable of sympathy for such enormous sufferings. Always elderly women, or postmenopausal, estrogen-deprived, aging and often lonely, living alone or with a husband that made for the equivalent of living alone . . . Look at Kate. How good she is, Bo thought for the millionth time, good to listen to this recital of ailments, taking Aunt Dillard's hand, shaking her head in sorrow and consolation. That's all Aunt Dillard wants. Her husband gone two years into their marriage, leaving her and their son, Christopher, behind, then Chris turning so wild and hell-raising, getting involved with meth dealers at college, in and out of rehab, then his death by cerebral hemorrhage at thirty-three, prompted by a reckless cocktail of drugs in his system. Bo figured no one had lovingly laid a hand on his Aunt Dillard since Uncle Randy left her, years ago. So here is her affection and human contact right here, Kate's little Christian performance, the clasped hand, squeezed tighter with each newly announced ailment.

"We've got an hour or so before dinner," Jerene said, now finished with adjusting the table. "Would you like to have a little lie-down upstairs?"

"More mountain climbing?" Dillard asked tremulously, contemplating the winding staircase of the foyer.

"There's a wicker couch in my office downstairs, if I move some papers off of it."

Kate and Jerene cradled Dillard to her feet and began walking her toward the little area that looked out to the back garden, a covered porch that Jerene called her "office," where mail and solicitations for artistic syndicates and charities could be piled unopened, where Bo and the other siblings had been forbidden to enter just as severely as Dad's Civil War Study and shrine.

Once Dillard was safely out of hearing, Uncle Gaston started in: "No such thing in my youth as fibromyalgia, although I suppose Victorian neurasthenia was the forerunner. Trilby-like women taking to the bed, invalidism. A long Southern tradition of this sort of thing before du Maurier ever wrote his novel popularizing it, sending legions of girls into faints and missed social seasons spent dying of mystery illnesses from the daybed."

Kate returned and then Jerene, glaring at her brother, miming a *ssssh,* finger to her lips.

"We had Geritol! Remember Geritol, Jerry?

And Father John's Medicine. And what was . . . Lydia Pinkham had a tonic, *good for what ails ya!* This stuff was advertised on TV. Pretty much alcohol and some mild narcotic to get Ma and Grandma through the boring stay-at-home day. I suppose it's like kids having attention deficit disorder these days — that's a crock too."

Bo began a conciliatory grunt. "Hm. Uncle Gaston —"

"She's sick," Kate interrupted. "That's all there is to it."

Gaston let his eyes go heavy-lidded and formed his lips into a disbelieving pout.

"If she feels all those aches and pains that the doctor can't find the source of, then she's sick. If she merely *thinks* she feels them, then she's still sick. If she's making every bit of it up for attention and has been doing this for a decade, then she's *really* sick. There is no way that she is not to be the object of our sympathy."

"Well said, Kate," said Duke. "Now where were we, Gaston? Making Annie's blood boil, I believe, laying out the case for Southern secession."

Bo was happy Annie was preoccupied fighting the Northern cause — that would keep her busy for a while, and off the topic of religion.

Did the North start the war by reinforcing Fort Sumter? President Buchanan refused to do it, declaring it a provocation, yet Lincoln secretly ordered General Winfield Scott to reinforce the Charleston forts even before his inauguration. What were the South Carolinians to think? If Lincoln freed their slaves — this fringe-party president elected in a four-way race with only thirty-six percent of the vote — then South Carolina would have a population of three million freed and mightily aggrieved blacks and fewer than a million whites. How to prevent the racial cataclysm? Come now, was not Lincoln's election a legitimate cause for panic among the whites? And wasn't secession — peaceful, orderly secession — from this so-called union a long-held right implied in the Constitution? Almost all constitutional scholars of the time reasserted the liberty of states to secede.

"*Do not* say the word 'liberty,' Dad," Annie erupted, "when you mean the liberty to enslave — that is a nonsense, a logical nullity. That is morally bankrupt and preposterous in the eyes of your — nonexistent, by the way — God."

Bo cleared his throat.

"I'm going to go help Mom and Alma in the kitchen," said Kate, seeking relocation.

"I ask the chairman," Annie said, smiling, "to advise and extend my remarks. Certainly no one thinks the Confederate God, pro-Southern, pro-slavery, is the God that should be currently worshipped in America, do they?"

"That god is not God," Bo concurred.

Uncle Gaston broke in, "Oh that God is just as real as any god any time. The only thing that evolves is the amount of wickedness you can do in the name of God. You can't enslave or lynch anymore, but the root, mob superstition just finds other channels to express itself. The chief attribute, after all, of the religiously deluded is credulity, fanaticism —"

"Uncle Gaston, please," Bo began.

Skip Baylor tried to participate. "It's like Mr. Johnston was saying —"

"When will you ever convert to calling me 'Dad' or at least 'Duke'?"

"It's like Dad says, the War was a lot about States' Rights."

"No it wasn't." Annie pounced. "It was about slavery and keeping black people as property on plantations and insuring the fortunes of the whites. Read CSA Vice President Stephens's 'Cornerstone Speech,' which explicitly declares the rebellion is about the God-given power to enslave."

Gaston, not fully committed, began, "Supreme Court Justice Samuel Nelson — from New York, mind you — had eloquently shown that union through coercion of the states was unconstitutional. There was a library full of legal documents supporting states' sovereignty which had to be conveniently ignored to pursue Mr. Lincoln's war.

"Why do you think they didn't try Jefferson Davis after the war for treason? President Johnson didn't pursue a trial because Davis could make the case for secession as well as the legality of slavery — not one court decision ever ruled against those principles. Salmon P. Chase would have presided over the trial and even though he was the first to let a black man argue a case before the Supreme Court, an abolitionist, a Free Soiler, Johnson understood that Chase would acquit Davis for the charge of treason thanks to the understanding of States' Rights. So there was no trial. Of Robert E. Lee, either."

Annie: "All of these States' Rights arguments are mired in spoiled-brat logic. I, the majority sentiment in the state, get to do whatever I want which includes trampling on the rights of the less powerful. I get to pollute or take mountains apart, top to bottom, to get at the coal, destroying the environment downstream for all the poor mountainfolk. I get to keep black people from voting or deny poor people Medicare they're owed or get to keep black schools inferior or get to criminalize gay people or order the state police apparatus to harass women seeking putatively legal abortions in Kansas and Oklahoma, and if you object, if you say it isn't just, I will wrap myself in a cloak of States' Rights and say, 'Even if we're prejudiced and ignorant, we get to trample the minority any way we please and how DARE you try to impose federal justice from above — States' Rights! States' Rights!' And you'll note that all States' Rights–obsessed states are antiquated hell-holes, Mississippi and Alabama and South Carolina, racist, backward plutocracies. And you'll also note when progressive states assert *their* rights — like Massachusetts allowing gay marriage or D.C. having strict gun laws or Washington State flirting with assisted suicide and euthanasia, then Bush's crowd moves the Congress and the courts, heaven and earth, to try to stop it. So what they really mean is States' Rights When Those Issues Agree with Our Theocratic Backwoods Yahoo Worldview."

Bo sat there as the older men tangled with Annie. She got the real brains in the family — if only his own sermons had her persuasiveness. And despite an oft-recited set piece or two, she was improvising, haranguing without a pause or a false start.

Jerene came in from the kitchen and banged a copper pot with a ladle, instantly commanding attention. "I heard the word 'Bush.' What did I say about Mr. Bush last year? We will not have one more family dinner descend into name-calling and ill feeling over George W. Bush. His name is no longer to be mentioned. We sacrificed 2004 to him, and we will not sacrifice 2007."

"All but a few of us, Mother, are in agreement he's the worst president in U.S. history. I don't know why —"

"Because I said so, Annie, and you don't get to eat if you're going to go on about the depredations of Mr. Bush or the Republicans." Looking at her brother and husband, already into a second bottle, she added, "Or the War."

"Good God, woman, this is totalitarianism!" cried Duke Johnston in mock outrage.

"Sic semper tyrannis!" cried Gaston Jarvis. "Jerry, what else will we talk about?"

"Oh come now, darling," Duke pleaded. "I don't get to see Gaston that often anymore . . . really except for a distant wave across the Nineteenth Hole, it's just Christmas and funerals. Can't we have a little more War?"

Bo heard the sadness in his father's smiling protest; he looked at Annie who looked back at him meaningfully, having heard it too.

Then Bo's father stood up, unsurely, raising a hand. "I say, as my ancestor Joseph E. Johnston said many a time, 'Retreat! Retreat!' "

"Perhaps we shall bivouac, Colonel, in your private study?" Gaston said, richly.

Yes, the Civil War Study, crammed with pistols, sabers, musket balls, medals, maps and period Bibles, Dad's inner sanctum, housing the Confederate relics the old men could venerate, toys these overgrown boys could play with. But also Dad's whiskey cache.

As Gaston lumbered to his feet, Jerene said with especial sharpness, "I'm calling a cab for you, Gaston, if you start slurring your speech. And you, too, Joseph — you can sleep it off at the Club." Dad's given name, Joseph, only came out in threats and warnings.

"I promise moderation," Bo's father said. "I've had the pistols restored and Gaston can inspect them for his next opus. Perhaps Cordelia Florabloom can shoot her way out of a Union garrison."

"Yes, but not before she's passed around like a blow-up doll, letting the officers desport themselves —"

"OUT," said Jerene. Then she turned her attention to her giggling children: "My Christmas wish is that you all would *grow up.* You'd never know any of you were in your thirties. Not including you, Jerilyn — you're the only well-behaved one in the family."

"Yes, Mother," Annie and Bo said in unison.

But to Bo Jerilyn did not seem well behaved as much as sullen. He asked, "Jerilyn, is something wrong?"

Skip answered for her. "Big-time cramps this morning —"

Jerilyn: "Oh shut up. Don't tell them that."

Bo and Annie, Skip and Jerilyn decamped to the dining room, where after a surreptitious pass at the first-course items on the server, a pick here, a nibble there, they sat at the table. Annie, Bo regretted, sat directly across from the seats he had picked out for himself and Kate, who soon emerged from the kitchen. Kate ferried a tray of congealed salads, red and green marshmallows suspended in an off-white gelatin, a Betty Feezor holiday recipe from time immemorial. She went along the table setting the small plates at the upper left of the three silver forks, engraved JJJ, at each place setting. "Are the boys still defending the Southern entry into the War? Are y'all gonna talk like this when Dorrie gets here?"

Skip asked to be reminded who Dorrie was.

"Josh's black friend," Bo heard himself say in a whisper. Why did he whisper *black*? It was the same way he would go sotto voce to say someone had *cancer,* or you know her husband *drinks* . . .

"His girlfriend?" Skip pursued.

Kate's eyes went wide, almost smiling. "No, they're just friends," she quickly supplied.

Annie crossed her arms. "Jerry, do you not know about . . ."

Now Jerilyn was whispering, so their parents in the next room wouldn't hear. "That he might be gay, yes, I know. How do I know if he's one hundred percent? For all I know that was a phase and Josh and Dorrie are a couple."

"I can assure you," Annie said, an edge in her voice, seeing a new campaign, "it is not a phase. And Dorrie's definitely gay, too."

Skip snorted. "Shit, why don't they just get married and have one of those cover marriages? I bet your mom would prefer that to, you know, the other."

Annie: "They won't do that because the calendar does not say that it's 1957 but rather 2007 and gay people don't have to do that bullshit —"

"Ssssh," said Bo, eyeing Alma and his mother through the doorway. "Let's not out Josh before he gets here."

"Why not?" Annie said. "You wanna talk about bullshit. The whole of Charlotte knows these two are gay except for Mom and Dad —"

"It's not for you to tell your parents," Kate said with too much haste.

"I wasn't going to tell, Kate, *my* parents about *my* brother's orientation, but it's nice of you to weigh in."

"Let's change the topic," Bo said, staring daggers into his older sister.

"Fine. This family needs to be issued a memo before we get together for these empty jump-through-the-hoop holiday meals about what topics are proscribed and what topics can be permitted to be dwelled on at a depth of one to two inches."

Alma burst in with a long silver tray of cranberry sauce. Everyone was quiet.

"I know you all are talking Civil War and slave times," Alma said with her level, unexcitable tone. "I can hear every word. Keep talking so God can hear what you're saying and take note."

"The boys are in the study," Kate said, "so the cannons have gone quiet."

"About the cranberry sauce," Bo mumbled, looking at the Jarvis traditional recipe with berry skins, seeds, orange peels, bitter walnut pieces.

"Yes, Mother's cranberry compost." Annie, each year, was determined to thwart her mother's twigs, seeds and kernels for the Ocean Spray can of molded gelatin, and in this, she had allies. "Shall we go get the Ocean Spray?"

"I have to drive or I get carsick," Kate improvised, staring desperately, telepathically at Bo. "And our van isn't blocked in the driveway, we parked on the street, so . . ." Bo and she furiously tried to think of a reason Annie couldn't accompany them.

Bo: "Yes, and you don't drive a stick, Annie. The van is manual. I'll go with you, sweetheart."

They were out the door before Annie could invite herself along and they had to invent a lie about why the sixteen-seater van didn't have room for one more passenger. They walked across the lawn without comment. They sat in the car and fastened their seat belts without comment. Kate started the car and drove around the corner and then permitted herself a scream: "Aaaaaaiiiiiii . . ."

Bo patted his wife's arm. "It'll be over soon. Just a few more hours."

"Annie tries so hard to make common cause with me and I suspect I agree with ninety percent of her views but I just hate her in the most un-Christian way! Her opinions do not spring from any constant source. I feel my faith — which she takes great pains to insult — informs all my positions and I understand having to fight tooth and nail with right-wingers who can't believe a fellow Christian doesn't agree with them, but I swear it's worse arguing with your own side. I think of my politics as humane, and I think her politics are just politics, just stances she likes hearing herself promote."

"I grew up with her. What do you think that was like?"

Kate was calming down as the Harris Teeter was coming into view. "She's so smart. I'm underequipped to tangle with her."

"You're not the one with three husbands, the current one which you'll note is a no-show for the umpteenth year."

"I'm not up to debating your uncle, either, who makes the Southern cause so reasonable. It was a fight to keep people in chains, lynching, hobbling, selling off the men, breaking up slave families, whipping, every sadism imaginable —"

"Save it for the table. I agree with you."

"I'm not opening my mouth one more time because I'm already non grata with your mother."

"My mom likes you!" Bo felt his mother did like Kate, but just like his choice of profession, would it have hurt him to marry from his own background? Someone who could be an ornament to his social standing, maybe invite the Johnstons over for a good dinner now and then, as families usually do? Kate refused to host Jerene and Duke — what was the point, she always said. I'd have to cater it. Or sneak in other people's cooking and pass it off as her own, and that just wasn't Kate.

They pulled into the Harris Teeter lot beside another van with a MCCAIN '08 sticker. "That's the first one of those I've seen," Kate said. "I'll get the cranberry sauce, you can stay in the car."

Bo thought, as he did in all solitary moments, about his next sermon. There was always a next sermon. The good thing about Methodism was that a minister could work up a few showstoppers and hit new congregations with polished chestnuts every few years after you moved churches, but there were no summer repeats like TV for a Presbyterian minister. Not that you didn't circle over familiar territory, time and again.

The run from Thanksgiving — let God be thanked for our gifts — to Advent — our Savior is coming — to Christmas — the Christ child is born — to Epiphany — the babe in the manger is divine — was cake. Just read the passages and sew together some heartwarming hokum, home for the holidays, a time of peace and good cheer, Christmas in our hearts, blah blah, blah blah; then came the onerous winter stretch.

Every year Bo wanted to do a series. It was good to do a series. Ten sermons on the Ten Commandments. Twelve sermons on the twelve apostles — one really had to dig for stuff about some of the no-names on the disciple backbench, though. For a month, Bo had been thinking about an eight-parter about God's manifestations in the Bible, how surreal, impractical, and often counterproductive they were. When God became flesh in Christ Jesus, it ended in Him getting executed, so God in His earthly appearances, we should admit, must take a very long view.

God appears man-like, without fanfare, to Abraham, though it's an angel that stops the sacrifice of Isaac. Jacob and the Wrestling Angel — except the Bible says it was a man and that Jacob comprehended that the man's face was the face of God. A burning bush to

Moses. Pillars of cloud and fire to the Jews freed from Egyptian bondage — good material there. A man with a drawn sword to Joshua. Balaam's ass. Chariots of fire. And then God starts showing up on thrones: First Kings, Isaiah, Ezekiel, Daniel — not much metaphor or poetry in God on a throne, an anthropomorphic comedown, really, God sitting in a chair like an earthly ruler. And then the writing on the wall in Daniel — you can get some rhetorical mileage out of that. But the last time he thought about Balaam's ass, he really stalled out.

Balaam is on his way to ritually curse Israel but God takes control of his voice and he keeps blessing Israel instead, despite the continued encouragement of the priests of Baal. When he sneaks off to perform another curse an angel appears that only his donkey can see. When Balaam can't get his donkey to go forward, he beats it, and God has the donkey speak to him, and then he can see the angel. (Why not have the angel appear so Balaam can see him, and save the circuitous route through the talking donkey?) Anyway, the angel says he might have killed Balaam if not for the donkey. Doesn't God have control of his angels? Would this angel have been permitted to kill God's prophet if God had not made the donkey speak? Bo read a number of rabbinical commentaries (all more ingenious than the ludicrous biblical episode upon which their commentaries were based), and also some Christian commentaries. The same Christian book went on to insist that Jacob wrestled Jesus, Abraham walked with Jesus, that Joshua's man with the sword must have been Jesus too, who is God, who was/is eternal, who is God's stand-in when he needs to incarnate.

And in a wave, a full complete conclusive rush of sense and reason, he knew all these fairy tales and myths and corrupted pre-existing pagan legends were all junk. A waste of time. He could see his expectant congregation befuddled, their upturned faces seeking an answer from the pulpit, wanting useful truth, meaning, and Bo couldn't very well say, "C'mon, you know this kind of biblical tale is nonsense." It was anthropologically interesting, the way Lord Vishnu becoming a fish or a tortoise says something about Hindu notions or Zeus becoming a swan or a white bull captures the salaciousness of the Greek imagination, but it's all lore and campfire legends, fairy tales, unlike the New Testament which is mercifully modern, pertinent to how we treat our fellow man, how we live now.

Though Bo, when in this mood, suspected that the magical baggage about Jesus wasn't true either, walking on the water, the Transfiguration, rising from the dead. If the authors of the New Testament sat down and set out to make the most *unconvincing* and incredible account of a resurrection, with a sometimes incorporeal appearing and disappearing Jesus, a Jesus no one much recognized, a risen Jesus who before the Roman authorities and the world can see him and bear witness to the might of God, has disappeared up into the sky — well, then you would have the gospel accounts of Jesus' rising from the dead.

The Rabbi-Spiritual Jesus was enough for Bo. He knew Kate felt and believed and lived the Resurrection Jesus. Bo thought the Jews were much nobler for not being moral in order to achieve an afterlife, no pie-in-the-sky payoff for earlier sufferings and sacrifices. Christian preaching usually dwelled in the land of Hell and Judgment, Antichrist and Apocalypse, and how we would never never never die, seeing granny and your dog Spot again at the Pearly Gates . . . all far from the message of compassion and living for others that Jesus embodied. He didn't want to preach about or dignify any of the Special Effects claptrap. He wanted the basement of Stallings Presbyterian to be a Hispanic day care for working mothers, legally or illegally in the country. He wanted to take over the Five Churches Soup Kitchen which was run so desultorily, held at arm's length from all the congregations, charity delegated, outsourced . . . every one of Stallings's congregants should be taking a turn at the soup pot. *I was a stranger and you did not invite me in, I needed clothes and you did not clothe me, I was sick and in prison and you did not visit me.* Who in his church, including himself, had visited one man in lockup at the county jail?

He saw Kate crossing the parking lot with a straining plastic bag weighed down with cranberry sauce cans.

I could leave the ministry, and I probably should leave it, Bo thought. I wonder if Kate would then leave me, too.

Another car — Joshua's beat-up old bomb — was parked in the street, so Josh and Dorrie had arrived.

Kate sighed. "I'm always eager to see what Josh is wearing."

Bo shrugged as they, not so quickly, made their way back to the front door of the house. "I thought the job in the clothing store was going to be temporary, but the years go by. I guess he doesn't want any kind of career, just a job."

Kate chuckled. "I would have loved to be satisfied with just a job. Why did we ever think we wanted vocations?"

"We were twenty-something and thought we were going to save the world."

Kate looked at him, squinting. "I'm still

gonna save the world. When did you drop out?" Before he could answer, she grabbed his upper arm and pushed him toward the front door. "We'll go save the world after we survive Christmas dinner."

When Bo and Kate returned, they saw Joshua and his friend Dorrie Jourdain were already drinking wine, ensconced at the table with Uncle Gaston, his father, and Aunt Dillard. Despite the fatwa against Civil War talk, the Gatling guns and cannonade were again ablaze.

"That's getting into history no one likes to talk about," Gaston was saying. "The freedmen blacks of Charlotte gave five hundred dollars, raised at their church, to support the Confederate war cause."

"Probably the best five hundred bucks they ever spent," Dorrie said. "Probably kept that little church from getting burned down. But you were saying about blacks and Indians who fought for the South."

Kate and Bo slipped into the kitchen and with the conspiratorial help of Alma were given a can opener and a silver dish to slide the molded cranberry gelatin into. They subtly positioned the contraband on the server, next to the seeds-and-peels cranberry sauce, and resumed their seats.

". . . because the Cherokees were slave holders," Gaston was elaborating. "The Creeks, Seminoles, Choctaws, Osage, all fought for the South. Colonel William Thomas and North Carolina's 'Thomas Legion,' with the Qualla band of four hundred Cherokee warriors and another two thousand mountain whites. General Stand Watie was a Cherokee brigadier general."

Bo then asked, taking his seat, "All those Indian tribes couldn't have owned slaves, though, could they?"

"No, but the Indians in Oklahoma didn't like what they saw with John Brown and Lincoln suspending habeas corpus, arresting landowners willy-nilly. They thought the South would honor their treaties where politicians from the North had proven more malign toward the native peoples. Oregon and Nebraska were free states where the whites grabbed Indian land with impunity. I keep coming back to this business about secession. Everyone down South thought they had the right to do this peacefully, and when Lincoln stormed into the South with troops that included prisoners and indigents gathered up in slum clearances of the Northern cities, troops that started burning and looting and pillaging, the Indians threw their cards in with the locals." Uncle Gaston turned to Bo's father. "Even after your ancestor surrendered to Mr. Sherman, sometime in April —"

"April twenty-sixth," Bo's father supplied. "Did I ever take you kids to the little cabin outside of Durham where Johnston surrendered to Sherman?"

Yes, Dad, said three out of four children simultaneously.

"Anyway, after April twenty-sixth, the Indian boys kept fighting. They sure didn't desert, like the white troops. Last shot fired east of the Mississippi was from the Thomas Legion, up in a skirmish in Waynesville. And Watie fought until June. Last Confederate general to surrender, in fact —"

There was a massive crash in the kitchen that stopped everyone cold.

Silence. And then, weakly, Jerene called out: "Um, no one come in, please." And after thirty more seconds: "Everything's under control!"

And then Alma stuck her head in the dining room from the kitchen. "There's gonna be a slight delay."

Kate began to get up. "You need any help in there?"

Jerene from within: "NO ONE come here, please. Everything is under control!"

"While my sister is occupied," Gaston said, now on his feet, "it is time for the decanting of the honorable Gaston Jarvis's renowned cellar . . . Why look, a 1989 Lynch-Bages."

History would show, Bo would conclude looking back, that this delay of an extra hour before dinner led to the horrors ahead. It set up Uncle Gaston in the role of Bacchus, filling the glasses tirelessly. Bo noticed Skip and Jerilyn took possession of their own 2000 Pape-Clément, and Gaston, permitting all, opened up another one, then another one. Bo counted empty bottles on the table . . . more than nine. Gaston must have had reserves in his car.

Annie exclaimed for all of them, "This is the best wine I have ever put into my mouth."

Dorrie concurred. "Clearly I have never even had wine, just . . . grape juice."

Joshua, the sudden connoisseur, was sucking air through his mouth with a mouth full of wine when he made eye contact with Dorrie and erupted in a laugh, spewing it everywhere on his plate of hors d'oeuvres . . . and in turn Skip nearly did the same thing, laughing at Josh.

"You know when Jesus turned the water into wine," Annie began, looking at Kate and Bo, "do you think it was this good? Would miraculous wine taste like this?"

"I'm sure it was sweet Jew-wine, like Manischewitz," Uncle Gaston suggested. "Speaking of the Levites, how go your real estate dealings, Duke?"

"Um, Mr. Yerevanian is Armenian, I believe." Duke then raised his glass to Gaston. "I can't thank you enough, Gaston, for what will prove a profitable introduction. We will, with care and reverence, develop the area around the historic site."

"The Battle of the Trestle," Dillard slurred. Bo and Kate had a momentary alarm she was going to pitch forward and pass out into her plate, on her cocktail of painkillers and Meursault-Genevrières.

"The Skirmish at the Trestle, my dear," Duke smilingly corrected. "We'll carry on with our historical re-creation next spring, and construction will begin soon after, leaving the site wooded with trails, a cannon or two, something. We'll solicit some landscape architects for a design for the memorial park."

Jerene burst in from the kitchen to announce that the goose was out of the oven and cooling; Alma — Bo could hear it — was flash frying the potatoes in the goose fat, ladled from the roasting pan. "Please help yourself to the starters on the server," she said, despite knowing they had been picking at the bounty for the past two hours. Bo felt he was — well, they all were — too full of wine and starters now to want the dinner ahead.

"Well," said Dorrie, piping up, "I'm sure my free ancestors had slaves and therefore next summer I want to participate in the Skirmish at the Trestle re-enactment, in complete dress gray. You'll have to help me, Mr. J."

Gaston noted, "My dear, there weren't any women that fought in uniform."

"I'll pretend to be a man. Every week at

the Harris Teeter the cashier calls me 'sir' because of my short haircut, so no one will know the difference."

"Actually," Duke said, looking at Gaston, "we re-enactors don't mind cross-dressing. We don't discriminate providing you appear to be a man."

"She makes a good one," Joshua concurred.

Gaston clapped his hands in pleasure. "You know, I think you'll make a fine Johnny Reb."

It was agreed that Josh would fight for the South as well, and they would bring some friends who could be aides-de-camp and slaves —

"Why can't I be a slave?" Joshua asked. "A white indentured servant?"

"That went out in the 1700s," Gaston said.

Dorrie nodded. "Maybe a very light-skinned slave who could pass. We might take you to a tanning bed so it's a little more believable."

Bo smiled. Dorrie was laughing at Uncle Gaston and his father, mocking them, and they couldn't even tell.

"And you, Annie," Dorrie said. "You could wear a big five-petticoat gown and call out after your beau, gone for a soldier."

"I want no part of your neo-Confederate shamefulness," said Annie.

Jerene entered with a giant platter of goose, surrounded, as if hiding in its own under-brush, by an array of verdure and vegetables.

Everyone applauded. Jerene went around to everyone's side and they served themselves . . . just not very much.

"Isn't anyone hungry after all this wait?" Jerene cried.

"We've eaten everything but the candles," Dillard cried out. Then she laughed drunkenly at her own joke.

"Glad to see someone's feeling better," Jerene said, making her way past her sister to Skip and Jerilyn, who also barely took a thing off the platter.

Annie served herself plentifully and began to eat.

"Annie, please wait until everyone is served and grace is said."

"I'm trying to soak up the wine," she said, "and whether the preacherman says his magic mumbo jumbo or not, the food will not be any different."

"It's not the food that becomes different," Bo said, now feeling the wine himself. "The hope is that your heart is different. That you take a moment to be appreciative of the blessing that a meal like this is."

Annie, while chewing, noted, "I am appreciative. Appreciative of this great food, the great wine . . ." She lifted her glass. "And most of all appreciative that I don't have to believe in some petulant deity in the clouds who needs to be sucked up to before every meal."

"That's enough, Annie," said Jerene Johnston, taking her seat at the head of the table. "No one's religious convictions need be dragged into the light. It's Christmas, after all."

Did she mean that to be a joke? Annie said, "Good God, Mother is right about something. Pagan, warmed-over Druidical tree worship by way of German animists, celebrated on the birth of the Manichean sun god? For once I agree — Christmas is no occasion to discuss Christianity."

"I'll make the grace quick," said Bo. "Father —"

Kate, oblivious, blurted out, "Annie, you look different."

Bo could tell his wife was drunk. He decided to soften what seemed like an accusation rather than a compliment. "You do, little sister. Every time I see you now, you look . . . better, younger."

"Almost like the billboard," Joshua said, snickering.

Dorrie whispered something in his ear and they were then both snickering.

"Thanks." Annie was curt.

"Do blondes have more fun, sweetheart?" Dad was trying to be light.

"I started seeing gray, so I . . . better blond than gray, I figured — *what?*" She turned to Dorrie and Joshua who, glassy-eyed with wine, were collapsing in laughter again.

"Nothing," Joshua said.

"Tell me," Annie insisted.

"Never mind," Joshua stammered. "If you did or didn't do something to your appearance, it's none of our business . . ."

Dorrie: "On the billboards — I thought, we thought . . . We thought it was just Photoshop or something."

"You want to know if I had work done?" Annie said, putting down her fork. "Like a boob job? I already got the biggest boobs in the family, maybe Aunt Dillie excepted."

Dillard blanched, her breasts referred to at table; she uttered a low gasp . . . and reached again for the red wine.

". . . oh maybe I might do *reduction* surgery before these babies go south."

Jerene, forgoing the grace, began eating and soon they all followed with their first bite.

"No, the face," Joshua corrected. He then sucked in his cheeks and pulled back his face to look like Norma Desmond in *Sunset Boulevard.* "It's not just the billboards then, huh, it's real life."

"I've lost some weight," Annie began unsurely.

"No one loses weight just in their cheeks," Uncle Gaston chimed in. "What's with all the hoo-hah? She looks lovely! Someone stuck a hose in and sucked all the fat out — what's the big deal?"

"For some reason," Dorrie mumbled, "I've

gone off the pimento cheese."

Mr. Johnston, slurring his speech now, looked very much amused. "Is tha' what you did, darling? Well, I think it looks marvelous. It's not dangerous, is it?"

Annie was quiet for a second or two. "Yes, I had some work done. Thanks to the genes contributed by two people at this table who will remain nameless, I looked saggy and forty-four years old at thirty-four and I thought who would buy a home from such a deteriorated old broad . . ."

"You looked fine the way you were," her mother said. "Perhaps a bit heavy but you seem to be losing."

"Thanks for that, Mom. I hadn't noticed I have a weight problem — which, scientific research is now showing, is also a genetic predisposition, so thanks for that, too."

"I'd be the size of a barn," said Jerene, "if I didn't watch what I eat. That's all there is to it."

Dillard: "No, you wouldn't, Jerry — you've always been a stick. Annie's right — it's the fat gene. Once you've got it you have to have a will of iron not to get fat, and if you get a set of those genes from *both* sides of your family, you're doomed. Like me." She gulped another swallow of wine. "Who knows how my life would have gone if I wasn't hectored night and day by my mother not to be fat, don't eat, don't even think about food or no man would have you. And Father . . ."

Gaston weighed in. "If this were forty years ago at the Jarvis dinner table, Father would be drunk by now and looking for someone to hit; Mother would be letting him do it, blaming us for provoking him. Who of us three ever heard a kind word from our parents?"

Jerene was stern. "It is *not* forty years ago, and that is another topic which can be added to the forbidden list. Why would we want to remember those godawful Christmases at home when all of us, even you, Dillard, have life so much better? Now someone pass the pumpernickel rolls."

Annie mumbled, still burning from having to confess to the vanity of her face-lift. "That's the Johnston M.O. Sweep it all under the rug."

"That's what rugs are for, sweetheart," said her father. "Some butter, Jerene?"

"No, thank you." And after a beat. "Watching my waistline."

"I think," Kate offered, trying to smooth over her opening the topic in the first place, "Annie, that you look great, procedure or no procedure. They can do anything now, so why not?"

"So you don't think it's wrong, condemned in the eyes of the God you serve, for me to have an augmentation or two of this body, this temple of the Lord?"

"Of course not."

"So it's my body, my choice to do with it what I wish."

Kate saw where this chute was leading. "Aside from Ecclesiastes reminding us that 'All is vanity,' I can't imagine much spiritual harm in cosmetic surgery, unless it takes over your life."

Dorrie said, "Promise you'll stop before the Michael Jackson limit is achieved."

Joshua: "Who is that society lady in New York who took it too far?" Joshua enacted his Norma Desmond stretched-face demonstration again.

"I've always hated how one's hands age," said Jerene. "When they can figure out how to keep hands young, I'll sign up for that."

"Amen, sister," said Aunt Dillard, holding out her own liver-spotted hands. "And these ridiculous drugs I'm on weaken the liver and make the spotting worse, I'm sure —"

"That's good," Annie continued, "because I never really am sure what your position is, Kate, on women's control of their own bodies these days. It seems in our previous discussions you want it both ways —"

"It's a nuanced position so, perhaps, you won't be able to understand it," Kate began, as Bo nudged her with his leg under the table. "I am pro-choice but very much anti-abortion."

Annie: "So . . . you know that desperate and poor women will have abortions but you want to reserve the right to moralize about their choice."

Gaston settled back in his chair and laced his hands on his belly, as if enjoying a spectator sport. Dorrie and Joshua looked at each other, as if to say *Now we're in for something.*

"No moralizing afterward, of course. But some strong counseling beforehand."

"So the Christians who gather at Planned Parenthood clinics to throw blood and yell murderer only differ with you in . . . in *method.*"

"They disagree with me in more than method for what they're doing isn't humane or Christian, and as I said but you steadfastly year in and year out refuse to hear, I am —" Kate hiccupped, inconveniently. "I am pro-choice, because I think there are situations that it is better not to bring a child into —"

"Speaking of children," Jerene interrupted, just as determined as the women were to have this conversation that it not be had. "I note another Christmas come and gone without any grandchildren."

Skip popped up to say he and Jerilyn were working on it. Then Jerilyn swatted his arm with a sharp look of disgust. When she moved her arm back she knocked over her water.

"Oh fuck," she said.

"Jerilyn, my land!" said Jerene. Skip and Jerilyn piled on their napkins to soak up the water.

Gaston said, "I think there's quite enough infantile behavior without another generation of squalling brats brought into the world. I'm anti-children. I think the Jarvis line should crawl moribund to its whimpering finale — can't speak for the Johnstons. Diapers, four A.M. feedings, kids turning out to be monsters, and the spectacle of them screwing up as adults while the loved ones watch the serial fiascoes. I'd be happy to provide money for any and all abortions, just give your ol' Uncle Gaston a call —"

Dillard: "You've just become so horrible, Gaston. That's the kind of thing Daddy would say."

Kate wasn't through. "I'm an army brat, as you know, up from a military trailer park in Fayetteville, North Carolina, outside of Fort Bragg. I saw desperation there — desperation in women's lives you can only imagine, Annie, although I suspect you *can't* imagine it. Real difficult, impossible situations poor women find themselves in. With my mom dead of cancer when I was sixteen, and my father out of the picture, signing up for endless rotations of overseas duty, I ended up working part-time and living in the Cumberland County Women's Shelter . . ."

Bo looked at his mother who regarded her daughter-in-law with a half-smile he had seen before. He could read his mother's mind perfectly. Kate had committed the unpardonable sin, which was not bringing up unsavory topics or having cumulatively drunk a bottle of wine to become thin-skinned and emotional. No, she had shone a light on class, reminded everyone at the table of their privilege and wealth. He could hear his mother thinking, *It's all well and good you came from nothing and married into something but you are not to carry the nothingness with you, drag it into our house when we have lifted you up, brought you forward. The past, and all that is low and sordid, is to be locked in the vault — just as we have no interest in reliving what transpired in the tyrannical homeplace of my upbringing, with my alcoholic father and enabling mother.* But then Kate did not support Jerene Johnston's under-the-carpet sweeping, her codes and strictures; he suspected his wife really didn't like her mother-in-law, even if she admired a certain fortitude about her. Maybe her feud with Annie was a substitute for the feud she dare not have with his mother.

". . . and in the shelter," Kate went on, "every day presented any number of blood-curdling scenarios, for which sometimes the only answer was an abortion, yes." Kate had a catch in her voice, and Bo had a horrified sense where this speech was headed.

Bo burst out, "Oh God, leave it alone, Kate!"

"I will *not,* it's important that we talk about this."

He felt a tide overtake him, saying intemperately what he would not say, had not said to her in private, now at the dinner table in front of the people he would least like to hear him say it. "Why can't you let this topic go? It's just like at church where they hate our guts because you cannot stop giving your complete exhaustive opinion when it's not appropriate. The Women's Circle and you going on about protesting the war, and they have sons in the military but your opinion *just has to* keep coming. You're as bad as Annie in your way —"

Annie: "Shut up, Bo. I love talking to Kate — she's the only one who'll talk about anything real in this whole family!"

Bo snapped back, "You don't like talking to Kate, you want to annihilate her rhetorically, like you do all of us. We all get to be crushed under the weight of your critical opinion no matter what we do. Forgive me if I don't think your life has cornered the market on perfection." Bo hopelessly deflected his temper to Annie but he knew he had done damage to Kate, and wished he could be alone with her.

"Oh I don't claim to be perfect, but I'd put my work over your work any day, preacherman, for the betterment of the community. I have put hundreds of Hispanic families, first-generation immigrants, middle-class blacks who've been shafted by the racist banking machine into their first homes, at affordable mortgages. You should see the tears of joy when they turn the key to their new homes. Out of the housing projects or the trailer parks and into a fine new home with their family — do you do anything on that level for people? Just stirring around the old lies and myths and three-thousand-year-old commandments about making graven images and thou shalt nots."

Kate, pointing to Annie with her wineglass: "Look, sister, you don't have the swightest — slightest li'l idea what ministering to a congregation entails. And you'll note we don't get rich off it, driving around in a sixty-thousand-dollar car for all our good deeds."

Annie: "If you don't like the rich, you shouldn't have married into a rich family, *sister.* Now as for what you were saying about abortion . . ."

Kate was weepy again. "I could give you an example of one . . . one sixteen-year-old girl, father in the army —"

Bo: "Katie, please, it's Christmas. Let's just . . ."

A very strange silence settled on the table. Then Annie pounced:

"So you had one. You had an abortion when you were sixteen."

Joshua and Dorrie simultaneously protested, this is nothing you have to talk about, no reason to pursue this topic, pass the rolls, pass the butter —

Annie went on. "I support you! If you were a teenager with no family around you, you no doubt made the right decision in your circumstances. I would hope you could make this decision without some church-person trying to talk you out of it and making the experience even more miserable than it was."

Kate stood up.

"Katie, it's all right, just sit down and —"

"No," she said, past any emotion. "I'm going to be sick." She ran from the table to the bathroom, leaving them in silence. There was the faint sound of retching from the bathroom.

No one said anything.

Perhaps, thought Bo, the worst was over.

Annie then said, "I had an abortion when I was in my twenties," causing Aunt Dillard to gasp a second time.

"Oh for Christ's sake," Duke muttered.

Gaston looked delighted, mumbling, "This just gets better and better," and poured some more red wine into his glass.

Josh put his head in his hands; Dorrie looked to the floor; Dillard gasped. Was this *ever* classic Annie, Bo thought. Kate's admission made her the center of focus, the authority on the radical topic at the table, so Annie had to pull even.

"It was when my marriage to Destin was over and I became pregnant, despite my usual regimen of precautions. It would have extended the marriage falsely. I couldn't have given it up for adoption because I'm sure Destin and his family would want the child —"

"But that was the solution right there," Dillard broke in. "That child could've had a home."

"And that child would know his mother wanted nothing to do with him, and I would be tied to Destin for the rest of my life. My twenty-eight-year-old life with no job and no money and my only choice of coming back here and being the pregnant divorced woman living off my parents and handing a baby over to my ex-husband who, by the way, would be a rotten father."

"Of course, you could have come home in those circumstances," Duke said soothingly.

And then Jerilyn, whom no one had noticed, spoke shrilly, verging on hysteria. "Oh that's just fine! That's just fucking great!" Now she was standing, swaying . . . Skip reached up to steady her and she swatted his hands away, glaring now at her mother: "You order *me* to get rid of my baby because 'think of your father, think how disappointed he'll be'! But Daddy wouldn't have cared — and of course, Annie . . ."

Skip was trying to steady and silence her.

"Now Jeri, we swore we weren't going to tell anyone about our little incident —"

"Oh it was a little incident for you, but it was a big fucking incident for me! You weren't the one with a vacuum up inside you . . ."

Duke was stricken, first looking at Jerilyn, then Jerene, who apparently knew all about it and had kept it secret from him, then Skip. It was easier to look at Skip than Jerilyn, so suddenly everyone turned to him.

Skip: "Um, it was like junior year. We used protection but . . ."

Jerilyn was swaying; she turned too quickly and knocked over her chair. Skip reached up to pull her back, so she wouldn't fall with it. He looked guilty and babbled for leniency though no one was accusing him of anything: "Jerilyn, now sit down, you're gonna fall — give me your hand."

"Don't you touch me!"

Aunt Dillard: "I know what! Why don't we all just . . . just let's all just stop talking abortions, how 'bout we all do that?"

Joshua: "Jerilyn, I'm so sorry —"

Annie: "Why should any of you be sorry? Having a child you don't want derails your entire life. Did Mom actually drive you to the clinic?"

Jerilyn ran from the room; Skip followed close behind.

"Does anyone," Dillard rambled, but more calmly, "truly understand the concept of 'none of your business' in this family? Hm? These are all private matters, and it used to be considered terrible manners to talk politics or mention body parts at a dinner table. Civilized people down South were trained not to do it!" She started swaying dangerously in her chair. Bo moved into Kate's chair to reach out an arm and steady her. Dillard, tearing up, muttered, "Maybe if I'd gotten rid of Christopher, my life would have been much happier."

Bo moved the wineglass she was reaching for out of her grasp. Dillard stifled a sob, and lifted the napkin to dab her eyes. Bo sighed: it was now officially worse than last year's Christmas dinner.

There was the punctuating sound of china smashing and everyone turned to Jerene, who had slammed a Christmas-patterned plate onto the edge of the table, shattering it. It had the treble sound of glass breaking.

Bo reflected inconsequentially that it must be really fine porcelain. No one breathed.

Then they watched as she broke a second plate.

"Apparently," she said calmly, crisp and clear, unfueled by even a drop of wine, "the idea that I could sit here in peace with my siblings and children and my husband and have a nice, quiet, respectful Christmas dinner for the holidays, after all the work Alma and I have done, is an impossible Christmas wish."

No one looked at Jerene. A mixture of shame, embarrassment, and abject fear seized the table; even Bo's father was avoiding his wife's eyes. Bo may have been the first to sneak a look at his mother, who presided at the end of the table with her level, inscrutable stare. She sat back into her chair, returning to her serious serenity.

"Well," she said, cutting the silence. "I see why we have no grandchildren, with everyone aborting their children left and right."

Gaston snickered. It was a dark joke but no one else dared laugh.

"Maybe Joshua and Dorrie are my last hope. Everyone knows there's nothing more cute in this world than a mixed-race child."

Annie, now wishing she had not played the abortion card, said quietly, "That's a little patronizing, Mother."

Dorrie cleared her throat. "But it's true. Mixed-race babies are pretty damn cute."

Silence.

"I'm gay," said Joshua.

More silence.

"Hm, I was beginning to wonder if you even knew," mumbled Uncle Gaston.

Dorrie raised her hand. "I'm gay, too, let's just get that out there."

"But you . . ." Duke Johnston sputtered out, sinking back in his chair. "You spend so much time together."

Nervous laughter from Joshua. "Yeah, but not . . . you know, screwing."

There was a snore. Dillard, crumpled into herself, was asleep (or passed out from pills and wine) in her chair.

Jerene brought out slowly, gently, "People are mistaken about these things all the time, Joshua."

Annie: "Oh for the love of God, Mother, he's gay gay gay! He's never had a girlfriend! His hair, his clothes, his . . ."

Then there was a *POP.*

And then there was a thud, of something, someone falling.

Dorrie asked, "Was that . . ."

Joshua followed up. "Was that a gun?"

Uncle Gaston sprang out of the chair. "Good God, Duke —"

"The pistols!" Duke sprang from the chair.

First Gaston then Duke then Jerene, all briskly walked-ran to the study . . . it was locked. Duke knocked loudly. "Who's in there? Jerilyn? What's going on in there?"

They all gathered at the door.

There was the sound of Jerilyn crying.

"Did you . . ." Duke was almost unable to find his voice. "Did you hurt yourself, sweetheart?"

"Open the goddam door this minute," ordered Jerene, and that got the job done.

The lock turned slowly, then the door

opened on Duke's Civil War Study to reveal Jerilyn with her blouse unbuttoned, holding a Civil War pistol. Skip, thank God, was nowhere to be found . . . Uh-oh, there was a groan behind the sofa. Skip was lying there, Skip was shot. Above the heart, and bleeding, and he was passing out.

Bo looked up at Jerilyn in terror. He tried to form a kind expression, look at her as a loving brother would, but he knew he was not convincing. Kate was clinging to his arm, now at his side, looking greenish but freshly adrenalinized, as they all were.

"I told you," Jerilyn muttered, maybe to Skip, "about thingy thing . . ."

"Maybe she should put the gun down," Gaston whispered.

"Only one ball and only one chamber," Duke assured them all as he walked to his daughter and relieved her of the weapon.

Bo and Kate drove home after a long vigil at the hospital. It was 3:27 A.M. They threw their coats over the sofa, and headed for the kitchen. Bo punched in the code for phone messages and there were more than fifty. Too tired to hold the phone to his ear, he trapped it against his face and the wall and let the messages play. There were a few let-us-know-if-we-can-do-anything offers of help, food, prayers. And then there were the others: *I hope next Sunday you will address how it comes to be that your sister, Reverend, is in the news for shooting her husband . . .* Biddies, busybodies, gossips, mean old men, all the familiars from their tenure at Stallings Presbyterian. Bo punched in the code to delete every message.

"Bet there're some good ones," Kate sang out.

"Yep. It made the local TV news. The congregation is all aflutter."

He looked at his wife who was boiling some water for some decaffeinated tea, her nighttime ritual, even on this night. She looked at him.

Bo: "This ought to just about finish us off at Stallings, don't you think?"

Kate: "We were doomed anyway."

"Poor Skip."

Since it was clear he wasn't going to die, they all had been much relieved. He was shot near the heart but with a weakly propelled lead ball. There was, naturally, an infection risk. If Skip died somehow, well, that would be the end of several worlds. Prison for Jerilyn? Bankruptcy for the family? "Liddibelle is a suer," Jerene told them both, riding to the hospital. Bo decided not to think about it. That is until he would get on his knees and pray about it, but he wasn't up to the heavy lifting quite yet.

Bo had been waiting for a quiet moment alone with Kate. "I snapped at you at the dinner table and I was wrong to do it. I didn't even truly mean what I said. You can say what you damn well please to the people at Stallings. I was drunk and I'm never drunk."

"No, I deserved it," she said, surprising him. "Drunk off my ass. Telling Jerene Jarvis Johnston about my trailer-park ex-army boyfriend knocking me up and getting an abortion at sixteen at *her Christmas dinner table.* You have the right to dump a whole pot of leftovers over my head. I will somehow, someway, make it up to your mom."

"You don't have to do anything. You were great at the hospital. She loves you, I promise."

The kettle whistled.

Kate shrugged. "Well, come on. We *had* to drink that wine. We'll never have better wine."

"Did you have the Lynch-Bages?"

She lowered herself carefully, so as not to spill the mug of tea, onto the deep sofa beside her husband. "I had it, all right. Tasted good going down and coming up — now *that's* a wine."

It was the first laugh they'd had in hours.

Kate nestled into his shoulder. "How do you think Jerilyn is holding up?" Kate asked despite knowing Bo didn't know either.

There were three parties after the shooting — the party that went with Skip and the ambulance to the hospital, who called Skip's mother, Liddibelle (Jerene did that unpleasant piece of business, cold as ice), who stayed until Skip came out of surgery and was transferred to the ICU; that group was Jerene, Bo and Kate, Joshua and, for a while, Dorrie. Then there was the party that followed the police car to the station where Jerilyn was being questioned — Duke and Annie; and then there were the escapees, Aunt Dillard staggering into Uncle Gaston's Porsche, getting as far from the scandal as they could, fast as they could.

"It wasn't an accident, I don't think," Bo said.

"I don't either," said Kate. "She didn't say it was an accident. Right when we came in, it would have been a good opportunity to get that story going."

"What was it she was babbling about?"

"Something about a thingy thing. She wasn't connected to reality."

"Do you think he tried to . . . do something violent to her? Her blouse was open. Maybe he put a hand to her."

"Nah. He was rubbing against her the whole dinner; he was running his leg up her leg, under the table — I was noticing. Maybe he tried something sexual?"

Bo: "In the next room, with the whole family coming and going?"

Kate shrugged. "That might have been the point. Something extra exciting. They're newlyweds. You remember how we couldn't keep our hands off each other. We'd do an old-folks-home visit and we'd almost have to do it in the car in the parking lot. Maybe they've got some kind of codependent control-freak thing going on and Jerilyn snapped."

"I have never gotten to know Jerilyn." Bo sighed. "Another black mark in my book. We're going to have to expand my black-mark book into a second volume, it looks like."

"You don't think it's going to come out," Kate then asked, "about all the fighting that was going on? I mean, there's no one who would tell the police or newspapers that we were all arguing, right? I mean, I don't want anyone saying we had a big family fight and somehow things got so heated that Jerilyn shot her husband, because that's not what it was like at all."

"No. Anyhow, she barely said a word during all the nonsense."

Kate rested a hand on his shoulder. "Let it come," she said, after a moment. "Let them fire us. Let's get a severance package and go do something God wants us to do. Médecins Sans Frontières, or Red Cross, or famine relief, or building a village water purifier in the south of Sudan. That church is done with us, but not nearly as much as I am done with them. I look forward to the next chapter. And I have some ideas about what we might do for God and they don't involve the Presbyterian Church."

It was because it was late and that Bo was exhausted by events that he thought something small and unworthy: *They're not so much done with me as they are with you, Kate. If you'd tried to function as a standard minister's wife, we wouldn't be at this pass.* Then he disposed of the thought. He was on her side, he would leave any church for her, he would always choose Kate, the best person he had ever known. Kate was where God was, over on His side. In the gentlest scenario, Bo would not have his contract renewed. The question was when. Actually, he perked up, a flash of sheer panic reawakening him; the most pressing question was what he was going to say from the pulpit — *tomorrow!*

After a surprisingly deep sleep of a few hours, Bo padded down the sidewalk to see if this little incident made the morning paper. A wave of foreclosures . . . questions about Bank of America's practices, Wachovia Bank, too . . . Then he flipped the paper over, below the fold.

Society Newlywed Shoots Spouse with 1854 Pistol

CHARLOTTE — In what two fine old Charlotte families are calling a regrettable misadventure, a young woman shot her husband of six months with a Civil War–era dueling pistol, during a holiday dinner.

Jerilyn Baylor, 22, daughter of former city councilman Joseph "Duke" Johnston, noted Civil War preservationist, and Jerene Johnston, trustee of the Jarvis Trust for American Art at the Mint Museum of Charlotte, shot her husband Beckleford "Skip" Baylor III, 23, in the study of the Johnstons' Providence Road home. Baylor is the son of Liddibelle Baylor and the late "Becks" Baylor, former CEO of Piedmont-Catawba Mill & Textile. Baylor was taken to Presbyterian Hospital where he is listed in satisfactory condition.

Police are investigating the incident, and Jerilyn Johnston was taken to the Providence Division offices for questioning and later released. Said Det. Jack D. Kessel, "We don't have any information to give at this juncture. I will say ballistics will have a time with this. This is the sort of injury we haven't seen since 1860 or so."

He would not confirm whether the couple was checked for alcohol.

Jerilyn Johnston is the niece of famed author Gaston Jarvis, noted for a series of Civil War–themed bestsellers. Jarvis was in attendance earlier in the evening but, according to family members, had departed the house before the shooting. He could not be reached for comment.

Duke Johnston, speaking to reporters from his front porch, identified the pistols as

Gastinne Rennetes. They are French-made pistols that were popular in New Orleans before the war.

"Like most dueling pistols of the period," explained Johnston, "they are designed to wound rather than to kill, so the men could walk away with honor satisfied. Ten grams of gunpowder, a small ball, and smoothbore, with no rifling or hidden rifling or else the wound would have been much more serious."

The pistol, when united with its pair, is valued at $11,500.

How the pistol came to be loaded, Johnston could only speculate.

Johnston said, "We go down to the Catawba River railroad bridge near Fort Mill, South Carolina, every spring to mark the anniversary of Stoneman's assault on Charlotte, known as the Skirmish at the Trestle. The pistol was likely loaded then for a target demonstration and our re-creators failed to make use of it or perhaps the powder became damp and never fired. I've told all my children, more times than they can count, not to play with the antique weaponry in my collection in the study."

No charges have been filed.

Bo and Kate entered the church from the kitchen entrance in the activity building. They made a hurried dash to his office and shut the door. He had made up his mind not to read anything prepared, he would just talk to his congregation. The words would come. If they rose up and demanded his resignation, then so be it.

The service began normally, with a prayer, with a hymn, and then he took the pulpit early in the order of service.

The silence was heavy as a stone.

"Heard any good stories lately? Anything in the news . . ."

That got a few chuckles.

"Well, here's the inside story. We have a lot of guns in our family. Living in this part of the country, I don't think growing up with rifles, shotguns, pistols, is all that unusual. Any gun owners out there?"

Predictably, about a third of the men raised their hands. Bet it was more than that, but some gun owners were too paranoid to raise their hands; the minister might be working with leftist forces to confiscate their weapons, naturally.

"When I was young my dad taught me how to shoot . . ."

Okay, skeet shooting at the club, but if they got the impression that he, manfully, had a history of blowing away small animals in the woods, he would let them believe that.

". . . and as they say in those NRA gun-safety courses, as it has been drilled into me a thousand times: there's no such thing as an unloaded gun. Right? So my father, you may, some of you, remember him, Duke Johnston, he was a Republican city councilman in Charlotte for many years. And he devotes himself now to the — well, you couldn't call it a battle, it's called 'the Skirmish at the Trestle,' where the locals faced down Stoneman's Raiders out at the Catawba River. Every year around April, they open up those grounds and they have a small ceremony and my father . . ." Why was he sounding like some prep-school snot? *My father. Oh Father, can't I borrow the roadster for the regatta?* ". . . Dad, he brings out all these antique guns and pistols and gets them ready for the big day, and they were lying out this Christmas, where our whole big family gathers every year for this incredible feed my mom puts on.

"There are so many people named Johnston in the world, you might not connect that the defender of the Carolinas, the last general to face General Sherman, was my ancestor General Joseph E. Johnston. The Civil War didn't end when Lee surrendered to Grant at Appomattox, it ended when my cousin, many times removed, surrendered to Sherman outside of Durham, sparing North Carolina the Sherman scorched-earth policy that South Carolina enjoyed. Charlotte, Raleigh, Salisbury, Gastonia, Lincolnton, all these old towns still standing and prosperous because General Johnston said, enough, it's over."

He didn't meet Kate's eyes. He hoped she was smiling. Some actors say they can feel when they have the audience, that a kind of telepathy transpires where you're linked — preachers have that, too. He felt the tide turning. He felt the old men who had written him off as some kind of liberal pantywaist taking another look, going, *Well whadya know?* He thought: this is Bo Johnston working the crowd here, running perpetually for class president of his high school, leader of the Student Association at Davidson, he can pander and manipulate with the best of them. He knows his audience and, when he wants to, he can push the right buttons. Republicans. Guns. Confederate sentiment.

"And so, there we were, talking Civil War, and Jerilyn and her husband head off to my dad's study where the guns are, and my little sister picks up a pistol — which should have been unloaded — and she's waving it about joking about shooting Skip, my brother-in-law . . . and bang. The gun went off. And nobody was laughing after that. Skip will be all right. He's in good condition at Presbyterian, and I think he has a sense of humor about it, bless him. I worry about Jerilyn. She can't forgive herself quite yet. Truly it was a Christmas miracle that Skip is still with us. It's also a miracle my little sister could get a shot off like that, one-handed."

Some real chuckles.

"I hope these two newlyweds can survive this. You gotta admit, folks, that's a strange start to a marriage: sorry about that time I shot you with that pistol from 1854 . . ."

Oh, you should have seen the congregation at the end of the service. An especially long line to shake hands, pat his shoulder, even the old goats who avoided him, who had pointedly refused to shake his hand, they were there. *You hang in there, Reverend.*

He heard about how Leroy Hargett got shot by his little brother by accident when he was sixteen.

He heard how Ray Crutchfield filled his father's behind with buckshot the first time he went hunting. *Hope this doesn't turn into one more chance for the gun control people to talk about takin' our guns, right?*

Elmer Gillette told him, *Would've liked to have seen your father go on and run for mayor and then governor, son.*

Lucille Gerster looked like she might faint, like she was clasping the hand of a movie star: *Had no idea about you and General Johnston — you gotta be proud to come from fine people like Johnston.*

And the old women, little hugs, little squeezes of the upper arm. *I'm sure those lovebirds will get over it. Don't let it depress you, it will all work out for the best.*

And from Ellie Ward Maynor, the snob of

the church: *Why Reverend, we didn't know you were from an Old Charlotte family — why didn't you say so?*

Kate hung back and let the lovefest continue.

She couldn't stop smiling and then laughing as they drove out to the nursing homes for the afternoon visits. "Wow," she said, at last.

"Stop saying that."

"Wow. That's all I'm capable of saying."

"If I'd known I could bond with my congregation so well, I'd have had a family member shoot someone much sooner."

"It's that they saw you were human, Bo. From a human family with human problems."

"No, that's not it. They saw that I was just like them."

"That's what I said."

"No, they think I'm just like them in the bad ol' Southern ways. Reactionary politics. Guns. Confederate sentiment. I won them over but it's with a false image of Reverend Johnston." And then after a second. "But that's not true either, Kate. I *am* just like them. Old Bobby Denning and Al Gerster, rednecks hanging on to what's left of white privilege, and Bo Johnston, who *is* white privilege. It was a great luxury to look down at these country rubes and feel because I'm going to vote for Barack Obama in next year's primary that I was more evolved, but the truth is that my life, rich, white, privileged, sheltered, segregated my whole goddam life from black people, Mexican migrants, poor white people, real people —"

"Whoa, hold on there, cowboy. You're channeling Annie here —"

"I AM their poster boy! I am what their politics derives from and hopes for, folks like me, to make me and my plutocratic existence possible."

Kate stared out the window. "I have quite a bit," she said softly, "quite a bit to say on this topic. But it will have to wait until later when you're a little less . . . enflamed."

They arrived at Mint Meadows, a retirement and convalescent home. It was outside of Mint Hill, North Carolina, but the idea of a mint-flavored meadow should have overruled the name of the place. It was not the nicest of homes, though the staff tried hard. Bo and Kate visited here first every Sunday and then finished up at the Presbyterian Home, always ending on the more monied, cheerier elderly community. A small bit of spiritual self-preservation in that. Kate would take the list of the male church members housed here, visiting each for a little while; Bo would take the women. Next Sunday they'd switch genders. They always brought a notepad since there were always small favors and requests, Life Savers, a magazine, could you see if my Social Security check was deposited, could you call my daughter and ask why she never visits?

Bo enjoyed the visits, grimly. He passed Kate in the hallway intersections, and she was still eyeing him like he might not have returned to his right mind. They strolled by way of the cafeteria, the plastic Christmas tree and empty gift boxes underneath, just props, ancient tinsel and paper chains draped from the fluorescent lights.

"Everybody holding on?" she asked.

"Miss Grace is probably going to lose her other leg, she told me."

Diabetes. Plus recurring cancer and heart disease. Grace Hough lost one daughter to diabetes 1, one son to the First Gulf War, one son to a liquor store holdup, and when her husband died, big-talking loudmouth Hank, he left her without a will. I mean what kind of villain assures his wife for thirty years that she's taken care of and then doesn't do it — no life insurance, dying intestate. The state is figuring out what she's entitled to — a case going on for years now — because Hank Hough's equally braying hillbilly sister is trying to get her hands on what little money there is. Miss Grace's life is one long string of tragedies and buffooneries, and yet she's so happy, so "blessed," according to her own account. *God doesn't send you anything you can't handle,* she says.

Bo hated that bullshit. God permits any

number of things no human can handle, every day, all the time. Try that in Africa where a woman can see her twelve children die of AIDS or famine. A tsunami or a pandemic or an earthquake takes out one hundred thousand in a flash — what kind of "plan" is that? To choose to see a tornado or a flood wiping out a town as a sign, a message, a sign of disfavor, a chance for God's faithful to dust off that faith and show God how well they can stick their heads up to get whacked again — how can anyone who knows God's love choose to see it that way? When hundreds of thousands of faithful die . . . that ought to make any sensible person question that there is any plan, purpose, meaning or God. A meteor will come out of the sky and take out human life as we know it and somewhere, clinging to a fragment of the extinguished earth hurtling into the sun someone will chirp, *God doesn't send you anything you can't handle!* What does Annie call Him? The Mean Old Man in the Sky.

"Poor Grace," Katie said. "I'll go see her during the week."

Bo didn't say anything right away, and Kate recognized in his face the dark places he dwelled. "Joan Maurner," Bo continued, "over at Presbyterian, is opting for more chemo. Don't know if I told you. She's down to a hundred pounds but she said she knows

God wants her to fight this."

It was Kate's turn not to say anything.

"When it's crunch time," Bo said, meaning death, "so few Christians really believe there's a world after this one. How they pray and plead not to have to go there and be with Jesus. We have to rally around the hospital bed and assure them more is coming. After eighty years, ninety years more, there's more ahead, we promise! What could be more important than more of Hank Hough. Grace can ascend to heaven and shake her finger, oh Hank, you scamp, you left me with nothing! But we're all together now with Jesus."

"I'm not sure Hank Hough is up there."

"Think how that would hurt Grace for him not to be there. He wasn't worth a shit, but he means something to her. Maybe God will let him slide . . . or maybe Mr. Mims can be resurrected as a consolation prize." Mr. Mims was Grace Hough's cat who had to be put down — Bo took Mr. Mims to the vet for that purpose — just as she was losing her first leg; she was more upset about her seventeen-year-old cat than her leg, Bo recalled.

"The trumpet will sound," Bo went on, "and up from the grave in Grace's backyard, Mr. Mims's body will be made whole again."

"Stop."

Bo fell quiet.

"Don't mock a belief in an afterlife. If

you're going to be a Christian preacher, that is."

Bo found her hand and clutched it. He closed his eyes. "Kate. When you experience grace, you feel the presence of Jesus, don't you? You sense a purpose and mission for your life."

"Yep. My grace is pretty much a steady state, but hey, kid, you had an actual voice-of-God moment. Praying in Duke Chapel," she reminded him, as if he could forget the moment that committed him to this path. "You were lucky to have had a Saint Paul experience. Most of us . . ."

"I was favored."

"Well, was it a con, or did you experience God or not? For your faith to sustain itself, does God have to keep performing special effects? Showbiz burning-bush moments — or can we tell the Lord that one revelation was blessing enough, and that your belief in God took." She squeezed his hand. "You should not be freshly debating your faith every week, every hospital visit, every encounter with some dumb redneck in our church. Are you inside the House of God or are you outside? If you're in, close the door behind you and roll up your sleeves." She stood up. "There is so much work to be done."

Bo sighed. "Lots of servants of God doubted and debated and wrestled with the angel all their days."

"Yeah, that's the Tortured Christian, and I was hoping not to be married to that guy." She held out her hand again, and as he reached for it, she plunged her index finger between his neck and collarbone, under the minister's collar, his most vulnerable spot. He sprung to life, tickled, laughing.

"If anyone's gonna torture you, Bo, it's me."

JEANNETTE

When her granddaughter shot her new husband, Jeannette Jarvis was down for her afternoon nap, which extended into evening because she had taken Christmas Dinner at Lattamore Acres — exiled from the family gathering — and the seared turkey and pecan and oyster stuffing and mincemeat pie with double Devonshire cream sent her into a blissful several-hour sleep. (Since the hiring of Olivier, their new chef, Lattamore Acres was every bit as good as some of these overpriced uptown restaurants that prey upon Charlotte these days, Jeannette was happy to tell anyone.) It was only when dear Mrs. Doaks knocked on her door to tell her that her family was on the local TV and that something bad had happened that she was roused to action. This turn of events made Jeannette Jarvis the subject of public interest again, her words and actions once again noted by the public. Well, didn't such things come naturally to her?

Jeannette strode through the main dining room of the retirement community the next day, marked, everyone staring, noticing her carriage and composure, wondering how she was bearing up. Jeannette wore her best violet pastel, somber but not lugubrious, light rather than dark, and an amethyst brooch passed down through her mother's side of the family, the Jellicoes of Salisbury, to remind people of her station. All of Lattamore, even the old harpies she despised, knew to cease hostilities temporarily to express support, because a larger conflict loomed in these situations: good families made to look like bad families, the quality made sport of by the rabble.

"In such a scandal," said Mrs. Bryan, "I bet your daughter must be turning to you now, Jeannette."

Jeannette concurred with a hum that she was at the center of things. "There's a phone call with new information every hour, but I advise as I can. There are lawyers, of course, who must be listened to."

But the truth was Jerene had barely said a word to her. Jerene called that Society-page nincompoop May Biddle Bridger at the *Charlotte Observer* hoping to ameliorate the coverage in the inevitable article. Jerene notified the Mint Museum and the ladies on the Jarvis Trust; she called the Charlottetowne Country Club and warned them that reporters might snoop around. She called the poor boy's mother and family; she called the older Johnston relatives; why, she called everybody on the Planet Earth, it seemed, but her own mother to explain what happened.

Jeannette insisted, "Jerene still needs her mother's advice, even at her age. This is not just any crisis, after all."

"Thank God she has you," said Mrs. Coggins.

"I would just die," said Mrs. Langford.

"We're made of stronger stuff than we realize," Jeannette had said, her lip trembling a bit as she turned to the window, nobly.

Some of the staff brought her extra sugarless cookies; even the doctors and Lattamore Acres counselors hovered around her, taking her hand, letting her know she would not be alone through this ordeal. But when the police announced that this was a misadventure, two young folk playing foolishly with a loaded antique gun and no more, that there wouldn't be any criminal charges, the tide of attention and sympathy began to go out. Jeannette, it must be said, felt the loss of it keenly — which was only a sign of how little attention she got from anyone anymore, of how her own blood relations had flung her to the far corners of their lives, like some old dray put out to the weeds, waiting for the death notice and the will to be read. (Yes, Jeannette had confided to a few of the ladies, there are going to be some surprises when that will is read, believe you me.)

But then came news that there would be a civil suit!

Liddibelle Baylor was suing the Johnstons for hospital bills, distress, trauma and embarrassment, loss of Skip's employment, future long-term health costs, and a host of other things that made no sense to anyone. They'd gotten some fancy lawyers who specialized in this kind of thing and they were going to fleece Jerene and Duke but good. Ruin! After all her labors to affix her girls into Society, and Jerene succeeding best of all . . . now that vulture Liddibelle Baylor, that tedious small-minded woman, already sitting on a fortune, was going to annihilate them. That was what Jerene's afternoon visit was surely going to be about.

Poor Jerilyn. She will always be the girl who shot her husband with an antebellum pistol.

Now. Some kinds of clever young things could make that an *asset,* carry it through Society with a sense of amused pride, almost, light self-mockery, threatening people who cross her in committee meetings that having slung her gun once, she might do it again . . . like Payton Disher's daughter who ran over the mayor's foot at his inaugural reception, as he was leaning in to whisper something to her husband — oh she rode that seesaw for years, laughingly retelling it at every occasion she could wedge it into. Oh, but dull little Jerilyn has none of that élan, nor for that matter did frosty Jerene or wounded, half-hysterical Dillard. Really, Jeannette herself could have carried it off, much in the way she had had to hold her head high after many of the celebrated verbal offenses and dipsomaniacal disgraces perpetrated by her husband. Of course, it would have been irretrievable if Skip had died — there would be little recovering from that. Like the Mainbows, and their daughter who drove her prom date, heir-to-the-furniture-empire Chip Gundy (in the passenger seat), into a light pole and killed him. Hard to escape that footnote following you throughout life, let alone forgive yourself.

"How are you today, Ms. Jarvis?"

Whatever would she do without Pilar? Pilar knocked and let herself in Jeannette's suite of rooms and made her way to the kitchen to put the daily installments of soda in the refrigerator. *Pilar, you're my pillar of strength,* Mrs. Jarvis liked to say, thinking it rather clever.

"I have your diet ginger ale, Ms. Jarvis."

Five years in this country and she still slightly says "CHarvis" rather than Jarvis — but Jeannette wouldn't hear a word said against her! Jeannette had been fearsome with many of her assigned attendants. The bed not made right. The breakfast brought cold. The mail not brought in a timely fashion when everyone knew it arrived at one every afternoon. Lax supervision of the Mexican cleaning crew, who could be told nothing in English. Jeannette was well aware what Lattamore Acres cost and yet nothing less than a base competence could be expected, when excellence shouldn't have been out of the question.

Jeannette called out, "Now don't forget your cans, Pilar!"

"No no, ma'am. Ha-ha, never forget the can."

Jeannette was so weak when she first got here, with everyone thinking she was only a few more months for the world, cancer removed from three places in her body, that she barely could utter a peep as insipid or inadequate attendants filed past. That dreadful Anne, with bad country teeth and no education in how she talked — low-church Christian, oh the bottom of the white barrel, snake-handling and foot-washing for all Jeannette knew, liable to launch into a backwoods sermon. Anne was good people, she supposed, sweet and always available when called. But to look at those brown, crooked teeth every day . . . it put one off one's feed.

Then lovely, lovely Carlotta, who was one of those take-charge colored women the world would have crumbled to dust long ago if not for the existence of, but her reign was short, just a year and a half.

And then when she retired, it was a parade of Hispanic women of some variety looking in on one, all with broken English and telling Jeannette about ever so many points of origin. Guatemala, Peru, El Salvador — two attendants from there, in fact, both named Maria, one following the other, for goodness' sake. And yes, there was one woman absolutely, for sure, who was let go as a result of Jeannette's complaints, but Guadalupe was a scapegrace from start to finish and her termination was only a matter of time. Many of the ladies had reported things missing and when Jeannette's pearl-inlaid hairbrush disappeared, she was fairly sure Guadalupe was involved because Guadalupe had mentioned to Jeannette how beautiful the brush was, had reached out to touch it and rub her hand along the spine of it, in fact. Anyway, water under the bridge. And now the Filipinos had invaded, including Pilar.

"You feel good today, Ms. Jarvis?"

"Quite well, considering all the aches and pains that arise afresh in this old broken-down sack I pretend is a body."

"You take your medicine today?"

"I'm still alive last time I checked, so I suppose I did."

Pilar wiped down the kitchenette counter, and there, sitting there, waiting to be hidden in the trash, but overlooked by Jeannette, was a ginger ale can: *sugared,* not diet. "You want me tell Dr. Sidhu you drink a sugar drink?"

"I'm in here parched like an old bone in the desert with this central heating, and my medicines are turning me into . . . into the Mummy. I'll drink whatever I please from the vending machine, and that's what I told Dr. Sidhu. Besides, your cans wouldn't pile so high if I didn't go to the drink machine."

The empty aluminum diet ginger ale cans were worth five cents apiece when you took them to a redemption center. Jeannette recalled seeing those homeless men pushing around shopping carts of cans, hoping to get enough for a liquor bottle, no doubt. But Jeannette figured Pilar made quite a little pocket change on the mountain of cans that she piled up. Jeannette could have tossed them out but she liked looking after her dear Pilar, since her own family didn't require her attentions.

Why, she'd barely ever had a soda before Lattamore Acres . . . oh, maybe a Coca-Cola back in the days of soda fountains where they mixed it with seltzer and syrup, like over at the Woolworth's uptown — my land, those were good. Nothing in a can could ever compare! But she had become addicted now to canned diet sodas, even though her doctors discouraged it. The only thing after the chemotherapy and operations four years ago, the only thing she could keep down was ginger ale, and then, with the diabetes, it had to be *diet* ginger ale, but she certainly kept Canada Dry in business! (That horrible country-Christian Anne would always bring her bargain-brand ginger ale and that is something you can *not* go cheap on.)

Jeannette had a special blue plastic bin for the cans and, if you made an inspection, you would invariably find some contraband sugared soft-drink cans amid the diets. There was a drink machine on the floor and Jeannette, when weighed down with a surfeit of quarters, would sneak-purchase the prohibited sugar-laden ginger ale, despite the severity of her diabetes. Pilar would tsk-tsk and threaten but she would never tattle on Jeannette to the doctors; they were conspirators, despite the banter.

"Oh my wonnerful wonnerful can, yes ma'am. How are we doing . . ." Pilar went to the light blue plastic bin and opened the lid to inspect her pile.

"You can take that bunch. Must be at least two dollars in there."

"Oh thank you, Ms. Jarvis. Every can help, you know."

"Oh yes I know. I know very well. I wasn't always rich enough to be in Lattamore Acres, it may surprise you to learn."

"Nah you say, Ms. Jarvis. You act like a woman born to be a lady through and through."

"Be that as it may, I was not raised with

very much money at all. But hard work will get you far in America. Remember that."

"Yes, Ms. Jarvis. What work did you do?"

Jeannette was suddenly tired of talking. "Oh this and that. It was my husband who really worked, who made the money while I made a home for him and three children. A country lawyer who made some very good investments in real estate and art."

"Art! Oh he musta been very very smart, Ms. Jarvis."

"That he was."

Pilar held up the white plastic bag full of aluminum cans, rattling it like a sleigh bell. "Thank you so very very much for my can, Ms. Jarvis."

Jeannette Jarvis smiled fully; the conversational ordeal was at an end.

"You want tea when your daughter come today?"

"Yes, when she arrives you can bring it up yourself. I don't want that oaf Melanie sloshing it all over the place."

"Yes, Ms. Jarvis."

Jeannette always looked forward to any family visit until about an hour before it happened, and then she wished she was left alone. Unlike some of the sentimentalists in this home who revivified from their coffins solely for visits by grandchildren and great-grandchildren, Jeannette was often *not at all* sorry that her family didn't visit more often.

Her own children were fractious and blamed her for everything that had gone wrong in the universe, and the grandchildren were a fright.

Dillard's only child, drug-addicted Christopher who died in his thirties, had stolen money from her purse. Jerene's brood were a strange lot, too. Jerilyn had been the most normal of the bunch and now look what she has gone and done. Annie the motormouth, the size, Jeannette Jarvis swore, of a blue whale, who wanted to unionize the Mexicans in Lattamore Acres' janitorial brigade. Jeannette had never met any of Annie's parade of short-lived matrimonies — that was an ignominious first for the family. Joshua, poor thing, who sat in her parlor with all the relish of a condemned man waiting for a call from the governor. Not bad looking, but no wonder he has had so little luck finding a girlfriend with so little charisma, fading into the wallpaper, invisible. (Hard to believe he is Duke Johnston's son.) And then Bo, who preached a sermon one Sunday here in the Lattamore Acres Chapel as a guest minister during which Jeannette Jarvis, *his own grandmother,* fell asleep. Jeannette liked Bo's perky little wife, Kate, though, alas, she wasn't from good stock.

The phone rang and the reception center informed her that her daughter had arrived and was coming up to her second-floor room.

Jeannette took a steadying, deep breath. She called the "assistance" number and asked the managers to page Pilar for tea service.

Jerene looked magnificent. You'd never know she was neck-deep in a morass of lawyers, filings, depositions with financial ruin lurking around the next corner. Whatever Jeannette did wrong as a mother, she nonetheless instilled in her daughters a sense of public presence. Neither Dillard nor Jerene ever so much as fetched the morning paper without being dressed and presentable to a world always rendering judgment. Much had declined in public manners since Jeannette's day but my girls, she thought, despite scandal and mistaken life choices, possessed a dignity of an earlier age — and surely that was Jeannette's great accomplishment. Jeannette lightly hugged Jerene at the door and bade her come in. "Tea is coming," she announced.

"I really don't think I'll be here that long," her daughter said, not shedding her winter coat or stylish leather gloves.

"The whole of Lattamore Acres is ablaze with talk of the civil suit. We'll be lucky not to have the activities director charter a bus to the Charlotte courtroom to watch the trial. Oh, that ungrateful bitch, Liddibelle Baylor. How could she turn on you like that?"

"Funny how people get when one of your children shoots one of their children."

"I could talk to her. Liddibelle's mother

and I go way back as well."

"I'd appreciate you staying out of it, Mother. It's all under control."

Jerene sat in the upholstered chair before the little table and Jeannette sat on the sofa with its matching pattern. "It doesn't feel the least bit under control. If you lose we'll all be bankrupt. And though I don't know what Duke knows about the law, I *was* your daddy's wife, and is it . . . is it true you have retained Darnell McKay as your counsel?"

"For reasons that must be very clear to you."

"But he is a tax lawyer, and perhaps not adept in civil suits —"

"Liddibelle's got her detectives going over us with a fine-tooth comb. He is as interested as I am in keeping certain things . . . Mother. I am not discussing any of this with you before we deal with the business at hand."

Jeannette raised her hand for a halt. "Why don't we wait until the tea arrives before we discuss things."

There was a rap at the door and Pilar entered with the tea, rolling forward a little cart with Wedgwood pot, cup and saucers, cream, and an array of finger sandwiches fanned out upon a platter, under cellophane. During the arrival of the tea, Jeannette suddenly swooned: she now knew what this visit was about. How she could have gone this long thinking it was about the shooting and not the more obvious thing? She had a very few defenses prepared but none of them was likely to save the day. Jeannette decided to play innocent, widening her eyes, and stall for time.

"Poor Jerilyn," Jeannette exclaimed. "Tell her that her grandmother is thinking of her. You know, young folks can get past anything. I'm sure by the one-year anniversary, they will be laughing about all this."

Jerene didn't say anything for a moment. "I do not believe there will be a one-year anniversary. They have already separated."

"The boy, what . . . Skip can't forgive her?"

"It's Jerilyn who wants out." Jerene appeared as if she hoped that might finish the discussion but her mother, waiting, stared holes in her, so she elaborated. "Skip demanded she go to marriage counseling and Jerilyn said no. Jerilyn insisted that Skip make his mother drop the civil suit and he said he had tried but he couldn't tell his mother what to do. He's right about that — Liddibelle is as stubborn as a cement block."

"But if it was an accident, when they were horsing around . . ."

Again Jerene looked burdened to be producing information she found distasteful. She glanced at Pilar who was pouring the tea. "Thank you, Pilar."

Pilar deftly slipped from the room, closing the door behind her.

Then Jerene resumed: "I don't think it was an accident. Jerilyn's romantic life, shall we say, was a series of misadventures with those . . . aggressive spoiled boys down there at Carolina. I won't shock you with details, Mother."

"What sordidness young people get up to could not possibly surprise me anymore."

"Well, you use your imagination — sordid is the right word for it. An assault, a pregnancy scare, many ill-considered relations, then she ran headlong back to Skip who she's known since childhood, I suppose, hoping for some comfort there. Jerilyn told me Skip sought counseling for drugs once upon a time — he has a compulsive personality. He was going to go to a sex addiction group, Jerilyn told me."

"Roly-poly Skip Baylor?" Jeannette shook her head faintly. "That's a little hard to picture."

"Jerilyn was drunk and upset, and Skip, I imagine, tried to hug and console her, then that led to him being inappropriately amorous — I'm just guessing here, Mother — and she snapped like a twig, grabbed the gun and shot him." They were both silent a moment. "So that's that," Jerene concluded. "I think that marriage is over and I don't imagine there will be a line of suitors queued up at Jerilyn's door anytime soon. For appearances' sake, they will wait a while to do anything official.

Fortunately, very few people know anything about the details of it all."

"They will when the civil suit goes forward. What's her name — Nancy Grace — will have it all over the national news on Court TV." (Jeannette never missed Nancy Grace or any courtroom show.)

Jerene examined her hands, having taken off her gloves. "As I said, don't worry about that suit. Liddibelle won't go through with it, when I talk some sense into her. We have a long history. I pushed for her to be in Theta Kappa Theta at Carolina when she transferred from Sweet Briar. I broke up with Becks and stepped aside so she could have a run at him. I gave her a perch in Charlotte Society by making her one of my trustees at the Mint. I gave her son and daughter-in-law a flawless wedding which she was moved to tears by. When she considers our long intertwined history, she will think better of the lawsuit."

"*You* should have married Becks Baylor and you would be a right bit better off."

"Becks was a boor. Crude and rough and a little stupid except for business. I was happy to set him up with Liddibelle. They were very happy together, before he died — and when he left her his fortune, she was even *more* happy. But speaking of money." Jerene was unsentimental. "We come to the purpose of my visit, Mother. You have to leave Lattamore Acres."

Jeannette said nothing. Tears would certainly not be effective, nor theatrics.

"Dillard, Duke and I can't keep you here any longer. It's been a huge financial drain for years now but with the lawsuit and the expenses, it's out of the question that we should continue paying for this resort."

"Leave Lattamore? But my whole life is here, my friendships, my . . . my doctors come here . . ."

"They can visit you in a new home, I'm sure."

"But the attendants on call know everything about my health — which is very delicate, as you may imagine."

"I imagine no such thing — you have proven indestructible. You are in sufficient shape to live to a hundred like a number of matriarchs in our line. No one has ever known how to die in this family and you are following in the tradition." Jerene serenely took a sip of tea.

"Can't Gaston — couldn't you ask him —"

"I did ask him, and Dillard pleaded with him, too. 'If not for your mother, then do it for us,' we begged. He has refused and wishes you out on the street in rags, and that is the nice version of what he envisioned for you. You see now the long-term disadvantage of allowing your children to be your buffer against a brute of a husband."

Jeannette's hand shook as she brought her teacup to her lips. Yes, in some quarter of her mind, she knew this talk would come. "You'd think my . . . my own family would . . ."

"Do you see them here? Do you see them gathered round you like a Christmas Norman Rockwell print? You do remember our last Christmas together as a family, don't you? What a celebration of good cheer."

Jeannette merely pursed her lips as she always did when the children were being disagreeable.

Jerene went on, "You wouldn't speak to Dillard for four years after she married Randy. And when her only child died you chose that moment to lecture her on child-rearing and how it was her own fault. You! You whose response to Daddy beating Gaston every time he got drunk was to blame us all for provoking our father. You could have left Daddy, but you were too . . ."

Jerene set down her teacup, her hands were clenched; Jeannette feared her daughter would crush the porcelain into powder.

"You were too *weak.* You cared more for your social station than whether we survived that hellish home you both made for us." Jerene gathered her purse, unfolding the coat in her lap. "You offered us all up," she added in cold recollection, now standing. "Better us than you. At any point, we could have gotten in the car and driven to Uncle Fred's and he'd have taken us in and not said a word about anything. Indeed, you could have stayed married to Daddy and not lived with him, that sort of thing was done all the time. But you had appearances to keep up. Apparently you still do. Well, those appearances are no longer affordable."

Jeannette blurted out, "We had a deal!"

Jerene seemed not to know what deal she was referring to. Then she figured what her mother meant. "Not a deal, an arrangement. I got to preside over the Jarvis Trust and we paid for you to spend the rest of your days in this palace. Did we not put you in the best possible place? This is a country club. Most people would spend their whole lives working to go on a vacation so they could live one single week like you do all the time. We chose this place so you could have a final few months of peace before what we thought —"

"I ruined everything, didn't I, by living! That's what you really mean!" She clasped her hands together tightly, not sure what to say or do next.

Jeannette Jarvis had been given no time at all to live in the winter of 2003. Her colon cancer was advanced. Radiation, an operation, then a follow-up operation, a colostomy, of course. Horror followed horror. She was tolerable company to the doctors who she understood were keeping her alive with all the medieval tortures, but she was awful to her family who tried dutifully to look after her. "I'm sure it would suit every one of you to a fare-thee-well if I up and died," she declared more than once, waiting for a contradiction . . . which her children noticeably never provided.

Before the second operation to remove another cancerous piece of bowel, the doctors discussed that if the operation did not go well, there was little more they could do. A failure here would mean a few more weeks — weeks, mercifully — of morphia-induced delirium until the end. And there was even a chance that Mrs. Jarvis might not survive the several-hour operation to come. Would she sign over medical and financial power of attorney so her family could make decisions for her? Defeated, terrified, Mrs. Jarvis did just that. She didn't trust Gaston not to suffocate her with a pillow at first opportunity, and she hadn't spoken to Dillard since Christopher's funeral, so that left Jerene who alone maintained a civil relationship and might be trusted not to pull the plug too gleefully.

After so many desperate strategems and procedures to stay alive, Jeannette came to fear a compromised survival, telling Jerene, "Don't let them bring me back full of tubes and hooked up to machines just so I can die slowly, Jerene."

"I won't let them do that, Mother," she

promised.

Gaston at last came to see her, figuring it would be a final encounter. Jeannette Jarvis was not sure what response he was after. And what a sight her only son was: bloated, fat in a female way, so unhealthy looking, some of that from drink, which she supposed came to him through his father, and some from general dissipation from his decadent habits. She tried to make peace with him, looking up at him sweetly, hoping to project a moment of pathos.

"This might be the last time you see your old mother, Gaston."

Oh she will never forget what he said and how he said it. It was just polite enough to pass in front of the nurses and doctors, but Jeannette knew just what meanness was intended when he said, "If that's so, Mother, just think. You can be reunited with our dear father for eternity."

Mrs. Jarvis had dwelled on that barb for years now, because no one, not even she, really thought Mr. Jarvis was anywhere other than the centermost fires of Hell.

And late, at the very end of visiting hours, came Dillard. Plump as ever! Well, none of the Jellicoe or Jarvis women except Jerene could keep the pounds off — it took cancer to do it. Jeannette needed to rest before the operation; she had been ordered to. And she knew talking had not led to much family harmony so she put out her frail hand for Dillard to hold, and Dillard took it, sighing. And there they were for ten minutes without saying a thing to each other, until Mrs. Jarvis said, "Thank you for coming, Dillie. I have to sleep now."

"I'll see you when you wake up, Mother."

Jeannette was an absolute wreck after Operation Number Two and didn't remember much — who was there, what was happening. She was slow to come out of the anesthesia, and when she surfaced she talked incoherently before lapsing into a coma, which everyone took to be the end, or the first stage of the end. But then she woke up.

And they really got all the cancer.

And here she was four, five years on, continually getting clean bills of oncological health while she piled up no end of lesser maladies — arthritis, skin ulcers, unexplained headaches, joint deterioration, varicose veins, diabetes 2. The colostomy and all its paraphernalia were deeply regrettable to a woman who had been so fastidious about appearance and presentation but then more distasteful was lying in the cold, cold ground.

Jerene's stint with power of attorney revealed something most unpleasant: Mrs. Jarvis was nearly broke. Not just broke but living on department store credit cards, a variety of VISAs and MasterCards from several sources, a second mortgage, a home equity loan. Jeannette suspected as much but none of her mild entreaties to the bank or to the credit card companies for more credit ever went rebuffed so she figured somehow she was successfully afloat. But Jerene called Gaston and Dillard and, after a family conference, began to liquidate the worldly possessions of Mrs. Jeannette Jellicoe Jarvis. The 160-year-old family house of the Jarvises had to be sold — or, more accurately, given over to the bank to sell. With Charlotte spreading to the east so completely, a fortune, a real fortune could have been had for that house in a few more years, Jerene told her in frustration. They did net several tens of thousands of dollars which were disbursed to her creditors.

Dillard and Jerene culled through the dishware and silver and rugs and porcelain to see if there was anything they had to have. There was very little they wanted from it, these monuments to propriety safe behind china cabinets and tucked in family vaults, things that had been exalted and protected while the family itself suffered under the depredations of Mr. Jarvis. Jerene already had the JJJ stamped plate in her possession and all the similarly initialed loot; Dillard, taking only the bone china, frankly declared most of the heirlooms too old-fashioned for her taste and for her small, already overstuffed house in Dilworth, and so the whole bundle was sent to a dealer, who gave them a good price. Or it was imagined to be a good price — who really knows with the dubious business of appraising and buying and selling desperate people's treasures.

The doctors were still saying (that fall in 2004) that it was "touch and go," that they "weren't out of the woods," all the clichés that led them all to think that she had no more than a year, a year in which she should be made comfortable. And so Lattamore Acres was the natural choice. Yes, it was more country club than retirement home. All grades of living conditions were available, from town houses with the briefest of check-ins by a nurse each morning to intensive-care beds on a hospital wing. Marble floors, a dark oak-paneled dining room, profusions of flowers in massive urns and vases and window boxes everywhere — never the smell of the hospital could be detected, nothing of age or deterioration was visible, except in the tenants themselves. You might have thought you were in a Mediterranean tennis resort. The food was remarkable, they took great care with the chefs, there were no end of amusements and activities, chartered buses to the museums, to concerts, for day trips to Salisbury for antiques shopping or Asheville for the fall colors . . . $3,500 a month — before medical charges — to rub shoulders with the doddering elite of Charlotte.

Jerene said, "Consider yourself lucky it lasted this long. Now. I'm going to the office and tell them that payment on your account stops this month."

"Where do you intend to move me?"

"We'll find another place. More affordable. Maybe a roommate is what you need."

"You're enjoying this! To tear me away from my home, the one place I have ever known peace, and send me to some charnel house!"

"Annie knows people in the moving business. I'll have her set up an appointment. You can leave in the dead of night, if you like, so no one will see you depart."

"Dillard has that house to herself . . ."

"She has declined to move you into it. I asked."

"And you and Duke have such a big place."

Jerene truly was bothered by an inability to escape; she wanted to be gone in the worst way. "Well, we were on the verge of handing it over to the bank. We took out a second mortgage to pay for Jerilyn's wedding and to hold on to Myers Park a moment longer. But thanks to Duke's newfound rapprochement with Gaston, Gaston has agreed to pay off that mortgage so we can sell it off free and clear."

"That Johnston house is legendary. Why would you sell such a grand place?"

"We will sell it so we can scrape together some kind of old age. We'll be moving to the gated community that Duke and that group of investors are building down by the Catawba River, near Fort Mill. A cozy condo, I imagine, and there won't be room for you there either."

Jeannette had one or two more gambits. "Where I go is the least of my concerns right now. You think me so monstrous, but it is something else that tears at my heart. That my children despise me. Now I don't expect Gaston to recover," Jeannette pleaded. "But Dillard and you . . . Mostly you, Jerene. You have never forgiven me. I couldn't control your father! Why should I be endlessly held accountable for his misdeeds?"

Jerene thought for a moment and sank back in the chair, setting her purse on the floor. She seemed . . . was that a smile?

"Oh Mother, you . . ." Now she laughed dryly. "You think it's because you didn't stop Daddy from beating us about and abusing us at will — that's really rich. He had fists, but you had your tongue. He had alcoholism as an excuse for being a monster, but what was yours?"

Jeannette drew her lips tight, hoping for a dignified mien.

"The commentary throughout our lives, the judgment. It was every bit as abusive as Daddy. At least when Daddy sobered up, he was tolerable company, and often very sorry for his behavior. He rained money and clothes and possessions down on us when he felt guilty. But when did we ever hear a kind word from you? We were too fat or too thin, ugly in some way, however we dressed. At college we were harlots or prostitutes for dating, and the boys we dated weren't good enough. We did nothing but shame and humiliate you. And we raised our children wrong, too." She thought a moment before going further, then she did: "Not counting the one given up for adoption forty years ago. Do I have to remind you of your commentary through all that? You'd found some low-country backwoods quack to cut it out of me. You couldn't kill it fast enough. It's a wonder you didn't rip it out of me with your own hands. I arrived in Asheboro without a dime too, thanks to you. Fortunately, Dillard scraped some money together."

Jeannette was silent. She now gauged the depth of Jerene's contempt. She had hoped, with no evidence, that Jerene was the child who was most sympathetic to her.

If she had been judgmental and shrill, there had been reasons for it, reasons grounded in her realistic fears of falling headlong out of Society and back into the peasantry, the white trash, to have once been something and then to go back to nothing again. If she had been too harsh, it was to prevent that! If Jerene and Dillard never felt the danger of decline, it was only because of the immense sacrifices

Jeannette had performed to prevent it. Now it hardly matters what Jerene and Duke's children do; the world of proprieties and respectabilities, the patina of Southern grace and elegant public bearing, all of that was nearly gone and smashed to bits. What the Yankees and the War and Reconstruction had not been able to accomplish, prosperity and time, modern mores and cable TV, had managed just fine. What a folly her whole life was, thought Jeannette, now smiling, too.

"Our whole lives," Jerene was saying, "we have been subject to your poisonous judgment, as if we all were criminals. And . . . just what is so funny, Mother?"

Now Jeannette was chuckling darkly, shaking her head. "Criminals! Oh, Jerene, if you only knew." Jeannette was feeling more steady now; she had a firm sip of unsweetened tea. "Sell one of your paintings. Come now, I won't be alive all that much longer."

"I don't believe I'm hearing you say this. Mother, you all but swore me to a holy oath that nothing could ever induce us to sell them. There'll be no more Jarvis Room in the Mint Museum if we start selling them to bail ourselves out."

"Sell the Church, it'll fetch the most. Never liked it anyway."

"I will do no such thing. Whatever we can hold together for a legacy for the children is in that museum. It's our calling card for

Society — my land, I'm sounding like you now! You would have me break up the collection just so you could play canasta with women you have assured me were awful?"

"Sell them *all.*"

Jerene huffed. "And what of Adeline Bell, hiding the paintings behind the settee, praying Sherman's men would content themselves with torching the barn."

"That story is all nonsense, Jerene."

"It may mean nothing to you anymore, but I feel an unbroken kinship with these Jarvis and Bell women who have held these paintings in our family for generations —"

"No! It's nonsense. I mean, the story. Your father and I made it up."

"I beg your pardon."

"We stole those paintings like we stole everything we ever owned."

Jeannette glanced at her daughter. Oh she was all ears now.

"Your daddy had a brother who died before you were born, your Uncle Demetrius. Believe me, in Waxhaw, North Carolina, the Jarvis boys were the eligible bachelors. The Jellicoes, as I told you, were an old, respectable Salisbury family but after the War we lost the mills, and in the Panic of 1907, Granddaddy lost the rest. But we covered up our indigence well, and my daddy spent his last dime on my wedding to your father."

"Yes, Mother, I know all this —"

"Oh but Demetrius, he was . . . he was touched by the gods. There was not a woman, married, single, widowed or dead, who didn't covet that man. And he married very well, into a fine family, one of those Virginia families so rarified and blue-blooded that they carried with them the genetic problems brought over from England, some inherited illness that got passed down from generation to generation. I suppose now we'd say it was some form of Huntington's disease. It left a good quarter of that family locked away in asylums, rocking and writhing spastically until their hearts gave out, poor things. Well, that was your aunt, Helen York Jarvis. People didn't have financial advisers in those days, instead they had lawyers, and your uncle turned to your daddy to fix things for him. What your father was to drink, your uncle was to womanizing and, I think, bastard children, black, white, brown, yellow and red, were proliferate all over the county. He had an insurance policy against accidents and, as you know, he died young."

"Yes, I remember hearing. Died before I was born. While cleaning his gun on a hunting trip."

Jeannette snorted. "Someone, some cuckolded husband shot him, sure as I'm sitting here. Your father patched it all up and made it look like an accident and collected the policy for Aunt Helen, several hundred thousand which was a fortune in the early 1950s. Then Helen's mother, Mrs. York, died and left her the house in Blowing Rock and the paintings in it. Demetrius swore your father to secrecy never to let Helen know just how much money she had. Didn't want her to get ideas about spending it."

"I see he and Daddy were a lot alike."

"Men liked their women helpless back then and a lot of women preferred being helpless — it made things much simpler. So she never knew quite what she was worth. And there she was fawning over your father — oh what would we do without deeeeear Gaston Jarvis, looking out for us so. Helen's brother died of the family ailment, leaving everything to her so she could be provided for, then Helen herself came down with it. Your father saw to it that she had a companion, someone who came to be with her as she lost control of her bodily functions and her mind went. There were three paintings then. The Church and the two Inneses, all in the York family."

"So after Aunt Helen died, we just kept her three paintings? But, counting the miniatures, we have twelve American landscapes."

Jeannette looked at her daughter impatiently. "The story is just beginning, sweetheart. Here is a dying woman who has ended up with her entire family's estate, plus some insurance money, plus the big mansion she lives in. All she wants is for her late sister's child, her niece — the last York heir — to be looked after in the event she gets the disease too. They all came down with it in their early forties."

Jerene did not bother to refute anything Jeannette said because it had the ring of truth, concerning facts she knew and what she knew about her father. "That was my cousin Patty. I barely remember her."

Jeannette continued. "They trusted your father with everything. As Helen got sicker, your father assured Helen's niece, Patty, that there was money there to take care of her beloved aunt. That she would get the best care and die at home where she wanted to be. Your father must have had his plan even then. Keep everything out of the public view, no state hospitals or asylums or anything that would raise attention or find its way into a record. So Aunt Helen died and then the whole York estate went to your cousin Patty."

"Not all of it, apparently."

"As far as Patty was concerned, the landscapes yellowing on the wall in Blowing Rock weren't worth anything. She agreed with your father that they should sell the mountain home and its contents. I'm sure, even back then, it fetched a *fortune,* and I'm just as sure your father told Patty that it sold for half that, pocketing the rest. He liquidated the whole York estate, and where the property or stock was in Union County, your father stole liberally. He'd slap the clerk of court on the back, ask to go find something in the files after a boozy lunch or golf game, change and alter and eliminate any form or receipt he needed to cover his tracks, down at the courthouse where he had free rein. But the one thing he couldn't do is deposit the money in a bank. A sudden surfeit of money would alert the authorities. He kept it in cash, in a burlap sack in the basement."

Jerene put down her teacup. Her face was showing signs of recognition; Jeannette saw, at last, that Jerene believed her.

Jerene said, "I see now why we were forbidden going in the basement. You told me it had something to do with deadly spiders."

"Well, there were fearsome spiders down there, too. Even your father was wary! Hated going down there. Once there was a spider with a body as big as a pepper shaker —"

"Mother, back to the story, please."

"Yes. So, your daddy and a bunch of his law school friends headed down to Charleston, South Carolina, for drinking mainly, I suspect, and he drove down there in a rented van with the three paintings to sell them for cash in the antique stores. He came back with those three and three more. 'Jeannie, those paintings were worth a goddam gold mine,' he told me. Art was a perfect investment. He'd go to Broad Street in Charleston or Royal Street in New Orleans and, between living it up, whoring and drinking, he'd spend the stolen cash on art. Trips to Richmond, Baltimore . . . Those dealers were happy to sell for straight cash, too, and I doubt there's a record of any of it.

"It was perfect. If Patty ever got curious and had another lawyer look into anything, your daddy was investing in art for the York estate; the paintings could be produced. If she never grew suspicious, then we had the paintings free and clear. 'These canvases are better'n bearer bonds, Jeannie,' he used to tell me all the time. And Patty was never curious. Your father set up a trust that paid her a very healthy monthly stipend, and she thanked and thanked him for it, oh thank-the-Lord what a savior he was."

"And he told you everything?"

"When I would ask him about it, even if he was drinking and in one of his bragging moods, he would sober right up and get that steely look in his eye. Told me it was none of my business."

"How'd you find out so much?"

"When he was passed out I'd look through the papers. Probably the only benefit I ever found to his alcoholism."

As Jeannette unburdened herself of these long-kept secrets, cousin Patty came into sharper focus in her memory. A short, pale, fragile woman, unlike many of the brawny Yorks, something doomed and apologetic in her quiet manner as if she had shown up to Life without a reservation and was shamefully aware of always being a bother. "Patty confided in me once," Jeannette said, "saying she heard of some clinic in Switzerland that had helped people carrying the gene, and maybe she could get your father to advance her some money . . . but then he talked her out of it, saying how he didn't want her in debt and it wouldn't do to chase false hopes. But she still went on about this clinic, and ordered brochures, was in contact with some German doctor. Your father ordered me to talk her out of it. She listened to me, trusted me."

Jerene didn't say anything, and didn't meet her mother's eyes.

"And that's just what I did," Jeannette said, having another sip of tea.

"Oh, Mother," Jerene said simply.

"And in the meantime, your daddy looked far and wide for some heir or claimant. Helen's family, the Yorks, were all but finished thanks to the disease. It was one of those things, some doctor told me once, that you get when brothers marry sisters, way back in the past. I felt sorry for anyone who got the disease, but that doesn't mean I really liked Helen, my sister-in-law. She looked down her nose at me, that poor Jellicoe woman from the family who lost their money. She didn't think I was quite on her level. But Patty I was sorry for. Sure enough, she got the disease, right on cue."

"What did Daddy do?"

"As she got sick and more scared, he had her sign a whole bunch of papers so she could be looked after, so funds could be transferred here and there. Then when it got where she couldn't control the spasms and tics, he had her shipped off to Butner."

The state asylum. Jerene frowned. "Mother, couldn't he have spared some money for a nicer place?"

"Figured it might hasten her end. I remember him saying if you slipped the Negro guards a twenty, there was one of them that would press a pillow over a patient's head — you know — when they had a disease like that. It wasn't about your father stealing the money; he'd already done that and tied up the loose ends, all clear and legal. It was about not wanting her to suffer."

"Did he pay that Negro man a twenty?"

"I never asked. I never asked about a lot." Jeannette finished her glass of tea, though it was cold and bitter in the cup.

"Do you think that's why Dad drank? Because he was guilty?"

Jeannette was wide-eyed, even laughed. "Merciful heavens! What a thought! Your daddy wasn't guilty for one little minute. He'd been waiting for a chance like this all his life. Your daddy drank because he was an alcoholic and that's what they do. I was the one who felt guilty. I waited for the reckoning, too. At every cotillion, every charity dinner, every trip to Raleigh for a cousin's debutante ball, every social occasion I waited for someone to tap the glass and clear their throat and announce that the most terrible revelations had come to light about the Jarvis family . . . and that some overlooked relative of the Yorks was pursuing remedies in the halls of justice. But that never happened." Jeannette laughed again.

"What's so funny about that?"

"Someone, sweetheart, could have made that very dreaded speech, and it wouldn't have made one iota of difference — not down South! 'Jeannie,' your daddy would tell me, 'everybody down South got rich doing something they shouldn't have.' I can name you the first families of the Carolinas who got rich on smuggling or selling to the British in the Revolutionary War — or the Yankees, mind you. Many of the cream of Southern society *now* were carpetbagging Northerners *then,* who came down here and bought mills and factories and deeds of land for a song from busted aristocrats whose money was tied up in Confederate scrip and were rendered penniless, and these families sit on their fortunes quite happily. The Hargett girls were here at Lattamore — Camille Hargett and her sister Leonore who, between them, simply ran everything in Charlotte for a decade. Head of the Debutante Society, over which they reigned as a ruthless fiefdom! The Hargetts made their money bootlegging — stills and moonshine. And Melissa Day Petty, who had started answering to Mrs. Day Petty rather Mrs. Petty, as if the no-account Days of pitiful old Bickettville, North Carolina, needed to be lifted up and constantly before us in her spoken name, such were their earthly glory!"

"Yes, I sent this year's Mint by Gaslight invitation to Mrs. Day Petty to humor her."

"They went around buying up poor people's farms in the Depression, hiring goons to run squatters off the land, had night riders in robes and hoods burning the colored folk out of their shacks. She told me about it herself, almost proud of it. And her niece, who she goes on and on about, is going to marry a Byrd of Virginia. How many times do I have to hear about her marrying a Byrd, a Byrd of Virginia, la-de-dah. When that first family of the colonies was nearly bust they turned to slaving. Hiring the ships and the slavers themselves. It is naïve to think anybody that has money got it without doing something really bad because it is much easier to be poor — that, my girl, is the natural state of things. Money runs out, money gets spent. To have so much of it that it doesn't run out or get spent means something . . . unpleasant had to happen somewhere along the way."

"And Patty had no heirs?"

"Oh yes, some cousins, distant, many times removed who lit out generations ago for Missouri, the Ozarks. Why should some bumpkin come to the door of his shack and get a notification that a branch of the family has left him a million? Why not our family instead? And we weren't even strangers. We were family by marriage."

"If someone were to audit . . ."

"It's over, sweetheart. We're talking the fifties and sixties, in Union County, North Carolina. You don't think your father was wily enough to cover his tracks?"

Jerene nodded, then shook her head, then stared out the window in shock, then seemed to come to. And then, perhaps, a smile played at her lips. "But Mother . . ."

"Yes, sweetheart."

"I remember when I was a child, you had a fund-raiser for the Jarvis Trust at the Mint, all of Charlotte was there and you thanked Grandmother Jarvis for her decades of work with the trust, and she stood up and took a little bow as they clapped."

Jeannette smiled back. "If you say something long enough — just like the Sherman's bummers story — people will think it's true. My mother-in-law was every bit the sot your father was, she just covered it better. It helps not to have much to say — no one expected her to speak at length. I pointed to her, she stood up every year, they clapped, she smiled, she sat down, she had another bourbon and ginger ale."

"My goodness, I've been peddling these bald-faced lies every single year."

"You didn't know they were lies, Jerene. And people like those kind of lies down here. They're good, entertaining lies — I suspect history is eighty percent those kind of lies."

Jerene was gathering up her things again. "I hate to break it to you, Mother, but art-selling is very regulated now. To sell any of the paintings, which I have no intention of doing, I have to attest to their provenance and a museum would hire an investigator to look into where they came from. To prove they're not forgeries, of course. I could *give* them away to a museum for a tax write-off but selling them would be a problem. It doesn't change your situation. I'll call Annie tonight."

Jeannette for a moment had no idea why Annie was being mentioned. Oh yes, she and her connections with movers and moving vans. "I'm not leaving here, Jerene." Now Jeannette stood, defiant. "I'll make a spectacle — they'll have to drag me out of here with the sheriff's deputies."

"As you wish. When my check ceases to arrive in the business office, I'm sure Lattamore Acres will deposit you on the sidewalk themselves."

"I bet I could find those cousins! I kept some papers, in my safety-deposit box! Those Ozark hillbillies could get the paintings and where would you be then?"

Jerene slipped on her gloves, calmly, undeterred. "You strike me as not very likely to reveal that you and Father were felons, ruining the thing that has meant most to you, your reputation." Jerene looked up, simply smiling at her mother. "Besides, you're right, I'm sure, about Daddy. He probably made sure there isn't a trace to connect the York money to those heirs. He was the Devil Incarnate and he never paid one small price for any of his devilment, so I don't think this will be an exception."

Jeannette staggered to the kitchen, yanked open a drawer and held a brown plastic pill bottle. "Do you doubt that two minutes after you leave, I will swallow every one of these heart pills — every last one of them? That will solve all your problems, won't it? Gaston can come dance on my overdue grave! Do you doubt for a minute I will do it, hm? You will have to explain how you threatened to throw your own mother out of her home and . . . it will follow you, this story, throughout . . . What? Are you laughing at me?"

Indeed, Jerene was laughing at her. "Oh Mother. You are not going to do any such thing." Jerene stopped buttoning her winter coat and came toward Jeannette, touching her cheek, tenderly. "You are expert at one thing, long as I've known you, and that is preserving yourself. You are the Queen of Self-Preservation."

Jerene walked deliberately to the door but Jeannette had one more thing to say: "You wondered why I didn't leave your father? Pile you kids in the car and go to Uncle Fred's?"

Jerene didn't say anything, but of course she was interested.

"Well, you do you want to know why?" Jeannette would make her ask for it.

"Yes, all right, why didn't you leave him?" Jerene's tense posture relaxed. She leaned against the door, her hand on the handle.

"Once your father and I were fighting and I said I'd had enough of the drinking and the violence — and Lord, he just slapped and shoved in those days. It was long before the real beatings. And that Christmas that just about killed us all. Anyway I said I would leave him because I was done being married to a monster. He said I could expect to live on the street because I would not see a dime of his money, and the children would starve. And I had no doubt he could figure out a way to circumvent all known laws and cut me off without a cent, despite my caring for three of his children. Which prompted me to say that if he was going to be that way, perhaps I would tell the authorities how he came by all our money, all they had to do was check into a few things . . . and he hit me so hard I lost a tooth. This one." Jeannette pointed to a front tooth.

"I was on the floor and he was right on top of me and he told me that he would not think twice about killing a woman who had no more sense than to turn on her husband. I crawled away, and he got more drunk, smashing things around in the kitchen. I think he was trying to decide if he should kill me now or kill me later. After all, he was going to jail anyway if I told about the Yorks. So he decided that maybe now was the time to finish me off, and just as he was deciding that, I was thinking about the gun he kept in the top desk drawer. And who knows what would have transpired if Gaston Jr. hadn't come home. You and Dillard, I take it, had the good sense to hunker down up in your bedroom, but there was Gaston — all of seven or eight, home from some church social or something. He saw your daddy start in on me, and he saw my missing tooth and the blood on my blouse and he just exploded and lunged for your father. Your daddy thought the spectacle of fragile little Gaston flailing and swinging away at his own father was hilarious and began to laugh and couldn't stop. He contented himself with shoving Gaston away and your brother went headfirst into the server in the dining room, bloodying his nose. It wouldn't stop bleeding so after Gaston Sr. passed out, I put Gaston Jr. in the car and drove to the hospital."

Jerene, no change or softening of her stare, not a flinch or ripple in her steady gaze: made of steel, thought Jeannette, made of stone.

"Now in those days, there was no social services or the like; the nurses and doctors knew good and well what they were looking at, battered wife and battered son. But nobody said anything. Gaston Jarvis was a respectable citizen and stalwart of the county, and nobody was going to cross him. So yes, darling, I stayed. I stayed so I wouldn't get killed, and I stayed so we wouldn't get cut off without a cent and live like paupers, and I stayed so some good could come of Patty's money. You went to Carolina and had nice clothes, a debut, that summer where you went abroad to France, and the Jarvis Trust and the Jarvis Room at the Mint and all the respectability you stand upon. That was poor cousin Patty's money. Dillard went to Salem and had a trousseau and Gaston had a Duke education, and all the rest. Did you see me spend any of it on myself? I couldn't give you a loving father but I could make it that when your daddy sobered up, and in those small windows of self-loathing and sorrow for what he'd done, I saw to it that he did the right thing and try to atone by giving you the makings of a respectable life. I could not have done that from Uncle Fred's, now could I?"

Jerene didn't move except to turn the door handle. Finally she said, "It's taken me a whole lifetime, Mother, to learn how to dispense with the past. There's been no room in my life for the past, not for years now. Not since you and Daddy, not since Asheboro."

And she was gone, out the door in a flash.

Jeannette still held the bottle of pills. She could — oh she might just take them all. But she knew she wouldn't. She set the bottle down.

Jeannette's circumstances were once again dire, her hold on comfort and peace slipping through her hands yet again. Other women, some grand Southern dames in Lattamore Acres, floated through the world like a rose petal on a stream, with an extended hand always there to help her up and down the small inconvenient steps of Life — but never Jeannette. Every small permitted privilege, every safe harbor had been paid for in blood and bruises, and now even at this advanced age, it would appear her finding sanctuary was still not settled and she would be tossed back yet again to the indifferent fates. Yet strangely, dire as this turn of events was, she had heart to wonder about her daughter Jerene. Gaston felt the past so keenly he tried to drink away its memory; Dillard spent her life medicated from aches and pains that were really spiritual rather than physical. But poor Jerene. Jerene had trumped them all, having turned herself to adamantine at some useful point.

Jeannette walked to her window overlooking the staff parking lot. Jerene often parked her BMW there because it was a shorter walk to Mrs. Jarvis's rooms from the elevator bank nearest the back. Jerene had indeed parked in the staff lot, and Jeannette watched her daughter march toward her car with measure and purpose, on to the next chore, pitching mother out of her retirement community checked off the list and now it's time for her hair appointment or a meeting with the caterers or something more important.

And not a minute after Jerene hopped in her car and drove away, there was Pilar, dear thing, leaving work for the day. Yes, Jeannette thought, smiling, Pilar was hauling her white bag of cans to her car, slung over her shoulder like Santa Claus, sounding like him too, clanging and jingling, all the cans colliding and rubbing against one another. Pilar stopped before the four recycling bins . . . and what, she . . . she was dumping the whole trash bag of cans into the blue bin for cans and recyclable metals. She won't get a cent that way! Why would anyone not want the two, three dollars that . . . Had she been disposing of every single can, for months and months? But why would she . . .

Jeannette steadied herself first against the windowsill and before she knew it, she was sitting on the floor, with her breathing becoming more shallow. She would probably have to be helped up when it came time to stand, she would have to call a nurse or wait for one to check on her, but she just sat there for a while, shaking a little, trying to remember one thing she knew for sure, one thing she could name that was true.

Joshua

Nonso : i dot have gay friend in lagos wey i live

JJ : There must be many gays in Lagos — it is such a big city!

Nonso : many whita gay

JJ : Really? That is surprising

Nonso : i have a whita frind 4rm holland is 59

JJ : That is good, yes? To have a boyfriend.

Nonso : he is rech bot i dot like his life n all the sexysexy

Nonso : he have 2 many gay friends

Nonso : so we brak up

JJ : Oh sorry. I think in Holland gays sleep with lots of men . . .

Nonso : we are no longar friend

Nonso : and i dot want 2 have a friend from nigeria

JJ : why not?

Nonso : da are all abot lay all da can see

Nonso : they tell u they love u bot all is lias

JJ : There are men like that here, too. Everywhere I think.
Nonso : But u no lik those men, yes U want reall love lik me

Joshua Johnston and Dorrie Jourdain were used to their exile, and had even come to bask in it — but only because they were along for the ride together.

For their final two years at university they had been inseparable, and then they parted for a while, worked in Charlotte and Durham respectively, and when they found themselves both in Charlotte, they re-cemented, connected like some married people never connect, lived just a block from each other. The incidents of their lives didn't even seem to happen if the other couldn't be the audience for them; their lesser friendships melted away and they didn't even really miss other people. Yes, everyone thought they were an interracial couple, which wasn't very exciting in the South anymore, except it would have been the less patronized template — black woman, white man. Occasionally they let that misapprehension stand in social situations where it made them seem like the coolest people in the room.

They both were gay and that had meant exile from the comfortable currents of high school, and university (though not so savagely, they both went to UNC–Chapel Hill where tolerance was performed nicely), and, of course, family. Josh had blurted out last Christmas that he was gay, and, dependably, not one word of follow-up, speculation, consequence, commentary or curiosity ever followed from it; all was as it ever was: *not discussed.* Dorrie told her mom after graduation from Chapel Hill (she and her mother were the whole of their family), and Mrs. Jourdain begrudgingly said it didn't matter to her and that she loved her daughter every bit as much but she would appreciate that Dorrie's future partner be a baptized Christian and that their kids be raised in the church. Dorrie smiled gently, knowing none of that crap — church or brats, or said brats being taken on Sunday for their weekly dose of homophobia from a black pulpit — was ever going to happen.

Their final exile was from the mainstream gay world of Charlotte. "We are bona fide race traitors," Dorrie frequently declared.

Dorrie liked white women, older, preferably with an aura of prestige and power, think Senator Hillary Clinton (Dorrie's beat-up Toyota was plastered with HILLARY '08! stickers), think Margaret Thatcher circa 1983, full professors who were experts in their fields. It didn't matter which field, as long as there was wisdom, probity, the eyeglasses slowly being taken off to answer a student's question with calm and authority, a hand on the podium (hm, no wedding ring . . .), a knowing smile at the edge of the mouth. Josh knew Dorrie's type well: white women who edited magazines in New York, white women in Brooks Brothers who dominated all-male boardrooms, grand High Southern white women who oversaw foundations, of which there was no shortage in the South, e.g., Jerene Jarvis Johnston, executive director of the Jarvis Trust for American Art at the Mint Museum.

"I would totally do your mom," Dorrie enjoyed announcing to Joshua in dull moments. "Hey, when she wears that black eighties shoulder-pad Faye Dunaway as Joan Crawford at Pepsico don't-fuck-with-me-boys number? Your mom is righteous hot."

Josh would respond in his established role: "Keep such ideas to yourself while I'm driving! You want me to wreck?"

"Hey Mrs. J.," Dorrie would rehearse, "no offense to Mr. J., but I bet there's certain things that ain't been attended to in a lonnnng time . . ."

"Stop, in the name of all that is human!"

And Josh liked black boys. Charlotte had more than its Southern share of black queens and snapping, attitude-wielding characters, but that's not what Josh wanted. Young, masculine, slim and smooth, loping, laconic, one of those yes-ma'am no-ma'am respectful boys raised by a hundred women, and the darker the better. Going down to Camp Greene Park to watch the pickup basketball tournaments, all the tank tops and rounded shoulders and smooth glistening black muscles fired by grace and energy — it was a friggin' porn film. Within this acceptable looks-model were: video-game nerds with computer engineering degrees from UNC Charlotte, the rare straight-acting hairdresser, no end of waiters and club bartenders, innumerable housing-project baggy-pantsed bad boys, true thugs and dealers, too . . . Josh had fantasies (and war stories, misadventures, misfires) with all of the above.

Josh was gayboy-beautiful in the face, articulated features like a theater actor in makeup, dramatic eyebrows and a sharp elegant nose, big brown eyes with long eyelashes, pale skin with straight black hair, but his face was the trump in an otherwise weak hand. Josh was thin, unmuscled, soft, occasionally fey and camp when the context was right, but you wouldn't call him "fem." Certainly no one thought of him as macho. There was a brief leather phase where he tried to butch it up but he was still a wimp in leather — besides, beyond the jacket and the boots, it started getting real expensive. No athleticism (and no plans to buff up), thin arms and legs, uneven and whimsically sprouting body hair (no, he was not going to spend fortunes having it all taken off in painful electrolysis like some guys), your standard-issue Southern scrawny Scots-Irish guy who sunburned and freckled easily, had bad skin in high school and felt his hair was already beginning to thin. Nor was he a good guy's guy. Hated sports, couldn't even play video games. God, that had replaced the after-sex cigarette: every twenty-something brightening and then suggesting that they could share a post-coital round of Grand Theft Auto.

There were dates and there were hookups.

Hookups. Josh had sex once or twice a week and he didn't always tell Dorrie about every quick encounter. While Dorrie strategized for months about her society white women, closed in strategically, worked out how to be in constant contact with her prey, Josh just clicked to the internet, went to CDL — that stood for charlottedownlow.com — looked at who was online, and then used the filter device to find African-American men of a certain age range (25–35) who were looking for or open to white guys. A few chats later and he was in the shower getting ready for a ride to the guy's apartment.

Ooh, you had to be careful. Looming over every encounter was the memory of Marlo. Josh was too lazy to cook for himself and too poor for anywhere too nice so he ate lots of meals at the all-you-can-eat Countrytyme Buffet two miles from his house. He knew all the waitstaff, who refilled your iced-tea glass and took your dirty dishes away. Marlo was always eager to saunter over, always bored and, frankly, too smart for this minimum-wage job. Didn't seem gay but he did hover and insinuate himself in a gay way.

"Never see you in here with no girl," Marlo ventured one day, with a bit of swagger which the Countrytyme faux-cowboy uniform seemed to support and undercut all at once.

"Because I like guys," Josh said.

"Maybe you need to come sometime right when I get off work."

Josh felt something was a little off. Maybe this was a hustle. Marlo would get Josh all worked up and then ask for money. And if Josh was horny and weak, he might peel off a twenty (or two) just to get this fantasy out of his system. That kind of encounter meant Marlo would let himself be serviced but probably do nothing back, which made you feel doubly used, but then Marlo was *fine.* It probably would mean, oh well, that Josh could never go back into the Countrytyme Buffet again. Horniness won out.

They got in Josh's car (Marlo took the bus to work) and Marlo said he needed to run by home to get out of the cowboy-waiter drag. As they drove northeast, the neighborhood declined, then got worse, then got worryingly bad. Josh didn't balk — he'd been all over Charlotte on hookups and knew a bad neighborhood from a merely poor neighborhood

— he saw a Sugar Creek landmark or two . . . then they arrived at a dark block without working streetlights, rows of tract houses, some boarded up and condemned, some lawns becoming weeds and a place to dump discarded rusted appliances. There were clusters of young men in the shadows, lingering on the corners. Marlo hopped out and ran into a house and was back in a flash, in the same clothes.

"You using this?"

There was a Diet Coke can on the floorboard of the passenger side. Josh shook his head. Marlo, newly frantic, groped around the car, the glove compartment . . .

"You got a pen?"

Josh handed over the pen kept in the unused ashtray.

Marlo used the pen to punch two pinpoint holes in the side of the Diet Coke can, then he bent the can so the holes were on the crease. Then he took out from a little plastic bag a crystal which he balanced on that crease in the bent can, then a lighter where he shot a flame sideways onto the crystal, then he sucked in the smoke from the can's opening. The acrid, burnt-hair smell of crack filled the car. Josh drove forward, his heart beating fast. In North Carolina if you had drugs in your car, no matter who brought them in there, the state could confiscate your car, and Josh saw a world of trouble and bad newspaper publicity and speculations that after his sister shot her husband, Duke and Jerene Johnston's fag drug-addict son went wild —

"You want some?"

"Get out of the car."

Josh drove several blocks from the drug-dealing corners. He was going to pull over . . . when he saw a police cruiser slowly moving down the street in the other direction. White kid in this neighborhood? Must be here to buy. Josh turned his head as the cruiser rolled by, praying for some magical invisibility. Marlo, watching his crack burn away, inhaled from the can again, making the coal glow — *as the police car passed by.* What degree of addiction would make you light up with the cop *right there*? Josh pulled the car to the curb once the cruiser was well behind him.

"Out! I mean it."

Marlo leaned back in the seat, free of all worldly cares and tension. "Chill out, brother. Ain't no thang."

Josh reached across him and undid the passenger door. As he did, Marlo weakly tried to push his head down to his crotch, his stale jeans with the cowboy trim. Josh reared up and undid Marlo's seat belt for him.

"Go."

Marlo stumbled out and Josh drove on, a little too fast, turning left, then right, then illuminating with his high beams a spray-painted street sign as if that would help him know where he was, then turning right again, into another, different block of young men idling, slingin', cars in front of him slowing, business being done at the car window. Josh could not calm down; he wanted to cry but was too scared to let it happen. Five more panicked and lost minutes later, he followed a glow at the end of another street, a service station, with metal bars on the window, a gathering of Mexicans out front, drinking from bottles in brown paper bags, *reggaeton* blasting from a portable radio. His car smelled of crack; he wanted to gag. No cop would mistake it. He gingerly picked up the Diet Coke can and buried it in the trashcan beside the gas pump. He drove until he found a twenty-four-hour drugstore and bought two air fresheners. Even months later, driving to his parents' house, going home from work, he would smell a molecule of the indestructible crack-smoke stink, still reminding him of his naïveté.

Joshua thought of his own first cousin, Christopher, Aunt Dillard's son, who died a few years back from his inability to get free of crystal meth. Chris liked slumming. He liked the danger, the bad side of town, heading out to the woods with guys with guns to see the rusted trailer where they cook it, he liked dealing to his college-educated friends. Chris thought we were all fools to be plodding along in the straight boring normal life when there was this wild-ass adrenaline world out there. Joshua had none of that in him. If he ended up in the occasional seedy housing project or hooking up with a gay guy with a drug problem — and, friend, they were legion in George W.'s America, where gay men were *so* admired, welcomed, embraced, supported — it was solely due to aesthetics. And the hope that Love might triumph over squalor.

But dating sucked, too. He kept falling between extremes. Josh, the English and Afro-American Studies double major with the 3.8 GPA, would end up spending evenings with the high school dropout he met at Starbucks, talked to for an hour, exchanged phone numbers. Nathan knew every word in "Bring Da Ruckus" but had never read one good novel. Then there was Horace, a charismatic professor who had been his customer at the clothing store, who invited Josh to his town house to be cooked for, in order for Horace to tell him about wine and wine pairings with food, as a mentor would . . . and that was just not what Josh wanted either. He was already cultured, knew a lot about wine and drink from his debt-ridden years at Chapel Hill, had his own fully formed opinions about art and literature, and he didn't want to be some black professor's decorative whiteboy at faculty dinner parties that fell to dry discussions of UNC Charlotte politics and speculation about budget cuts.

The solution for the moment was the bed-buddy, the sweet good-natured minimum-wager coming over for a regular *thang* after his shift was done, curled up together on the sofa, a six-pack and a pizza from Papa John's, watching the NBA game (whose tip-off made them rush the sex an hour before), with the young man's cell phone buzzing throughout, his woman nagging him about something, diapers for the baby, when is he coming home. In the last five years, the most regular guy was Silas, who would pop by in his Bojangles uniform after work, smelling comfortingly of chicken grease.

"You see," Dorrie said once, "there's the big difference. I can go out to a classy wine bar with my older white sugar mama and we can talk about art, literature, whether the symphony played the *allegretto* in Beethoven's Seventh too slowly. What are you gonna talk to Deshawn about?"

Josh was patiently resigned to lots of earnest conversations about what working-class young men did for a living, in exhaustive detail. Together, he and Dorrie had lived through Samir's getting his hours cut back at the Flower Hut, Dwayne having to go back to court for not seeing his parole officer (a marijuana arrest), and Rudy's Jiffy Lube closing down on Independence to make way for lane-widening. (Rudy made the Jiffy Lube uniform *work,* even Dorrie was impressed.)

"I like RayRay," Dorrie said, sitting beside Josh on the couch, perusing the goods on charlottedownlow.com, in her advisory role, ready to sanction or forbid an online contact.

> WAT IT DO MY NIGGA. . . . . WAT IT IZ??? YO wudup fellas ya boii RayRay b outta brooklyn nu yurk. new 2 tha downlo system checken shyt out. da kidd iz mad laid back luv 2 blaze, smoking treez, and most deff a FREAK. and all wayz lookin 2 meet new headz. if u read my joint & wana know more screem atya RayRay.

Ray let his face picture show; had the thug thing down, he was fierce and hard and buff as any gangsta rap star. God, what Josh wouldn't give for one night with one of these guys. Not a middle-class Kappa Alpha Psi frat boy at Emory pretend-thug, but a *real* banger.

"I'd get in that stream," Josh said.

"I hear that."

> YO, SUP WIT YALL? DIS BE DAT ONE AND ONLY NIGGA TRELL, HOLDIN IT DOWN, ON HURR COME AT ME CORRECT AND YOU'LL GAIN MUCH RESPECT, I DUN BEEN THRU ALOT WIT PEOPLE ON DIS HERE MADHOUS! DONT HAVE

TIME TO DEAL WIT NO FEMS, IF DAT WAS DA CASE I WOULD FUKK MY GIRL, EAZYSKETCHIN', PRODUCING, SUPERVISIN MY KORNER KREW, GETTIN BLAZED, DICKIN' BITCHEZ. O U WANNA PLAY GAMES BIIIIATCH? JUS LET YOU KNOW,,,, NIGGA ABOUT TO GET BROOOOOKKKE OFF. . . . . THAT'S RIGHT, YO BOY FROM NEWTON IS IN DA HOOOOUS MUHFUKKAS

Dorrie shrieked before ranting: "What — this gangsta is from Newton, N.C.? *Newton* in da house? Negro, this is metro-fuck-you-politan Charlotte, North Carolina! You come correct to *us* with your two-bit Dollar Store played-out country ass from *Newton* . . ."

Josh loved it when Dorrie went ghetto on someone. Dorrie who had spent three summers abroad studying the old masters, in Paris, Madrid, and Florence respectively. "Newton stays out in the yard, it don't *get* in da muthafuckin' house," she muttered, the storm over.

Every once in a while, Josh thought he recognized someone from a bar or high school; Dorrie was sure *wideopen* was an elder in the church she grew up in. One after the other, at the bottom of the profile with stats, invariably it read:

Out? No
Married or living with a woman? Yes
You identify as . . . Straight

And a little farther down, after height and weight and endowment, circumcised or not, was a stat for preferred sexual role:

Preferred position? Bottom

"Ha!" Dorrie laughed. "All these b-boys with their bling and signature NBA jackets and eight-hundred-dollar shoes, looking to take it in the hiney. Maybe they got used to it in jail."

"I need to get sent to jail," Josh whispered.

"One of them down east Sampson County brokedown jails in the swamps, niggas still in there for looking at a white woman in 1949. Where all the guards are black and mean as shit, letting the gen pop take turns with that new pretty whiteboy prisoner from Charlotte."

"Stop it — that's totally turning me on." They indulged this idea for a few minutes more, inventing dialogue and adding a new character: Warden Dorcas J. Jourdain, who managed the nearby women's correctional facility — with an iron hand.

They clicked on a few regulars they kept track of. There was *pledgemaster,* this hot Italian-American guy named Joey who wrote

Josh fairly regularly, bemoaning Josh's exclusive search for black guys when what he really needs is to meet "Little Joey." Then there was the now legendary Tyrell, who went by the dignified user name *sucknips69.*

"Yeah," said Dorrie, "still got that lame-ass picture."

Tyrell was as cautionary as Marlo. Josh chatted online with Tyrell, whose profile located him in "Charlotte," only to drive twenty miles into the sticks and find a man ten years older and fifty pounds heavier than the antediluvian Polaroid he had scanned for his profile picture. The bad thing was, Josh would tell Dorrie, was when you've thrown a night away like that, your card-carrying gay man will always decide oh-what-the-heck and go through with it. Tyrell, the photo-fraud whose every stated statistic was off by half, led him inside . . . past his grandmother, who sat on the sofa in her nightgown in the outer room of the shotgun shack.

"Evening, boys," she said.

Josh entered the bedroom to find several months of laundry piled on one half of the bed, and the unwashed sheets smelling strongly of . . . Tyrell. Sitting at a small desk was a thirteen-year-old boy who was typing away on the internet gay hookup site that Josh had used to meet Tyrell. Until seeing that, Josh never imagined he could have been chatting with kids some of the time. Tyrell told his cousin to move along; Tyrell's cousin gamely tried to interest Josh and Tyrell in a threeway ("I know how," he promised, in an adamant soprano), before being told to go watch TV with grandma.

"Nah, she don't know," Tyrell assured Josh. "Grams don't think that way."

Whoa, and Josh thought *his* family was steeped in denial. Josh told Tyrell that he could not have sex with every sound being broadcast to Tyrell's grandmother one thin wall away; Josh could hear her labored breathing even with Tyrell stomping about the room, moving piles of dirty laundry so they could have a small surface for lovemaking. Plus, Josh assumed a *Dateline* camera crew on the hunt for pedophiles would burst into the shotgun shack at any minute. Pudgy, unshowered Tyrell who hadn't brushed his teeth in an age was truly disappointed — he probably hadn't gotten anyone as far as the bedroom in years. Figured it'd be terminally hopeful/terminally horny Josh, thought Josh, who achieved this distinction.

Dorrie squealed with amusement every time he relived this encounter. "And you know he uses his little cousin as his fallback. Heh-heh, you took a trip to Jim Trueblood's cabin, yes you did."

Josh laughed too. But if Tyrell had been hot, Josh knew he would have gone for it, copulated quietly as possible, gathered himself up as well as he could and walked past grandma with an "Evening, ma'am."

Calvin Eakins Sr. was an African-American Democratic city councilman representing District Three when Josh's father was a Republican councilman. Unlike Duke Johnston, Calvin Eakins made a life in politics and moved on to being a state senator, then a powerful committee chairman in Raleigh, then a figure rarely off the front pages for rumors of corruption, graft, kickbacks, illegally obtained campaign contributions — but that was only the last few years. He was indicted early in 2007 and, as the case got harder for prosecutors to make, they started indicting his family members (in whose bank accounts he had laundered his ill-gotten gains) throughout 2008, in hopes of squeezing the truth out of the patriarch: his youngest daughter, his younger lawyer son, and his oldest son, Calvin, fellow alumnus of Mecklenburg Country Day, of no steady profession, unless you count low-level playboy.

Calvin called Josh and left a message on his landline. They hadn't spoken in nearly eight years.

Driving uptown, Josh looked up to see one of Annie's smiling, soft-focus billboards. Berma Bigglefield was another woman with a billboard: BERMA'S BAIL BONDS. You saw

Berma coming off I-277 heading toward the Mecklenburg County Courthouse. Again, the airbrushed shot, the trademark photo haze that all self-employed women on billboards required for their likenesses to meet the public. It was hard to tell with black women how old they were. Berma could have been . . . late forties? Maybe sixty? He'd have to ask Dorrie, if he ever decided to tell her about what he was doing.

He walked into a small bungalow, with a neon sign in every street-facing window: the one word blinking red BAIL and in the next window OPEN 24 HOURS, while in the one attic window a glowing blue neon that simply announced BERMA. And sitting at the crowded desk in a cheaply paneled room was . . . Berma herself!

"I came down here 'cause I saw your picture, Ms. Bigglefield," Joshua said. "You look even prettier in real life."

"Ain't you sweet? What can Berma do for you, sugar?"

Joshua had never been to a bail bondsman (or bondswoman) before. Calvin's bail was $20,000, sort of a slap on the wrist. But neither his daddy nor his family was in any state to come bail him out. Obstruction of justice. Just $2,000 and Calvin could be released. Joshua figured — no, he knew, it was $2,000 down the drain. Joshua had a few

IOUs that dated back to their days in high school.

"Now if he fails to appear in court," Joshua asked, "does that mean I owe all twenty thousand?"

"That's right, sugar. Berma's gonna always get her money back."

"Where do I sign?"

Joshua was then supposed to go to the lockup and present this to the assistant warden's secretary. Sort of exciting, wardens and jails, all this official court lingo and big stone edifices of columns and judicial severity. Lawyers looking smart and stylish, and all the strapping, thuggish defendants in orange jumpsuits, the occasional media person, a camera crew setting up outside the courthouse steps.

"Only you, Calvin, could come out of a jail looking like a *GQ* cover," Josh said when his friend emerged.

"Shirt needs pressing," he said.

They walked in the unseasonal February warmth to the parking deck. No one said anything during the walk but that was from overabundance of topics.

"You still driving this piece of shit," Calvin hummed, getting into Joshua's 1996 Taurus.

"I've kept it on the road for over ten years."

For what Joshua put into the deathmobile, Calvin explained, he could have leased. What followed was one of Calvin's patented how-to-look-rich-for-no-money scams, how to legally welsh on a lease agreement, how to get out of a payment or two while being seen in a BMW. Joshua nodded as he threaded the car through the narrow concrete spiral ramps leading to the pay station. All this lifestyle savvy and inside dope had gotten Calvin nowhere. No job lasted very long, no good first impression was left untarnished.

"Why'd you call me?" Joshua asked, interrupting a speech on how Josh was a fool to rent an apartment when he could own.

"My brother and I aren't speaking."

There was a pause, as if that were sufficient. "Well," Josh prompted, "that's *one* out of ten thousand people I would have thought you'd call before me. Mother?"

"Total meltdown. When Dad got arrested she took to the bed."

"Why not someone on your dad's staff?"

"Shit, they're all trying to keep out of prison themselves," Calvin said lightly, showing no signs of worry or concern for his own fate. "Or they're looking for new jobs."

"College friends?"

"Too embarrassing. Bound to give my enemies satisfaction."

"Your little black book? What was her name . . ."

"No no no. A girl gets you out of jail and then you're *really* indebted. Almost like a marriage proposal. She sees her pathetic ass sitting by your side at trial, dabbing her eyes with your handkerchief." Calvin pulled the seat forward, then bent it back to lie down, staring at the roof of the interior. "I'm not seeing anyone anyway." An odd pause.

"How about you?" Calvin asked.

"Eh, nothing serious. Just a regular-sex thing." For some reason, Joshua felt his heart race, wondered if his face was coloring. Was this a swoon? He wasn't sure what a swoon was. "Maybe once a week —"

"I envy that. Just a sex thing. Never could get that arranged with any woman. They wanted to marry me and reform me and generally domesticate me. Sad to say."

"So why'd you call me?" Joshua tried again.

"I knew you'd come get me."

"We haven't talked in about, what, eight years."

"But we're still friends."

"Oh I still like you," Joshua said, all smiles, "but friends keep up, don't disappear for years at a time, and then only call to get bailed out of jail. Money I'm fairly sure I won't see back."

"You didn't have to do it. Why did you?"

Just to see, Joshua thought. See what he looked like. Reintroduce a character back into his life, despite the surefire wear and tear and drama that hovered around Calvin. Who was left in Joshua's life who remembered him from his rich-kid private-school goofy, nerdy, smart-kid, class-outcast, school newspaper, drama club, band-geek days? "I was happy to do it," Joshua told Calvin, to keep the conversation going. "Where am I taking you, by the way?"

"A motel, I guess."

"You have money for a motel?"

"Nope."

Joshua pulled into a service station parking lot. No sense driving aimlessly. Calvin hopped out for cigs and a giant Coke. They dehydrated you in jail. The cell-block water fountain tasted funny — and God knows what you were catching, drinking after the scum of the earth — and then they barely air-conditioned the place. Calvin walked a few yards then circled back around to Joshua's driver's-side window. "Uh, can you lend me a five?"

Joshua handed a five over.

I'm being used, Joshua thought as Calvin walked away. Used *again,* to be more precise. Big surprise, there. Take a number. Calvin had previously been the screwup of his family. Now, with State Senator Calvin Eakins Sr. under corruption and racketeering indictments, that distinction was a little harder to obtain. His father's whole public arrest and downfall must come as a relief to Calvin. So much for living up to his daddy's impossibly high standards. But still, as dysfunctional as Calvin is, Joshua thought, I must be more so to keep dealing with him. Joshua decided he wouldn't offer Calvin his sofa. For one thing, Calvin might never leave. Joshua would end up the pathetic-ass friend in court, following the proceedings, dabbing his eyes with a handkerchief. Second, it recalled an old social desperation, dorky Joshua wanting to be friends with cool Calvin more than Calvin wanted to be with him. Oh for God's sake, Joshua told himself, high school was a quarter of a century ago — offer the guy your couch!

"I was going to quit," Calvin said, bouncing into the passenger seat, shaking his box of cigarettes. "But what's a racist show trial without a good smoke?"

"So your dad's innocent?" Joshua pulled back on the boulevard.

"Hell no. I'm sure he was skimming just like every other crook in Charlotte or Raleigh, but you see how the SBI is only making a case against the powerful black state senator, right?"

"They just convicted the white Speaker of the House, Jim Black. They're putting a number of powerful Democrats in jail."

"Believe me, race is in the mix."

Joshua nodded. Dorrie's much offered opinion on any celebrated black trial was that blacks had been railroaded and scapegoated through the decades for so much that they didn't do, that if they could play the race card successfully to get out of a few things they *did* do, well, it's sort of karmic redress. Still, a crook is a crook.

"So, uh, Josh. Can I use your sofa for the night?"

Joshua smiled a little.

"Poor homeless black boy," Calvin intoned melodramatically. "Nowhere to go . . . probably go down with *ma brothas* at the homeless shelter down on Tryon, get a urine-stained cot."

"Your family is twice as wealthy as mine. You don't want to be with them?"

"I want to be with my funk soul brother Josh-oo-a. Ain't you my *wigga*?" Calvin crossed his arms like he was in a rap posse. "JJ is pretty fly for a white guy." Calvin wove together several hip-hop phrases, all out of date. Joshua was more up on black music than Calvin, if anyone wanted to know. Calvin talking gangsta — that always played nicely with his white coterie in high school, Joshua thought. For a bunch of soft white innocents, Calvin was dangerous and uncharted racial territory, but if he tried to hang with Charlotte's notorious Hidden Valley Kings? He'd be dead.

". . . and I promise not to have any crack ho's over to your crib, dawg. I'll turn my bi-atches out somewhere else . . ."

"Oh Jesus." Joshua tried not to laugh, or be charmed again.

Calvin returned to his normal smooth

baritone: "I'll flush the toilet. You can keep a stack of separate glasses and plates so you don't have to eat after me and get any of my black cooties."

"It's already a little late for that."

Calvin went quiet. Joshua pulled to a stop at the light, then looked over to see if that remark was over the line. But Calvin was smiling slyly. He exhaled Winston smoke, keeping his level, inscrutable gaze on his friend. Big brown eyes of great mesmeric power, eyes that once moved the stars around in the sky. "Don't go there, baby. That was a long time ago."

By making an allusion to their teenage homosexual experimentation, Joshua detected that he'd gained a little power, the power of the person who might say what was never said. "All right. But no running around in your little thong underwear," Joshua pursued, extending his run. "No flopping out of your shorts, teasing the gay guy."

"I can't help it if I've kept myself up, got the body of a twenty-year-old." That he did. "But that was . . . you were the only one that kinda shit happened with."

"Now now. You can tell me about the fun you had in jail."

"I held the niggas off. Your boy is alllll man."

"I'm all man, too, Calvin."

"You know what I mean."

"I certainly do."

Josh had achieved a mastery of getting out of family occasions.

The store made for a good excuse. Josh had established the story that his temperamental boss, Mr. Mundy, was always calling him to work on weekends, at all hours of the day and night — Josh could invoke each branch around town (and miles north at Concord Mills) as a site of a crisis that required him to speed away and miss whatever family requirement he had begrudgingly committed to.

"I believe I shall have to have a word with that slavedriver you work for," his mother said once, quite cross when Josh skipped a Mint by Gaslight one year.

Truth was, Josh worked exactly when he wanted; Mr. Mundy was a softhearted old queen who let him do as he pleased. Josh wasn't sure the clothing store made any money at all. It was called Uomo Modal, and the flagship store which Josh managed was prominent in the South Park Mall. These stores featured mostly silk Italian-cut shirts and ties, plus terribly expensive faux-European accessories with Italian names, Bulgari platinum tie clips with an inlay of tanzanite — what was tanzanite? Josh sold that stuff without having a clue — Raffaello cuff links, Armani Executive sunglasses.

Joshua assumed Mr. Mundy was independently wealthy and the stores were a front for importing something criminal . . . *or* a losing enterprise convenient to Mr. Mundy's tax portfolio . . . *or* an excuse for constant trips to Italy, where a whole lavish vacation to Fashion Week in Milan might be a business write-off . . . *or* an excuse to hire and be surrounded by lovely, mostly indolent Southern gayboys who looked good in Italian clothes.

Josh usually worked alongside Manuel, who dabbled in drag on weekends. He was just starting to compete in pageants. He barely had to shave and had that African-American lean smoothness which is the envy of the drag-performing world — no Adam's apple, too. Manuel put on a wig and he was halfway there. A lovely young man, but not macho (or dark) enough for Josh to obsess about. Josh had heard that some clerks (i.e, Manuel) and branch managers had "grown close" to Mr. Mundy; some had even gotten to come along to Milan some years.

Dorrie would say, "I'd get in the stream, if I got to go to Milan."

"Can't do it. Can't get in that stream," Josh said glumly.

At thirty-two years old, Josh felt the full weight of having no career to speak of. Maybe Mr. Mundy would let him take over the empire when Mr. Mundy retired. Maybe Josh would one day be the soft, overdressed old queen with too much cologne, wearing rose-pastel-tinted linens, silk shirts with cravats covering the aging throat, hiring young twinks to be clerks and cashiers. Josh played this scenario of life failure to goad himself to greater ambitions, but it never worked. Didn't sound so bad, actually.

Anyway, the Golden Age of Family Avoidance was done. After Jerilyn's infamy as the Christmas Dinner Shooter, there had been lots of family interaction, a circling of the wagons and SUVs. Dad was on TV with regularity as the family front person — good Lord, his father was charming, that comforting buttery North Carolina accent soothing and explaining away every rough edge.

"Your dad must've never lost a court case," Dorrie said.

And all the bad Jerilyn publicity had proven good publicity for the Skirmish at the Trestle Civil War Re-enactment coming up April 19, 2008. Dorrie, whose profession was setting up attractive webpages, was summoned to help Mr. Johnston expand and improve his event site, so people could register (with a credit card), commit to permitted commercial activities (hot dogs and funnel cakes, horseback rides for the kids), sign oaths not to shoot real ordnance, promise not to be drunk, use foul language — this was a family event — and promise not to come as a Confederate general. That was a real problem in Civil War re-enactments, no one wanted to be a grunt, everyone craved rank — generals outnumbered privates at these things, if you didn't curtail it. And no one wanted to play a Yankee soldier, because that would mean investing in a Union uniform, which was not how the ardent Southern re-enactor chose to spend his disposable income.

The real estate tycoons and Mr. Boatwright, though they might be every bit the shysters and crooks that Annie made them out to be (and she would know), had done the Johnston family the great favor of revitalizing their patriarch. Josh loved to hear his father talking with the other committee members on the Catawba River Trestle Historical Preservation Society (a group of old Civil War–crazy codgers, like his dad), at the Charlottetowne Country Club, in the doldrums of a big Sunday lunch.

"But that's just it, Ben," he heard his father tell Mr. Badger, "if the grounds were simply a public park with some picnic tables and a plaque, think of how it would be graffitied. Kids would come and drink beer there, gangs would make drug deals. But as a preserve within a gated community, the land is especially preserved. Anyone can be permitted to visit the historical park," Duke added with animation. "School groups, historical societies — I have the developers' word that the gatekeepers will let anyone through to a proposed small parking lot near the clearing, and the riverfront and trestle."

"Well, it *would* be advantageous to keep the riffraff out," said Mr. Haslett, a man who wore his white beard in flowing nineteenth-century fashion. All the better to portray his many-times-removed ancestor General Jubal Early. With the passion for *J* names in the family, Josh was quietly happy not to have been named "Jubal."

Said Mr. Haslett, "You get your college liberal types who might want to protest a Confederate shrine, so a shrine on private property might not be such a bad thing. I suppose we can vote as a committee to allow this development deal."

By February, the family house on Providence Road had become command and control, a barely functioning chaos. Preservation Committee members came in and out of the house at all hours (according to Alma, who was beckoned to provide hospitality regardless), small crises erupted and the phone rang into the night (according to his mother), otherwise habitable venues were turned into war rooms, maps and posters and battle diagrams draped over sofas and propped themselves against lamps . . .

"I'm putting everyone to work!" Duke Johnston declared, enlivened by a steady flow of coffee. "You're the English major," his father pronounced, hands on Joshua's shoulders, pinned to the chair at the dinner table. "Be nice to get something back from my exorbitant investment in a Chapel Hill education."

"Dad, I think you know I did nothing but drink and spend money on expensive restaurant meals and home décor while I was in Chapel Hill."

"I was indeed aware, but I have always hoped that you might have brushed against the English language from time to time."

Josh, conscripted, was in charge of Written Materiel.

April 19, 1865 . . . the War was winding toward defeat for the Confederacy and Richmond, Atlanta, and Columbia lay in ruins. Charlotte was now the only major city of consequence left standing in the South. Sherman burned Jackson, Mississippi; left three buildings standing in what was once Oxford; dismantled and razed the whole of Meridian, pulling down churches, schools, private homes. From Chattanooga to Atlanta to Macon, he famously plundered in a 60-mile-wide blight of scorched-earth destruction.

Then he turned to South Carolina. "I almost tremble at her fate," wrote Sherman, the *her* being South Carolina, "but feel that she deserves all that seems in store for her." After Orangeburg and Columbia, which

Sherman watched burn to the ground, it was Charlotte's turn, and the city braced itself for the inevitable William Tecumseh Sherman treatment.

Gold and silver were buried in backyards, jewels hidden, women and children packed off to points north and west (the famed diarist Mary Chestnut was sent to Lincolnton), while the men formed militias. Norfolk had fallen long ago but its famous ironworks, the forges that made artillery, shells, bullets, had been relocated to Charlotte, and the trains that steamed to and from Charlotte were laden with arms for the final battles of the long conflict. Columbia was merely ninety miles away — how could Sherman resist Charlotte?

Yet General Sherman could not resupply himself or his colossal army or the phalanx of freed slaves forming another army behind him. So after a feint or two in Charlotte's direction, he headed east for the sea.

For the moment, Charlotte's rail supremacy remained untouched. Foodstuffs, clothes, medical supplies, all were transported along the most important rail link left to the ravaged South, the line that had supplied General Lee before his surrender at Appomattox, the line that now shipped supplies to the cities smoldering in Sherman's wake. And this mighty iron highway had but one vulnerable passage, the longest river bridge on any north-south railway, the trestle over the Catawba River at Nations Ford, ten miles south of Charlotte in Fort Mill, South Carolina.

"It's just too terribly exciting, isn't it?" Mr. Johnston said, clapping his hands. "And Joshua, it's properly 'Nation Ford.' A colonial-era Indian reserve was made for the Catawba Nation; Fort Mill was built to defend them against the Shawnees, who kept attacking. Somehow the Ford picked up the *s* after the War."

Union General George Stoneman, whose rogue operations and sneak attacks throughout the South had made fearsome legends of "Stoneman's Raiders," steadily advanced down the Catawba River Valley with a goal of destroying this essential trestle. A band of Raiders under Colonel William J. Palmer, with just four hundred men, crossed the mountains, marched through the foothills, and traversed the river valley, encountering skirmishes at Morganton and at Statesville.

The Charlotte Home Guards, valiant men who for years had dreaded the war finally coming to their community, who had trained for just such an assault, built fortifications on the Charlotte side of the river; Confederate General Sam Ferguson and the Third

South Carolina Cavalry made their way to Charlotte.

His father weighed in: "Not much of a force, but we'll not advertise that. Or what a slowpoke Ferguson was. He marched his South Carolinians to Charlotte doing God knows what, while Palmer slipped easily past him to the bridge. Did Ferguson imagine Palmer was going to march the Raiders right down Tryon Street? Of course, Claymore Ferguson, his ancestor, will come with the Ashley Dragoons from the South Carolina Third — oh that will be quite a show. This website is not the place to question General Ferguson's failure to go straight to the trestle."

Josh and his father spent the morning writing and rewriting. Finally, their ramble came to the Skirmish itself. Shots were exchanged. Palmer set fire to the trestle, and that put an end to the rail link. The Skirmish at the Trestle . . . over in a few minutes, from what it sounded like. Fortunately, his father and his cohorts were planning for this historical profundity to play out over an entire weekend.

Duke and his confederates had checked the train timetables to make sure the proposed cannon display did not coincide with the afternoon hundred-car freight runs. Norfolk & Southern were anything but cooperative. No person shall walk upon the tracks; any occupation of the bridge over the Catawba itself will be considered trespassing and the person subject to immediate arrest. In fact, N & S assured them they would have an extra cadre of railroad cops on duty for the weekend.

None of that stopped the Skirmish plans from turning baroque. "Major" Badger wondered if a stuntman could be hired. Five Yankees could take the bridge, brandishing explosives, but before they could do their dastardly work, the Charlotte Home Guards would heroically appear on the bank and impressively pick them off. Oh, the four nonstuntmen could fall on the trestle, but the stuntman could stagger to the edge and plummet forty feet into the river. Didn't they make Hollywood movies down in Wilmington now? Couldn't someone find a falling-off-a-trestle specialist? A month was put into this project only to learn that no stuntman was interested in plummeting into the rocky two-foot depth of the mighty Catawba. They could perhaps fasten a giant foam landing cushion to the nearby rocks but that . . . that sort of lowered the tone, somehow.

What about, Colonel Haslett suggested, one of those stationary fireworks displays from the trestle? Pinwheels and fountains of sparks and a few noisemakers booming away from the top of the bridge? The families and kids would love that!

"Mr. Johnston," said the representative of

Norfolk & Southern, this time making a quite serious home visit, standing in the Johnston family foyer. "Under no circumstances is anyone ever to set foot on the railroad trestle, a railroad, I might add, in constant use through the day and night. Every bit the vital link in 2008 that it was in 1865." Josh drifted away from the scene, leaving his father to it when the railroad lawyer pulled out papers, injunctions, cease and desist court orders. He heard mild defeat in his father's tone: "Oh really now . . ." and "You think all this bother is necessary?" and "Why don't we sit down and talk about it over some of Alma's legendary chocolate chess pie?"

A final hush-hush secret mission was undertaken to bribe the nearest stationmaster to turn a blind eye on the day of the event. Attempts to appeal to Southern Civil War sentiment failed, mainly because the line manager had strict orders and, inconveniently, was African-American. Very well. The railroad didn't object, did it, to the trestle being illuminated in red shimmery lights in the evening to suggest its being burned down? The line manager gave the go-ahead for that, receiving the thanks of a grateful Confederacy. They offered him free entry passes for the whole family. He politely declined.

Duke Johnston and the high command surrendered on all plans involving the trestle; there was a note of sour grapes when Major

Badger said, "Well. Why even bother illuminating the trestle? What are we celebrating — its destruction by Yankees?"

"We'll stick with the cannon," said Colonel Haslett.

Joshua knew, from his homework, no cannon were fired in the historic fateful half hour in question, but it would be nice to see cannon go off. Contentedly, Joshua sat at his computer, in his boyhood bedroom, polishing and typing and answering e-mail queries from as far away as Worcester, England. And when Dorrie and his father were in his Civil War Study hashing out the web design downstairs, Josh sneaked a look at charlottedownlow.com. He smiled. There was a message from Nonso.

CDL had a following of twenty thousand members but some of them were white worshippers like Josh. The gamut of North Carolina's African-American closeted world was here, professionals, church deacons, married men, athletes, teachers, the hunky guy at Home Depot, the assistant vice president at First Union. Many profile photos did not show a face since this was "on the down low," and some went straight for the crotch shot, letting it all hang out.

"Damn, the black thing is surely true," Dorrie observed.

"Yep," said Josh.

Josh couldn't care less about endowments. That was the inevitable sneering summation of his gay acquaintances when they found out Josh was into black guys. *Oh,* their expressions (and sometimes extended banter) would say, *another size queen.*

When Josh was growing up, their housekeeper Alma's son Jeffrey would come over and he and Josh, both the same age, would play cowboys and make forts and sit on Josh's bunk bed looking through picture books on rainy days. Nothing was as important as Jeffrey coming over — he asked every morning if Jeffrey was coming to the house, and since Alma only came three days a week (but varying days), mostly Josh was disappointed. At Mecklenburg Country Day School there were just one or two black kids at that citadel of white privilege, including his lab partner, Ronny. Josh manipulated his teacher, his classmates, the planets and the stars, to end up "by chance" being assigned Ronny as a lab partner in seventh grade. Ronny was his first love and was oblivious. Then there was Calvin Eakins Jr.

Josh remembered that Calvin's school-age pursuits were mainly devoted to martial arts films and white girls but, during a sleepover or two, Calvin prodded Josh for some hormone-driven homoerotic touching and rolling around. It was all Josh could do to put up a mild resistance as if he didn't want to do this more than anything. I don't know, Josh remembered saying, aroused to new extremes.

"What do you mean, you don't know?" Calvin whispered in the dark bedroom, prodding without any malice. "You're a hundred percent fag."

Josh's love of African-American boys was primal, congenital, conceived in utter innocence of sex stereotype, some mystery in the beautiful skin itself that drew him, would always draw him as close as he was allowed to get . . .

Calvin was now residing on Josh's sofa, rarely leaving the living room, never more than a few yards from ESPN. Josh discovered Calvin had ordered some pay-per-view without asking but, aside from that, he was a pretty low-key houseguest.

"Lakers versus Celtics in five minutes!" Calvin yelled from the sofa, a room away. "Anybody in the mood for a pizza?"

"You paying?" Dorrie yelled back. Silence. "Thought so," she said, before whispering to Josh, huddled at his laptop, "Any estimated time of departure?"

Josh shrugged.

"I hate to think you actually blew that loser in there —"

"Sssshhh!"

"Okay then," said Dorrie, "show me your Favorites."

On CDL you could click and drag a profile to a door graphic on the left (a closet door, presumably) labeled MY FAVORITES. A click on the door would bring them up.

"Um. There're some weird choices in there that I cannot justify to you."

"I'll withhold savage commentary about the miscreants you're in negotiations with." Then she grabbed the mouse and clicked on the closet door before he could stop her. The standout was a Nigerian boy with the most out-of-proportion blinding tooth-filled smile to his lean oval face.

"Whoa, look at him," Dorrie marveled. "It's like one of those racist minstrel-show posters. Somebody go get dis chile a slice a watermelon!"

"How could anyone not want to see that first thing in the morning?"

"Africans have great teeth," Dorrie said. "Then we got dragged over here and started eating American crap and it's dentures by the time we're forty."

"I think he's adorable."

Nonso was from Lagos, Nigeria, and the six photos revealed a slender, chiseled body and his skin was purple-blue dark, which made the perfection of the big smile all the more striking.

"And . . . oh no, kid. Uh-uh. Sorry to say, he is a certified nutjob," Dorrie pronounced, while reading:

HELLO AMERICA HE MAKE ME CRYING SO MUCH WHEN I WANT REMOVE MY PROFILE FROM HERE . . HE WAS SO ANGREY AND HURT IN SAME TIME WITH ME . . . I NEVER BEEN SEE HIM BE LIKE THIS . . YES HIS REALLY LOVE ME SO MUCH . . AND I BELIVE IN THAT HERE IS SOME FROM HIS RO-MATIC EMAIL FOR ME------->>
-------((My Dearest Nonso,

How I love you from afar. I wish I could snap my fingers and make you appear beside me. Meeting you online has been one of the highlights of my life. You made me smile during the darkest times of my life. You made me laugh when all I wanted to do is cry. You are so much more than just a friend to me. Words can not even begin to say how much you being in my life means to me. Always know I am with you in spirit.
Love you always, forever and a day.

from Bob

!!!!!!!SO THAT IS WHY I BACK AGAIN HERE !!!!!!!!!I
^^
NOW FOR ABOUT ME
---->>((PLEASE TO READ MY PROFILE))<>------
1/ IAM SINGLE
2/ SEMPLE YOUNG

3/ SO VERY HANDSOME
4/ HONEST AND SERIOUS AND
5/ VERY ROMATIC
6/ VERY SWEETY ANF FRIENDLY
7/ SO SINCERE
8/ I VERY VERY SINCETIVE
9/ HERE IAM FOR FIND TRUE LOVE
10/ NON WASTER OF THE TIME
11/ ENOUGH OF HURTING ME
12/ BE HONEST AND SERIOUS WITH ME . . OR . . LEAVE ME ALONE.
13/ IAM POOR BOY BUT HEART IS VERY VERY

RICH OTHER SEID OF ME/ WELL IAM VERY LOVLY ONE . . WHO LIKE JOKE AND LAUGH . . VERY ROMATIC. SOME GUYS HERE . . THEY THINKING IAM VERY SADLY ONE . . YES THAT TRUE . . BECAUSE IAM LONLEY . .

looking for white americcan boy for reall love.

my life nothing without love.

"I thought they spoke English in Nigeria," Dorrie said, engrossed.

"He's from some tribe," Josh began, not sure which one or why it didn't speak English. "Hey, the Skirmish at the Trestle. You really think —"

"I'm still reading the African Queen here.

Don't try to change the subject."

some time i meet gays here but only SECRET life here. no desco here . . . some groups gays make it partey some time here . . but i dont like go there. because i know they what looking for . . I WISH have even a old man from usa who is very honest and serious for find about true love.not just sexy sexy . . . my dream is to study in USA and learn my better englsh.
---->>((. . . U KNOW SOME TIMES WHEN IAM BED . . I THINKING WE GO TOGATHER OUTSIDE AND SHOW THE USA GAYS PEOPLE HOW MUCH I LOVE YOU. HOW NICE WHEN HAVE SHOWER TOGATHER . . HOW NICE WHEN I LOOK AT UR BEATFULL FACE IN SLOW PLACE WITH BLUE CANDLES AND VERY SLOW MUSIC . . .
IAM SO SORRY FOR LONG MASSEGE . . AND ALSO SORRY FOR MY ENGLISH BECAUSE DONT HAVE GOOD SPEAKING . . but WILL LEARN IN USA NO NAUTY FOTOS OR SEX ON TELIPFONE OR SEXY THING ON SEX CAM. . . .YOU MUST KNOW IAM FOR LOVE.

nonso

"Whoa," Dorrie said at last.

"I wanna get in the stream."

"You are NOT getting in that stream."

Josh was quiet a moment. "I'm not sure why he posts his profile in Charlotte. He may want to come to school here. I was thinking of sending him a link to —"

"I absolutely, as your Designated Black Friend, forbid you from taking up with him, if he somehow makes it over here. We cannot have that kind of hysterical gay drama in our lives."

Josh sighed. "I don't think there's much of a chance of Nonso being admitted to our exclusive social circle."

By mid-March Dorrie's Skirmish at the Trestle website had garnered 95,000 hits. Cynical as they were, even Dorrie and Josh looked forward to it, checking the site daily to gauge its popularity, and answer queries.

— Officers are expected to bring sufficient troops to justify their rank.
— Any brigade, battalion or unit commander directly disobeying the order of their respective overall commander will be subject to removal from the event.
— Officers have a responsibility to know the medical condition of the men in their commands!

"I imagine," Josh said, "this is a mecca for three-hundred-pound armchair warriors out there in the heat, clad head to toe in wool when it's eighty-five degrees. The death toll will exceed the death toll of the actual skirmish."

"Your dad said they'll have an ambulance driver hiding in the bushes somewhere."

— Unit colors must be full size and correctly constructed according to each army's standards. Unit colors will be carried during battle scenarios only with the approval of event military staff.
— No tent camping is allowed in the parking area. Hookups for RVs will not be available.
— Bedding straw will be provided for purchase by the event host.

The farm collective that owned the land on the other side of the river was gung ho. They would lease their field for the campers and RVs and modern campsites and set up concessions. The farmer's son would drive a shuttle bus back and forth to the north side of the Catawba River, so he needed to be specially insured and indemnified, too. More details, more contracts, more paper, more stacks of paper, more lost stacks of paper, more doomed cries of "Alma!" and "Jerene, darling!" asking where the lost stacks of paper had run off to.

— Women may portray combatants with the approval of their immediate commanders. Every reasonable effort must be made to disguise their gender.

"Some of us," said Dorrie, "won't have to work that hard on our disguise."

She was still on for going in drag as a Confederate soldier; Duke Johnston was contributing the uniform, scabbard, powder horn, and the insignia of a North Carolina unit that had black Confederate soldiers. "I'm nervous now," she told Josh. "I'll be traipsing around in a thousand dollars' worth of museum antiquities. Not much time for rape and pillage of the local white women."

— Modern eyeglasses will not be tolerated on the battlefield. Those needing period eyewear should make the needed arrangements prior to the event to acquire same.
— All uniforms should be constructed of natural fiber materials. Uniforms should also be of a proper design or style.
— Shoes and boots must be of the proper construction. Jefferson boots, brogans, and period cut boots are highly recommended. Modern military combat boots, cowboy or work boots will not be allowed. All re-enactors will wear shoes of an ac-

ceptable fashion.

— Bayonets must remain sheathed at all times.
— No horses will be ridden through camps or sutlers' areas at any time during the event. Riders are asked to be particularly careful around the large number of spectators expected for this event.
— All horses/mules will be properly groomed and shod.
— Horsemen will maintain control of their animals at all times.
— Horsemen will bring their own feed and provender.

Provender, thought Josh, reading his father's notes. *Sutlers.* Even the words were romantically archaic and exciting.

Dorrie and Josh were spending every weekend at the Johnston house in the month leading up to the Skirmish. Getting the credit card PayPal hooked up to the website was proving an ordeal, so Josh left Dorrie and his dad at the downstairs computer and went up to his childhood room again. He lay on his short, teenager's bed, stared at the shelves and the way the streetlight projected a shadow of the window frames on the far wall, squares stretched to rhombuses. In a year or so this room of secrets that, somehow, had not incinerated from all the adolescent longing would belong to some other person.

Mom and Dad, Josh understood, were going to sell this home (*had* to sell it, given their finances) and move to the new gated community on the Catawba, when it was finished being built. The developers would start construction on the site the Monday after the Skirmish re-enactment. Going to visit Mom and Dad in some South Carolina faux-antebellum-themed enclave, Josh thought, would be different, though, and a little sad.

He remembered coming back, a decade ago, to this house after five years at Chapel Hill. This was the beginning of his year and a half separation from Dorcas Jourdain as constant companion and adviser. To leave gay-friendly Chapel Hill was to be shown the door of Paradise by the flaming sword, condemned to his room in his mom and dad's house where loneliness had been practiced and perfected. Joshua dutifully had carried the box of college artifacts up to his room but his photo album was too incendiary for prying eyes, so he deconstructed it, peeling out the more salacious photos. Birthday parties where cute boys made out with him in the coat room, amateur theater openings and the endless post-performance parties, weekends at some rich boy's parents' house at Wrightsville Beach, where he sat until three A.M. on the cottage's steps with his arm around Alex Blayton, the only black guy on the UNC tennis team that year, talking about whether Alex might be gay or not. They ended up kissing, so you'd think that would have constituted an answer, but Alex was ignorant of what he wanted to an unusual depth. And that shot of him tongue-kissing Sanjay Patel on his birthday. Very shy and self-effacing and barely speaking above a whisper, a painfully thin boy whose effect was dependent upon his large liquid brown eyes and tremendous eyelashes that, Joshua thought, you could hang Christmas ornaments from. Well, at least the Patels were loaded, his dad one of the richest surgeons in North Carolina. See, Mom? Only the queers of "quality"!

Where had those photos gone? For years he would give the search one more try, hoping under some desk drawer or in the back of some closet the too-well-hidden envelope would miraculously show itself. Maybe Alma found the photos and destroyed them so his mother would never see them. Alma always stiffened when Josh asked about her son Jeffrey and how he was getting on, always was quick to mention how much he was dating, dating all those women, so many girls. Josh once asked for Jeffrey's e-mail address or phone number so these childhood friends could be in touch and Alma affected not to know it. Yeah, Alma threw those pictures away.

■ ■ ■ ■

"I'd a been here sooner," Josh told Dorrie, "but I got the good-for-nothing black girl at the Wilco, talking on her cell, not knowing how to work the credit card swipe."

"Why can't it be 'a good-for-nothing girl'? Why does it have to be 'the good-for-nothing *black* girl'?"

"Because when I say 'good-for-nothing black girl' you know just what I'm talking about. Long enamel fingernails painted fuchsia, crazy hair straightened and then molded into something that looks like a melted black ice-cream cone, talking on the cell to Shenequah or Lakeesha. You said one of those last week."

"When?"

"When I asked you why it took so long for you to come over, you said that you got behind a 'slow-ass old white man' on Tyvola Road. Why not just say 'slow-ass old man'?"

"Because it was a slow-ass old *white* man, in an old 1970s junk car and there he is wearing *his hat* to drive — you know what I'm talking about."

"And you know what I'm talking about when I talk about the good-for-nothing black girl behind the counter."

"Speaking of. When you gonna throw good-for-nothing Calvin out of the apartment?"

Dorrie followed with. "Gettin' sick of his sorry, sorry ass being around all the muthafuckin' time."

"He'll be moving on soon. My porn collection is, strangely, not to his taste."

Dorrie and Joshua would drive to the mixed neighborhoods of Charlotte when they were bored and play black-house/white-house.

"Oh this ain't even close," Dorrie would say, waving it away. "Black house. Yard looks like shit, grills on the windows, porch railing painted black. A white person would have painted it white."

And down the block, Josh's turn: "It's a white house. Appliance on the porch — never fails. Black people would worry about it being ripped off, or they'd take the old nonworking washer out to the country and dump it —"

"Next to one of those NO DUMPING ALLOWED signs," Dorrie concurred. In North Carolina, that particular sign had an opposite effect on the population.

"But an old white man," Josh went on, "thinks he's gonna fix that piece of junk one day and so it stays on the porch. He thinks it's valuable."

But there was a several-years-old black Cadillac in the drive. "Not so sure now," said Dorrie. "No white people drive black Cadillacs."

"I think it depends on the interior."

Dorrie hopped out of their car and ran over to the Cadillac in the drive.

"Don't get shot," Josh called to her, listlessly.

She cupped her hands to the glass, peeked inside and hopped back to the car. "Maroon and velvety."

"Black house!" they called out in unison.

Dorrie was laughing at a profile:

> LET ME SAY SOMETHING TO ALL YOU PEOPLE THAT HIT ME UP AND ACT LIKE YOUR ASS CANT SPEAK TO A NIGGA AFTER WE MEET WHEN YOU PLAINLY SAID YOU WANTED TO BE CHILL AND HANG OUT AND BE FRIENDS AND SHIT. NOTHER THING. THIS SITE IS BOUT 5% TOP AND 95% BOTTOM, AND HALF OF THEM TOPS, YOU GET THEM HOME, THEY BOTTOMS TOO.

"Don't get me started," Dorrie began, "on straight black women and what shit they'll put up with. The blindness. Oh Oprah and Maury and Jerry Springer, everybody can do a show on down-low brothers but nobody thinks it's *their* man."

"Send those sex-starved women to me," called out Calvin, stretched out on the couch before the TV, in T-shirt and sweatpants, the same ones worn yesterday. “I’ll make up for all that faggot dick.”

Dorrie called back, “Uh, Calvin, I think these women are looking for a dick that can get hard.”

“I’m hard right now, Carpetmunch. Whyn’t you come sit on some’n that isn’t plastic for a change?”

“Triflin’ ass-under-indictment waste of space,” she uttered under her breath. Back to charlottedownlow. “Hm, Josh, he’s cute. Might have to get in that stream.”

“Yum,” he said, looking at a handsome thirty-two-year-old man, who was brave enough to post a face picture. “Oh I’d get in the stream.”

Calvin interrupted: “What’s all this ‘stream’ business you guys keep saying? ‘Oh I’d get in the stream.’ What’s up with that?”

> Das right bitches all u fuckin fem sissi-boys, throwback looking, fat stank ass cheese puff niggas need NOT apply because aint shit yall can do fo me aiight Wit dat said all da niggas who got a bit of morality get at me. i dont kno wat to think . . . tried to be serious wit 2 many guys . . . and got thrown out like dirty drawrs . . . im sick and tired of bein sick and tired of all the games and gamepla-yas . . . DO I LOOK LIKE A MO-

NOPLY BOARD . . . if u real and serious bout wat u want get at me baby

Josh was touched by the plaintive "baby" at the end of it. Alas, the guy had checked the "married" box so that ruled him out. "What does 'cheese puff nigga' mean?" he asked Dorrie.

"No idea, but I'm gonna start using it. Hey Calvin!"

Dorrie let loose a string of insults culminating in the new one, and she was repaid in kind. Josh decided it was as good a time as any to go to the toilet. His friends continued to squabble, and he lingered a bit in the hallway to monitor the exchange of abuse. But from his vantage point in the hallway, he could watch Dorrie snooping; he saw that she clicked on a box called MESSAGE HISTORY which would let you see your correspondence over the last three months. Her click would reveal a few pages of his back-and-forth chat with Nonso, endearments and sex talk, talk of Nonso applying to a Charlotte-area school, talk of them being together.

Dorrie turned around to see if Joshua had caught her snooping; they looked at each other. Rather than act sheepish and apologize, she was stern. "What did I tell you about this project?"

■ ■ ■ ■

Joshua had seen dawn a few times staying out late in the clubs — well, not Charlotte's clubs, but New York and Fort Lauderdale — but he had rarely woken *up* for dawn. Freeways empty, the drive-thru espresso place not even open yet, streetlights still on, the Charlotte skyline still glowing like Christmas for no one to see it, except himself on this Saturday morning, the only person awake in the whole world.

From Friday afternoon, the banks of the Catawba had become populated with campers and re-enactors; cars parked on both sides of the narrow U.S. 21, RVs and trailers were installed on the Rock Hill riverbank, the people with tents made their way down a red-clay path half a mile downstream on the Fort Mill–Charlotte shore, away from the busy U.S. route. Josh turned his car into the dirt road leading to the riverbank (newly bulldozed by the developers), he checked in with the two martinet parking managers who needed to see ID and "proof of uniform" — no one got in the historic zone without authentic period attire. Josh let them inspect the dry-cleaning bag lying on the seat with its gray woolen Rebel uniform; his being Duke Johnston's son counted for nothing. These re-enactors were serious folk.

Once the car was committed to the nearly hidden parking area deep in the trees (ah, there's the ambulance), he began his search for his father. Throughout this swath of Piedmont deciduous forest sloping down to the Catawba were lean-tos and campsites, campfires, murmured morning conversations. Howdys were exchanged with men with chest-length beards, men smoking long-stemmed pipes, men shaving with a straight razor by lantern light, one man gently playing an old melody on a harmonica; the smell of wood smoke and rashers of bacon permeated the woods.

"Good show," said his father, in full military regalia, looking like he walked out of a tintype. Duke clapped his son's shoulder. "Today's the day!" A tin cup of ink-black coffee was pressed into his hand.

Around eleven A.M., Dorrie arrived — with Manuel, or, more precisely, Manuel in drag. Manuel was in a long blue house-servant dress, his wig neatly arranged under the do-rag. Josh pointed out that the eye makeup was a little too fabulous and Dorrie took to the mascara with a tissue.

"Manuel?" he accused Dorrie.

"Calvin isn't coming, so I didn't want the ticket to go to waste. How do I look? This takes my being a race traitor to a whole new fucking stratospheric level, you think?" Dorrie had cropped her hair quite close for the occasion and ran an Ace bandage around her breasts. She looked magnificent in the Rebel gray uniform.

"I'm almost turned on," Josh said. "Shame you didn't have a gay little brother."

Manuel broke in: "You two could get married and have a baby . . . but . . . but Massa, I don't know nuthin 'bout birthin' no babies!"

Josh: "Manuel. *Any other time,* I would be for camping it up and having some fun with the crackers, but this is my dad's big day, so please —"

"Okay Josh, don't worry, baby. Let's go to the big gathering over thataway. Idn't no shortage of hot white daddies up in here."

As they walked to the sutlers' fair, Josh asked Dorrie, "Calvin sitting on my couch watching sports instead?"

"Calvin has left the building."

"He's gone?" Joshua stopped walking. "What did you do?"

Dorrie's face was lamb-innocent. "Let's face it. There wasn't room in that apartment for the both of our black asses so I requested *il se déplace loin de chez nous.* C'mon, Josh. He wasn't going to give that ass up again, so good riddance."

The sutlers (merchants who followed the battles) were amazing. There was a booth for the sale of Civil War–era jewelry, glassware, hip flasks, photos and pendants and lockets, hats — my God, the hats!

"Mm, baby," said Manuel, at a millinery stand, "I've got to have one of them belle-of-the-ball cotillion ladies' hats! For my whole Scarlett O. Horror routine." Manuel then ran a hand over a top hat while the haberdasher gave him an evil look.

"That's real beaver," said the hatmaker.

Manuel gave an exaggerated glance to Dorrie.

Dorrie raised her eyebrows in a warning that whatever Manuel was about to say better not find voice.

Amid the carnival atmosphere, Duke Johnston spotted Josh and Dorrie and waved from afar. Josh's Uncle Gaston, in a double-breasted suit that would not have looked out of place on Cornelius Vanderbilt, was with his father, walking to a booth where he would sign autographs for his Cordelia Florabloom novels. Another Norma inspiration. A crowd was already gathered so perhaps Uncle Gaston would really cash in today.

"Hey, look at Robert E. Lee," said Josh. "Near Uncle Gaston's booth."

"Damn, he does look like Robert E.," said Dorrie.

"This guy lately shows up to every Gaston Jarvis signing. My uncle hates him."

"That's Ted," said Manuel, nodding.

Both Dorrie and Josh stared at Manuel.

"He's a regular at the Eagle," Manuel

continued. "He's got a cop uniform, a German Nazi uniform. I'm into silver daddies but I'm not into uniform-play. Child, I'm the only one allowed to play dress-up. Still, he's a good-looking ol' white man, yes he is."

Dorrie watched a group of four women, all in nineteenth-century dress with bonnets, carrying a loom, walking it slowly to their booth. All the women were in their forties or fifties, laughing, attractive . . . and another middle-aged woman brought up the rear with some fine woven blankets and scarves, presumably made on the loom and for sale, in a pull cart. "I do declayuh," Dorrie said in her plummiest white Deep South, closer to Foghorn Leghorn than Shelby Foote, "these flowers of Southern femininity may need an assurance of the manly protection that I intend to provide for them."

Josh: "They might actually think you're a guy."

Dorrie pointed to the one in the dark gold skirt. "She's looking a little dykey to me."

"You gonna go get in the stream?"

"I aver, upon alllll my Southrin' honor, that I shall go down to the rivuh, and get into the stream."

Manuel: "What you two always talking about? 'Get in the stream.' You call up at the store and he gets on the phone with you and all I ever hear is 'get in the stream, girl.' "

Neither said anything for a minute. And

since Manuel pressed and the topic was before them, Dorrie told her story:

Dorrie had an older, rich white lady friend, Mrs. Spangler, who was the chief patron of a series of women's halfway houses, including one for women who had been prostitutes. Helping them to leave that life, escape their pimps, get some different life skills and a bus ticket to somewhere else, et cetera. The women and their counselors uproariously traded stories and Mrs. Spangler, without too much cajoling, could give chapter and verse of who among Charlotte's elite frequented prostitutes. It was often what you imagined — the ministers with high-priced call girls, the politicians who felt there'd be less chance of detection by frequenting prostitutes working a street corner, rich men, rich men *and their wives* cruising in their BMWs along the industrial zones aside I-85 which became makeshift red-light areas. Anyway, there was this one rich white man with lots of prostate and circulation issues beyond the reach of Viagra, but he would call an elite call-girl service when he felt he could manage an uninterrupted flow of urination — preferring women of color, by the way — and would pay a generous rate for a girl to bask there in his weak stream, writhing in pretend ecstasy. He was in his late fifties, and a *writer,* living on the edge of Myers Park.

Manuel smirked, casting a glance at Gaston

Jarvis's booth. "You mean . . ."

"Yeah," said Josh, giggling, "it's gotta be Uncle Gaston. He's such a wreck."

Dorrie smiled. "Who is surprised he's some kind of perv? But the man knows his wine."

"So," Josh continued, "whenever we see someone we like, if we really really want them no matter what they'd demand of us, we say we'd 'get in the stream.' "

"Y'all are nasty."

"Oh come on, Manuel. If Sean Connery called?"

He thought about it for three seconds. "Okay, I would get in that stream."

"Someone's fording a stream?" It was Duke Johnston, suddenly upon them, all smiles, so proud, brass buttons and ceremonial sword, everything polished until it blinded. Dorrie, Manuel and Josh all jumped a little at the instantaneous appearance. Duke Johnston took Manuel's hand and brought it to his lips. "And who is this vision of loveliness?" He kissed Manuel's hand. "Colonel Joseph Johnston, at your service, miss."

"Enchanté," Manuel flirted back.

Dorrie raced to change all subjects. "Um. So, Mr. — Colonel Johnston, did the cannon people arrive?"

Colonel Johnston was on his way to the riverbank now to see the firing. Would they all like to accompany him? Josh quickly inserted himself between his father and his friends, feigning interest in cannonading, allowing Dorrie and Manuel to slip away. Manuel soon commenced pursuit of Robert E. Lee. Dorrie drifted across the field to the loom women.

Part of the cannon show was going to be the ten uniformed men whose job it was to roll the caisson up the riverbank on a little path, a gain of about thirty-feet of elevation, turn the cannon upon the high promontory by the trestle, aim for the imaginary Yankees, light the fuse, and boom. A drummer already stood at the promontory tapping out a steady martial rhythm.

They got about halfway up the path when one of the wheels fell off. The cannon (on its intact wheel) slid back down to the bottom of the bank with the men diving before it as human stops trying to keep the cannon from going into the water. Soon there were twenty uniformed men gathered, with rope, with tools, to reattach the wheel . . . and twenty minutes later, another roll up the hill was attempted when the wheel came off again. This time, ten men fell upon the cannon and kept it from rolling; the loose wheel, however, pretty as you please, bounded down the bank and into the river, where it flopped on its side and began fitfully, catching on rocks, to float downstream. A unit of another ten were dispatched to rescue the wheel while the other ten huffed and heaved the one-wheeled cannon up to the promontory.

"I only offered two hundred dollars online for a cannon," Duke said soberly to Joshua. "I suppose this is the sort of cannon one gets."

Half an hour later, the caisson's missing wheel was jammed into place and it was time to fire the cannon. The men whose uniforms were wet from the river retrieval got the privilege of lighting the fuse. After an ear-shattering blast, the cannon flew backward and upended itself in a bank of kudzu and overgrowth; the loose wheel in a perfect repeat of its earlier performance rolled like a girl's hoop down the embankment and half-way across the Catawba before falling on its side and floating, again, downstream.

"Oh well," said Josh's father, imperturb-able, "we got the one, at least."

The firing of Cannon One had taken nearly ninety minutes, so no one dispersed knowing it was nearly time to fire up Cannon Two on the other side of the river. No one in the plan-ning had seriously considered just how wide the Catawba was at the ford. One had to squint to see the cannon on the other shore. This firing was bedeviled by trains. Duke's research concerning train times on the trestle had proven fanciful; the tracks habitually groaned with freight every few minutes. No sooner had someone with a bullhorn an-nounced to those gathered in the muddy marge of the riverbank that it was time to shoot Cannon Two, than another train would show up clanging along, blowing its horn, upstaging the military show. It would finally disappear and then they'd start again . . . and here came a train from the other direction, banging along, chugging, blaring its horn. All the kids in the crowd, in long skirts and little leather breeches, bonnets for girls and straw hats for boys, waved and waved to the conductor, who blared the horn even more and waved back. Finally, a railway respite. And then sprinkles . . .

"Thought it wasn't going to rain," Josh said, wondering how it would be to be trapped in damp wool for the rest of the afternoon.

The shower wasn't serious and cleared soon enough but the powder had become damp over at Cannon Two. The fuse was lit and there was the muffled sound like a champagne cork followed by a wisp of blue smoke rising up. People were not aware that that was, indeed, what they had waited hours to see, and the man with the bullhorn broke the news.

Against all agreements and understandings, at four P.M., five Union scoundrels did run out upon the trestle whereupon the Charlotte Home Guard, now two hundred and some strong (possibly two hundred more than originally showed up to defend the trestle in 1865) started blasting away with their blanks.

The Union re-enactors gamely fell on the tracks or staggered back to the ground away from the trestle before collapsing dramatically . . . before the excitement in the next five minutes of a train coming and the corpses making a quick retreat to the riverbank, with cheers and laughing applause all around.

"That's it for this year," said Duke, a little crestfallen, slapping his son's shoulder. All this shoulder slapping and clapping was apparently the new official father-son gesture, Josh thought. "The trestle is soundly defended, son."

"But the Yankees destroyed it in the original skirmish."

"Eh, but we got 'em this year!" he said, returning to ebullience.

Joshua walked through the sutlers' camp with his father, afterward, hoping to run into Dorrie.

Boy, there was no end of gun stuff. You could get actual Civil War–era formula gunpowder, antique weaponry, musket balls, and — whoa — Civil War–era *unexploded* bullets ready to be fired by a Civil War–era gun.

There were seamstresses who made the rounds of re-enactments in the South to sew on period buttons to period costumes. Most of the costumes (particularly for the modern fellow, who was much bigger than his nineteenth-century counterpart) were contemporary, made from blends of fabric as close to the period as possible. But that didn't mean you couldn't have the era's buttons, medals, handkerchiefs, bootlaces. (How did they get the 1860s bootlaces?) And there was a brisk trade in tobacco products and antique pipes, pipe stuffers, cans of tobacco from the period (the pipe tobacco inside was fresh, presumably), and flints and lighting devices although the safety match was invented by the time of the Civil War, but these guys liked doing things as old-fashionedly as possible.

You could buy food — some stands advertised "modern" food, and some sold hardtack and biscuits and cured meat. Josh wondered if the people running the stands went out and bought a load of beef jerky for the occasion, but his father put him straight — everything was cooked on an old wood-burning stove or cured in a smoke-cured barn, just like it would have been in the 1860s.

"Did the barn have to be around in the 1860s," Josh asked, "or is that pushing it too much?"

His father, unsmiling: "There is no 'too much.' "

Then Duke Johnston wandered toward Gaston's stall, receiving the handshakes, cheek kisses, the thanks of a grateful Confederacy for his masterminding of such a lovely afternoon.

Dorrie found Josh. "You'll be happy to know Manuel and General Lee have undertaken a walk in the woods — toward the general's mini-van."

"Now you see there. If Lee hadn't been in his tent getting blown by a black drag queen the third day at Gettysburg" — Josh now switched to his own overblown Southern accent — "I say, we might have won this war and spared ourselves the ruinous conflagration . . ."

"I got Harriet's number. The loom lady."

"I expect at least a scarf out of this. Hey, where did Calvin say he was going?"

"To his sister in Atlanta."

"He doesn't have a sister in Atlanta. The younger one lives here in Charlotte and the older one is married to an importer in Jamaica. What'd you say to get him to leave?"

Dorrie looked straight across the way at a blacksmith's forge as she said lightly, "Saint that I am, I paid for his ticket."

Josh appeared worried. "A ticket to Jamaica?"

"No, Atlanta. Calm down. He ordered it online and we used my credit card . . ." But now her expression was unsure.

"Did you actually see what destination he typed in?"

"Um, no. Well, damn, that *was,* I thought, a pretty expensive plane ticket to Atlanta. I figured he was going prime time, business class — it didn't matter. I wanted his sorriness out of our lives."

Josh felt his head go light. "Jamaica."

"Who cares if his broke ass is in Jamaica? Whatever, wherever . . ."

"I'm out eighteen thousand dollars, that's what."

"Excuse me?"

Josh confessed that he had paid Calvin's bail and the forfeit was $18,000 in addition to the $2000 he paid. Calvin was going to hide out until his father's trial was over, unavailable to testify, in a country with limited extradition rights. The State Department was not going to move heaven and earth over a petty obstruction case, a son refusing to rat out his father.

Dorrie exploded. "How was I supposed to know you were doing a dumbfuck thing like that? Since when do you keep a secret like that from me?"

There were a number of things Josh never told Dorrie about.

Silas, for example, who among Josh's stable was Dorrie's favorite. He was goofy-cute, shaved head, one big pirate earring, slender with big hands going every which way as he told stories, totally cute in his Bojangles uniform, and his brother got him some of the best pot in town, which he'd also bring over. Dorrie and Silas whooped and carried on; Josh was often a bystander but this was like, he supposed, other people's family gatherings, these were his loved ones and it pleased him to watch them laugh and dish.

He paid Silas. He never told Dorrie, and Silas would be mortified if Dorrie found out, but at one point Silas said, "Look, I'm gonna need a little something if I keep coming over here." And so, Josh would stop at the ATM and, in some private hallway moment, would slip Silas the forty/sixty bucks and get a kiss for his trouble, as well as some certainty that Silas would not disappear; he'd be back for more sex, more fun, more money. Silas — was this just delusion? — seemed to care about Josh (and he loved Dorrie) but there were men out there who could slip Silas a hundred or more. A good-looking boy like that had a market value; it's just what it was.

Josh heard from a Spanish exchange student once that most of the Mediterranean world worked like this, the richer man secreting the working-class lad some money for regular visits, but that didn't mean it was impersonal prostitution, and those arrangements often lasted a lifetime with the benefactor giving elaborate presents when the boy got married, and the boy looking in on the benefactor when he got old and isolated. Josh thought of the tons of money he had never spent because he never dated women — the expensive dinners, Valentine's, birthdays, anniversaries, the obligatory schedule of mercenary prove-you-love-me gifts. He decided he was getting off cheap with Silas.

And he knew Dorrie didn't tell him everything, either. Josh knew all about one secret that didn't stay very secret: Renee. Sometimes Dorrie tired of her months-in-the-making seductions and would simply go to Women's Night on Thursdays at the Nickel Bar and Renee would be in place, waiting. Renee was Dorrie's most egregious romantic detour. Renee was older and white but not powerful or impressive; she was needy, neurotic, clingy, hyper-emotional and in and out of recovery. She always advertised that she had "just club soda" in her glass but often it was something else clear. She was a fixture at the Nickel and Dorrie knew she was always willing, and if all else failed (and many of Dorrie's seductions and strategems failed), Renee was there idling, sometimes even smug about it: "You know, Dorrie, you're gonna end up with me in the end." She was reportedly masterful in bed, not unattractive. It was the morning after when the clinging started and Dorrie would swear that she would never be so expedient again. Twice she'd had to change her cell phone number because of Renee filling her phone with drunken *I-thought-you-loved-me* messages. Twice she had tried to get to Dorrie by communicating with Josh, pouring her heart out to him. But Josh never passed any of it on to Dorrie since that knowledge would make things worse.

And there were things Joshua barely thought to himself for fear they might be telepathically perceived:

Josh was sixteen. The only open flirting he ever did was with a gay art teacher at Mecklenburg Country Day, but nothing would ever come of that. He was dying to be an adult, a gay one, free of the suffocations of being a Johnston. So he went up to UNC-G to visit Annie, to have a wild college weekend. Annie wagged a finger at him. "No drinking, it's against the law . . . that is, if I see it."

Annie had a party at her house, full of actors and History majors and artsy types. No parents anywhere! God, what freedom — why wasn't every single night an orgy for university kids? He watched Annie flirt with all the boys, and they loved her right back. Annie, to tell the truth, annoyed him most of the time, but he wished he had her confidence. You know who was really nice? Annie's boyfriend.

He must have been under some instruction to take Josh under his wing, make sure he didn't get too drunk or dragged away by carnivorous females. That could have happened, too. "Your little brother is a doll! I just love him . . ." Lots of hugs, cheek kisses, breasts pressed into him . . . what a waste. Annie's boyfriend was hunky but not really Josh's type. Josh had his eye on a probably-gay black Theater major holding court in the living room.

But by two A.M. everyone was very drunk, drunker than Josh who had held back out of fear of embarrassing himself. No one else was concerned, apparently, with making a fool out of himself. Annie's boyfriend collapsed on the sofa beside him, nestling into his arm. "You know what's funny. You're prettier than she is."

And later: "If you were her sister and not her brother, we'd be out back doing something about it!"

Josh left for another room. Annie's boyfriend's directness and proximity made him nervous but also aroused. Josh rooted himself to the very public kitchen where nothing secret could happen. He saw the black Theater major leave the party with a redheaded boy, their arms around each other's necks, which released some chemical of longing and recklessness into Josh's being. After beer number five, Josh stumbled away from the noisy house, into the dark backyard woods for a pee, and suddenly he was joined by Annie's boyfriend. He stood right beside Josh as he urinated, doing it in an exhibitionistic way, not putting it away when he was done, doing the "Sure am horny these days" line, which led to Joshua taking his own hand away to show that he was aroused. Next thing he knew, Michael — yeah, that was his name — was on him, pinning him to a nearby tree and giving him oral sex.

"I'm sixteen," he said, a minute after it began.

Michael stopped, then mumbled, "Oh well, too late now," and kept going.

That should have been the end of it, but then Josh wanted to perform oral sex on Michael too, since it was an evening for firsts, so Michael leaned against the tree, invisible to the party, hearing Annie call Michael's name from the back porch while Michael greedily held Josh by the hair and moved his head about for his maximum enjoyment. Josh wasn't sure if he enjoyed doing it or not; he was fairly sure he was terrible at it but Michael quickly finished up, kind enough to withdraw before he ejaculated.

"Michael! Where arrrrre you?"

Josh dared to peek up at the house; Annie retreated inside and closed the door. As they both zipped up, Joshua saw Michael wasn't meeting his eyes and was beginning a whole "Wow, didn't see that happening" speech, when Josh cut him off:

"I'll never tell anybody, if that's what you're worried about."

Michael reached out to touch Josh's face. It was all Josh could do not to kiss him, melt into him. "Weird. I can't help but noticing. You and your sister sort of taste alike."

"You should break up with my sister."

"I keep meaning to do it, man."

"End of term, maybe?"

The rest of that party was spent watching Michael hang all over Annie and Annie, later on, confiding to her baby brother in the kitchen that she and Michael might go to New York and live together after UNC-G.

Joshua heard two weeks later they were broken up.

Josh was cleaned out — 20K in the hole. Though despondent, he was able to hug his father at the end of the Skirmish and tell him what a triumph it was. His father intended to camp another night. He too had brought an antique flask with some fine sour mash, a single-barrel bourbon distillation in a Sauternes cask, which he and Major Badger and Colonel Haslett were going to sip, sitting by the fire and reminiscing about the glories of re-enacted battle . . . or was it Colonel Badger and Major Haslett?

Josh's father wondered if he might ask one more favor. Could Josh call a taxi on his cell phone (once out of the historical zone)? His Uncle Gaston was hammered. That would be a fifty-dollar cab ride easy.

"Wait. I'll be happy to drive him," Josh volunteered.

Joshua got Uncle Gaston to his rusting Toyota, with the help of some moonshine distillers. Josh winked at General Lee who looked on with hauteur from a nearby tent. By the time they reached Myers Park, his uncle had had a good thirty-minute nap. Joshua reached over to gently shake him.

"Home already?" he slurred.

"Uncle Gaston," Josh began anew, walking his uncle to the front door. "There must be a long line of greedy relatives and acquaintances always asking for a handout but I fear I have to add myself to that long line, and I wish —"

"How much you need, my boy?"

Josh needed $18,000 to finish off Berma's bond. But he blurted out, "Twenty-four thousand." But it was not because of greed or anything he hoped to spend on himself. Well, not directly.

"Hoo hoo hoo," said Gaston, standing up straight, looking rumpled like he'd slept on the streets. "Twenty-four big ones. I know you didn't get a girl in trouble."

Joshua smiled. "Most assuredly not."

Uncle Gaston fumblingly opened up his house and careened inside. "You're not being blackmailed, are you?"

Josh followed. "You remember Calvin Eakins, the city councilman?"

"Charlotte's very own race man. Big loud shakedown artist, went on to become one of the crookedest amid the crooked Raleigh Democrats — which is saying something."

Josh explained how he had bailed out Senator Eakins's son and how Calvin Jr. had betaken himself to Jamaica and how he owed

Berma Bigglefield the forfeit of the bond.

"Come to the kitchen. We'll see if we can find which room I left my checkbook in."

Josh, like many visitors before, was struck with how desolate the undecorated first floor of the mansion remained. He was escorted toward the kitchen-dining nook and there resided proof of residence, mail stacked in piles, manuscripts and galleys — sent for his blurb or review or goodwill — stock statements, corporate brochures, the kinds of things people with money and investments receive. Dishes in the sink, about a score of whiskey glasses abandoned in various corners of the room, catering and delivery boxes from the upscale bistros and brasseries that deliver.

Josh felt he had better gush. "Oh thank you, Uncle Gaston! I promise never again to pay anyone's bond."

Uncle Gaston chuckled. "Except if I need you to pay mine one day."

"You go commit all the crimes you like. I'm your bail."

"I doubt you'd have the money for the kind of crimes I may yet commit," he groused, searching the cluttered tabletop. "Still have a mind to burn down the *Queen City Times.*"

Josh's heart was lightened, he felt infused with helium, needing to be affixed to something earthbound before he floated skyward.

"Here we go!" Uncle Gaston lurched for the dining room table and bent over the surface to write the check, which also allowed him to stop swaying. "Twenty-four thou, you say."

"Yes, sir."

"Do I make this to that bail woman or to you?"

"To me," said Joshua quickly, not wanting the extra six thousand to land in Berma's lap.

"Does Miss Berma look anything like her billboards or is it like with your sister Annie, a wholly created computer fantasy?"

Josh laughed. "Berma looks more like the picture on her billboards than Annie resembles her billboards. Have you been down I-77? And seen the billboard for Lookaway, Dixieland?"

"No, can't say that I . . ." Uncle Gaston froze.

"They've started advertising for the place. Big fuzzy shot of a Southern antebellum mansion through the mists, exclusive homes starting at five hundred thousand and above. And there's a faded cannon imposed over the left half . . . Uncle Gaston?"

There was a full thirty-second silence. "Lookaway, Dixieland?"

"That's the name of the gated community on the Catawba that Dad and Mr. Boatwright are developing. They're going to keep the area around the trestle as some kind of memorial park with plaques and, one day, a monument. Though I don't think anybody died there."

"Lookaway, Dixieland?"

"Corny as hell, but they're going for that Old South hokum theme. Dad came up with the name."

Uncle Gaston was still as a statue. "He did, did he?"

Joshua saw that something was amiss. Uncle Gaston had written the check but not signed it. Now Uncle Gaston was staggering toward the kitchen counter for a new glass and in the cabinetry below was a liter bottle of Four Roses bourbon. A stop at the fridge to gather a few ice cubes, and then a healthy pour, and then he teetered toward the telephone on the kitchen wall. He swigged, he dialed, he dropped the phone, he tried to pull the receiver close to him by reeling in the tangled cord only to drop it again.

"Can I help?" Josh asked. He stared at the unsigned check. He reached down and tore it from the checkbook. "Um, Uncle Gaston, if you could finish this out."

"It was just so he could stick the knife in," his uncle mumbled. "All the friendliness, the camaraderie like old times, just so he could . . ."

His uncle was unwell. "Okay," said Josh, sounding stupidly cheery to himself, "let me get you to write your name on this and I'll leave you to do whatever you are, um . . ."

But Uncle Gaston had stormed from the kitchen to the nearly barren living room.

There was a conventional phone there on a small table against a far wall, one of two pieces of furniture in the whole long chamber. Uncle Gaston began to dial, then stopped, then stumbled toward the hard-backed chair (the other item of décor) and collapsed into it, murmuring, "No . . . no, I'm not going to give him the satisfaction of . . ."

Josh stood in the doorway with his unsigned check. He circled back to retrieve the pen from the kitchen and approached Uncle Gaston timorously.

"You were going to sign this, Uncle Gaston."

Uncle Gaston stared into the far wall, his face drained of color. "Who do I make this out to?"

Josh realized he thought he was at a book signing. "Just a signature will do . . . right here, on the line . . ."

Uncle Gaston mumbled, "I'm not . . . This signing is over. Norma!" he called out.

Josh backed away. Josh wasn't good with mental health episodes. He would bring back the check another time, perhaps.

He let himself out. Josh stood near his Toyota and looked up at the empty, lightless two-story mansion surrounded by giant oaks. They could be a hundred miles out in the country except for the nightglow of the metropolitan sky. The turret at the end, the mansard roof . . . this may have only been built in the 1990s but it was a good candidate for being a haunted house on a Hollywood back lot. Just then the trees took up a breeze, swaying and rustling, an impermeable wall of shifting darkness surrounding the creepy old house.

Josh reflected that he didn't deserve his uncle's money. He abused his uncle's overblown neo-Confederate novels, privately judged him, hated his politics, and mocked him about his sex life from a tidbit of information which might have been untrue, but he and Dorrie continued with the libel anyway, and, what's more, whispered it to anyone in Charlotte whom they wished to entertain and scandalize. And yet, here he was, shamelessly begging for the man's money which he generously gave — almost.

He felt bad about his uncle's sad life and he felt bad about his own disloyalty, but he didn't feel bad about the check. Josh was still holding the pen. He had seen his uncle sign a million books. He had his uncle's autograph back at the house on some book on some shelf, he was fairly sure. Yes, he was going to forge this and cash it and if his uncle accused him, he would thank him profusely as if nothing were amiss, or protest and remind him how drunk he was.

A few weeks later in May.

Dorrie had a key but she had never come

into his apartment alone without it being an emergency before.

"Hey," said Josh, entering his apartment, clutching a bag from Pier 1. "What's up?"

"Nonso."

"Huh?"

"He's coming to America and you're bringing him, right?"

Dorrie was good on the surprise attack; Josh couldn't lie well under pressure. "Well. Heh-heh. You see, he got into a program for African nationals at Johnson C. Smith. So yes, he's coming. How did you know?"

"Back at Chapel Hill, you wrote that final World Lit paper on *Things Fall Apart* and then I borrowed it to write *my* final English paper . . . and then a few months ago you were over at the house going through disks and boxes of papers trying to find 'something' and I wanted to know just what you were hunting for, and you finally tell me it's that ten-year-old term paper and I ask myself, I say 'Dorrie, why would Josh need an old term paper about a Nigerian novel unless he was applying for grad school or something,' and then it clicked. You were applying for our little smiling friend."

"Um, it worked. They accepted him."

"And you filled out his application and wrote him an essay about his hopes and dreams. You've seen the guy's English. What? You're gonna write all his term papers for him so he won't flunk out?"

Josh thought a minute. "Once he's here they'll work with him. Even Carolina had all kinds of lame foreign students who could barely speak English. They have tutorial services —"

"And so he lives *here,* with you? And you run him down to J. C. Smith every day? You feed him, you clothe him, like a pet, a little Nigerian boy-doll. And he's totally dependent on you?"

"There are other African students there. He'll make new friends —"

"And you'll sleep with him and . . . it'll be just like slave times. Thank you, Massa, for bringin' my jet-black ass over from the Dark Continent so I can better m'self among allllll da white people. Would Massa like me to warm his bed tonight?"

"Aw come on, that's . . . that's a little harsh. I'm trying to help him out."

"Uh-uh. That's not what you're doing. Have you thought for two minutes how this affects me? Aside from dealing with his backward African dumb ass all the time, you won't have any money for vacations, for film festivals, for our going to New York. All our beautiful world will be sacrificed so you can . . ." She didn't finish because she didn't want to have a friendship-ending fight with Josh. She fished around for something neutral to say. "What's in the bag?"

Josh sighed and reached into the crumpled Pier 1 bag and slowly brought out one of the contents: a long elegant blue candle. There were five blue candles in the bag of various widths and scents.

Dorrie looked askance. "Thought I smelled bayberry."

"Look, I've talked with him on Skype, with the camera, he's . . . He's so sweet. I'm just trying to give him a chance to be gay in a country that doesn't persecute him for it."

"Oh yeah, you're a regular Peace Corps. So how much was the ticket? Presumably, you've booked him a ticket."

"No," Josh said with fervor, like his buying a ticket would truly be a step too far. "His older brother is going to pay for that. The deal was if he got into an American school, his brother would buy him a plane ticket. I offered but he said no."

Dorrie cocked her head sideways, squinted, almost said something, then pursed her lips, shook her head.

"What, Dorrie?"

"Oh my darling innocent boy . . ."

"What?"

"It's a scam. A romance scam. The internet is full of them and Africa is the capital of them, usually Nigeria."

Josh thought he knew what she was referring to. "No. I've talked to him with a webcam. He's not just a photo some con man put up online."

"I wonder how many old queens, sitting with their lapdogs, nursing a G and T, around the country are online with this boy, agreeing to help him out. You haven't sent him money yet?" There was enough hesitation that Dorrie pounced: "So you have. He wouldn't take an airline ticket from you because he couldn't get cash out of that. So what was it? Money to bribe an official?"

Josh sat down, setting his candles gently on the table. "Nonso said to get a passport in Nigeria there's nothing more to it than handing some government guy a bribe."

"How much?"

"Twelve hundred dollars."

"Jesus Christ. Okay, these guys start small and then get you committed and you keep sending because you've already sent so much. This official will need more money, so Nonso will be back in tears begging for another installment."

Josh blankly stared at the bookcase. Nonso had already asked for some more money. "It's hard to think that . . ."

"These guys are *good.* They prey on lonely queers and desperate straight women, sometimes church philanthropy types who think they're helping someone. No shit, it's a billion-dollar industry; the biggest home-based industry in Nigeria. Cheating soft-hearted Westerners. C'mon, Josh, this is the home of the Nigerian prince who writes you by e-mail to share his immense fortune if only you'll send him some money first."

Josh breathed heavily. "Can you go now?"

Dorrie, correctly, heard no anger or resentment in the request, just defeat. "Yeah, baby. I'll go. Call me later, okay?"

She let herself out.

Immediately, Josh turned on his laptop, waited for the endless assault of windows asking him to upgrade and renew programs he never used or didn't know he had . . . the interminable wait until the wireless signal was captured and connection to the internet was achieved. Josh went to charlottedownlow.com and logged on.

Some guys sent him a smile, a flirt, stupid little emoticons popped up that some men hoped would lead to an online chat, a hookup.

An hour went by, then another. Josh stared at Nonso's profile, that ludicrous smile, waiting for the green dot to glow in the corner, showing that he too had come online.

Another hour went by; it was getting dark in the room. An overweight older guy, *bigblk4white,* sent him a message telling him he "was lookin fyne." A previous lackluster hookup, *hoodstar,* sent him a "wasup?" It would be after midnight in Lagos, but that's when they often talked so Josh continued to sit and stare at his screen.

Finally, Nonso was online. Within a minute, a message arrived in Josh's mailbox.

Nonso: hello my love it is nt long for we be toghter in Charlote

After they moved over to Skype, after an hour of accusations and tears (Josh's and Nonso's), and after some very complicated explanations, Josh and Nonso understood each other perfectly. As the blue candles burned down, as the webcam images got darker and fuzzier, Josh said good night and immediately went to his online banking site and transferred into Nonso's account another eight hundred American dollars of Uncle Gaston's check money.

Dillard

She lived on Elderflower Drive. At first she found mockery in the name, some bloom turned ancient, something for the potpourri basket, wilted, desiccate . . . but then she came to like the name. Elderflower: a flowering in old age, a late and splendid blossoming that the world would find unlikely. Dillard understood that no elderflowers bloomed in North Carolina or anywhere nearer than England. Once she had a friend very much a bore about tea and tea-making who brought her some dried elderflowers and prepared a tisane. It was divine, she recalled, but how precisely was it divine? She remembered a sweetness, some sugary floral taste without citrus or sharpness, a weak perfume, gentle.

Dillard of Dilworth, went the family singsong, like Tess of the d'Urbervilles or Catherine of Aragon (to name two other women disappointed in love). Dilworth was a venerable neighborhood, one of the most respectable in Charlotte, though it had never been particularly monied, or rather, the old families within it had not been conspicuous with their money. A mix of two-story Victorian frame houses, brick bungalows of the 1920s and 1930s with a hint of Asian influence in the roof tiles, properties politely separated by magnolias and clusters of azalea, ill-considered modern apartment blocks of the 1950s, brick ranch homes of the 1960s with big yards to be mown, each sweltering summer abuzz with mowers and teenage boys doing their expected chore or making a little pocket change in the yard of the nice old lady next door. Her own Christopher, shirtless, gleaming like a Nordic god, used to mow her entire cul-de-sac; the hustler in him had cornered the market.

Dillard owned one of the 1930s bungalows with a large bay window facing the sloping front yard down to the street, as well as a large bay window looking to the backyard and the small strip of woods behind. The living room received light throughout the day. One could sit in Dillard's living room and face either of the two views, one capacious — the suburban street with the Bank of America Tower jutting above the neighborhood poplars — and the other cloistered — the cozy backyard against a small bank and its grouping of trees that, when the shadows lengthened, seemed like the edge of a greater forest.

That theoretical guest in the living room could also face north, to the portrait of her paternal grandmother, or south, to the fireplace and the mantel which at one time was a shrine to her son, Christopher. No other room in her house had so much to delight or sadden or provoke Dillard, but there were not many days when she didn't come for a brief sit-down to be with her thoughts, or to empty her mind into the passing view, the bird feeders, the neighborhood children in the street growing up with tricycles, then bicycles, then skateboards, the prowling of an orange tabby in her backyard, the chattering chase of squirrels in the lower branches . . . these were the visual accompaniments to the sharp ticking of the chestnut cabinet clock on the mantel. There was no need to turn on the television, she often thought — right here was all the stimulation she required.

Dillard's entire social landscape had changed since Christopher died. At times she felt a pang of loss for it, felt some last lifeline had been coiled and stowed out of reach. There was an annual gathering of Salem College alumnae in Charlotte, a springtime get-together, lots of gossip, shopping, dining, an en masse escape from families and husbands, which she had in the past looked forward to until this year when the day implacably arrived and Dillard found herself contacting the ringleader and begging off appearing, crediting “an unspeakable efflorescence of my fibromyalgia,” from which she suffered.

She had quietly withdrawn from the Sunday school class at Sedgewood Presbyterian; the sermon was sufficient and the gauntlet of greetings and well-wishing to and from the sanctuary was social whirl enough.

And there was her sporadic employment at Parminter’s, of course, but she had cut back her hours there. Lily Parminter herself called the house once, asking if she was all right, why they hadn’t seen her at the store in ages. Why, the new girls don’t know the first thing about pre-war china, and regular customers — wedding planners, caterers, old-family matrons maintaining a Smithsonian Museum’s number of china sets, always looking for rare, matching gravy boats or tureen ladles — they were *all* asking after her: “Lily, where is our Dillard?” But it was never as if the china shop paid her a living wage; she only had dwelled so long among the glass cases and cabinets for the social aspect, the antiquated spinsterish element that suited her. The all-female preserve of china, replacements, no-longer-made things, fragile things, beautiful things with hairline, barely detectable cracks, small flaws of art that eluded even the finest German or Asian porcelainist and yet there they were. And the little stories of loss, or how someone’s two-year-old pulled at the tablecloth and sent the priceless Sèvres cup and saucer to the floor, told and retold as if an epic tragedy had occurred, accompanied by female keening fit for Greek drama ("Oh you poor darling — and you just watched as it happened!") and the final show of sympathy, Lily Parminter removing her chained glasses, pressing her delicate aged hands to the hands of the sufferer, with her assurances that a salad plate, a cream urn, could be found to match just perfectly, just you wait. That must have been the appeal of the place, the idea that losses could be met with restoration, not easily, but eventually. And there was esteem there for Dillard, a deference, an acknowledgment of her expertise. She, who had been so useless in the important matters of life.

Socializing with family was less avoidable but Dillard had made tactical withdrawals there, too. She had to be forcibly dragged by family, for Sunday lunch, to the Charlottetowne Country Club which she didn't approve of, down deep, the origin of her social follies, the setting for her initial courtship with the roustabout Randy Revelle. (She remembered Joshua, her favorite of Jerene's children, innocently asking about "Uncle Randy" and Annie piping up, asking, " 'Randy Revelle' was really his name? Who was naming people back then, John Bunyan?" Well yes, his name alone should have foretold all that she was to endure.)

She had two very infrequent family visitors. Gaston would sometimes be overwhelmed with fraternal feeling and stop by the house when he was headed uptown, giving no more than five minutes of warning before he appeared at the door, and rarely staying for longer than twenty. He always offered money. Gaston's social currency was his money — he would be pointless without it. His mountain of money, she imagined, must weigh on him when he considered his little sister, left a ward of the family, her solvency subject to stray generous gestures.

They would perform the same Edwardian parlor drama each time: her refusal to be a burden, her rejection of his latest offer, she simply couldn't go on being such a charity case, his bluff insistence, her faint assertion that her work at Parminter's brought in enough, his threat to go down to the bank and simply put it into her account without her permission so she might as well take the check he was dangling in his right hand. If Gaston had recently appeared at a family function drunk or had been especially nasty to everyone — he usually could not recall if he had particularly offended her among the many people he had certainly offended — then he would rise to extraordinary gestures, like paying off her home's mortgage in 2001.

"I'm sure," he said, "that my agent cheats me yearly for more than this little check I am writing." He gave each check his oversized flourished signature honed at countless book signings. "It is nothing to me except that it could bring you a little security." He looked up, suddenly shed of his half century, suddenly the bright-eyed boy she grew up with. "And I'm sure I got walloped half as much because you were there to head Daddy off at the pass."

She was not in a position, in their long-playing melodrama, to actually refuse his money for reasons of pride — pride which she had dispensed with long ago. On this bit of charity she was serene: he had money, he was family. Any other avenue to money had some shame or degradation attached to it, or worse, sheer bother. Dillard had passed the age of bother, of complication.

The second family emissary was her niece Annie the barbarian who stormed Dillard's citadel of quiet. At first so welcome, such an unexpected youthful envoy. Annie brought laughter to the house, talking at her high boisterous volume — and food. Naturally, poor Annie, like all fat people, Dillard speculated, wanted partners in gustatory crime. Annie would have a newly discovered ice-cream flavor she had brought or a fabulous ethnic find, a Persian pastry with pistachios and honey, this Chinese cake from the Asian market, a pound cake of sorts soaked in lychee juice — in Charlotte, North Carolina!

In this backwater! — always a new discovery for poor Dillard, who never gets out much, who never goes anywhere, who probably, Annie must imagine, subsists on gruel or pet food.

"What possessed you, Annie, to think I need one *bite* of those cookies, let alone a hundred?"

"I wanted to bring you something, Aunt Dillie," she said, setting the cookies on the kitchen nook table. "You hate flowers and said not to bring you any more knickknacks or bric-a-brac."

"I don't need to be brought something like some potentate of the East every time you want to come see me." Dillard broke off half of a cookie and popped it into her mouth. "These are good, though."

It was a way, Dillard reflected, of Annie justifying the pig-out (since Annie always ate four fifths of what she brought over), disguising it to herself as a mission of mercy. Dillard's house had become a no-comment zone for eating, no scolding, no consequences, just us girls and our secret chocolate. Maybe she thought calories eaten in the service of keeping poor old Aunt Dillard company didn't even count.

Last month her niece was desperate to confess her difficulties with her third husband, Chuck — oh what was she now? Annie Johnston Costa Winchell Arbuthnot, my goodness. A presumptuous solidarity with Aunt Dillard who made the bad marriage just as she had, the two reckless romantic outcasts against the rest of the family — that seemed to be the gist. Dillard did not accept this retelling of the myth. Annie had arisen in an age of complete freedom from social constraint and societal inquisition, where girls tried out their men pre-maritally, where they took themselves off to Europe for the summer and discovered all there was to know about sex and related misadventures. Annie, unlike sheltered naïve Dillard, who was seduced handily by Randy her junior year at Salem and was instantly pregnant, Annie had no excuse for her bad choices. Annie had followed one bad marriage with two others! At least Dillard had held it to the one. Another thing, Annie was always floating some disparagement of her mother, longing for her aunt to join in and be an ally with her against Jerene, who she feels is a perpetual outrage, some monster. Her visits were becoming a nuisance.

Among the younger generation, Dillard wished Joshua would visit more. Dear Joshua, so soft and sweet she continually wanted to hug him. How odd that the world had destroyed her rugged, athletic, hale and hearty son but had spared tender Joshua with his permanent look of bullied hurt on his face. Bo came by a year ago, and what a plodding sincere thing he was — though his wife is a firecracker. She wished she could get to know Kate better, but Kate was in motion continually, inexhaustible, dawn to midnight, doing church things, world-saving things. Kate had even taken over Dillard's chair at the Jarvis Trust for American Art meetings — surely as a kindness, since what could she care about paintings and the rich-lady gossip of Jerene's handpicked circle of sycophants. Yes, that too Dillard had quietly removed herself from. "You're not to become a cat lady," Jerene had said, rather than begging her to stay on the board. "You may not get strange and eccentric past a certain point, Dillard — I won't have it."

So few, so very few visitors in recent years. She had not encouraged people to look in on her or trouble themselves. Perhaps the shrine, as Jerene had termed it, had scared off her acquaintances. It had begun as five or six framed pictures of Christopher as a boy, leaving out his ragamuffin teenage years, his drugged-out twenties. He was such a fair-skinned boy, so blond in coloring, that he looked in many of his later photos like he hadn't slept, like he was glassy-eyed and on something even when he wasn't. He was too easily marked by his abuses, creased, reddened, hardened to the point that by twenty-five his smile was permanently cynical and sneering. She had stopped keeping photos of him by then. Oh she would take them, against his will, his offering up to her a cross or compromised face; she kept taking them in hopes of capturing the angelic boy she had raised single-handedly. A year after he died, Dillard had created a chronological diorama of photographs from childhood to young adulthood. Yes, she had gotten carried away for a while, added his Little League trophies, a debating plaque or two from his middle high school years, field day second-place ribbons, a sash of merit badges. It was all tastefully done, she thought . . . but Jerene disapproved.

"Dillard," she had pronounced, surveying the mantel-shrine at its maximum growth, "I say this out of love. Take this down or move it to the bedroom — better yet his bedroom, not yours. There is too much to dwell on here, none of it happy or helpful."

Dillard defended her display to Jerene, but within a day she came around and dismantled it. Anyway, all of her collection, save a single school-era class photo, was in the hallway closet, easy to hand if she wished to reconstruct it and risk people thinking she was unwell. Because, of course, she was unwell. She had lost her only child. She had powerlessly watched him corrupt himself and deteriorate, her angel seeking out the gutter, beholden to people who were only too eager to drag him further down into it.

Yet there were days, after all, here in the living room, here where she spent so much time thinking and remembering, that she was very cold about Christopher and his life choices, even unforgiving: *I gave you life and you threw it away. Have it your way then, Chrissy. Don't expect me to sacrifice the rest of my life to your selfish nonsense, your inconsideration. I don't suppose it ever occurred to you how it might be for me watching you become a methamphetamine addict. It never passed through your mind, even once — I'm sure of it — what will my poor mother think if I keep going down this path. How sad she will be, how devastated.* Well, she thought, when she swept her shrine into a cardboard box, you see, don't you, Christopher, how I am not so devastated that I cannot pack you up and put you in a closet for a little while. I can get on with things, I have moved forward and have done so in fairly admirable fashion. Yes, they say, poor thing, poor Dillard, how does she scrape through? But they also say, she suspected, that she'd made the best of it, been able to soldier on and function in the world you and your father left me.

Sitting in her living room today, listening to the dry tick of the chestnut clock, giving just a glance to the surviving Christopher photo, she relived all her inescapable soliloquies and dialogues with . . . with whom? Who was "they" who were in constant commentary about how poor Dillard was doing, how she soldiered on? Charlotte society, she supposed, once upon a time, was "they." But "they" had written her off some time ago, when she married young and stupidly. And when Christopher died and his tragedy and crimes became news for the City page (front page of the B section), the obituaries (page 43), little noticeable in the plentiful pages of the *Charlotte Observer,* then she found herself receiving a little more pity — oh, she hated pity! — a little more judgment. In every Charlotte family of note, in every generation, there is a black sheep or a screwup or someone solely mentioned by people as a lesson, a marker in human unhappiness, and Dillard Jarvis Revelle had fulfilled that role for her generation and her son, Christopher, for his.

That chestnut clock. How it had accompanied her unpleasantly through life. She should sell it. Apparently it had great value, that's why it wasn't already destroyed — her brother was willing to take a hammer to it, but she and Jerene spared its life. But how had she ended up with it? It should be over with their mother in Lattamore Acres.

When they were children, their mother made them dress up for dinner. Their father felt if he had to suffer the indignity of coming home for his evening supper then it should be a bit of a ceremony, and his little girls should dress up. They sat in the parlor of the homeplace, staring at the clock. Four-thirty would be the sign that they had to run upstairs and slip on a Sunday dress. And then they'd return to the parlor and wait until five when Daddy would appear. How they'd stare at the clock, and in return, how the clock would lengthen the minutes. Dillard was sure the clock was louder sometimes than other times . . . it couldn't be proven of course, but sometimes the dry tenor click of the minute hand was like a stiff playing card being played upon a card table, sometimes that noise filled the whole of the room. With each passing moment that Daddy did not come home, the more everyone's fate would darken. By six it was clear Daddy had made a detour to the country club or Harlan's Tavern down near the Union County Courthouse to gladhand with other lawyers and judges, and it was clear that he would come home inebriated. Oh every once in a great while, he'd come in sweet and docile, kissing Mother and saying he had gotten held up and he hoped we weren't starving, but those times were so rare as to be memorable.

The usual routine was his coming back at nine in a fiercely bad temper — who knows what transpired to make it so. They would all be chastised for something in turn, not eating vegetables, putting a stain on a dress, or maybe he would be furious that something was cold, despite its being served so late. Father slinging a plate of mashed potatoes against the dining room wall was particularly vivid to her; usually, he would just shove things to the floor. Dillard remembered her mother, who conducted herself through all the bad behavior by not acknowledging it, running to stop him only from smashing a soup tureen to the floor: "God no, Gaston, that's worth a fortune!" Such interference spared the tureen but got her face slapped. And Gaston Jr., her little brother, would enter into it to defend his sisters and mother, God bless him, and that got him sent to his room without dinner, and later there would be a follow-up for that backtalk with a belt. By that time, their mother would be in hiding downstairs, again, expert at that small stoic expression that nothing bad was happening, nothing need move her to intervene. She was a pure coward, Dillard reflected. Better her little boy and daughters slake her husband's pitiless rage than herself.

"Did you ever stop to think," Mother would bring out mournfully, "that if you didn't annoy your father, he wouldn't be like this?"

So each night we combed out our hair a little longer, tied the bows a little tighter, pulled up our white socks a little higher, learned to sit up a little more straight, as we sat there in the parlor, Dillard reflected, watching that clock keep time on our childhoods. And here that cursed thing is still astride my afternoons, preparing to tick-tock me into old age, Dillard thought calmly. Probably the last fool thing I will hear in this world. It was 4:26. She might take a hammer to that thing yet —

Then, the doorbell.

Dillard's heart skipped a beat; she steadied herself and pushed her bulk out of the chair and saw, through the bay window, that Jerene's BMW was in the drive.

"Sorry to break in on you like this," Jerene said, storming past the foyer and into the kitchen. Dillard simply followed her.

"That's all right. I can tell something's wrong, Jerene."

Something was wrong because Jerene was uncharacteristically frantic, and Dillard's sister was never frantic. Jerene paced the dining nook, circled the kitchen island, rustling the shopping lists and newspaper clips on Dillard's small bulletin board, then, declining all the while Dillard's offers of coffee, iced tea, a Diet-Rite cola, Jerene did a circuit of the living room, her kelly-green swing coat sweeping around her like an impresario's cape. Jerene held a sealed manila envelope.

"Would you like a fat-free granola bar?" Dillard asked, primarily to see Jerene's expression of horror.

"I hired a detective," she said, settling on a couch.

"For Duke?" Dillard sat in a straight-backed chair beside her.

"Why would I hire a detective for Duke?"

"I thought that's why people hired detectives, to spy on their spouses."

"Oh what do I care what Duke does. I should have said that my lawyer hired him, Darnell McKay."

Dillard leaned forward to convey gentleness. "Are we pressing Darnell into service again? I know why you want him looking out for your interests, but are you sure he is up to negotiating a civil suit with Liddibelle's pack of wolves?"

Jerene was on her feet again, pacing toward the kitchen, still clutching the manila envelope. "Duke has left sorting out everything to me, and among Darnell's attributes is his having detectives on his payroll."

Dillard, with effort again, a twinge of sciatica announcing itself, got out of her chair and followed her sister into the kitchen. "And this detective is supposed to find dirt on the Baylors?"

"*Their* detective is investigating Jerilyn to make her out to be some crazed madwoman with a past full of reckless action, and there was a . . . some unpleasantness at Carolina, some misadventures where boys were concerned. I don't want any of Jerilyn's past — or my past or your past or Annie's past — making its way to a civil suit as part of a larger attempt to suggest that the women in the family are unbalanced or hysterical and shouldn't be in the same room as a weapon."

Dillard didn't approve of dueling detectives, let alone dueling teams of lawyers, but said, "Perhaps none of us should be in the room with a weapon. I would shoot Randy Revelle between the eyes without a trace of guilt." Dillard opened the refrigerator and got herself a Diet-Rite cola; Jerene shook her head again that she didn't want one. "Now Jerry, you simply *must* settle this case — have Liddibelle name a price and get it over with. It can't go to court! I thought she was a better friend to us than that."

"I am dealing with Liddibelle directly and I think that will put an end to it, but in the meantime, her detective can learn much that we all do not want him to learn. Darnell, as I was saying, brought in this detective . . ." She sighed. ". . . and I thought, what an opportunity to have a detective to look into various and sundry matters."

This couldn't be good. "Oh Jerene . . ."

Jerene sat quietly, running a manicured hand over a pleat repeatedly. "There are a number of things," she continued slowly, "that we don't speak of in our family and God knows I am most thankful that we *don't* talk about them."

"Yes?"

"Asheboro," Jerene said simply.

Dillard nodded soberly. "The baby. Your daughter."

Jerene reached for her sister's hand. "I couldn't have made it through without you being there with me, Dillie. I remember Mother was on the warpath, wouldn't hear of you accompanying me but you did anyway."

"Of course I did." Dillard squeezed Jerene's hand back.

"And you helped scrape the money together for Miss Grace and Halliford House. Bless your heart."

Neither said anything for a minute, surprised by the power of this wordless moment, this minute of closeness, when in truth they hadn't historically been overly sisterly at all. They had mutually survived their home but that gave them closeness of soldiers in a battle, and often soldiers return from wars never choosing to see their comrades again, preferring to start fresh once their war is over, and it had been that way for them a bit, formal, cordial, respectful in allowing an envelope of space to re-invent and assemble another life. Their formality was a final act of survival and coping, but when it had counted, when one needed the other, they were indeed sisters. Dillard and Jerene, though, had not completely honored it until this moment.

Jerene slowly opened the manila envelope and slid out the few sheets of paper inside. "He found out about *her.*"

Dillard put her hand over her mouth.

"Yes," Jerene said.

"What are you going to do?"

Despite declining the Diet-Rite, Jerene reached for Dillard's can and took a small sip. Jerene found her reading glasses in the pocket of her overcoat, then she read: "Shawna Jane Mabe, born September third, nineteen sixty-six."

Dillard sat again, at the other end of the breakfast-nook table, putting the length of the small kitchen between her and her sister. "September — I remember that hot-as-Hades September."

"The adoptive parents were Jane and Edwin Mabe of Fayetteville, North Carolina. He was in the service. That seems a gamble, letting a soldier and his wife adopt in the middle of the Vietnam War, but that's what the Children's Home did. The father's dead now, according to that next piece of paper."

"My goodness. What do you intend to do now that you know she's . . . she is alive, isn't she?"

"Forty-one years old. She got married late, at thirty-two, to a Kyle Crotts, but is divorced. Two kids by him, a baby from somewhere else. Living in Matthews, North Carolina. Darnell's man got me an address. Carolina Acres . . . Could be some kind of gated community or something."

Dillard shook her head. "I suspect a trailer

park, more likely. You're just going to drive out to Matthews and say, surprise, here I am, your long-lost biological mother?"

"I have no idea what I will do so I've barged over here to ask my big sister."

Dillard felt an unaccustomed giddiness: Jerene seeking the counsel of her big sister. In the last decades, the polarity reversed itself; it was always Dillard coming hat in hand to Jerene, and Duke, and Gaston, who lent her money, then just flat out gave her money, money they'd never see again for her divorce, her setting up a new life after Randy, and then once for a drug treatment clinic for Christopher. She became the classic poor relation. No one that one would go to for help.

"I suppose," Jerene said, "we should drive down there and take a look."

"Sneak around in the bushes? And if we like what we see, knock on the door . . . and then what?"

"Get your car keys. Let's go, and we'll think of something."

Dillard drove Jerene in her Toyota, reflecting how she much preferred others to drive her places. The deep joint pain associated with fibromyalgia could flare at any moment but perhaps adrenaline was holding her pervasive physical maladies at bay. This unexpected expedition, however serious, was also a bit exciting and Dillard found again that earlier sense of giddiness, almost so overwhelming that she thought she might laugh the way others might sob, unbidden, up from the diaphragm.

"I'm worried," Jerene said, "about the Jarvis Trust, Dillie. All the time. I lie awake wondering what will become of it, after we're gone. Since we're halfway to the poorhouse."

Dillard didn't quite see the connection to events at hand.

"I wonder about this Shawna Crotts, what she's like . . . if she has an eye for art, perhaps."

Now Dillard was dumbfounded again. "Jerry. *That* is what you are thinking about now?"

"Among a long list of other things, yes."

Jerene's sense of vulnerability had passed once they were on the road. She had transformed into the sister Dillard was most familiar with, Jerene's face aimed determinedly, lips set, eyes narrowed, the committee woman taking charge, the military commander with a plan under way.

"Annie has made a joke of the Trust for years," Jerene continued, "saying she'd sell off the collection, and now that she's struggling with her real estate business, she really would sell the lot and recoup her losses, I predict. And Jerilyn, poor thing, can't be in charge of it, since she's a walking scandal —

she'll always be the woman who shot her husband, even decades from now."

"That might be why you should let her do it, so she could find some social redemption."

"Do you see any gift for speaking or dealing with the public or . . . She's my own dear little Jerilyn, but she is not a charmer. She is earnest and thoughtful and . . . after this civil suit is over, she has mentioned she might go to graduate school very far from North Carolina and start over."

"She needs to talk to a therapist. It sounds like she has a world of trouble she has not dealt with or processed."

"I agree, but Darnell McKay says she shouldn't see a therapist until the trial is over. The fact that she is seeking counseling will be seen as a sign that she has psychological problems, that she shot Skip on purpose and is only now dealing with her anger issues or male-hatred issues or whatever the prosecution will come up with."

"What is she doing with herself all day?"

"Sitting in her room upstairs. We take every meal together. She just drags around the house, watches a lot of TV. She and Skip went to their seventh grade prom together, then he came down from Carolina to escort her to the senior prom, then he was her guest for the Debutante Ball at Charlottetowne, then she dated him in Chapel Hill, then they married — has she ever been apart from this boy?

But now she acts as if she doesn't care if she ever sees him again. She's not lonely for him, never takes his calls when he rings up. But back to the Trust, Dillie."

Dillard, who had ceded her seat on the Jarvis Trust for American Art to her nephew Bo's wife, Kate Johnston, was happy the Trust and all its bureaucratic drama was out of her hair. So far from being offended that she was "passed over," that her little sister had taken over from her mother in the running of the Trust, she was *elated* to be spared the importuning curators at the Mint or the half-competent caterers or the unctuous fund-raising consultants or the empty-headed society grandes dames that Jerene had packed the committee with. Dillard then saw on a sign that she was eleven miles from Matthews, and they still didn't have a plan, but Jerene was determined to talk about the Jarvis Trust.

"I suppose," Dillard suggested, "your sons *could* end the female tradition. Dear Joshua might be suited to it."

"Yes, it will likely be Josh to take it over. But I had always thought it should be something for the women of the family. Some added piece of security, some status, some reason for them not to simply be decorative Southern women while their men decided their fate in every other aspect of life. It would make it up to her, don't you think? This . . ." She looked at her Xerox again.

"This Shawna Jane Mabe Crotts. My land, those are ugly names all together."

Dillard was slow to see her meaning. And then she did. "My dear, dear, poor deranged sister." Dillard allowed herself a laugh. "Oh my. Are you suggesting this woman raised in military housing in Fort Bragg, North Carolina, married, divorced, and no doubt with a house full of children and no husband, living in Matthews, working . . . where did that say again?"

Jerene looked straight ahead without a flutter. "The detective's report said she had part-time work at the Dancy Corporation. Maybe she's middle management."

"That's just a prettified name for Dancy Mills. She probably does shift work on the line, Jerene. Maybe on food stamps and government aid!"

"Perhaps she will not be right to take over the Trust but I don't see why I shouldn't hope for it. She is a Jarvis, after all. One would like to think a certain intelligence, certain survival skills fought their way to the surface genetically, whatever her adoptive circumstances."

Dillard decided to concentrate on driving, and not say any more.

It was a nice trailer; the faded exterior, the sad metal rusted at the eaves belied a rather cozy home inside. The furniture was old but comfortable; there was a smell of dog and boiled pasta. The dog outside was barking.

"Magnum, shut up!" Shawna yelled. "He hates missing out on the party," she said, smiling.

Both Dillard and Jerene heard it, a speech impediment of some kind, mild, an inability to convincingly do the *t* in hates and party, which came out *pah-ee.* Dillard looked briefly at Jerene, who held a pleasant expression, but her eyes had already passed through regret and rejection and she was spiritually long gone from this trailer.

"Y'all can understand me, right?" She wiped her hands with the dishcloth and set the colander in the sink, steam rising in plumes. "You can sort of tell my jaw's not right. And I have to sit on this side of you. Deaf in this one." She pointed to her right ear.

If there was any doubt she was kin, Dillard thought, her leaning forward, fixing them with her eyes, her smile — it was Daddy looking back at them.

Dillard laughed lightly. "It doesn't seem to have slowed you down any."

"No, s'pose not. Pa always tried to get me to go on disability." *Dis-a-bee-lee.*

"Disability," Dillard said, getting it in a second.

"But I said disability was money for people who really were disabled, and I'm not disabled. He always felt so guilty about it. There were other things that made him take his own life but I'm sure all that info was in your file."

Jerene's file had mentioned the adopted father was dead, but the suicide was news.

"My my," said Dillard, feeling useless as she said it.

"How sad," Jerene said simply, real sadness in her voice.

"It's an old story, I guess. Soldier back from Vietnam."

"Yes," said Dillard. "You say he was guilty . . ."

"Now I think the VA does a lot better by the Iraq and Afghanistan boys, but it's still what they went through and they have to all live with what they seen and done. I'm sorry, you were asking something and I didn't get it." She leaned in with her good ear.

"Nothing. You were saying he felt guilty about . . ."

"You read his file, right?"

Jerene cleared her throat. "Actually, we weren't permitted to read the file, not being with the VA but an auxiliary organization."

"Well, I was five. And he was back from Vietnam, right from when it was going to complete hell and, um, we were all so happy to see Pa get home. And he was sleeping on the sofa, and I just loved him to death — I barely ever saw him, you know, except on leaves and holidays and little letters he sent me. So I snuck up on him to crawl on the sofa beside him and he just exploded. Forced his hands out quickly, the way you would if you were sleeping in-country and someone touched you." She laughed. "It's good, I guess, he wasn't armed with a knife or something — I'd be dead. As it was, he broke my jaw, severed a nerve so my tongue is lazy and my hearing, just in this ear . . . well, he didn't mean to do it. Ma just about left him over it. He carried me crying all the way to the base hospital — I mean, we both were crying. All that's in the file, of course."

Jerene and Dillard sat still a minute. Jerene then went into her purse and brought out a checkbook. Dillard assessed her sister's calm deportment. Money would be her escape plan — a quick check for some too big amount and then they'd get out and that would be that. Jerene had no intention of revealing she was Shawna's mother. It ended the minute they drove into the trailer park and the speech impediment finished any hope of appeal. It wouldn't do, would it, for the head of the Jarvis Trust for American Art to have a speech impediment.

"Well now," said Jerene, taking out her pen.

"I am a bit confused," said Shawna. Now the dog was barking again, and the baby in the playpen began crying, too. She hopped up to get her bawling son, his nose now running profusely. "I thought . . . now hush you, it's some of Daddy's friends here, hush Magnum. Hush both of y'all. I thought the insurance people said there couldn't be a settlement because he took his own life within two years of the policy. I have a stack of letters that say it over and over."

Dillard had no idea what to say.

Jerene didn't miss a beat. "Well, we're not your insurance company and we're not the military, but we're the Veterans' Auxiliary and we can do what we please. It's not maybe what you were hoping for, but . . ."

Shawna laughed, now that her son was quieting down. "We don't hope for too much 'round here, do we, Nathan?"

"May I ask the rent here?"

"One-twenty for all the utilities. I own the trailer."

"Here is five thousand —"

"Oh my God!"

"Five thousand will tide you over a while and keep you in diapers. It's a very small gift for your father's service to this nation, but the Mecklenburg County Auxiliary of," she took a breath as she made up the organization's name, "the Veterans of Foreign Wars wants you to have this."

Dillard was sure her scorn was written on her face. Such adept lying.

Suddenly, along with the dog, there was a racket from the back of the trailer. A nine-year-old girl, her hair the identical straw color of her mother's, and a ten-year-old boy ran down the short hall, slamming into things, screaming accusations, she cut me on purpose, no I did not . . .

"You two? Terry, what did you do to yourself?"

The boy was bleeding on his hand. "She smashed my hand into the broken Coke bottle."

"Well, lordamercy, why is there a broken Coke bottle back in your room?"

"He's got *all* kinds of stuff he's hiding!" tattled the girl.

Now the baby was crying again. Shawna looked pleadingly at Dillard. "I don't suppose you could change a diaper, could you?"

"Why yes. I'd . . . I'd be happy to," Dillard said, leaning forward, hoping without too many grunts or theatrics to get to her feet, standing slowly, and then going to meet Shawna and take the infant to the kitchen counter. Shawna reached to the top of a shelf to get first-aid things and lectured both children to be quiet, to behave, but judging by the children's volume and general air of disobedience, that seemed rarely the case around here.

Dillard turned to Jerene . . . who was not there.

The screen door was just pulling closed. She had escaped.

Write a check and run, Dillard thought.

Facing the vicissitudes of life, of other people's lives, was hard work, she said to herself. Dillard had done more than her share of staring into the shadows where human lives take residence, she thought with stern pride, as she undid the synthetic pants of the boy, the first time she had changed a diaper since Christopher. It was all cloth diapers in her day, and a truck that drove around Charlotte trading soiled for clean. The little boy was laughing, reaching out to touch Dillard's nose, engaged by her. Dillard nuzzled him back. And then an even stranger thought . . .

A thought which stopped her, froze her in her task.

What if she told Shawna that *she,* Dillard Jarvis Revelle, was her biological mother? Shawna looked more like her than Jerene. What if Dillard were to enter the world again, the world of motherhood and, given the mob inside the trailer, grandmotherhood. There would be visits and news of the children, little gifts and cards and celebrations. They could say she was a great-aunt — nothing too complicated or upsetting need be told to the children until they're older. What would Jerene say? Who cares, in this instance, what Jerene would say, when there is such a good deed afoot. Ha, wouldn't that be something, Dillard thought, straightening up the diaper, then holding the boy Nathan close to her bosom. He was content to be there, not crying, gurgling peacefully. Wouldn't that be something, to dive back full force into life. She would, of course, have to do less with the fibromylagia support group —

"Lord, I can't thank you ladies enough," said Shawna, now washing blood and iodine off her hands in the sink. "Changing the diaper was *way* beyond the call of dooey," she added, meaning *duty,* followed by her strange nasal laugh. Dillard wondered if she properly heard her own laugh, how strange it was. "Um, where's your friend?"

Dillard smiled weakly. "We have a few more stops and she's out on her cell phone, I suppose, lining it all up."

Shawna reached over and took Dillard's hand. Shawna looked like she might cry, but she leaned forward and kissed Dillard on the cheek, and said in a ragged voice very quietly, "What good work you ladies do."

Dillard thought she might cry, too. But she blathered to hold it off: "Servicemen and their families do not get nearly enough from the government. We, the ladies of . . ." Oh for God's sake, she couldn't come up with Jerene's made-up organizational name. "We hope what little we do will help." Dillard leaned in to kiss her biological niece's cheek in return. "You take care now."

Would she do it? Would she declare herself Shawna's long-lost mother? But the truth would come out, wouldn't it? It was Jerene, not Dillard. And resentful of Jerene as she was, that was still her choice to make, to own and include a daughter and her unruly brood into the Johnston family. No, what a foolish whim, the more she thought about it. Maybe that's what Jerene understood. Maybe that's why she left before she said anything that would have consequences, consequences of family dynamics, of scandal, of money. The family secret, so close to the surface, visible for anyone outside looking in, slowly began to return to its home below the surface, down to the dark reaches unfathomable, where secrets belonged.

"I'll show myself out," Dillard said, tears playing at the edges of her eyes.

It was late and the sun was low, blinding everyone with the gift of sight, reflecting off the rows of white trailers. Dillard nearly stumbled from the small broken wooden porch, making her way to the visitors' lot, in such a swirl of light and heat. She wondered if she might faint.

Dillard took a few wrong turns between the rows of mobile homes before she found the visitor parking spaces. Dillard's Toyota was still there, but no Jerene. After wandering back and asking the trailer park host who had first given them directions, it appeared the nicely dressed lady with the dark hair had called a cab and gone on her way.

Dillard fumbled with her car keys, barely

able to put them into the lock. She drove home — the merciless sun in her eyes all the way from Matthews, refusing to set, tormenting her from the west. She parked in her driveway; Jerene's BMW was still there.

She opened her front door.

She turned on the living-room light, but that seemed of a piece with the taunting sun, so she turned it off. Dillard felt light-headed but otherwise intact, but she suddenly was completely exhausted. Not hurting, not in pain. She slumped into a soft living-room chair.

Did all of that just transpire? It had played out so quickly, like a little theater piece, and now here she was back to the normal quiet of her own house. Was she normal? Her heart was beating faster. She heard, as if amplified, the tick of the mantel clock.

The phone rang.

Dillard leaned to the end table and picked up the receiver.

"I'm back in your driveway," said Jerene. Dillard could hear a taxi drive away.

Jerene said, "Sorry about my disappearance. I couldn't take another minute of it, not a second."

Dillard's heavy breathing must have told Jerene that her sister was exhausted. "It was very awkward to get out of there, Jerene."

"I deserve your scorn, I don't deny it. Part of my punishment was paying for that

Matthews-to-Charlotte cab ride — there'll be no Christmas this year."

Dillard wasn't amused but then she knew Jerene didn't say it to be amusing. Neither sister said anything for a while. Dillard sighed a few times, not knowing what to say or how far to push.

"I'm curious about something," Jerene said at last. "When I said I hired a detective, your immediate thought was that I hired him because of Duke. As if Duke were cheating on me."

"How should I know, Jerene?"

"On the principle that everyone knows all kinds of things that aren't their business. Just simply tell me if you know something. I cannot be surprised *anymore* by events this year."

"Duke's not the type to cheat," Dillard said, meaning it. Duke could not be credited with genitalia, far as she was concerned. "I haven't heard anything like that at all. You told me — you were the only one brave enough to — that Randy was cheating with women all over town. I didn't want to hear it, but you told me and even proved it to me. I would perform the same service for you, if I ever heard something that could be credited. But this is Duke we're talking about. Duke who worships you."

"Thank you," Jerene said, adding, "For everything."

Then she hung up.

Dillard set the phone on the cradle, still not quite sure the day that had happened had really happened. How quickly the hurricane had worked itself up — three hours ago, Dillard was waiting for the clothes to come out of the dryer, then Jerene tore through, leaving her usual wreckage, then they were in a trailer park, then there was a long-lost daughter, surveyed, judged and found wanting, no better than the official offspring, tossed back in the pile, then it was back home for Dillard, sorry to trouble you, never mind.

Imagine, Dillard thought, heading instinctively toward the mantel and the picture of Christopher, imagine having another child out there to love, like a spare tire, an extra. Dillard would pay all she owned for such a youthful mistake if there were another child to be a mother to.

The picture of Christopher was a school photo, sixth grade, before he became an impossible adolescent. The usual aquamarine background, the feathered 1980s big hair that boys desired, the polyester blends in sports coat and dress shirt and wide tie. That had been one of his father's ties and she remembered going to Belk's to buy that sports coat, with him dragging his feet all the way. She smiled. No young man wants to shop for clothes with his mother.

Duke

Duke's first conscious thought was to fumble for the alarm clock, but it was not the alarm clock. Nor the phone. Oh God, the cell phone.

Jerene stirred beside him in bed. It was 3:30 A.M. She rose up on one arm, prepared to receive an emergency.

"Shouldn't have let the kids talk me into one of these things," Duke said, going through clothes, trying to find which pocket held the cell phone. Not in the trousers . . . not in the sports coat . . . wait, in the breast pocket.

"Hello?"

No one was there.

"Hello?"

"Wrong number," Jerene mumbled, collapsing back to her previous position.

"It's three-thirty in the morning," Duke said to the silent caller with a sigh.

"You know what you did."

Duke glanced at Jerene and slipped into his

bathroom, pulling the door softly behind him.

"You couldn't resist just one final show of contempt."

After a bit more of this, Duke interrupted: "Gaston, you're drunk. You won't even remember this phone call in the morning. I didn't give you this number. How did you get it?"

"Norma had it, the old trout. You were supposed to be there with me, Duke. When I wrote it. We were going to write it. You knew I couldn't do it without you and then you go and name that . . . name that place in fucking South Carolina . . ."

"Good night, Gaston."

"I was like Lee marching off to Gettysburg without Jackson. You — you abandoned me."

Duke held down the red button and turned off the device. Gaston had left a few drunken messages on his study phone; Duke had erased them, not telling Jerene about them. But now she had better know.

"Tell your new mistress not to call so late," she said.

He sat down on the edge of the bed, his eyes not accustomed yet to the dark after the bright white bathroom. "Gallant of you, darling. That you can make that joke at this hour." He paused, a final reprieve of quiet before the talk to come. "It's your brother. Quite inebriated. And still aggrieved."

"I'd managed to go a whole three hours —

that would be the hours I was asleep — without thinking about him and the house."

Jerilyn's wedding, the house renovation, the engine overhaul of the BMW, all of it led to a second mortgage on the Johnston house. For a while their meager income flowed to servicing their mortgages but then it became clear there would never really be enough to pay it down on the schedule planned. An attempt at renegotiating the first mortgage failed, despite Duke's best charming manner — midway through the interview with the bank officer, who was all of twenty-five, nervous and not making eye contact with his elder, his collar too big for his thin neck, Duke felt he was coming off like some sponging British aristocrat out of P. G. Wodehouse, trying to smile and glide his way to stiffing the bank on his borrowing.

So, Jerene one night asked Gaston if he would loan them a six-figure sum to pay it off, and he surprised them by saying he wouldn't make it a loan, but rather he'd pay their loans and mortgages off as a gift, that they should again own the Johnston mansion unencumbered. There was an accompanying Gastonian screed, naturally, demanding no cent of his gift should indirectly work its way to the care of their mother Jeannette Jarvis, but Jerene and Duke expediently agreed and they thought the matter was settled. Those were nights they both slept soundly, knowing that they could, if they chose, in their own sweet time, die in their bed, within these very walls. And all was briefly right with the world again: the restored friendship of Gaston Jarvis, Duke and Gaston, back to being pals, old revels and vices rehabilitated, drinking buddies talking late into the night in his Civil War Study, convening for dinner when Jerene had a meeting, the revival of a golden age. What had happened? What had yanked away the promise of Gaston's bailout? They would lose the house in October 2008, by Duke's calculations.

Now their landline phone rang.

Jerene erupted from the tangle of sheets and blankets to grab the receiver. "Gaston. Yes, I can hear that you are drunk but it's no excuse for waking us up so . . ." She listened. "I will not put him on. And you will not call this house again this late or . . ." She listened a bit longer then put the phone down quietly, Gaston having hung up first. She unplugged the phone jack that snapped into the base of the phone.

She resumed lying on her back, with a sigh. "Lookaway, Dixieland," she said after a moment.

"Yes. We can get an unlisted number when we move to our condo in South Carolina."

"No, Lookaway, Dixieland is what he is furious about."

Duke now lay down beside her in the bed,

also looking up at their ceiling. "Yes. I know. In my own defense, darling, this is a crisis I wandered into rather innocently."

His fellow investors had been musing aloud for a name of their development on the banks of the Catawba. They had drawn up a list, most having the word "trestle" in it. *Shadows on the Trestle. The Trestle 'Cross the River. Trestle Crossing.* Bob Boatwright ruled that he didn't think "trestle" was a poetic enough word to be in a name of a high-end development. It called up images of hobos; it made people think of the noisy passing freight that would rattle their china cabinets. No, said Bob, it had to be in line spiritually with nearby Tega Cay. Duke, like most Charlotteans, thought calling anything a "cay" on an inland catfish-and-red-clay riverway dammed by a concrete embankment was ludicrous. Tega Cay, South Carolina. It sounded like some lost exotic islet off Turks and Caicos, a nighttime soap setting . . . *Reginald, I refuse to let you and Topaz steal Mother's cabana on Tega Cay . . .*

The neighboring development was the Palisades at Lake Wylie. Did the people who named that imagine there was anything palisade-like around? A fence of vertical, spike-ended tree trunks around a fort? Anyway, the Palisades was one of the most glamorous addresses in the Carolinas, five minutes from a Jack Nicklaus golf course, homes from the $800,000s and connected to the Ranch (hm, no poetic ambition in that name) for the one-acre-plus mansion lots. The Palisades Boat Club. The Wilkinson Tennis and Swim Club with Pete Sampras and Mats Wilander as visiting tennis pros. No, said Bob, we need to carve out a niche of exclusivity, gentility, the Old South . . . *Cannons on the Catawba. Battlefield on the Rivershore. Ramparts on the Catawba.* Maybe just *The Ramparts.* And it was then, freed from some long-unutilized corridor of Duke's brain, that "Lookaway, Dixieland" sprang out. They didn't like it at first, then they thought about the lines dropped from the lyrics of "Dixie," then they liked it, then they liked it a lot. A whole theme took shape. The sign resting upon white neoclassical columns, the plantation house engraved behind the logo, the mini-Tara-like gate and uniformed attendant to keep the riffraff out. *Old times there are not forgotten,* intoned Bob Boatwright, sweeping a hand out as if there were a view in the conference room to behold. *Lookaway, lookaway . . . Lookaway, Dixieland.* Duke didn't think about Gaston's great unrealized literary project of the same name, in mothballs for the last forty years. Gaston surely thought it was some cruel jibe, but Duke had honestly not remembered Gaston's so-called book, that book that never was, that never will be.

Jerene fished through the covers to find Duke's hand.

"If we lose the civil suit," he said, voicing all their fears which needed no voicing, which were always with them, "then Liddibelle will be very surprised, as will Charlotte, to find out we're completely bust. We'll have to declare bankruptcy."

"I'll take care of Liddibelle," his wife said. "Don't worry about that. I just keep thinking how we will miss this house. Somewhere your grandfather is shedding a tear."

"This house was always a refuge for me," said Duke.

Grandfather Johnston built his house in 1897, on a bluff that could look back on the uptown of Charlotte, and in the 1920s, developers and city boosters surrounded their farm with the developments of Myers Park and Eastover and Wendover. All those years, his grandfather's Providence Road estate had sat regally on its hill, watching the elite of Charlotte nestle around it. By the time Duke's grandmother died, the house was occupied by Duke's maiden aunt who lived into the 1970s, by which time Duke's own father was suffering from strokes and dementia and not in a fit state to inherit the property. The estate settled equally on Duke and his brother, Carrington. Carrington was happy in Maryland so Duke bought out his brother's half. Duke's work as a lawyer brought in comfortable money to keep the place up; his time on the Charlotte City Council was not unprosperous. But after that, to make ends meet, Duke sold off the parcels of land surrounding the house until their white two-story house with the elegant, columned screened-in side porch appeared to be just another nice home, another half-acre lot in Charlotte's rich folks' neighborhood.

Then they took out a mortgage. Then a second one.

Duke scooted closer in the bed toward his wife, squeezing her hand. "How I dreaded going to Virginia on those weekends home from university. I stopped going to Virginia altogether by my last year of law school, speeding away most Fridays to come here and be with my grandparents instead. My grandmother was a sumptuous cook."

"Yes, I only met them once, but I liked them immensely."

Yes, his grandparents had left him a monument, Duke reflected, a small respectable Southern estate. And Duke had fumbled it away.

Duke's own childhood was in Caroline County, Virginia, near Fort A. P. Hill where Major Joseph Beauregard "Bo" Johnston trained soldiers in the Officer Candidate School. Major Bo had been trained there himself before deployment in North Africa with General George S. Patton. Operation Torch. Task Force A. Two Army Corps. Duke would tell his schoolmates at Hampden-Sydney these designations with pride. After his World War II service, Duke's father had returned to A. P. Hill to train officers for the European bases until after the Korean War, when he was then part of the Engineer Officer Candidate School that prepared young officers for Vietnam.

Duke's full name was Joseph Beauregard Johnston, too. Major Bo spent a good deal of time correcting people who wished to familiarize the name and call either of them Joe. "Never let anyone call you 'Joe,' son," his father instructed. "Joe pumps your gas or fixes your sink. Joseph is the name of statesmen and generals." Duke was glad that in college he got the nickname "Duke," since the farther he could get from identifying with all the glorious ancestors, the better.

Duke's younger brother's name was Carrington, named after their Revolutionary War ancestor Lieutenant Johnston's great friend and partner in youthful mischief, Clement Carrington. The Carringtons still existed in Charlotte and Duke knew them socially — it was their one worn-thin topic of affable conversation each and every Mint by Gaslight. By marriages, throughout the 1700s, the Johnstons married into the Henrys (of

Patrick Henry fame), the Prestons, the Woods, all manner of Virginia aristocracy with sons educated at Hampden-Sydney (founded, in fact, on a parcel of land given by John Johnston in 1777); these young scions inevitably matriculated at William and Mary, UVA or West Point. The wilds of the Virginian Piedmont was where Peter Johnston and Lighthorse Harry Lee rode and camped and hunted — two military greats whose greater sons, Joseph E. Johnston and Robert E. Lee, would also be close. It was Robert E. Lee who was chosen to break the news to Joseph when his favored nephew Preston died in the assault on Contreras in the Mexican-American War. They write that Joseph fainted to the ground, had to be carried to his tent, such was his grief for the boy he had loved like a son. A photo of Preston accompanied Johnston everywhere, from the bivouac tent to his civilian offices. Perhaps that is why Joseph E. Johnston had no children of his own, Duke had always speculated.

General Joseph did, however, have nine siblings and, somewhat obscurely, there was a sibling who wandered to Tennessee, from which their corner of the Johnston clan descended. At some point, Duke's great-grandfather moved to Charlotte, thereby avoiding a return to the bosom of family connections that was Virginia and its high-society snares. Both Virginia and South Carolina were obsessed with colonial lineages and dynastic marriages. North Carolina offered nowhere near the privileged-class blood sport of its neighbors.

Suddenly — and this was happening a lot lately as he got older — another flash from Duke's university days unspooled to his conscious mind: an evening in his beloved Arcadia attic room, Gaston sprawled upon the leather couch that was more comfortable than any bed or bower known of before or since, Duke at his desk, a law book open and unattended.

"I suspect," said Gaston, "that North Carolina's lack of high society pretensions has to do with its rivers." Gaston then quoted the famous description of North Carolina being a pleasant "vale of humility between two mountains of conceit," the windy summits being Virginia and South Carolina.

"That's Governor Vance, isn't it?" Duke asked at the time.

"Some say Alexander Hamilton said it — it sounds like Hamilton. Maybe it was William Byrd, the eighteenth-century one. He didn't have much nice to say about North Carolina. Said we were lazy."

Duke now was sideways in his throne of a desk chair, letting his legs dangle, head dangling too, staring up at the eaves. "Lazy? What slander."

"Said our women were of loose virtue."

Gaston swirled the ice in his glass. "I've regrettably not found it so."

"I believe I have found it so, just not lately. You were saying about rivers."

The James River and Chesapeake Bay in Virginia made for an ideal system of shoreside plantations which could get their crops to ports. Charleston in South Carolina as well, a tangle of bays and rivers, leading to prosperous plantations. A great place to get rich. And here is poor North Carolina surrounded by the Outer Banks, Cape Hatteras, the Graveyard of the Atlantic. Waters much to be avoided as the points of land would suggest: Cape Lookout, Cape Fear. Those shifting sandbars enclose the Great Dismal Swamp, as the colonists named it, dense, dark, dangerous, full of snakes and alligators, several mythical monsters including a fire-breathing giant raptor. The Old North State became the haven of escaped slaves from Virginia and South Carolina, escapees from the numerous shipwrecks off our coast. Better selling than *Uncle Tom's Cabin* in its day was Harriet Beecher Stowe's follow-up, *Dred: A Tale of the Great Dismal Swamp* about Dred, a fugitive slave preaching uprising and revolution. (Maybe she felt a little bad about creating the passive Uncle Tom.)

"Indentured servants, debtors, petty thieves, seducers and bigamists, escaped prisoners — they all ran headlong into the swamp sanctuaries of our beloved state. They *are* our true aristocracy," Gaston added, toasting them. "The tobacco magnates came later, of course. Just white trash made good."

"I don't think you should share that theory with the benefactors of this fine university," Duke had suggested.

How was it that Gaston wished to deprive himself of their friendship? The ease and rich flow of conversation, the reading, the small investigations, the discovery of new bottled pleasures. Having dwelled in Arcadia, how could one leave? And how much longer, Duke would wonder, would they both be alive? Duke was coming up on sixty-four this very weekend, Gaston was five years behind him but looked older. Duke himself had neuropathy; his fingers and feet were often numb, he dropped and fumbled every device or medicine bottle he put his hand to. He was on a number of medications that weren't terribly serious — for blood pressure, for cholesterol — and he had a regimen of mild blood thinners and aspirin to prevent the strokes that did in his father and led him to dementia. He could only imagine what Gaston's ailments were, if he even went to a doctor.

"Gaston and his money were our last hope," Duke said, sounding pitiful to himself. "And I managed to set him off again."

"He likes being set off. If it wasn't one thing you said, it would have been something I let slip. We were children to imagine he would follow through on that gift."

Duke heard their downstairs phone ring again. They had not left their warm bedroom to go unplug it.

"My brother," Jerene said calmly, "is in the late stages of alcoholism, the treatment of which is complicated by two or three personality disorders."

"I think that's a low estimate."

"He likely needed counseling from the time he was fourteen, so." It wasn't a sentence that really needed a predicate.

"I suppose, darling, you should prepare yourself. The end of this particular downward spiral might well be quite ugly."

"Norma will work something out," Jerene said, out of more hope than knowledge.

They both darkly knew how it could go. He would commit a fatal hit-and-run while drunk, wake up in an emergency room with the police handcuffing him to his bed. An alcoholic coma from which he does not recover. Wandering drunkenly in front of a bus. A tumble down his foyer stairs and, as he lies there, a coronary. His esophagus so raked by acids and alcohols that it perforates and he bleeds out into his throat. That, Duke remembered, is what happened to Gaston and Jerene's father.

Mortality, mortality. God, a birthday this Friday — how Duke hated it. He hoped it had been forgotten utterly but there'd be a dinner somewhere, some foolishness. Jerene's hand had lost its tautness; she had fallen back asleep. He gently released her and turned over . . . now wide awake, of course.

The talk of bodily deterioration made Duke think about his father, Major Bo. Duke never relived the beatings, replayed any of the unsettled grievances or the constant refrain of military-themed belittlement that he and his brother endured as boys. It was a part of him he rarely accessed, half shrugged off and forgotten, half retained in some locked part of the heart. But Duke had been thinking lately of his father's physical decline. A series of strokes that made him bedridden, and finally, left him with dementia. Duke remembered the VA Hospital in Hampton was where he and his brother, Carry, took him but he had become so aggressive with orderlies, so unpleasant, that the VA shipped him briefly to a mental institution that specialized in violent dementia. After a spell there, he was calmer. Whether that was through drugs or electric shock, Duke did not investigate.

Duke declared he had no intention of taking his invalid father into his home in Charlotte. After some soul-searching, Carry said he would at least try to take care of Dad, and moved the old man into his Maryland home. Duke, once he had broken off relations with his military father, escaped at university into fine clarets, whiskeys, the best cigars, indulgences like Civil War pistols and first-edition nineteenth-century books — the secular Southern-pagan world that beckoned with wine, women and song. Carrington escaped, too, but into a deeper religious faith and that led him to try to make a lasting peace with his father. So he moved Dad, stroke-ridden, his left side limp and useless, into his home with Rhetta and their three kids.

Two weeks later, Dad was moved out again, into the Baltimore VA hospital.

"He only had use of one side of his body," Carry told Duke by phone, "but he managed to bloody Rhetta's nose with the good hand. I went in to lay down the law and . . ."

Duke heard a catch in his brother's voice. Duke didn't say anything, to give Carry time to tell what he needed to tell.

". . . and when the kids were at church, and Rhetta was at Circle, I went in there and said, 'Look, you fucker. This is my house and your days of victimizing any of us are over.' And he said some things."

"Of course he said some things, unforgivable things. That's who he's always been."

"And I punched, him, Joze. I punched my own bedridden father in the face. And it felt good enough that I did it again, and again. I think I was saying 'How do you like that, old man?' and . . ."

"Carry, I couldn't have lasted as long as

you did."

"He just laughed at me. Anyway, he's back at the VA."

And that's where Major Bo stayed until he died.

"You were braver than I was," Carry would always say. "You committed to go to Vietnam and I was always the shirker, the soon-to-be draft dodger."

Duke knew he wasn't the brave one. He thought the war was being badly fought in addition to not being worth fighting but he marched dutifully toward it, not able to imagine a world where he did not do as his father commanded, or live up to his ancestors. He didn't have the courage *not* to go to war. He was hoping, in scenarios steeped in self-contempt, that becoming an officer might lead to survival, a desk to hide behind, a small command in Europe staring down at the Russians staring back, all of it far from Southeast Asia. He lay in that hospital bed after his football injury, emerging from his coma, and he breathed an easy breath for the first time in his life: *Thank God, I am out of the war.*

Duke put on a good public show about not being able to serve his country but he was inwardly delighted. It was nothing less than spiritual liberation, a heavy door now flung open to all possibilities and unreckoned futures. He would not be a soldier, nor train to be an officer, nor be measured against his father's heroism; he would not be killed or torn to pieces by land mines or ripped apart by grenades, nor would he have to kill anyone, for which he was almost as grateful. His life was his own. Now as a man on the eve of his sixty-fourth birthday, he wondered why he did not always see that his life was always his own. Perhaps a fatal pattern was set, though. Duty calling and an excuse presenting itself.

What he dreaded was Christmas, going home to see his beloved mother and his father, always spoiling for a fight. Christmas 1969 was his last appearance. He had met Gaston's sister by then, Jerene Jarvis, and among her many enchantments she had forsworn ever going back home for a visit again, dating from Christmas 1965. Gaston also had boycotted return visits — they had a little parents-hating club, almost.

Solely to see his much put-upon mother, Duke summoned his will and drove to Virginia for the holidays. The year before, his father looked at Duke walking with his neck brace, his walking stick for balance when there was vertigo, and started in. "Don't think because you fell down on a football field that you even begin to matter as much as those men who left an arm or a leg on the field of battle."

On the last Christmas that Duke appeared at their bungalow in Fort Hill, before the schism, before he told his mother he would not be coming home as long as his father was alive, he sat through a last long dinner where his father summed up the worthlessness of his sons for the table's benefit. And when Major Bo got around to mocking Duke's stylish walking stick, some nineteenth-century thing bought in a Durham antiques store, saying how he shouldn't imagine his little sufferings were anything compared to the men who left an arm or leg on the field of battle, Duke looked up and said, "Why didn't you leave one, Dad?"

"What?"

"There was a lot of carnage in Morocco, in Sicily, right?"

His father stood up, shaking the table, sending his water glass on its side. His eyes already blazing. Duke would recall that look — that was the look that got Dad into the mental institution — deranged, pure uncontrolled hate and rage, flailing around for something to pummel. But that Christmas, Duke was determined:

"Soldiers in Two Corps were falling like flies but you managed to stay out of harm's way, didn't you, Dad? Tell us. Did you hang back a little? Let the enlisted shield you a bit . . ."

By that time, his father was on him but Duke got a blow in first. He remembered his mother's cries, and Carry sitting there, still too cowed to move. There were a few back-

and-forth blows before he pushed his father into the cabinet full of military awards and plaques. His mother ran between them to intervene, and Duke flew from the house.

He would call his mother when he was sure his father would be at a veteran's parade or a VFW event. He begged her to get in the car and meet him a few miles away at a restaurant for lunch, but she wouldn't. She couldn't lie successfully to his father, and if he found out . . . His mother was ground down like dust. Died suddenly. Both he and Carry got a call from his father, spitting out the news, a hint of blame in his voice as if maybe they had participated in their mother's demise in some conspiratorial way. Duke did not go to the funeral. His mother would not be there and would not know he wasn't there, so what was the point? Carry reported that his father was a wreck, crying, sobbing, maybe embracing for the first time a vision of how helpless and alone the remainder of his life would become.

Duke and Carry made the arrangements to have the major buried at Arlington. Duke and Carry attended without their families. The army is good about this stuff — they ginned up some kind of crowd. There was a band, the caisson, an escort, and a few of his surviving buddies, who assured his sons, with still-strong handshakes, with tearful eyes, what a brave man their father was, such ingenuity at the Kasserine Pass, such fearlessness at Monte Cassino.

"Glad at least someone got something good out of him," Carry mumbled, on the way back to his car. Duke thought of how his last encounter was him accusing his old man of cowardice. Felt good at the time — didn't feel so good now, walking amid the crosses of Arlington.

"You take care, Joze," Carry added, with a brief pat on the shoulder in what was almost a hug.

It had been fifteen years, and the brothers had not seen each other since. Granted Carry has his kids, Duke doesn't travel much. Oh they talk on the phone, holidays. And birthdays; he'll probably call this Friday. And Duke was sometimes sad about it but he knew they would likely not see each other anymore until there was a summons from a wife, a dire scene in a hospital room one day.

The phone rang again downstairs. Duke craned his head to see the alarm clock. Four-thirty A.M., now.

Duke (and Gaston in the old days) could get almost as worked up over hush puppies and barbecue talk as they could about Civil War talk. The closer to the coast you get, the more cakey and desserty the hush puppies get. Good Lord, Duke could remember Gaston declaring, the hush puppy should be savory, gritty with large-grain corn meal, fried to a crispy brown, NOT of a consistency "like a piece of deep-fried pound cake," and never *ever* sweet. Now the coast itself — where hush puppies accompany fried seafood — often has exemplary hush puppies, i.e, Tony's Sanitary in Morehead City, probably the best hush puppies made. Duke had been fishing with his law partners twice in his life, playing at being Papa Ernest, a charter boat out of Morehead, big talk of marlin and tuna in the Gulf Stream, the entire operation soaked in beer and, later, whiskey to avert seasickness. All Duke came back with was three sacks of hush puppy mix from Tony's — two for his family and one as a gift for Alma, whose job it would be to recreate the hush puppy excellence in the Johnston kitchen. Gaston once said, "It is a hush puppy wasteland from Lexington to the sea with a few notable exceptions."

The twin ideals of North Carolina barbecue — the phrase "pork barbecue" would be a redundancy — divide down the line where the flat and sandy, piney coastal plain meets the rolling red-clay, deciduous-forested slopes of the Piedmont. Piedmont barbecue is pork shoulder, slow cooked, eight or nine hours over hickory coals in what's known as "Lexington style." Down east, they roast the *whole hog* on a spit in a smokehouse, letting the organs and marrow flavor the meat, which becomes more tender and delicious than any pork recipe known to man. The pork is light as ash on the tongue — a *mousse* of pork, aerosolized. Both methods are delicious — there is virtually no bad barbecue — but Duke and Gaston, after the requisite sticking up for their native Piedmont style, spent many a university Saturday in spring on forays into the flatlands of the east to go "whole hog."

Duke wondered whether he could patch things up with Gaston by proposing a two-day barbecue run to eastern North Carolina, stay overnight in some swank golf hotel . . . or more fun, some country club of a Podunk town, letting the old ladies swarm Gaston with copies of his books to sign, amusing themselves with the redneck fineries and parochial *société.*

Slaw. Just as important for Duke and many North Carolinians is the slaw. In the Piedmont there is "barbecue slaw," which uses the juices of the pig and vinegar and sometimes cracked dried chilies to make a red-tinted, spicy slaw of chopped cabbage. When combined with the chopped-up shoulder on a sandwich or just side by side on a tray, where one can intermingle the piles alchemically on one's fork, well, you have as North Carolina patron saint Andy Griffith would've said, "Goooood eatin'." Slaw down east is mayonnaisy cole slaw, which often, even in the greatest of barbecue shacks, can taste store-bought from the supermarket deli counter. Sadly the best slaw (the Piedmont) and the best pig (down east) are never found together in the same operation. And then you got South Carolina. They can cook pig south of the border, too (Kingstree, Manning, Hemingway), and they tend to cook whole hog over wood chips like the east. Some barbecue joints make a hash out of the coarse ends of the chopped barbecue pile which is then turned into a stew and served over South Carolina white rice . . . which is right up there for satisfaction with first love and winning the lottery. Anyway, they have a mustard-based sauce and that might not sound good but it is: creamy, tangy, sharp with a latent heat.

On Nations Ford Road, right over the South Carolina line, Duke and his daughter Annie, in a red vinyl booth Annie barely fit into, were gorging themselves at Daryl's BBQ Palace. The owner loved to see Duke coming because during the Skirmish at the Trestle historical re-creation (two more miles down the road), Daryl's did record business. In fact, Duke was trying to wave and capture Daryl himself's attention, but to no avail.

Annie had a large chopped plate, red slaw, fried okra, a little bowl of Brunswick stew and some collard greens she loaded up with vinegar. "Dad, I feel guilty taking you out for barbecue. Cholesterol, salt, your blood pressure. I'm sure this is forbidden. Just as . . ." She reached for her Styrofoam cup of tea. ". . . my pre-diabetic state would forbid this glorious sweet iced tea."

The waitress came by and asked about dessert. They had blackberry or peach cobbler with whipped cream, except she didn't say "whipped," she said *whup cream.* Annie's eyes sparkled as she and her father exchanged smiling glances. Annie asked for the banana pudding.

Duke: "I'll take an extra Lipitor and you shoot yourself full of insulin and just enjoy yourself, says Doctor Dad. Really, the whole glory of being alive right now is that they have pills for everything. You can be just like your grandmother. She eats a slice of chocolate pie at the Presbyterian Home and then stabs herself with an insulin pin. We're paying doctors all the money in the world to fix what we broke, so we might as well make the pharmaceutical companies work for us."

Annie had missed the Friday birthday foray to a steakhouse, but had shown up Saturday morning, unusually, idling around the house, reading old magazines. She brought him a present — a navy blue Duke University hoodie, "like the cool kids wear," she said, but perfect for his mandatory walk-round-the-block regimen of exercise on cool days.

He began, "I keep seeing where Charlotte

hasn't had a downturn —"

"Oh believe me, we're gonna get it too. The banks at the center of this cluster . . . um, big steaming pile of . . . um, mess are in Charlotte so we'll feel it last, but it's coming. I can't sell any of the properties I own, and they are losing value by the hour."

"I thought you just sold on commission. You actually own properties?"

Annie looked caught out. She'd not told her father anything about her business life except that she was wildly successful. "The housing bust finally is coming to Charlotte," she admitted. "Starting and spreading out from Ground Zero, my pocketbook. Let's not talk about my situation," she said with a wince. Duke assumed he would hear if Annie was teetering toward bankruptcy like so many other people in real estate. Annie made no secret of her sufferings, as a rule. But maybe this, financial failure, after she had been riding so high, was too much to advertise.

"But speaking of real estate," she began, "and I'd like an answer unvarnished, if you would."

"I'll do my best, sweetheart."

"Are you and Mom losing the house?"

Best not to temporize: "Yes, by the end of the year. The bank will own it — they already do, in a manner of speaking. You may have heard that Gaston was going to help us, but he's feuding with us again."

"I could go try to speak with him. Uncle Gaston likes me."

For one thing, Duke had heard Gaston berate Annie recently in the unkindest of terms — loud, vulgar, materialist, a woman who had wasted her magnificent intelligence — and second, Duke hated for any hope to be revived, even to be attempted. He and Jerene had made up their minds to leave and they would leave. "We don't really need the house anymore, darling," he said. "It's big and expensive. Property taxes, the yard, Alma's getting older like we are and will retire upon our departure. Our children are all grown up and gone."

"Your children are *not* gone. We're all bankrupting ourselves in turn and will come home with great frequency."

"I beg your pardon. Bo has a lovely manse courtesy of Stallings Presbyterian."

"That Nazi church is always about to fire him. Josh says they're shutting down stores at *Uomo Modallll.*" She over-performed the Italian name of the ridiculous place. "And Jerilyn needs a place to hide out until the court case has gone away."

"And you're planning on returning again, are you?"

"You never know." She changed tone. "Dad, it's a lovely old house that's been in the Johnston family forever —"

"Just over a hundred years, let's not exaggerate."

"I'm surprised you want to sell it. I'm doubly surprised Jerene wants to lose her perch in Myers Park."

"Very shortly, your mother and I hope to be in Lookaway, Dixieland. It will have a guest room for your cyclical bankruptcies."

Annie was fooling neither of them; she hated fundamental change, only preferred it around the edges. She couldn't stand to be without the house she grew up in. "But your Civil War Study with the fireplace," she wheedled. "You're not going to have such a nice period room in some pre-fab condo somewhere."

"I'm surprised to hear such concern for my Civil War Study. You said once if you could bring General Sherman back from the grave you would do so in order for him to burn down my study."

"Gimme a break, I was a teenager."

"That was just a few years ago, sweetheart."

"This development sounds dreadful. Gated community, snobby, exclusive . . ."

"Just the ticket, for your mother."

"Filled with South Carolina Republicans."

"We should hope so."

"I've seen that billboard on Seventy-seven. The house on the sign is like a mini-Tara, white columns and foyers that'll be impossible to heat or cool. Three-car garages, tacky chandeliers in high-ceilinged rooms that don't have any more floor space than McMansions in Huntersville and Morristown that are half the price. God. What do you suppose the guy in the gatehouse will be forced to wear? White-powdered wigs and breeches with stockings?"

"I was hoping for a girl in a hoop skirt." Duke saw Daryl, the proprietor, emerge from the kitchen — he waved. It seemed Daryl saw him, looked right at him, but turned around back inside. Must be busy. But it was two P.M., a bit late for lunch, and the dining room was not that crowded.

Annie was still ranting: ". . . and I'm ashamed to have parents living in South Carolina. North Carolina has worked very hard *not* to be South Carolina and here y'all go and sink to their level, in a gated community — and these enclaves represent nothing less than Southern apartheid. Maybe that slogan can be a selling point for Mr. Boatwright and his crowd: *slavery still permitted here.*"

"I'll suggest it to the residency association."

"Are we really out of money? I mean, as a family. Have we gone bust? I think I have a right to know."

"I think it is debatable whether our finances are much of your concern. We've clothed and fed you, we've educated you, inasmuch as that took, and we've been generous as we could be throughout. And we're done, darling, we're just simply done." He didn't mean to sound harsh. Duke smiled again, his trademark twinkle. "Yes, we've gone through it," he went on, "in the tradition of great Southern families."

"But Mom could sell some of the paintings," she ventured.

Duke stared at her. That would be the very last thing that could transpire with her mother still breathing. "You know that's not going to happen. Any more than I'm selling my pistols or muskets."

"But they're just things —"

"Yes, things that mean a great deal more than houses — which, by the way, are also things. Cars are things. Annie, why don't you sell your BMW and chip in? That is two years of property taxes sitting in the parking lot."

Annie said slowly, "If it could save the house . . ."

"Oh don't even pretend you would sell your car so we could pay property taxes. No one in this family sacrifices anything for any greater good — it's not how we've ever operated. Your mother would rather have the Jarvis Room at the Mint than sell paintings for . . . for what? Taxes, groceries, deodorant? The Jarvis Room is her legacy." He had actually stuck up for Annie, too, trying to convince Jerene that she would do well by the Jarvis Trust for American Art. Of course,

Jerene always knew best — Annie would have the paintings at the pawnshop by mid-afternoon on the day she got her hands on them. He continued, "I intend to hoard my Civil War artifact collection until I am a near-corpse and give it to some museum that will display or care for it. And you'll be driving around . . ." Duke pointed to the parking lot again. ". . . in that overpriced car that tells your clients you are successful until you trade it for the next spectacularly overpriced car. There is no point pretending things are not as they are."

There was nothing now but a desperate emotional appeal. "Dad. I can't stand to think of our home with other people in it."

Duke wondered if she would say the thing no one in the family would say to his face. Even Jerene in recent years stopped hinting or expecting there would ever be a change: if only Duke Johnston would go to work again. Resume his law practice.

"It's the bottom of the market, Dad." Annie sighed. "A terrible time to sell. Might make the difference in one to two hundred thousand dollars."

But then a male voice: "You, sir, have some nerve coming in here."

It was Daryl. Duke thought it was somehow the beginning of a comic riff, and stood up to introduce Annie. "Daryl, my friend. This is my daughter Annie Johnston —"

"Father or daughter," said Daryl, "no Johnston is welcome in here. We all trusted you, Duke, to preserve our heritage."

Duke now gauged just how upset Daryl was.

"I believe I —"

"Have you seen what they're turning the battleground into? I remember you pulled five hundred dollars out of me — sacred earth, blah blah blah. Where Charlotte fought, blah blah blah. And you swore that you'd keep the developers off that site, and damn if you weren't part of the team developing it all along. Hope you got your thirty pieces of silver."

"I haven't seen what they've done, Daryl. I —"

Daryl grabbed their bill off the table. "This is on me. Consider it a payback for all the business you got me in April. I guess there'll be no more re-enactments, thanks to what you and your rich buddies've done down there. Now, if you've finished up, I'd like it if you folks got on your way."

They drove toward the trestle in silence.

Annie broke it one time saying, "You know, Bob Boatwright and that crowd are douchebags. It shouldn't surprise anyone that they didn't do anything they said they would do. I hear things. I hear . . . that like Beazer Homes, they're all being investigated. Predatory practices, false estimates of value, secret lot-splitting after the assessments, big bonuses paid to partners out of development money, earnest monies paid in cash back and forth to each other. I hope they all go to jail, Dad."

Duke sighed. "Well. Not at least until we move into our home and the ink is dry on the deed." He cleared his throat. "Then we'll build a scaffold."

Oh God. Oh no.

Worse — much worse than he feared . . .

The riverbank that had served as the "historical field of battle" had been denuded of all grass and trees; some of the great riparian oaks were now fresh stumps. It had been scraped bare by bulldozers, acres of topsoil and red clay exposed; Duke wondered how many shells or buttons or artifacts had been churned under the soil by the earthmovers. That element was, at least, reparable. So they replant their field with grass and make it more of a lawn . . . all the better to re-enact upon. But Duke walked farther down the shoulder of the roadway to investigate: there were wooden stakes and cement blocks which marked out the dimensions of a tremendous building about to begin its construction. Duke remembered this, a columned porticoed faux-antebellum mansion/activity center for wedding parties, balls, meeting rooms, a high-end bar and restaurant, with a riverdeck outdoor restaurant . . . But it was supposed to be farther upstream! Placing it right in the middle of their field would leave fifty yards or so between it and the makeshift ramparts. The re-enactors would be virtually on the back patio.

Duke never brought his still unfamiliar cell phone anywhere, so he borrowed Annie's. She looked as downcast as he was.

"I'll pay you back for these directory assistance calls," he said.

"Jesus, Dad. Don't worry about that."

Calls to Bob Boatwright turned up a secretary who, after delay, her hand over the receiver, muffled voices and a TV broadcasting CNBC running in the background, returned to declare Bob was traveling on business. Calls to Mr. Yerevanian never picked up. Calls to Mr. Brownbee didn't even get to a message box. Duke called the landscape architect that he had spoken with before, Mr. Arens, and he indeed was in his office. But he told Duke he had been let go from the assignment, and that others — he didn't know who — were in charge now of designing the area around the trestle. They (Bob and his fellow investors) had asked that the clubhouse and restaurant be moved closer to the trestle as a sound buffer for the homes; when the new embankment downstream raised the Catawba River twenty feet —

"What embankment? They're going to flood the whole area?"

Yes, said Mr. Arens, they envisioned a marina to come out from the ramparts so the fisherman-motorboat crowd could take advantage of new waterfront.

Duke heard his own weak voice. "But what of the historical park to be made around the trestle?"

The former architect said that it had been in his design, but that design was rejected. He was sorry he could not be of more help. Duke nonetheless was gracious to the man who had drawn such a heartening design for the path from the parking area to the trestle, a monument near the ramparts, a circular sawdust trail for an eventual statue, perhaps, and a paved trail through the muddy marge under the trestle that would lead to an outdoor display, a series of three plaques, the pictures on which would be chosen by Duke — with text by Duke Johnston as well. All of that, Duke knew in an instant, was never going to happen.

"What have I done?" he said simply to his daughter. "They couldn't have gotten the building permit without me. I raised a small fortune from friends, family, the Charlottetowne Country Club, to preserve this site and then . . . I was instrumental in destroying it."

Annie didn't insult him, at least, by saying he was some blameless victim. "They were awful men you were dealing with, Dad."

"I suppose you should take me home."

They rode in silence again. Duke didn't feel the gloom lift even when he saw the familiar WELCOME TO NORTH CAROLINA sign.

Annie said quietly, "You could sue."

"Nothing was in writing, darling. It was all gentleman's agreement stuff, handshakes and promises. I've known Bob at Charlottetowne for ages. Besides, my compensation for my help with this development . . ." Here Duke raised his hands to cover his face — he was overwhelmed by what was happening to such a long-held dream. "My compensation was held in an escrow account which I would transfer back to them when I took possession of our new home. They had worked out this legal way to give your mother and myself a condo for our troubles. I can't sue them and expect them to pay up."

But now Annie was sniveling. "I'm so mad at myself."

Duke was surprised she was so upset. "Oh it's my folly, sweetheart. No need to be so upset. Not the first time what I've done has come to nothing."

"I'm upset over *my* folly," she said. "Oh bother." She was tearing up enough not to be able to see properly, so she pulled into a Kangaroo service station lot, parking off to the side. She fished through her purse for some tissues. "I had to make these last stupid, stupid house purchases. So fucking greedy — sorry about the language."

"It's all right. I'm fucking mad at fucking Bob Boatwright."

Annie laughed, at last. "Fuck those . . . fuckers."

"Yes, absolutely. Fucking . . . what did you just call them?"

"Douchebags. Fucking douchebags."

"Fucking swine, fucking low-life criminals."

Annie laughed again, wiping her eyes. "The F-word doesn't sound dirty coming from you. Why is that?" She sighed. "I knew the market was sinking but I went all in. I had tens of thousands on hand last year. Thousands I could have lent you and Mom. I might as well tell you a fantasy of mine. To buy our house through a third party and turn around and give it back to you as a surprise. But then you said Uncle Gaston was coming through so I spent it all on three homes in Lakewood. They've lost half their value since I did it, too."

"Oh darling."

"I so *wanted* to give you your house back." She hit the steering wheel, biting her lip, then wiping another tear. "And maybe make up for my loud, misspent youth when I put you and Mom through the wringer."

Duke shook his head. "You spend your own money on your own life — your mom and I have had our time in that house, in Charlotte. And it's time for a new phase." He didn't much believe it himself, but it was the view from where he now stood. He surprised himself by adding, "*I* am the only utter failure in the family, sweetheart. Not working these last twenty years. I should have gone back to the Law, much as I didn't like it." Duke felt his own eyes filling, in pure self-loathing and disappointment. Couldn't this one thing — the Skirmish at the Trestle, the memorial park — couldn't this one project have succeeded? The world had strewn petals in Duke Johnston's path that he might make something of himself, every skid greased, every impediment removed, and nonetheless he had assiduously failed the cheering crowds at every turn of the race. Every aspiration muffed, every earnest stroke of ambition shanked, he was a bumbler and a flop. He put a hand out for a tissue. He didn't want to cry in front of Annie, so he said something about needing to blow his nose and pretended to do it while dabbing his eyes, and she pretended not to notice, although it made her start crying again.

"We had a very privileged upbringing," she said at last, "and you gave us that, so you're off the hook for that one, really. If we haven't made a great success of it, it's our fault, not yours." She blew her nose, composing herself. "It's never been about money for me — or for any of us, Bo, Josh, Jerilyn. I guess we had Mom the Materialist who kept her eye on the checkbook."

Duke did not like the note of judgment in Annie's voice, but he was not going to argue with her now over how she treated, always treated, her mother. "Someone had to, Annie. We all managed because Jerene was the one providing for the family. We'd have starved without her."

Annie was quiet a moment. "I envy you two. What you guys have I will never know. Nor Josh or Jerilyn, it looks like. We all took for granted you and Mom, married forever, happy, ambling along. All of our peers' parents were getting divorced, once, twice, serial divorces, half brothers and stepsisters and all kinds of convoluted family arrangements, and you guys . . ." More tears. "You guys were the Rock of Gibraltar. That's where I fucking dropped the ball, where I couldn't follow suit."

Her father patted her shoulder. "You are too harsh with yourself." Duke then waited, sort of knowing what was coming next.

"Chuck and I are divorcing. Or, he informed me we were. He's taken up with a lawyer in Nag's Head, Olivia Something, and she has convinced him he is entitled to some of my commission money, since he floated me for the first year when I got up and running here."

"Convenient, then, that you've run out of cash just as Olivia Something is trying to take it from you."

Annie pressed the tissues into her eyes again, stifling a sob.

Duke offered comfort: "I didn't think Chuck was the sort to cheat on you. I didn't know him well — you saw to that. But I thought he would not have done that to you."

Without looking at her father, she said in a small voice, "I cheated first. With some of my real estate partners. No excuse, but we had too many late nights and late dinners and . . . Chuck was three hundred miles away in Hatteras. So he can have his money. If he can find any of it." She recovered, the confession made.

Duke wondered about Annie somberly, just as he had after her abortion pronouncement at Christmas dinner last year: had she ever made a discrimination that something was too personal to tell or that a parent might not want to hear it? And now, with the confession made, Duke could see that she was lighter in spirit. After all, it was now his to dwell upon, not hers; she had dropped her adultery into his lap.

"About the money," she was now saying, "I don't care — this is capitalism, right? Boom and bust, bubble and pop. But in the matters of the heart I should have imitated you and Mom. I should have held out for my generation's equivalent of Duke Johnston, instead of the foolish choices I did make."

Annie started the car again, meeting her

father's eyes anew as they gave each other a warm, exhausted smile.

Then Duke turned away, looking out the window at the dreary suburban sprawl of south Charlotte. Most of it developed now, what used to be fields. Only briefly would a vacant farm lot appear, fallow acres filled with weeds, a FOR SALE sign, some distant trees not yet subject to the axe.

Her name was Miranda Mabry.

He had been re-elected for the third time to the city council of Charlotte in 1983. People were beginning to talk about his taking on one of Charlotte's congressional seats . . . that is, if he didn't want to make a run for mayor, and from there, governor. A fellow city councilman who was going back to his law practice, Bud Shackleford, approached Duke about this shining star in his office, this bright, capable, lovely young woman named Miranda Mabry, who had crafted three legendary resolutions that overhauled the city finances, the means of school board funding, and parks and recreation respectively. Charlotte was a largely black, largely Democratic city, a city of trucking and freight and salvage, mill workers and farm folk, and if the Republicans could hold their own outside of Myers Park it was because of the party's populist-but-reasonable, frugal-but-progressive reform agenda, and Miranda was its mastermind. She was certainly going places but maybe the first place she ought to go is Duke's office so they could find an issue to catapult him into greater prominence and maybe the mayor's chair. She's a looker, said Bud. Just about sank my marriage over that girl, he confided.

"Bud, now really," Duke said at the time, smiling. "I hope Thelma didn't get wind of it."

"Wasn't even a proper affair, Duke." Bud put his hand behind his head, a nervous gesture, as if he were wiping his neck. "Just blowing off some steam at the suite at the Hilton. I'll never know for sure if Thelma found out or if she didn't, but it doesn't matter now because I'm leaving City Hall. I'm just warning you. You'd be a fool not to take her but find wherever they installed your libido switch and turn it to 'off.' No man is safe around that girl."

That proved true. Superbly dressed each and every day, just the right amount of flirty and sultry with the men, in that patented Southern-belle-getting-her-way model. Miranda seemed to have no life outside of the furtherance of Duke Johnston's political fortunes; she was there before the day began and she was the last one out of the office . . . which sometimes led to an end-of-a-project drink at O'Donnell's, where the city government and staff went to wind down and network each other. She had fine light brown hair that fell in tresses to her shoulders. It could go up in a bun which sensuously disassembled itself throughout the afternoon, stray hairs coming loose to be swept aside with her pale, delicate hand. And that mane smelled always of spice and herbs, some pricey salon shampoo that mingled with her perfume.

"Hm, I believe," Jerene said, one evening, lying beside him reading in bed, "that that's Fabergé's Babe. How long has your affair, with a woman undoubtedly in her twenties, been going on?"

Duke kidded about it at the time, claiming assignations at Byerley's Travel Court, Route 73, on the shores of Lake Norman — an established joke when they needed to refer to a place that was the bottom of the barrel. "Alas, darling, it is merely Miranda's perfume and she lives in my office, forcing me to sign papers and read things."

"And you thought the city council job would involve 'no work at all.' Best-laid plans."

Miranda would sit across from Duke's desk and talk about what it would take to be mayor of Charlotte. But good as that was, her true long-term interest was in going with him to Raleigh. Jim Martin was a Republican who actually stood a chance of winning the state house, if Reagan's landslide materialized. But any Republican who had any prayer of dislodging the state Democratic machine had to have intrinsic real-folks appeal but mixed with some polish, like President Reagan . . . and who was more like Reagan in North Carolina than Duke Johnston? The gridiron associations, a charmer, a storyteller, witty, well spoken, and a wife with style, plus the bonus of his heroic Civil War associations. Day in, day out, Duke allowed himself to listen to his own sterling Reaganesque qualities, his own inevitable greatness. Miranda made him believe it.

At home, Jerene was more discouraging and practical. She didn't know if she was up for all the glad-handing, the parties, the public appearances, the constant scrutiny — there were family matters that bore absolutely NO scrutiny, as he was well aware. What of the children? Their ups and downs might be fodder for the newspapers. And she would have to leave Charlotte for Raleigh, which she didn't fancy much, where she didn't know anyone, and it would all mean time away from the Jarvis Trust and the Mint Museum. But of course, if this was his destiny, then she would stand beside him and be an ornament.

Was that all it was? Jerene was her busy, practical, unexcitable self, while Miranda believed in a dream in which he starred, adored him, looked at him the way the young women who visited Arcadia used to look at him, with admiration for his present as well as his future. He felt it again, the heady ambition, the foretaste of great things close at hand.

Duke did not think, looking back, that his most disloyal moment was actually sleeping with Miranda. It felt wrong and went wrong and both of them knew it, sensed the mismatch of it immediately. Of course, no wife would see it that way — the act of adultery was always the most objectionable, disloyal thing. But his real treachery was to, however briefly, envision a future with Miranda by his side, two political animals, two shrewd operators seeing how far up the political ladder they might go. After the governorship . . . who knew?

What heady, empty talk it all was. Miranda would close the office door and sit on the arm of his chair. She would lean into him and dial a number of a potential backer. After he had shaken down the latest donor, Miranda would hug him, kiss his cheek, congratulate him for inching them one step closer to their mutual dream.

But all of his memories of politics led to 1984 and the one unforgettable memory, which he had cause to replay almost daily in his mind. Miranda had arranged a night at an uptown steakhouse, a private room where Duke and the little lady could be inspected by the men who would invest in a Republican mayor with an eye on the governor's mansion. It was a big boozy affair, open bar, a short, handsome Mexican bartender working the small drinks table in the corner of the conference room, and a leggy blonde ferrying the drinks back and forth to the real estate and trucking tycoons, who reached out for a pinch or a pat. While Jerene entertained one banker, and Miranda laughed uproariously at another one's jokes, Duke leaned into Paco (it said that on his name tag) and said, "It's all a little ridiculous, isn't it? Politics."

Paco, not understanding him, just smiled.

"Make it a double bourbon," Duke said. "I have to tell my wife some very bad news tonight."

Somehow, three sheets to the wind, they got back home safely.

Jerene was suitably gay from the champagne; she untypically left a mess for Alma, kicking off her shoes in the foyer, flinging her coat toward the living room, musically laughing, now shedding her suit jacket on a banister . . . "So that's what it's like, having an evening with the moneymen, hm?" She dropped herself into a plush padded chair in the living room. Duke remembered following in, marching to his grimmest task ever. "I hope there's many more of them. For one, I adored the absence of trophy wives, decorative molls, boring 'better halves' that I would be forced to converse with —"

"Jerene."

"We haven't even won the mayorship yet and here they are talking what you'll do when you get sworn in at Raleigh! Martin gets eight years and then you're there to succeed him — what would that be, 1992? Good heavens, they can't really plan that far ahead, can they?"

"Jerene."

"You'll have to decide just how corrupt you will be, of course, and stick to it. I'm not so naïve to think —"

"Jerene, darling, please."

She focused on him, and her smile faded to match his own expression. She knew something bad was about to come.

"We can't go any further without my telling you something."

Duke remembered his last cowardice, that he virtually had her guessing it, hinting at it, hoping she would say it aloud first, but she wouldn't. "You'll have to tell me, Joseph," she said, now crossing her arms, finding the living room chill. "If you've done something to disqualify you from political life, let's have it."

"You always know how to make everything right," he said glumly, sitting on the edge of the sofa, not feeling entitled to any real comfort. "But you can't make this right. Since it was against you, that the . . ."

She waited for it, lips drawn tight.

"I had a fling which is over now — the

chance of it repeating, I mean. But the consequences persist."

Jerene didn't flinch. No doubt, she had figured it out from all his approximations and stalls. "Some woman has had a child by you, or is pregnant?"

"No, nothing like that. It was a drunken evening, everyone celebrating Reagan and Martin getting in with such big margins. You left the party, you'll recall, early."

She never let him out of her titanium gaze. "Apparently I should have stayed behind to prevent you from screwing somebody and sacrificing your political career to a drunken moment."

"I wish you had." He took a deep breath. "I went up to my office to find some aspirin, since I'd surely had too much, and I collided with my chief of staff, Miranda. In our excited state, we . . . we kissed." Duke shrugged, hoping the rest could be implied.

"You wouldn't be confessing to something as pointless and forgivable as a kiss."

"No. Then we fell onto my sofa and rolled around a bit."

"And?"

"There was just one other time. We never said anything, both pretended it didn't happen, and then one afternoon . . ." He wanted to offer up a number of small expiations. The talk of his political future with so many Republican bigwigs and moneymen, the lunches and cocktail parties of being taken around and shown off like a prize bull, the steady mantra of Miranda's praise and predictions, something like a dictator could expect in Stalinist times, forward with Duke, our man of the people, *General Johnston may have surrendered to Sherman, but Duke Johnston will reign victorious as he takes the battlefield for North Carolinians fighting for the American Dream,* this sudden head-turning world of worship and fawning, the crass sloganeering . . . all of it wrong, all of it heaped upon someone so unworthy. Sleeping with Miranda was an exercise, yes, in ego — yes, he was flattered and megalomaniacal in the light of Miranda's attentions — but there was a flip side to it. It was the act of a man who knew he was a fraud before he began, a weak vessel. This was his way of shattering the tablets. But none of that could be said or should be said. There was no acceptable excuse even if there was an excuse.

"One afternoon?"

"One afternoon we got it out of our systems. The tension had grown to take up the entire office, every breath of air in the room was charged and we, as if besotted, went to a hotel and tore each other's clothes off. It was terrible, of course, darling."

"Mmm. The sex was terrible, was it? I'm so sorry for you. You should have had Miranda buzz me and I could have given her some pointers."

"I didn't mean that, although the sex was truly awful. Some part of me, some notion of myself and who I was, what I represented . . . well, it died. I would have said before that afternoon, I was a more or less good person, the proof being my home, my family, the love of simply the finest woman I've ever met, and now I was worthy of none of it." He was feeling unsteady, so now he did, at last, slip deep into the sofa, seeming to shrink down into himself. "If I am to lose all of it, the political career I care so little for, the home and good opinion of my family, the marriage that sustains me . . . I can't even feel sorry for myself, because that's what I deserve."

Jerene finally looked away from him. "I know who you are, Joseph Johnston. You forget how long we've known each other. Back at university when we were dating, there were a few stray women, a few sneaking one-last-times. Your patterns, and libido, are known to me. I'm not wholly surprised. Miranda is beautiful and smart — at least, you don't insult me with some bar girl." She looked at her hands. You would never know she had been given devastating news. After a moment, she looked up. "You said consequences."

"Well. Whereas I lay there utterly in despair, wondering how soon it would be appropriate to give that speech of ships-passing-in-the-night, just one of those things but we can't do it again, maybe she should find work in another office — all of those speeches. I was rehearsing them even then. But she had other plans. She wanted to be a 'power couple.' Bob and, um, the Transportation lady — what's her name? — from up the road in Salisbury."

"Bob and Liddy Dole."

"Yes, some big political power couple. She had a plan."

"I'd like to hear this plan."

"First, I am to win re-election on the city council up through 1987, then immediately announce for mayor. I am to divorce you after the mayoral campaign. Then after a respectable interval, marry her in time for the '94 race for governor. She had given some thought already to what causes she might promote as North Carolina's First Lady." Jerene shook her head and smiled faintly; Duke wasn't capable of seeing the humor yet in anything. "So, the Monday after the hotel romp, I gave all those speeches I had been rehearsing. Maybe she should find another office, our little fling was a mistake, and so on."

"She didn't agree, I take it."

"No. She said she had well-placed journalistic sources whom she would leak information about the affair to. I suppose it could be proven — hotel receipts, closed-circuit security cameras and all that. She would make it so I had to get a divorce. I refused and told her to do her worst, since —"

Jerene was ahead of him. "Since she craves power and could hardly stand to be in the paper as some politician's floozy, some other woman."

"Yes. Then she said she would go away and work in Raleigh with a state senator she had her eye on but such a move would require some funds. She named a five-figure sum. As I temporized, the sum increased. And now she seems willing to make good on all threats at once. We're up to six figures. I thought about . . . Jerene?"

She had stood and was walking to the phone table. As he had seen her do a thousand times, she took off one big earring.

"Who are you calling?"

With one hand she held the phone, as the other riffled the address book. She punched in a number.

"Hello?"

A pause.

"Hello, Miranda Mabry? This is Jerene Johnston, Duke's wife. You remember me from the re-election party and a few hundred phone messages you have been good enough to take."

Another pause.

"Yes, well, you can save the laughing anecdotes. I know about the little affair. My husband will not be leaving me. And I understand there is a sum of money you require to keep quiet."

Duke felt his head go light. But this was, at some level, what he yearned for. Jerene handling it.

"That seems a bit steep. I think you know what city councilmen make."

She listened.

"You overestimate our vast estate, my dear. And if we don't meet your sum?"

More listening, though Jerene stared at herself in the mirror, rearranging a strand of hair.

"That would be the whole of our savings."

A final pause before the return fire.

"Well, I hope that you will now listen to me. You may know that before Duke was a city councilman he was with a law firm, Munford, Mehta, Rankin. Duke was made the youngest partner in the firm's history at just thirty-two years old, and for a season it was Munford, Mehta, *Johnston* and Rankin. Jon Munford works now for the state attorney's office. Patrick Mehta's son, Clarke, is the assistant attorney general for the state of North Carolina. You are a blackmailer and we have ample acquaintances and close friends who will happily prosecute you for it. Indeed, this conversation has been recorded. Some years back, in Duke's first term, we were getting someone making death threats and we added a recording device to this line. Which I am using now. The SBI will enjoy your quoting me those exorbitant figures."

Jerene listened impatiently.

"No, you are mistaken. We have nothing to lose. You will be in jail, or in any event disgraced and blackballed from your intended life as a political operative if not a politician yourself one day — you seem to have the mettle for it. Duke will not lose his marriage — I assure you I am going nowhere — and he will not be running for re-election, and so there is no political consequence to your threats."

Whatever Miranda said, Jerene interrupted her:

"You find me in a civil mood, Ms. Mabry. Future encounters with the full force of the law on our side will strike you, I promise, as less pleasant. You will resign your position by mail and your severance, I'm sure Duke will oversee, will be in keeping with what is expected. Any more contact with me, my husband or this family, or any *hint* of any sordidness appearing in the local papers, and this tape will be in the SBI's hands by nightfall. Have I made myself clear?"

Jerene's level expression suggested that Miranda enjoyed a state of perfect clarity.

"Then this concludes our business. Good night, Ms. Mabry."

Duke now felt he could breathe normally.

Clutching the armrest, he tried to get up but found his leg strength had deserted him, as if his circulation had been on hold. But Jerene set the phone down and then pulled off her other earring, standing in the doorway to the living room. She had dealt with the impertinent Ms. Mabry and now she would deal with him.

"You will not run for re-election. Nor will you accept these newfound friends of ours' invitation to higher office. No congressional race, no mayoral race, no governor's race. You are out of politics. It is the price of keeping me as your wife."

It was all over — like that.

The political future that had been assumed, worn grandly like a cape, throughout his young adulthood, brandished in his confident striding through his thirties, the club, the law practice, was torn from his shoulders by her words. No, his destiny was annihilated by *his* actions — her words merely followed his folly. But it was Jerene who made the decision. And he acquiesced. He had relived the moment almost every day of his life and he, in each iteration of the scenario, still sat there acquiescing but he said more eloquent things, asked to be heard, recited the reasons that once Miranda disappeared, they would be safe to pursue political office again, but even in his fantasy do-over, she nonetheless would say what she said that night:

"Politics brings out the worst in men, and I do not need to be standing beside you at some press conference, supporting my man while he confesses to some liaison with a call girl or some tabloid-fodder love child or a tango in the reflecting pools with exotic dancers. I am not that wife. You'll go back to your law firm and our normal life, which, you must admit, had a superior tone to the circus we live in now."

"Quite."

"I thought you might protest my edict."

"I will never protest anything you dictate ever again, Jerene. I am your unworthy but grateful, loving husband."

"For this weekend, you can sleep in your study. We'll be back to normal, eventually." She paused. "When her perfume is one hundred percent gone. Gone from your clothes, your hair."

"I'll burn all my suits in the yard, and go buy new clothes."

She would not be charmed, and reconciliation, words passing between them that were not freighted with extra meanings and latent accusations, were still months away. "Good night," she said, as crisply as she'd said it to Miranda. Then she climbed the stairs. Then she closed the bedroom door — not a slam, but there was a discernible increase of force in it.

There was a brief appearance at the old law

firm; it was not exactly welcome that he return and divide the profits of the firm by another partner, but having been a city councilman, he would be in a position to draw new business . . . but it never happened, his return. The matter was left to drift and a reprise was never formalized.

What occupied him, for the next moment, and then the rest of the 1980s and most of the 1990s, was the undeveloped land around the Catawba River trestle south of Charlotte. Duke lent his considerable popularity to the cause of raising money and buying up the marginal land not owned by industry or the railway. Then he met with those industries and those railways that used the trestle to see if they would support his plan for a memorial and a park and a regular re-creation of the skirmish there. The most hard to persuade of any group were the developers who had their eye on the surrounding land. No one then imagined luxury homes could be in view of the trestle — the noise of freight, the association of boxcars and hobos — but they did have leases and water rights and hopes that the train track might be relocated so there had been some just-in-case purchases and Duke had to use his smooth, easygoing charm to talk them into selling, as well as selling to his not-for-profit foundation for a reasonable price.

So many expectations and hopes for the life

of Joseph Beauregard "Duke" Johnston, and he whittled himself down to one project, distilled his considerable advantages and gifts into a single trifling purpose, and now look.

Annie pulled into her parents' driveway. She looked at her watch again. "I think I'll come inside," she said. "Dad, perhaps I should warn you that . . ."

"Perhaps you should warn me of what?"

"Nothing. Let's go inside."

Duke saw she wanted to tell him something more, but he had borne enough events and revelations for one afternoon. Even though Annie had a key to the front door, she hung behind, making him get his keys out of his pocket and open the door for her.

Surprise!

"Oh goodness!" Duke said, laughing, clutching at his heart like a pretend heart attack.

There was Joshua and his friend Dorrie, who had been so helpful with the Skirmish website. There was Bo and Kate. There was Dillard, looking like her old self. There was Jerilyn — all of them laughing, pleased with themselves. Alma was now lighting the candles on a cake on the dining room table; the dessert plates were set around the table for nine.

"I thought I expressly forbade any notice being taken of my birthday," he said, shaking his finger at them all.

"It is," Jerene explained, setting linen napkins by each plate, "the day *after* your birthday."

"Ah, that is why Annie was checking her watch — she was the shill sent out to occupy dear doddering Papa and bring him back home at precisely five P.M. Very clever, very clever." Annie almost told him about the party as they walked inside — wanted to give him time, perhaps, to pull himself together. Well, he was together. How could he not be with such adoration.

"Where are your cars?" he suddenly asked.

Parked around the block, they told him.

"Happy birthday, Dad," said Bo, who with Kate gave him a five-volume set of *The Army of Virginia,* one more History Channel retelling of the winning-then-losing campaigns of Lee and company.

"Happy birthday, brother," said Dillard, presenting a lovely cashmere cardigan. "Now don't smoke your pipe around it and turn it into a walking ashtray."

"Sister, I intend to do exactly that," he said, kissing her cheek.

"Happy birthday, Dad," said Jerilyn, who gave him, in a ring box, a bullet she had ordered from a Civil War collector's emporium in New Orleans. "This can replace the one I shot," she said, as everyone slowly laughed after they saw her laughing. "Is it the right caliber?"

"Good Lord, it is!" he marveled.

And after the applause, "Happy birthday, Mr. J.," said Dorrie. She had brought him some kind of spyware-spamware-virus-stopping device for his Skirmish at the Trestle website. Ah, alas, the Skirmish would have to live on solely on that website, he thought, with a fresh new pang. That was now all that there would ever be.

"Happy birthday, Dad," said Joshua, who had something wrapped in beige packing paper that was either a fishing pole . . . no, a walking stick . . . no — as Duke tore into the paper: a flagpole. One of those flagpoles you install on your front stoop. And wrapped around it was the state flag of North Carolina.

"Y'all can move down to South Carolina," Josh explained, "but we want you to remind all those rich neighbors where your loyalties truly lie." Widespread *yeahs* and booming agreement. A little more laughter, but it soon died down as Duke stood there, momentarily speechless, starting to say something, then not. Then crossing his arms.

"About that. I don't think we will be moving to South Carolina, after all."

Jerene popped her head up, all ears.

"General Joseph E. Johnston, our Civil War ancestor, never forgot the magnanimity of the surrender terms offered by Sherman. He came to respect, even love General Sherman in post-war years. When anyone dared say a word against Sherman — and you can still hear people condemn Sherman even now — Johnston refused to tolerate that sort of talk. They shared a wonderful, superb correspondence . . . as you know, one or two of the letters I own. And they remained close until the end of their days. Sherman died and Johnston was a pallbearer. He went to New York City where it was very cold, very rainy. You don't cover your head when you're a pallbearer, and people at the funeral came up to Johnston and said, sir, at your age, you *must* put your hat back on, you'll catch your death of cold. And he said, 'If I were in his place and he were standing here in mine, *he* would not put on his hat.' And so he didn't. And he did catch cold. And that cold became pneumonia, which, weeks later, killed him.

"Johnston is often said to have failed the Confederate cause by his timidity, his unwillingness to fight the big battles — certainly Jefferson Davis thought so, and General Hood, some others. But that last gesture, toward the general that defeated him, showed honor."

All of them now were watching him. He searched their faces, settling on Kate who projected her considerable warmth; perhaps she was even moved by what he was saying.

"So," he concluded, "I can find no honor in taking that home in South Carolina, since the developers have violated every agreement we had, made a mess of the historical site. I would not be happy living there, having gained such a home at the expense of a bit of earth I sought to preserve."

Annie knew his situation better than the other children. With real concern she asked, "But Dad. Where are you going to go? You have to live —"

"If he doesn't want to live in South Carolina," Jerene interrupted, "I, for one, am happy not to go there. Never liked the idea anyway. Now cake is served."

So much laughter and relief that night at the Johnston household. Everyone said they had to leave, but no one left. People stayed to tell more stories and remember the house, the house that would soon remove itself from all their lives. Annie's five-year-old trip and fall down the foyer stairs and ride to the hospital in the ambulance where it was shown that nothing was broken or injured — but it was Duke who banged his head on the ambulance door frame and had to have stitches! Bo, at seven, breaking the front window grand-slamming a baseball that Duke had pitched to him. Not just that: the ball breaking the window, flying onto the dining room table, destroying the centerpiece, then bouncing into the china cabinet, taking out the protective glass and a porcelain statuette. Jerene was a firestorm of indignation, bursting from the house, confiscating the bat, sentencing son and husband to the hard labor of cleaning up their mess, while they giggled and she grew more enraged, which made them giggle even more. Joshua with a Super 8 movie camera playing director, getting out the ladder without permission and filming an overhead shot from the roof and then being too terrified to climb down, staying up there for hours until his parents came home.

"Dillard's sweater must be woven of Persian cat hair," Duke said, after a second slice of cake, after a burst of familial laughter. "Let me go get my allergy medicine before my eyes turn red as coals."

He padded up the stairs to the bedroom. He locked the door to the bathroom.

He was not going to take allergy medicine. He was weeping, tears pouring out in profusion. Of joy or self-pity he wasn't yet sure. What a worthless old father and husband he had been, what a fraud, an inconsequential dabbler, a muddle. And they loved him anyway! Hadn't it nearly always been that way, once he escaped his father's home? Hadn't he been liked and admired and had people drawn to him all his life? At Hampden-Sydney, at university, how they streamed into Arcadia to be with him. People elected him to office, people made him partner in a law firm, people invited him to everything and brightened when he entered a room. Downstairs were eight people, eight wonderful dear people, who were anxious that he should return because they loved him. Love that was not the least bit called for or deserved. To be loved for no good reason — well, he supposed, that was what love really was, but still, how remarkable to be on the receiving end of such bounty, such largesse.

He pressed a towel to his face. He laughed a little. This is what that elusive quality must feel like, he convinced himself: accomplishment.

Kate

She knew things. That was her gift. Others had the gift of music or cooking to comfort people, some Christians had prophecy and healing, but her gift was small yet ever with her. A woman would say "Good morning" to Kate and she'd ask what was wrong and twenty minutes later, they were discussing the dissolution of the woman's marriage. A boy would complain about being mediocre in his math class and a half hour later he was telling Kate that he suspected he was gay. People confessed to her, confided in her, sought her counsel. They knew she would not judge, or if she disapproved of something (stealing from the petty cash, sneaking pills out of mom's purse, texting nude pictures to the boyfriend of the moment), she would at least be corrective in an unhysterical manner, always clear, always lucidly laying out the moral precept to be considered — you would never say she was ethically squishy or lax —

but always patented, unjudgmental, loving Kate.

Lately she had been thinking about taking a hiatus from Stallings Presbyterian and going to work for three months with some of the foreign charities in the developing world. She needed another Peace Corps fix. She wanted to dig a well and get the water pump working. She wanted to put a permanent metal roof on the community center where there were now palm fronds. She hungered for it and could talk herself, most days, into thinking this is what God wanted her to do. But then there'd be another young teenager in the church who was cutting herself and told Kate and no one else. A wife who had slipped into an affair with a co-worker and told Kate and no one else. That child in the family just moved here from Maryland, where an uncle had touched her inappropriately and whose parents did not believe her. Was she certain this call to mission work was really what God wanted or wasn't she where He wanted her, right here, doing what she alone could do at Stallings Presbyterian.

She might have counseled herself to sit still successfully but then the church Monthly Bulletin fell into her lap when Stewart quit. Stewart was a youth counselor and assistant; they shared him with Gold Hill Presbyterian. Stewart was smiley and full of energy and, though thirty, sort of a big kid himself, which maybe meant — Kate was never sure — that he bonded well with the youth group in the church, but she uncharitably distrusted all that bouncy energy and guilelessness, kept waiting to hear he was molesting the girls, suspected him of bad things which she never confided to Bo because it was nothing but un-Christian malice.

But then Stewart quit, getting a full-time youth director job at an uptown Charlotte church.

"Look, I'll take the kids to Carowinds," Bo volunteered. "I know you don't want to do that."

"Ride roller coasters for Jesus, no, thank you."

But putting together the Monthly Bulletin was the drawing of a short short straw. She'd never paid much attention to the little magazine, but now that she did, she was appalled. Senior Spotlight. Look, the seniors are going to Concord Mills outdoor mall on a field trip, God be praised. Calling all young adults! Hoops4Him. "Basketball for Jesus, really?"

"That's an interchurch activity. We've been doing Hoops4Him for years." Bo paused. "You don't approve?"

"Don't recall the twelve disciples playing one-on-one."

The Book Group was reading some piece of Christian fiction with a serial killer in it. The Covenant Class was renting and discussing Mel Gibson's *The Passion of the Christ.* It's time for the Young Men's Retreat. *Between bouts of sock wrestling, log throwing, skeet shooting and paintball war, fifteen young men of the faith will grow closer to each other and to God. Participation fee $45.00.*

"I don't suppose any slight hint of working toward Christ's kingdom could trickle into our scheduled activities for our congregation."

"Hey, the church is getting along again. Bonding. All this is good."

"No, it is not good. What are we? Cruise directors? We're becoming like that awful Charlottetowne Country Club you used to go to, except for lower-middle-class people."

Bo sat on the edge of her desk. "I think it's great that we can get a turnout for these social activities. Not long ago, the church had too many battle lines to do any of these things."

Kate, silently, continued to typeset the issue left up in the air by Stewart's departure.

Bo cleared his throat. "Um, you want the Men's Group to go visit the prisoners in county lockup. You want the Women's Group to take a shift at the women's shelter. You want the youngsters not to go to Carowinds but to eat their vegetables."

Kate wasn't finding him charming today. *"Choose for yourselves this day,"* she said, while typing, *"whom you will serve . . ."*

"Oh boy. When you start quoting Bible at the preacher, I know it's time to clear out."

". . . whether the gods your ancestors served beyond the Euphrates, or the god of Carowinds or the Harry Potter movie marathon at seven tonight in the Activity Building or the graven idol the Amorites called Putt-Putt Miniature Golf. *But as for me and my household, we will serve the Lord."*

But dissatisfied as Kate was, that was nothing compared to how she felt when Bo made a unilateral decision for both of them. A complete betrayal — not asking her about it first. Because, of course, he knew what she would say.

So, in divine payback, she would indeed tag along on some mission project or undertake a three-month service contract with one of many developing-world charities that were out there. Médecins Sans Frontières, CARE, Red Cross — heck, Red Crescent. That'd get the old geezers talking. And she would commit herself and present it, as her husband had done his little surprise, as a fait accompli. Odd. She was more nervous about telling Jerene, her mother-in-law, about this detour than she was her husband.

Kate admired Jerene — she really did. She admired her devotion to the Trust, her family, their place in society. She was fascinated by Mrs. Johnston; she was worthy of a sociological treatise, anthropological research, a kind of Southern woman not long for the twenty-first-century world. She also feared Jerene. Bodies were surely buried in her backyard, enemies had no doubt drunk poison from her crystalware.

Maybe Kate could begin her temporary withdrawal from Johnston family life by degrees. The first thing, she figured, as she found a place in the Mint Museum parking lot, miles from the door, was that she should be excused from this committee. Why in God's Holy Name had she been invited to be a part of the Jarvis Trust for American Art in the first place? Who was less qualified than she? She knew nothing about art, nothing about trusts, had no business at a high-society rich-lady gabfest at some precious overpriced lunch emporium, with Jerene at the end of the table presiding, a queen in her court. (Mind you, the fried oyster salads at Noble's were out of this world.) Anyway, Kate had never properly understood why the Jarvis Collection even needed trustees — didn't all actions flow from Jerene, the Maximum Leader? No doubt there was some tax advantage beyond Kate's comprehension, but it looked for all the world like Jerene had merely selected some girlfriends from school, some Charlotte grandes dames, maybe a rival or two, and positioned them around her for show, to have her own glory reflected back upon her. Payton Disher. Belle Bennette. Kitty King Haywood. God, even the names of the ladies spoke of an old dying matriarchal regime.

Or maybe it was not so vain because it was not so serious. Maybe it was merely how Southern society women did things, an excuse to socialize, meet, play at importance while the men were at the club golfing or out shooting something, away from the little ladies. Kate had decided additionally that she was done — done for the *rest of her life,* mission project or no mission project — with Southern-lady rituals and the sooner she got back to straight lines, plain speech, hard work, the happier she would be.

But as she entered the Mint and was greeted by the longtime docent, Miss Maylee, ghostly frail and in her seventies (if not eighties), she felt a twinge of importance.

"I think, Mrs. Johnston, you are the first to arrive," said Miss Maylee.

Kate was about to insist upon being called "Kate" but she was brought up short, realizing she did not know Miss Maylee's name either. Was that a last name or was — as Norma taught her — she a younger sister and was Maylee her first name?

"And how is Reverend Johnston?"

"Bo is fine, thank you for asking," Kate said, smiling back. Miss Maylee had one of those minds for people and their kin, could connect all the cousins and knew husbands' and children's names. Kate did well at church but she could have used a dose of what Miss Maylee had; so many of their congregants were just familiar faces to her, classified in her mind by type of complaint or illness.

"The other Mrs. Johnston hasn't called to say whether she and Mrs. Baylor want tea. Do you have any idea?"

"I do not. Wait, it's not all the trustees? Just Jerene — um, Mrs. Johnston and Mrs. Baylor?"

"Yes, that's what I understand."

Land o'Goshen. Maybe Kate could disappear before the two titans battled it out. Although . . . an initial dread soon gave way to curiosity. Having studied and speculated about Jerene as a zoologist would study a rare species, Kate supposed she owed it to her accumulated knowledge to observe what she could.

She strolled around the museum, waiting for the titans. After she quit the Jarvis Trust she may never enter this place again. Once she had imagined Jerene asked her to join the trustees in order to educate her in the ways of women of a certain station, to make Kate a protégée since her daughters had disappointed her in this regard. But that wasn't it. Jerene never covered up Kate's dispossessing past or apologized for her rougher edges; no

Pygmalion-like instruction was ever attempted. Kate even once wondered if this was an unconscious cruelty on Jerene's part, a way to force Kate to contrast herself with the wellborn others and see how she would never "fit in," should never have married into Southern society, for that matter. But Jerene wasn't petty; she didn't waste time on elaborate insults or passive-aggressive gestures. Jerene was aggressive-aggressive, nothing passive about her.

Kate looked up to see the name JARVIS embossed in gold above the door to Jerene's gallery. She once again walked around the room looking at the collection. The portrait by Cropsey, some grand Tory lady of the late eighteenth century, the landscape by Inness (one of his "storm" series, gray roiling skies over a farmhouse), a Church tropical valley from his mid-nineteenth-century Andes tour, landscapes by Heade and Whittredge.

Kate stared at the misty vale rendered by Frederick Edwin Church, the precipitous slopes of palms and flowering trees, the frothy torrents raging between the peaks, joining in a verdant valley and cascading into a great bottomless seam in the valley's floor, the mists rising from the falls, joining the morning mists, the mists around the ice-bound Andean peaks . . . pure fantasy, Kate suspected, an artist finding paradise and then exaggerating it on the canvas to produce an awe equal to his own. Kate hoped a year from now she was in the tropics. There was no returning to the Peace Corps, her happiest time, when her youth and undiluted faith all combined for a full heart, for real joy. Once the heat and humidity kick in, once she is trapped for the night behind mosquito netting, might she even miss the Mint Museum and these genteel afternoons? Kate wondered if she had been too knee-jerk about the Jarvis Trust. The shallow society-woman nonsense was all silly but there was a breath of civility here, refinement, an escape from the muck of ministerial duties. She checked the eyes of Cropsey's grand colonial lady and found complicity.

Kate heard distant laughter and she walked back to the lobby. It was Liddibelle Baylor sharing pleasantries with Miss Maylee. Kate wagered to herself that when Liddbelle sees Jerene they air-kiss each other's cheeks, take each other's hands, lament this unpleasant business that will be over soon . . . while each woman could, if granted immunity, cut the other one to pieces with a razor. I won't miss that about High Society either, Kate thought.

And now Jerene appeared. "Liddie . . ."

"Oh my dear Jerene . . ."

Yep, thought Kate, with something not quite a smile and not quite disgust on her face, watching these women hug and clasp each other's hands.

Jerene: "How have you been holding up, my dear? I know you're not a suing person and this must be distressing for you."

Liddibelle: "Can you ever forgive me, Jerene? My lawyer's put me up to it, and the insurance people. I keep being told it's the way to proceed."

Jerene: "Well, I've secured Darnell McKay — you remember him, all those years ago, after I ceded the field with Becks to you, we double-dated at the Founder's Cotillion, you and Becks, Darnell and me —"

Liddibelle: "Of course I remember *him*! I was secretly envious of you — he was so handsome, and I thought to myself, now Liddie, you cannot date all of Jerene's boyfriends when she's done with them, she'll come to resent it."

Jerene: "I could never resent you, Liddie — not even for this! We go back too far, and have come through so much together." Jerene offered Liddibelle her arm as they strolled toward the conference room where the Trust meetings were held. "Oh hello, Kate. So good of you to make it. And Miss Maylee, lovely to see you. I thought there would be tea made."

"Tea, why of course," said Miss Maylee, looking a little confused and abashed.

Jerene had said nothing about tea to this woman, Kate understood, but Miss Maylee laughed lightly and said she must have forgotten, she would see to it right away. So many small sacrifices of justice and surrenders of pride to attain this highest level of Southern manners, Kate thought, knowing her nature had never adapted.

Jerene cried out, "But not another word before you tell me how Skip is."

"He's bearing up," Liddibelle uttered. "He's never been disabled in any way; the boy never had as much as a cold growing up."

Kate, following the women into the dark wood-paneled room where the Jarvis Trust met, had heard elsewhere that Skip was up and about, driving his car, out on the town, so the idea of him as some kind of invalid struck her as false as it must have struck Jerene. But Kate sensed Jerene's sympathy was genuine. "And so he doesn't know how to recover properly, hm? You have to be willing to let the rehab people and the doctor tell you what to do."

"He wants to hop out of bed too soon and go jogging or something foolish."

"Of course he does! And he will be able to, soon, Liddibelle. I pray he'll be back at it in no time and all this will be just a little blip in his wonderful life."

"I do hope so," said his mother, whose eyes seemed to dazzle.

"Now what we have, this lawsuit, this is *business* and it will play out however it plays out, but you must know, Liddibelle — you must know, as long as we have been dear dear friends, that I think the world of Skip. I just love him to death. I wouldn't see a hair of his head harmed, and nor would Jerilyn, who's in an awful state."

Liddibelle blanched at the mention of Jerilyn, but her manners won out and she asked, "How is the poor thing?"

"Just a mess! She's lost a boy like Skip which would be tragedy enough for one lifetime, but you can imagine how upset she is. Oh I suppose when this is all over we might have to see a counselor — I'd take her to see an African witch doctor if I thought it'd help but . . . but she's not getting over this. And between you and me, Liddibelle, who is going to come courting now? The girl who accidentally shot her husband."

Liddibelle nodded, maybe feeling a pang of sympathy she hadn't counted on.

"And you know, Liddie, I have always looked out for you."

"I know that, Jerene."

"Whether it was my parting ways from Becks so you could date him or putting you up for Theta Kappa Theta or inviting you along to be a trustee or making that phone call for the Myers Park Country Club —"

"Of *course,* I know so well all that you've done for me." Liddibelle put both hands on top of Jerene's nearest hand. Kate wondered if maybe Jerene's nonchalance about this lawsuit might, after all, have been justified.

Liddibelle Baylor seemed quite pliable under Jerene's barrage of talk.

Jerene went on. "And even with this business between us, I am going to look out for you as I always have, as you shall soon see." Jerene had been holding a manila envelope which she now set before them on the table.

Liddibelle didn't seem to notice the envelope, saying, "Well. This might be the one time, my dear dear sister — and that's just what you are, just like a sister! — but this may be the time where we have to let the lawyers do what we pay them to do. However disagreeable."

Jerene said this with such a level tone, it was hard to know if she meant it as an accusation or a mild question: "Like your detectives looking into our past? Apparently my bank records have been opened to you like a children's book."

Liddibelle reddened, but composed herself. "Oh the lawyers said that was necessary too. I hope you . . . I know you . . . Well, I know you know, Jerene, how *little* I credit of what they told me. These lies some people were telling."

Jerene said nothing. Kate saw that Liddibelle was steelier than she thought. She was warming up to blackmail Jerene Johnston. Was she after a big settlement so the civil suit and its attendant revelations would not go forward? Liddibelle then glared meaningfully at her. "Maybe you don't want Kate, Jerene, to hear what we both know they have turned up?"

Kate shifted to excuse herself when Jerene touched her shoulder lightly. "Why Kate and I are family, and there's nothing that you might discuss that she is not allowed to hear."

"Well, those audits. By the Mint. Some talk that much of the Mint by Gaslight money went into your personal account."

"My name is on the Trust's account, of course, so you see the confusion. All of that was looked into and dropped."

"And big five-figure payments from people who . . . Well, Mecklenburg Country Day said they paid out ten thousand because you were going to press an action about that art teacher making a pass at Joshua, which later proved to be false —"

"I believe he was eventually dismissed."

"And when your daughter Annie had a marriage annulled, you received a five-figure payout from the Costa family of Salvador, Brazil, you didn't report on your taxes."

"There were certain expenses . . ."

"And this business in Durham," Liddibelle went on, checking her notes again, clearly uncomfortable. "That awful man who said that Jerilyn . . . that you were going to make a rape accusation against his son unless you received thirty thousand dollars in hush money."

Jerene let out a puff of surprise. "Don't these sound preposterous on their face, Liddibelle?"

"I swear I didn't believe that or any of the things about Jerilyn. The behavior at Carolina, the reputation she came to have, of promiscuity —"

"Oh now you know today's young women, Liddie. You didn't have a daughter. But they're all down there on the pill, having a Roman orgy. Now *we* were the sixties girls and we weren't exactly prim little virgins ourselves. Or do I have to remind you."

Liddibelle laughed, and looked happy to have an excuse to be light. "Oh goodness no, our mothers would have killed us if they knew what we did on some of those weekends."

"So what some bitter sorority sister says about Jerilyn or Skip for that matter — Jerilyn told me that he was quite the ladies' man. The Zeta Pis had a designated sex room in their house and Skip — well, never you mind. And marijuana and cocaine down there, and Skip . . . well, your detective may have filled you in on your son's reputation in that regard, but neither of our children needs for those sorts of youthful indiscretions to be dragged out in court. I know it suits your lawyer to make my Jerilyn out as some crazed, psychologically damaged hussy, but what does it say about Skip that he would marry someone like that?"

Liddibelle was quiet a moment. She looked at Kate, again concerned.

"Well, the lawyer thinks . . . wants to put forward that perhaps there was an instability in the family."

Again Jerene, her face perfectly pleasant, said nothing.

Liddibelle, her eyes darting between Kate and Jerene, fell to a whisper: "You *know* what I'm referring to."

"I'm not sure I do, darling."

"Like mother, like daughter, I think is what the lawyer wants to say."

Jerene gave a small social, insincere laugh. "That is your lawyer's case? That the women in the Johnston family are a bit off? I've never shot anyone. *Yet,* I mean." Another theatrical laugh without any mirth behind it.

"He thinks there is a certain lack of control, an impulsiveness." Liddibelle was truly distressed. Jerene was exacting a price by making her say these things. Liddie closed her eyes and whispered, "September third, 1966."

Kate had had just about enough of this small, vicious, cowardly woman and her shakedown attempt. "Mrs. Baylor," she began —

"Kate." Jerene sensed what was coming and stopped her. Then she announced: "I had a child out of wedlock. Given away for adoption back in the sixties."

Kate was now speechless.

There was a knock at the door. Miss Maylee and the tea service.

"Your generation had abortion as an option," Jerene followed up, "and we didn't as a rule, though my mother had found a woman in South Carolina who did those things. I insisted instead on a private, anonymous country house in Asheboro where a young woman could finish out her pregnancy and they would take the child to the Children's Home. Lots of white girls from Charlotte went there. I was not being heroic having the baby, or particularly moral. It's just that I had heard of another girl in another sorority who had a private abortion from a man somewhere down east and who bled to death a few days later. I was too scared for it, so I hid out in Asheboro. Dillard was with me."

Another knock at the door.

Kate said, "I'm so sorry, Jerene."

"Why on earth should you be sorry? I paid a very small price for what could have been a ruinous mistake. The child was put into a proper home, we all got on with our lives. Kate, if you would be so kind to bring in the tea?"

Kate unsurely got to her feet. Fertile bunch, the Jarvis-Johnston clan, Kate found herself thinking. Jerilyn's abortion that she announced at Christmas Dinner, Annie's abortion (well, if she didn't make it up for show).

Aunt Dillard, who had to marry a ne'er-do-well husband and delay her college graduation when she had become pregnant from a single post-cotillion tryst.

And Kate thought about her own quickly ended pregnancy at sixteen, how she was taken to the clinic by her censorious aunt. Bo suggested this trauma had made her swear off ever having children. He knew her preference when he married her — she was not interested in childbearing — and yet he had been hinting again about them possibly having children. Another reason to get out of town for a while. Do the Lord's work in Honduras rather than one's wifely duty in Charlotte. But is it really the Lord's work, that familiar voice inside asked, a voice she had never been able to get rid of or silence and she had come to think of as God, if the true purpose of your performing charity is running from your husband and the issues of your marriage? Kate pinched the bridge of her nose, before taking a breath and then opening the conference room door.

"So sorry to bother you," said Miss Maylee, tremulously. "Here's the tea."

Kate remembered there having been a tea trolley that the tea things were rolled in on, but to her horror Miss Maylee was holding — had been standing there for some time holding — a silver tray with three cups, bowls of different sweeteners, a small ewer of cream, and a heavy silver teapot. "Oh my, Miss Maylee . . . no, let me . . ." Kate took over the tea tray a handle at a time. It was heavy for Kate to lift! "You are stronger than you look, ma'am."

"Just habituated to that ol' tray. That tray has been here long as I have."

"Well, you're both indestructible."

Miss Maylee smiled and went back to wherever it was she worked. Did they give the docents an office? Kate with difficulty turned and tried to sideways push back the stiff door which was adjusted to swing shut automatically when open. She brought in the tea things and set them down on the table. But . . . now Liddibelle was standing, gathering her things. Jerene now stood, too.

"I cannot find the words to tell you, Jerene . . ."

"I know but, darling, you had no way of knowing."

"But I should have. I don't know why I . . ." Liddibelle was panting, out of breath, excited.

Jerene put a firm hand on her shaken friend's shoulder. "We will pay all outstanding medical bills for Skip. Any rehab or physical therapy or any treatment of any sort that his insurance will not pay. And we'll do more than that, if it's reasonable, Liddie."

"That sounds fine — *more* than fair!" And then she threw herself into Jerene's arms. "You'll have to forgive your silly, foolish old friend! It's like you said, you always look out for me."

"I do, Liddie, and I always will."

Liddibelle turned to Kate and extended a hand. "You'll have to forgive me, too, Kate. What a bunch of carrying on you've had to witness today!"

"I take it," Kate said, "everything is now settled?"

"Yes, yes!" exulted Liddibelle, genuinely relieved. She hugged Jerene again and kissed her cheek, adding strangely, "I'll go call Hester and Hutchens, call off the dogs. Now Darnell won't . . ."

Jerene shook her head benignly. "No, why would I want any of that information anywhere but between you and me."

Liddibelle nodded back and clutching her tissue and her purse made for the door.

Jerene sat down and began to fix herself some tea. First she poured the milk into the cup, then a spoonful of sugar. Then she opened the top of the teapot to smell, to see if it had steeped properly, then she poured herself a cup. "And you?" she asked Kate.

Kate now sat down. They were going to fucking sit here and *have tea*?

"I know you are a tea maven, Kate, just like me. Or so Bo tells me."

"Yes, please," she said. She took the full teacup on its saucer elegantly extended to her by Jerene. "So it's over?"

"Just as I have been telling everyone for ages, she would drop the suit. Liddibelle and I go back a long way."

"What made her drop the suit?"

"We said we'd cover all hospital costs, rehabilitation."

"You said that four months ago."

"Well, now she saw the goodwill behind the gesture." Jerene sat back in her chair, holding her saucer and teacup. "Liddie was worried, I think. She'd suffered a bit of negative publicity engaging in a suit. You generally don't sue your own family or family-by-marriage. The first families of Charlotte have always worked things out among themselves rather than drag one another through the mud in court, like the new money do. People were saying what a greedy old thing she was, already sitting on so much of a fortune. But that's just it. The fortune that Becks left her has been spent down considerably." Jerene brightened after a sip of tea. "Wasn't there something you said on the phone, something you were going to tell me about you and Bo — some news?"

Now it was Kate's turn to be silent.

"I had hoped it was an announcement that you were pregnant, but that's not it. You don't have that glow, that happiness that pregnant women have."

Kate sipped her tea. "It's nothing that . . . we can discuss it another time." Kate was determined to know what had just played out. "So your lawyer, Mr. McKay, found something out about the Baylors that trumped what their detective found? Some equal scandal?"

"No, nothing like that."

Kate realized that Jerene had disposed of the lawsuit and now didn't need Kate for whatever purpose she had intended, so she didn't have to tell her anything at all. But maybe even Jerene who played her cards so closely, so privately, needed one other person to confess to, to absolve her . . . or merely to observe her victory. "Come now," Kate said, using a brand-new tone with her mother-in-law. "Had to be more to it than that. What's in your manila envelope?"

Jerene sipped her tea.

"If it's not dirt on the Baylors, then . . ."

"I merely told Liddie, when you went to the door to get the tea, that she wasn't thinking chronologically about the baby. And the implications for both families."

Kate gave that some thought.

Jerene topped up her cup of tea. For a minute there were no sounds but the china cup on the saucer, the silver spoon chiming the edge of the porcelain as Jerene stirred in sugar.

"The baby was yours and Becks Baylor's?"

Jerene was impassive.

Kate continued, "That folder contains a birth certificate that shows it's yours and

Becks's? And you told her that."

"Not *precisely.*" Another luxuriant sip of tea. "But of course, she guessed it right away."

"And I suppose she wanted to see the proof of it, see that birth certificate."

Jerene, still taking her time, answered, "I told her if she saw it then she would have to, legally, be responsible for the implications of the information. And we all, you and I, would be witnesses that she saw it. That's partly why I asked you here. So you'd be a witness. I told her it would be best if she never saw who was listed as the father."

Kate wasn't all the way on board.

Jerene spoke simply. "Becks left his considerable fortune divided between his wife and sons. I had my detective check. You see —"

"You hired a detective?"

"Of course I did. Anyway, Liddibelle got the houses and property at the shore, but the portfolio, where the big bucks were, was divided evenly between Liddie and her two sons. But the language of the will directs the fortune to be divided among the 'heirs.' "

Kate nodded. "And Liddie would have to carve out another fourth of that portfolio for this newfound heir."

"To win a few hundred thousand from us, she would sacrifice a few million to some stranger."

"My. What a payday for that other son living somewhere."

"It's a daughter. Perfectly happy where she is. There is no interest on the part of either of us to have a relation, if that's what you're about to ask."

Jerene gave out the last sentiment rather quickly as if she were still convincing herself, Kate thought. Kate looked into her teacup. *Jerene Jarvis Johnston got knocked up before marriage?* This pillar of respectability . . . But Kate's old instincts took over, the Kate that counseled the young girls at church about their unplanned pregnancies. It would have been the 1960s, and Jerene had been truly banished from her home, lying low in a halfway house of unwed mothers in Asheboro until it came due, then she would have handed her own child over to some state Children's Home functionary, then have to rejoin society, race back down to Chapel Hill and the social whirl of her sophomore year with lies and subterfuge. Kate had imagined her mother-in-law constructed of ice, but back as a teenager she would have been like any other scared girl, heartbroken, coerced, made to suffer with no one having any sympathy, terrified of scandal and ruin, judged by her high-society clan and judged by herself. Suddenly, the steely woman of resolve Jerene Jarvis had become made tautological sense; she must have vowed never to let things veer out of her control ever again. Kate felt tears crowding her eyes —

poor Jerene!

With a waver in her voice, Kate asked, "Who knows about this?"

"None of my children knows. Of course, my sister who went with me knows everything. Duke knows some of it, I told him when he asked me to marry him and he said it made no difference. We kept it from Gaston, too. My mother knew, who wanted me to abort it even if I got carved up like the Sunday roast. She wanted it gone and maybe me with it. My father never found out. That was our greatest fear." Jerene reached for a butter cookie; she broke it in half but did not eat either piece. "I cannot command that you keep secrets from your husband. You have to decide whether Beauregard will be a happier person knowing or a less happy person."

"I keep a lot of secrets from Bo. People tell me things in the church that I make a decision not to pass on to the preacher who may . . . feel compelled to act." Bo and she weren't gossips and they didn't enjoy trading their congregants' foolish choices and long-running miseries. Some mothers or daughters especially would plead, *Please don't tell Reverend Bo,* and she didn't.

Jerene stared at Kate, taking this measure. "That is one of the less commented upon wifely duties, Kate. Men are only good at duplicity when sex or money is concerned. Women grow up having to sham and artifice their way through life; we have a high tolerance for secrets, despite our reputation for gossip. We go to our graves with an encyclopedia's worth of things we chose not to tell our husbands, our families. For the sake of tranquility."

Kate lately was seeing the truth of that.

"And you might wonder," Jerene began again, maybe sobered herself by the return of these topics, "the whole reason why I included you in this episode today. Well, I think that church life keeps you plenty busy but I want you to consider that one day, after I'm too old for this, that you should take over as the head of the Jarvis Trust for American Art." Jerene, for effect, sipped the last of her tea. "I don't think Jerilyn wishes any public pedestal in Charlotte after what's happened. And Annie — well, we know about Annie. Josh, I am assured, is not likely to marry. And so I turn to you, Kate."

"You should let Josh do it. I'm hopeless about art."

"It has always been my plan to pass it down through the women of the family. I think you and Bo are the only ones likely to have children, in a normal fashion, in a loving and steady home, and perhaps one of your daughters will take it over after you."

Kate reached over and took Jerene's hand. "Jerene. *Mom* — you're as close to being a mother as I've ever had. I am so flattered and moved by your offer. But I think I am the wrong person for this job."

Just a small decrease of light in Jerene's eyes. "But you'll promise me, you'll think it over?"

"Of course."

"Another reason you're here, to hear all this dirty laundry. You have to know everything about the Trust, all the detractors, the enemies, the secrets, so you won't be caught unaware."

Again Kate thought of the simplicity of building a health clinic in a remote jungle location. How easy it seemed beside the Jarvis Trust suddenly, abysses forming on all sides.

Jerene stood up and reached for her purse and the manila envelope. "Did Bo bring you? I can give you a ride."

"I drove myself."

They walked through the lobby of the Mint. Materializing from her perch or warren, Miss Maylee magically fluttered alongside them to wave farewell. "Shame about the rain," she said.

A monsoon had established itself.

They waited a minute at the entrance hoping the rain would subside a bit. Kate watched Jerene absently deposit the manila envelope in an overly stylish chrome trash receptacle, squeezing it so it would fit through the round hole. It must have been a Xerox copy of the birth certificate inside. Funny that she didn't care if anyone found it in the trash. *Not precisely.* What had Jerene meant by saying she didn't tell Liddibelle outright . . . ?

"Jerene."

"Yes."

"Why not just show Liddibelle the birth certificate knowing she would never notify any authority about it?" Kate laughed. "I'm sorry, but you . . . You don't have to tell me but I think . . ."

Jerene gazed out at the marble stairway, slick with rain, the edges of the parking lot forming puddles by the storm drains.

"Was Becks's name really on that birth certificate?"

Jerene continued her study of the rain-filled parking lot. Was that a smile, just a hint, at the corner of her mouth?

Kate resuscitated her new carefree tone. "Just a hunch, but I . . . I think you pulled a fast one."

In a very dry whisper, Jerene asked, "What do you think was in my envelope?"

"My guess," Kate said, waiting to be contradicted, "is that envelope held a blank piece of paper, the way you threw it away a moment ago. Who did you date about that time you were with Becks Baylor? The next fellow." Another small laugh, but not so loud as to attract Miss Maylee's attention. The family friend, dear dependable Darnell McKay, the tax lawyer who had never handled a civil suit, but the lawyer whom Jerene insisted upon hiring anyway. "Darnell McKay," Kate brought out, marveling. "Who has been working round the clock on the case. Bo and I figured your legal bill would be very large, so we were, privately, going to offer to pay some of it for you and Dad."

Jerene continued to stare at the lot. After a full minute, she said, "That's very kind of you, but Mr. McKay's fees are very reasonable, as he is an old family friend." Kate bet they were reasonable, as in free of charge so he, too, could keep his and Jerene's out-of-wedlock daughter a secret. So another estate and portfolio didn't have to be divided, or a wife told the truth about a lie forty years old.

"That," said Jerene, after another minute, "is why I thought you might be up to the challenge of managing the Trust. You have very good people instincts. You know things." Jerene smoothed her skirt. "Let's run to my car, and I'll drive you to the end of the parking lot."

That's what they did. Jerene got to park up front near the handicapped spaces twenty yards from the front door, given her primacy at the Mint. Once inside Jerene's warm BMW, Kate directed her to the last row near the entrance on Randolph Road. But Kate did not hop out right away, and Jerene seemed in no hurry to deposit her. Kate noticed that she was gripping the steering wheel very tightly.

"I won't be telling Bo," Kate concluded.

"That might be best," said Jerene, sounding strained, the high spirits early in the day, the accomplishment of her victory, now extinguished.

Kate reasoned: Bo would want to know the older sister he never had. He would want to ask Mom about what she went through. It would turn into a Sunday sermon, a homily with many moralistic conclusions, a month of sermons. He would flog it and use it and squeeze the ministerial juice out of it just as he did his sister's shooting of her husband; it would all be *material.* That was a terrible way to think about her husband, crass, exploitative, but it is what would happen. Did ministers really have a choice, having to cough up a life lesson every Sunday?

And Bo would feel the urge to air out this honest impulse everywhere, and Jerilyn and Josh would also soon know about their mom's out-of-wedlock birth, and Annie — Annie who would use this very human foible as a club to bludgeon her mother with, some future Christmas dinner . . . which Bo would insist should include the given-away child, re-embraced and gathered up into the family bosom, whether this woman wanted that or not. Yet this revelation and all the public Christianizing wouldn't make Bo happy, to know his mother had suffered this. He adored his mother — too much, in fact. It's a matriarchy in the South — you can't convince a Southern man his mother isn't perfect if that's what he thinks. She wouldn't tell Bo. That was for Jerene to do. She would add that to the pile of things she wouldn't tell her husband lately.

Like that she was contemplating really leaving him. She might choose to tell him once she got out of the country on some UNICEF project, from deep in a rain forest. She thought they were almost done with Stallings Presbyterian and were, mercifully, only a year or two away from real roll-up-your-sleeves inner-city work or a mission assignment or something true, and *without telling her* he allows his name to be put up to replace Zephora Hainey at the synod. As soon as she heard that, she understood Bo would not only get the job but he would continue climbing ever upward until . . . until he was the Pope of the Presbyterians. Bo would run for class president all over again — and again and again. That was not the work directed by Christ, as far as she was concerned. The work of Christ was elsewhere besides synod politics and doctrinal debates and agreed-upon articles with other less reasonable branches of the ever-divided Presbyterian population, and her husband would get lost in all of it, and Kate would be lucky to ladle one bowl at a soup kitchen with him by her side.

Another secret: she had heard from Ellen Markowitz, her former lover and former Peace Corps partner, who had shunned her when they got back to the States, who had married and pleased her Connecticut family, who had consumed heterosexuality like medicine. Ellen had written to say that she was divorced, she was an out lesbian now, she had written to beg forgiveness and make amends to Kate, and she was heading back to Central America with the Red Cross, with her nurse's training. The mission fields. Well, that was Kate's name for it, not Ellen's, who was Jewish, atheistic. Right up there with Jesus in Kate's salvation was Ellen, whose sole gospel was *feed, clothe, heal,* and there was a place for Kate in this work. If she could make an escape.

And another thing: her faith was getting stronger and more directed as Bo was losing his to church-domestication, plain and simple, and another thing: that she didn't want to have children and he did. And also, she felt she might be happier working, living with, loving a woman. Not so much the sex thing but the consanguinity, the being on the same page, starting from the same emotional place. Oh God. Had Jerene proven contagious? Had Kate caught the Southern disease? She was now full to the brim with secrets, just as full of cover-up and turmoil as the poor congregants at Stallings Presbyterian, the cutters and the adulterers and the victimized girls.

"Jerene?"

Jerene had returned to her stony stare forward, gripping the steering wheel.

"I'm glad to hear, actually," Kate said slowly, gently, "that Darnell McKay was the father."

Jerene said nothing.

"Because, well, perhaps it's a habit from my counseling, but I counted back. Back from September third. Nine months before would have been around Christmas. When you were, presumably, home."

Jerene stared straight ahead.

"And I wondered if, from all I heard about Bo's grandfather, who was apparently a violent man, a drunk, there might have been a possibility that *your* father was your child's father. That he committed a violence against you."

Except for a tightening of her hands on the wheel, Jerene stared straight ahead, her expression untroubled.

"It's the sort of thing I have heard many times. And if that were the case, how you might need one other person to talk to."

Kate heard nothing but the rain drumming the top of the car, the defrost whirring, keeping the windshield unfogged.

"Or, if not me, then someone." Despite the

defogger, Kate saw, the car was fogging up anyway. "But you say that the father is Darnell McKay, who you began dating soon after Becks, so that is certainly . . . That is . . ." Kate didn't know how to wrap up. "But if it were the other thing . . ."

Jerene, at last, spoke. "We'll be meeting again with the full Jarvis Trust next Tuesday, at noon. Can I count on you to be there?"

"Yes, ma'am."

■ ■ ■ ■

Book 3
Scandal Redux

2012

■ ■ ■ ■

Dorcas

Dorrie Jourdain was proud of her family, preferring to trace the free Creole family line that ran back to New Orleans and maybe further back to Haiti although the thread became murky after that.

Most whites in North Carolina couldn't be too sure who their ancestors were in the 1700s, let alone most blacks, but Dorrie was sure of her Louisiana roots. Let's see, the 1700s are about ten generations ago, meaning she could trace back any of a thousand great-great-et-cetera-grand-ancestors, which meant that every abuse and cruelty and outrage of slavery, every brand, shackle, and lash of the whip haunted the majority of the Jourdain lineage, but much of that history was lost. Her romantic view of herself ran in the one detectable direction, the industrious French Creole ancestors made good. It's why she took French in high school.

Free people of color made New Orleans possible. Most whites didn't last longer than five years in the French colonies back in the late 1600s and early 1700s, in Mississippi and Louisiana — malaria, plague, yellow jack, scarlet fever, not to mention the profound lack of air-conditioning, to put it mildly. But the colored folk, with an African or Caribbean past, could take it, and they became the basis of society in New Orleans, becoming the government workers, soldiers, toll-takers, tariff administrators. White and free black mixed very well. Given what English colonial slavery was like, France's Code Noir was pretty civilized: no selling off slave family members, slave marriages consecrated by the Catholic Church were honored and protected, and once free, you could not be re-enslaved. You even had the right to sue your master for cruelty.

Maybe it got a little tricky to tell who really was black, so slavers importing humans from Africa were encouraged in the contracts to bring the darkest Africans they could find. That darkness scale fell apart too, mainly because Frenchmen manumitted (freed, after a while) their slaves, as was encouraged by the colonial society and Code Noir. It was Spanish custom (and New Orleans, people tend to forget, was Spanish only five fewer years than it was French) to free all slaves upon one's deathbed, leaving a little stipend or legacy for them to go make a life as a freedman. If you were a slave (of any hue) who fought the Indians — the Natchez proved strangely unwilling to become Frenchmen — then you won your freedom as well.

No one, apparently, was more into the caste system than the *gens de couleur libre,* the free people of color (born into freedom); they married among themselves and did not marry former slaves. The French were pretty adamant about white not marrying black, but the Spanish, already part Moor and semi-Africanized in skin tone and hair, turned a blind eye to interracial marriage, so North America had its own little Brazil of beautiful exotic golden-skinned people . . . and, as anyone knows who has seen the parade of Mardi Gras Indians and their spectacular feathered-and-beaded costumes, the escaped slaves who took up with the Choctaw made for some pretty red-brown people and fascinating traditions, too.

The politics of skin color, and whims of population (women of color were double in number to men), played a role in the Jourdain Family history. There was an Augustine Jourdane (people weren't so particular about spelling then) listed as a *placée* girl in a document of the 1760s, and dating from the 1770s, on Esplanade Avenue, on the edge of the French Quarter where the free people of color lived, there is a Jourdane House. By the 1790s, there's a Jourdain Importers in the French Market, where there are records of cane and cotton and other commodity trading.

But back to being a *placée* girl. That this happened in the US of A still impresses: *plaçage* was a system by which lovely mixed-race girls got "placed" in concubinage to young white men. Most white men would not marry until they came into their inheritance (their thirties or forties) at which time they would marry a much younger white girl, pure as virgin snow. In the meantime, to keep away from prostitutes (disease) or the slave girls out back (immoral), they went to madams who, with the girl's mother, would negotiate a contract. The young Creole girl would be his lover and in return, he would provide her a house, and their children education (usually back in France), and these arrangements lasted a lifetime. Many white wives must have heartily hated those beautiful tan temptresses down in New Orleans whom their husbands would go visit on trips to the big city, away from the dullness of the plantation. Young planters' sons and city-dwelling young men of promise would attend the Quadroon Balls in the French Quarter where the mixed-race beauties would be on display.

There were accounts of men being so besotted that they married their *placée,* consequences be damned; some men left more to their Creole family than to their white family in their wills. Well, it took the concupiscent

French and colonial slavery to make such a world; the dreary Southern Protestant mentality would begin to put an end to all of this when Louisiana became American property under Thomas Jefferson (who had some *plaçage* action of his own, come to think of it). Dorrie amused herself to imagine being a lesbian *placée* who found herself in the arms of the exquisite and powerful Doña Isabela de Pontalba Leblanc . . . but a better fantasy was to be disguised as a young, wealthy freedman shopping for a girl at the Quadroon Ball, no one knowing Dorrie was a woman, not even the *placée,* until she brought dear Euprosine or Philomène or Clémence (*loved* those Creole names!) home to her own elegant town house in the Faubourg Marigny. Hey, this *plaçage* system sure as hell beat what was happening elsewhere in the South: granddaddy dragging the newest slave girl out by the woodshed to rape and impregnate.

If you said Creole in the 1700s, it meant mixed race or black, with French-Spanish-Indian ancestry in the mix. By the 1800s, whites wanted Creole to mean the original European settlers, so that's what it started meaning. Sixty years of redefining mixed-race people began, so there would be just Black and there would be just White. Whites were outnumbered by slaves one hundred to one on these mega-plantations, cotton and cane mostly, and after several uprisings in the

1820s and 1830s, the whites figured it didn't pay to take any chances — any drop of Negro blood made you black. Free colored folk had to carry papers that proved they were free, at all times. There were deportations of free blacks — don't care where you go, folks, but you can't stay here. Colored could not testify against white in court. A law forbidding "favorable stories" about people of color was passed. My my, Dorrie thought, learning about all this, white people seem to have such a tenuous hold on their whiteness; how they could own and run and possess absolutely everything and *still* lie awake terrorized by downtrodden, oppressed and marginalized — criminalized — blackness is a long-running mystery.

There was a free Celestin Jourdain in Natchez, trading cotton through the 1850s when the whole King Cotton boom played out. And one of his sons, maybe moving north up the river while the getting was good, opened a mercantile in the black section of Cairo, Illinois, which was known as a prosperous black city in the 1800s. There is a grainy black-and-white photo still in the family possession of a brick general store, Jourdain & Lavalle Dry Goods, a trio of black men in suits looking proprietary, three women in long white skirts by their side, everyone a little out of focus.

From what Dorrie could see, the family had

darkened back up, hence her own dark coloring. After one drop was good as being half- or quarter-black, given one's rights in society, why not marry who you want? Dorrie understood the mulattoes in New Orleans, descendants of the true Creole, still marry within their ranks, never marrying white, never marrying black. Dorrie visited New Orleans to see some early Edgar Degas paintings (he joined his brother there in the 1870s, and his painting of the New Orleans cotton market was his only piece to get into a museum in his lifetime). There was an older Creole woman who, depending on the light in the room, looked black, looked white, looked Indian when she held her head back, looked French when she pursed her lips and scolded. Dorrie was ready to quit school and move to New Orleans on the spot. *Maman de sucre . . .* what do you suppose the French term was for sugar mama?

There's a black historian who says all the miscegenation in the South is not, as you might expect, solely due to masters raping slaves; only eight percent of whites in the South owned slaves. Most of the mixing — no surprise to Dorrie — was just people not able to keep their hands off other attractive and legally forbidden people. In the remote rural areas of the South, no one seemed to care what the poor folk got up to. And now, in 2012, that the social barriers are almost wholly gone for race mixing, from the president on down, white people, Dorrie predicted, are gonna get more and more tan, just you watch.

So. From Cairo to Kannapolis, North Carolina. Her grandfather had worked in the mills there, making towels, and her mother had been an employee until textiles collapsed as an industry due to ubiquitous Chinese imports. Tobacco, textiles, furniture — just when the blacks were getting somewhere in these traditional North Carolina businesses, splat, the bottom falls out of these professions. Thank you, globalism.

Dorrie got some idea of why her people might have left Cairo when she took a Twentieth-Century Black History class at Carolina. In 1909, Willie James was lynched there and the whites who made it into a big public event couldn't control the forces they'd unleashed. The hanging was played out in a fairground atmosphere, electric lights for the scaffold, refreshments sold, souvenirs for sale, ten thousand whites cheering and jeering. After the hanging, the white ladies lined up for a turn of dragging the corpse through the streets, heading to a pyre where they would burn the body. But just the one death was an anticlimax, so this mob went looking for more blacks to lynch. And when that pool ran dry, some good-for-nothing whites. The class read a defense written by a

Cairene for *The New York Times: . . . This negro population, coddled as it is, is a constant menace to the town. No white woman dare venture outside of the house at night alone for fear of assault. Many outrages of which the world has never heard have been attempted. This is why, as Mayor Parsons says, the effect of the recent lynching will be "salutary." Altogether it is not surprising that a lynching took place in Cairo. The only wonder is that one did not take place long ago.*

There was always, and is always, some white woman alleging a black man done raped her or done flirted with her or done looked at her or done brushed against her sleeve. Like Greenwood, Oklahoma, in 1921, where hundreds were killed and ten thousand blacks were burned out of their homes, thirty-five city blocks incinerated. After thousands of the black homeless were put in camps by authorities, some fool got out his airplane and dropped homemade bombs on them for good measure. The great Chicago race riot in 1919 stemmed from a young black man paddling his paddle-boat over to the white side of the pond; that was worth a week of death and destruction. Two racist Democrats competed for the Atlanta mayoral election in 1906, law and order, keeping the blacks in line, and they both tried to outdo each other in inventing black-on-white outrages, fueled by the newspapers of the day. When it appeared that nude photographs (commercially available) of white ladies were found in a black tavern, then it was time to lynch and burn some stuff down.

In 1919 in Omaha the whites worked themselves up into such a frenzy they burned down the courthouse demanding the release of a black convict so there could be a lynching, trapping the white police and city workers inside. The hostages kept moving up, floor by floor, to avoid the flames. The mayor, who was a reformist and constantly libeled by the newspaper, which was in the control of local oligarchs — newspapers have a *lot* to answer to Black America for, you better believe it — said nobly, "If you must hang somebody, then let it be me." They took him up on it, clubbing the white mayor and stringing him up. And weren't there some Greeks and Eastern European immigrants who needed to be taught who was really white, too?

This was just the twentieth century, with laws against vigilantism and laws asserting black men's rights held up by the courts — you don't even want to know what shit went on in the nineteenth century. When Lincoln drafted men to fight the Southern rebellion, in New York City the Irish and others too poor to pay a fee to get themselves out of the war marched straight on the black neighborhoods and two thousand dead black bodies later, the army had to be sent in to calm things down. A bunch of Irish guys went to the black orphanage and set it on fire. A building full of children. Every once in a while you can't even imagine how any human being would . . . but then you can.

East St. Louis, Rosewood, Hamburg, the thing is that these were the model places, this is where the Good Negroes were living, working hard, making a prosperous community, keeping out of the whites' way, agreeing, almost to a citizen, not to vote. From 1898 to 1904 in North Carolina, it was simply illegal for blacks to vote — the whites made it that way, and Washington, D.C., didn't move a finger to stop disenfranchisement. So blacks said fine, we won't vote because it will antagonize the whites . . . and it didn't matter because, let's face it, whitey *likes* being antagonized. No behavior was so good that the nightriders and the lynch mobs couldn't march into a black neighborhood near you.

Don't get her started. Just look around at these fanatical right-wingers today — same old shit, mad as hell, stoked up on made-up racist fantasies, ACORN and voter fraud, reverse racism, sharia law, a resurgent Black Panthers — all two of them — and President Obama, white-deranger in chief — who is barely barely barely left of center — some kind of totalitarian socialist communist treasonous closet-gay Black Power Islamist working with the terrorists. It's time to "take our country back." You there, ugly white lady — hold that misspelled sign up high with the letter *N* turned backward, show radiant Michelle Obama as an ape-woman or another Barack Obama photo in a bull's-eye or with a Hitler moustache. Blacks are fortunate, Dorrie supposed, that this inextinguishable American howling white mob, for the moment, has turned its attention to gays, Moslems, and Mexican immigrants, but they'll be back in force. They'll circle back around, they always do.

That was her mother's rule: 20%. "One in five whitefolk are no good, baby," she always said. "Now that means four in five are all right, and you gotta remember that in your dealings." George W. Bush's approval rating after he wrecked the country, 23%. The Urban League did a study on employment discrimination when whites were interviewing; they sent in the most qualified, perfectly dressed and well-presented blacks as well as very unqualified, intentionally bad-at-interviewing whites to see how often the whites got hired anyway. *Twenty percent* of the time, the lackluster white person got the job. One in five — that's the mischief proportion in American society and, if you look for it, you see that number repeat itself *a lot.*

So, yes, when solicited for an opinion, Dorrie was unhappy to see it play out, the rise and fall of the Johnston clan, she really was. But like most African-Americans, she was loaded up like a pack mule with the history of people darker than they were light in North America; sometimes she didn't feel the burden, sometimes it weighed her down and brought her to a stop. Didn't change how she dealt with people; it certainly didn't change her game plan to sweet-talk some of Charlotte's *fine*-looking white women into bed neither — but that burden was there, just reach around and feel for it; it never goes anywhere. The Jourdains had been through the storms, had waded through the high turbulent waters, and though it was a shame a little bit of rain finally fell on the Johnston Family, it wasn't like white people hadn't made it exciting for her folks through the centuries as well.

And yet, c'mon now, the Johnstons were Dorrie's Designated Crazy Whitefolks — for a while there, she was virtually in the family. And having been away from their orbit, she couldn't help missing them, worrying on their behalf.

Late one night, three A.M.–late, coming home from a romantic evening, Dorrie drove down Providence Road and sadly beheld the old Johnston place she would now never enter again, and then she turned on Wendover Road to cruise by the huge overgrown one-block wilderness where Gaston Jarvis built his mansion. You couldn't see his house from the street, thanks to the wall, and beyond that, the giant oaks and leafy maples, but she saw the gate was open, so she turned in, inching up the driveway, aiming her car and its headlights toward the house. She realized that she might alarm whoever was still inside, if they were awake, so she cut her headlights and waited for her eyes to adjust. The lawn was a wild tangle, Gaston Jarvis's Porsche was under a tarpaulin, there were no lights or signs of life; around the side was Duke Johnston's Mercedes. So it's true, she thought, they're squatting in Uncle Gaston's house while he is away in some Swiss clinic drying out. She put her car in neutral and rolled backward to the street, heading on her way home, feeling a chill from the lonely old house.

Dorrie had heard from Josh a lot of the drama surrounding all the fireworks with Uncle Gaston. Back in January 2009, Norma drove by the Johnston house and saw the moving vans, Jerene out in the yard supervising. Norma learned that weekend there would be a yard sale. A *yard sale* — Jerene Johnston selling her end tables and lamps, her chrome kitchen items and decorative glassware, out there for God and everybody to see in a *yard,* taking 50 cents for something worth $50 just to get rid of it . . . Dorrie couldn't imagine it. Jerene's following through with this indignity made Dorrie admire the woman even more, but at the same time, that spectacle, the false cheer, the rolled-up sleeves, the sadness in the eyes, would have been heartbreaking to behold.

Norma must have thought so too. She sped to Gaston's house and roused him and must have given him a hell of an ultimatum. *You go over there this instant and write those dear people a check that wouldn't even dent your smallest checking account. Does family mean nothing at all to you?* Norma had a backup threat, Josh recounted. Norma had a sister, widowed, retired in Arizona who had asked her to come out to live. She would do it. She would pack her bags and go, leaving the Cordelia Florabloom enterprise to founder and Gaston to go to hell. And Josh heard that Gaston pulled out his checkbook and said, *You're right, Norma.* He wrote her a check for the plane fare and said, *Don't let the door hit you on the way out. Be careful around the cactus, and watch out for rattlesnakes.*

And Norma left. At some point, even Norma had had enough abuse and neglect. She stopped by the Johnston house, rooms empty of furniture, FOR SALE sign in the yard, Jerene and Duke camping out more or less, and said her goodbyes. There were long hugs and expressions of mutual sympathy. What could any of them do? Gaston was who he was. And Norma left for Scottsdale.

Dorrie's conquest of 2009, Hazel Moultrie, head of the English Department at UNC Charlotte, didn't last too long (she was separated from her husband of thirty years, but still closeted, didn't want to tell her teenage kids). Hazel offered a shaft of clarifying light. As Dorrie recounted the adventures of Gaston Jarvis — Hazel loved literary gossip — they discussed how Norma had a potentially successful lawsuit if she wanted to sue for some of the Cordelia books' profits, since she virtually produced them. As they cuddled, Hazel added, "And I'm glad Miss Norma wised up. Now we await the day you will wise up."

"Me?"

"Why are you micromanaging the social life of Joshua Johnston? It's like you're his minder, like you're hauling Benjy Compson around in a cart all day making sure he doesn't get into trouble. I'd let that go, sugar. See to your own happiness." Then Hazel pulled her closer as if Hazel herself constituted that future happiness, which Dorrie knew even then was not the case.

It troubled Dorrie. With what passion she scrambled and arranged on Josh's behalf, paying to get rid of Calvin, stationing herself nightly beside him at the laptop to condemn or approve Josh's online entanglements, trying to head off the ridiculous Nonso at the pass, so — for what? — she could have Josh, platonically, all to herself? Because Dorrie knew best what would make Josh happy? What made it easy to take a step back was that Nonso *did* bring his skinny black ass over from Nigeria for that program at Johnson C. Smith, he *did* move in with Joshua, and they did seem, actually . . . happy.

Oh it was pretty impossible not to like Nonso, he was a walking feel-good African smile, festive in his dashikis and kofi hat, spewing naïve declarations of love and friendship ("If you love Joshua, then I have to, sister, love you. You are already very much my so very good friend!"). But Dorrie didn't relent for a long time.

Nonso, she surmised, having scammed Josh for money back in Nigeria, was now over here to clean him out completely. When Nonso went back to visit his folks, with money given to him by Josh, Dorrie predicted he wouldn't come back. But he did, and on his own dime. It may have started as a Nigerian online scam — Dorrie refused to believe otherwise — but clearly Nonso decided Josh was the (relatively) rich white man for him. Dorrie was hard on Josh throughout, comparing Nonso's importation to some kind of late-in-the-game slavery operation; when Nonso flew back from Lagos and they met him at Douglas International, Dorrie asked, "So, how was your Middle Passage?"

Snide, snarky, full of invective and rants . . . at some point she heard and saw herself and remedied the situation by a retreat into her own career and life, which, by the way, had been languishing. The women who ran their website service had sunk into conventional lesbian drama — breakups, an office love triangle, a counselor-conciliator brought in, mandatory sessions were required of everyone, all to make sure the employees could "support" and "nurture" each other, *When I hear you say you can't work with T.J. what I'm hearing is that you still feel hurt and wish to communicate your pain back to Mare, that your personhood is not being respected,* blah blah blah. Working there had passed through tiresome and landed smack into torturous.

There was an assistant curator opening at Charlotte's Afro-American Cultural Center which was being refashioned as the Harvey Gantt Center, named for the accomplished black architect and mayor of Charlotte, the two-time Democratic standard-bearer nominated to run against the Devil himself, Senator Jesse Helms. The Gantt Center was part of the uptown renaissance, near the new branch of the Mint and the Bechtler, in a dazzling new building by the Freelon Group, the go-to architects for high-end African-American cultural projects. It was time to get in the forefront of things she cared about, so she applied for the job and she needed some letters of recommendation. Jerene Johnston, as an art trustee, would be a good recommender. It had been a year since she'd laid eyes on her fantasy sugar mama.

Jerene was still Dorrie's ideal. Exuding will, she was a distillation of rich-white-lady force who could eat her social inferiors for hors d'oeuvres and probably took no notice of anyone younger or anyone black, let alone younger and black and gay. Yes ma'am, Dorrie marveled, the upkeep it took to be Mrs. J. To speak like she did, hold herself with that carriage, to look like she went to bed and got up the next morning with every hair in place, makeup perfect. Dorrie was doing well to wipe the sleep out of her eyes. Tank tops or T-shirts, no bra (and not much need for one), worn-through jeans, everything loose and comfortable, ratty Converse sneakers, hair cut close to the scalp not for politics' sake but for convenience. But just imagine such an unfashionable jeans-and-T-shirt tomboy forcing Mrs. J. to the bed in her pearls and fashionable Burberry trench coat, clutching that Kate Spade purse, Dorrie removing one suede pump after the other and throwing them across the room. *And just what do you presume to do, young lady?* Mrs. J. would ask. Would Jerene Johnston suddenly fear she was dealing with some ghetto-girl banger who was going to take her purse and her credit cards? *Hell* no. Mrs. J. could stare down a drug lord of a Colombian cartel. She'd know what Dorrie had in mind, the day Dorrie followed her up to her plush, rich-lady's bedroom. *I'm gonna rock your world, Mrs. J. If you haven't had an orgasm to date, prepare to have one because you're not getting out of this bed until I make it happen.* And Mrs. Johnston in this oft-returned-to fantasy would fix Dorrie with that squinty, steely look and ever so slightly relinquish some of that power, relax her grip on the reins, and say, *All right. But it better be a good one. I've got to be uptown at the new Mint in three hours.*

What needled Dorrie was that the Jerene-fantasy was not absolutely one hundred percent remotely out of the range of things that happen in this world! Dorrie had been with enough older, charming, dazzling white society women — all married, married, married — to know that there were certain women, long out of the bedroom-business thanks to age-dwindled husbands, women who were susceptible, curious, maybe always bisexual but deprived of appropriate circumstances and venues for it to find expression. And when Dorrie was on her game, really, who could resist her?

Jerene surpised Dorrie with an earnest hug, and they adjourned to the conference room at the Mint Museum. Some ancient white docent, not a hundred pounds, brought in a silver tea service.

"How's Mr. Johnston doing?" Dorrie dutifully asked first.

"He's out of the wheelchair, which pleases him. Using a walker now, sometimes just the cane."

In 2009, Jerene and Duke moved away from atop Providence Road and rented a unit in an upper-middle-class condo development Annie found, on the south edge of Charlotte. It was one of those lavish two-hundred-unit housing tracts that bankrupted their owners in the downturn. Where once investors hoped to make $450,000 a unit, they were settling for $220,000, and then, more desperate still, they started renting the units. Annie, who would go bankrupt herself later in the year, smelled a bargain and directed her parents to rent a place until they knew their next move. Dorrie and Josh went out there once. It was a ghost development, three-quarters of the units unsold, no cars in driveways, no lights on in windows. They had bulldozed away an old-growth Piedmont forest and an ecologically valuable stretch of what is known as Piedmont Prairie; in place of that, each unit had a spindly just-planted sapling, and the entrance drive boasted a line of the so-common-as-to-be-vulgar Bradford pear trees, none of the landscaping well attended or groomed. It never stopped looking just built. Josh described it as like being in one of those evacuated Chernobyl towns — all it needed was a loudspeaker playing staticky Russian martial music echoing between the empty condo units. Three weeks later, Duke Johnston had a stroke, paralyzing the left side of his body and slurring his speech.

"And his speech," Jerene reported brightly, "is a lot better. We can understand what he says most of the time. What is not better is the depression. We still are trying to find a medicine that won't knock him out, sleeping away each day."

Dorrie smiled sympathetically, a little surprised at Jerene's frankness. She couldn't imagine Duke Johnston so reduced and unhappy. Dorrie always thought of Annie as the ultimate daddy's girl, exhibit A for the Elektra complex. But soon after his stroke, Annie cleared out for Berkeley, getting in the master's-doctorate program there in History. Dorrie decided that Annie couldn't stand to see her father debilitated so she just removed herself geographically. Dorrie didn't quite judge her for it, because she didn't want to see Duke Johnston that way either.

Dorrie asked after Bo and Kate.

Jerene was brisk. "Same as ever. Bo is running for something, Clerk of the Office of the Presbyterian General Assembly, something like that. Spending a lot of time in Kentucky.

Kate's still in Honduras, serving the heathens or some such."

Dorrie knew they lived apart. "Well," Dorrie said, enjoying her cup of tea, feeling civilized again, "I'd like to see Kate sometime when she passes back through on a visit."

"I don't think she'll be coming back," Jerene said without inflection.

Jerene set down her teacup and began quizzing Dorrie on her new duties if she were to be curator at the Gantt Center. Did she hear about the acquisition of drawings on paper by Romare Bearden, the most nationally famous of Charlotte-born artists, whose works were in the Mint as well as the Gantt Center? Was the Gantt Center up to providing a room that could preserve the drawings regarding heat, humidity, mold, the elements? But also Henry Ossawa Tanner — had she investigated where and when some work might still be acquired for the Hewitt Collection? Dorrie realized that Jerene knew an astonishing amount about art but her angle was purchase, scheduling exhibitions, negotiating the loan of paintings, restoration, preservation . . . Dorrie had been a little naïve to think that curating would be like a great big art history exam, all about appreciation and understanding the art. The museum world was not the academic world. She parried Jerene's questions the best she could, and she correctly saw this as Jerene preparing her for that first interview, going through a checklist on what she had better get up to speed. Jerene wrote the recommendation letter. Jerene made phone calls. Jerene, Dorrie was to hear later, showed up at the Gantt Center as a Founder's Circle contributor, making a $2,000 gift. Had that helped Dorrie? Dorrie did get the job.

When she called Jerene to thank her, she got Duke Johnston on the phone. He was very hard to understand. "It'd be luff-ully to see . . . you . . . again, my dear . . ." Duke was short of breath, and his voice had dropped to a lower register, but the worst of it was the sense of ragged exhaustion; it was an old man's voice, not the buttery Southern baritone of old.

And then two more years passed by. Dorrie had flourished in the assistant curator's job, and after her dynamic boss and mentor moved on to a cultural center in Anacostia, Dorrie was made one of the head honcho curators. The Center loved her and she loved the Center.

As an added bonus, she got to host evenings and galas and fund-raisers, and got on the circuit for other arts fund-raisers too — frolicking in a well-chummed sea of rich, powerful white ladies. She didn't even bother with the long con anymore, the incremental seductions — she was a known Charlotte cultural quantity, was becoming a "character" people talked about, the out-lesbian Dorrie Jourdain. She swooped down upon heiresses and matriarchs, wealthy widows and silver-spooned spinsters, aggressive and flirtatious, and when she didn't get a phone number or an assignation, she often got a contribution. Probably made these married old girls feel risqué and modern, writing a check with the sassy black lesbian leaning into them, a little close for hetero comfort — cheap thrills. And for every ten women she charmingly scared off, she got one or two who were curious, who arranged for a lunch date, who were slowly putting themselves into position for Dorrie to take charge and drag them the rest of the way over the line. Who knew so many white wealthy women could be curious about a butch (but with makeup, a softening touch here and there) dark-skinned black woman?

It was Barack Obama's fault. Every white lady in town wanted to vouchsafe to Dorrie that, yes, she really really did vote for Mr. Obama. It almost made up for the monstrous, hysterical backlash of birth certificates and Islamo-Kenyan conspiracies and the Fox News–yokel uprising that shut down the man's presidency before it began.

Hell, she cried too, when he got sworn in. And North Carolina, of Jesse Helms fame, in the electoral college went for Obama! Man, did she ever lose a bet with Annie (who never collected on it); Dorrie didn't think the country would elect a black man. Look what the New South done up and did. Like her mama said, "George W. made such a darn fool mess of things that a white war hero couldn't even beat a black man." Best analysis of the Election of 2008 that she'd ever heard. She wondered if Jerene voted for John McCain and Sarah Palin. Dorrie decided that Palin would be a Jerene deal breaker — she represented a change of national tone worse than what Obama threatened, so she bet that the Republican former city councilman's wife voted for Obama, too.

As the years passed, she wondered a lot about how Jerene was doing but that didn't quite translate into calling or seeking her out for a visit. She saw Josh once a month and, if it was evening, that meant Nonso would be in tow (damn, he was getting more queeny and swishy each passing day), so she often proposed lunch when Nonso was at classes. Josh was getting older but letting it show; gray at the sides and in the beard stubble, thinning hair. He used to go on for hours about how he was off to Hair Club for Men if the thinning got any worse, but he didn't seem to care now. Someone loved him just as he was. And Dorrie, exhaling, finally let herself feel happy for him.

And then, one autumn night, October 2012, there was the phone call. It was Jerene. Would Dorrie be so good as to do her a favor?

"Sure," she said, still indebted for the recommendation letter. "I can get Josh along too, if you like."

"No, just you will do. I'd like to discuss something with you. But there's also a chore. I need you to pick up Gaston, my brother, at Douglas Airport."

"I'm sure I'm free, Mrs. Johnston."

"What did we agree to last time?" Dorrie wasn't sure what she meant, it had been two years since she had last seen Josh's mother. "You're to call me 'Jerene.' We're colleagues in the Charlotte art scene now."

"Okay. Jerene." Dorrie wondered why Gaston couldn't take a taxi home. She knew in his final touching-bottom descent he had gotten a second DUI from the police and his license had been taken away. Just as the Charlottetowne Country Club had revoked his membership for some terrible public behavior.

"And I'd appreciate it," Jerene added, "if you could come straightaway here, no stopping at bars or ABC stores."

Ah, that was the rub, thought Dorrie. Bring him back sober.

So, she went to the airport where Gaston Jarvis's evening flight from New York would land, he having left Zurich last night. But as for the soberness, that plane had already flown. Mr. Jarvis had been drunk when he got on the plane, drank heartily throughout the flight from his first-class perch, passed out from the expensive wine and the sleeping pills he had taken, and when they couldn't rouse him after everyone had deplaned, just as they were about to call an ambulance, he stirred and stumbled to his feet.

Dorrie, who had gone to meet him, saw at once he was red-faced and drunk. Otherwise, he must have got healthy for some length of time: he was fifty pounds thinner, sleek, if jaundiced, in the face, his clothes looked good on him. Jerene called out, "Mr. Jarvis!"

"Do . . . do I know you?"

"It's Dorrie, Josh's friend? Mrs. — uh, Jerene asked me to come get you tonight. I was at Christmas Dinner with you about four years ago."

"Don't remember," he mumbled. "You're not the woman that . . . no, you're not."

It flashed through Dorrie's mind that maybe he thought she was one of his alleged escort-service girls. *Not gettin' in the stream,* she almost mumbled aloud.

They plodded to the Baggage Claim. "Are those your bags?"

They were. The last two left in the carousel. He took the small one and Dorrie understood that it was for her to lift the heavy one. They went outside to the curb of the terminal. Dorrie had parked some distance away and she could see that Mr. Jarvis wouldn't make the journey, so she advised him to sit right here on this nice little bench, sit with his luggage, and she would be by in five minutes with her car.

Gaston muttered, "It's cold . . . I'd forgotten North Carolina got cold."

She went to the deck, paid the parking ticket at the booth and then entered the loop road that would take her by the Domestic Arrivals terminal. She pulled up just in time to see Gaston climb into a taxicab.

"Shit," she said aloud, having failed her one and only Jerene-mission.

She followed behind the cab, waiting for the turn north on Billy Graham Parkway, but the cab went south, and then turned, and turned again . . . she was right behind them . . . and there they came to an ABC store, moments from closing.

"Oh no," she said. She pulled up behind the cab who had been told to wait. She negotiated to get his bags out of the trunk, and soon Gaston emerged with a bottle of Dunlap's Hundred. "Can't get decent bourbon in Europe. Isn't that odd, that there's a Bourbon family, full of claimants to half a dozen European thrones, but you can't get a decent bottle of the nectar named after them."

He let Dorrie transfer his bags to her car, and paid the taxi driver. And soon they were back on Billy Graham Parkway. Dorrie asked if he wouldn't like some coffee; he would not.

He sipped freshly from the bottle, having shredded the wax seal with his house key, raining the debris on the floor of her car.

"I always knew something was screwy about that claim, my friend's, my so so wonderful friend . . ."

Dorrie sighed. "Not sure I understand you, Mr. Jarvis."

"Had a lot of time on my hands in this joint, in Switzerland. Lot of lakes over there. You go to a clinic, they wheel you out and make you look at a lake for an hour. Rest, they tell you. I mail-ordered myself a laptop and got to researching. That's what I did."

"Hard at work on a book?"

"Fuck books."

"I'm going to take that as a no."

"My research is right here. And you'll want to see their faces when I tell them."

Dorrie sped her way down I-85, then turned for the Brookshire Freeway. Gaston beheld the lit-up skyline of Charlotte as if for the first time.

"Almost pretty," he mumbled. "When I was a boy there was none of this city stuff, none of it . . . All new people in this town." Then after a cruise down Randolph from the city center, they turned for his street, and the big dark house surrounded by enormous trees.

"Home sweet home," said Gaston. "I see my poor relations didn't sell off my Porsche. Might as well have, since I won't be driving anymore. Good God, who is responsible for the lawn service — this is a jungle out here."

It was hard to see, since there was no porch light or streetlight; the house showed no signs of occupation, except for a dim orange glow in the living room. The Southern cacophony of insects overpowered the drone of the nearby thoroughfares beyond the ring of trees and the high brick walls.

Dorrie had never been inside Gaston Jarvis's house; she'd heard from Josh and others about the famous emptiness of it. She indeed saw an empty room to the left with merely a phone on a small table and a chair in it. Jerene and Duke Johnston had brought some of their furniture from the old house and filled the living room, but the furniture looked dwarfed by the high ceilings and long room; the furnishings gave out before the room did. There was a fire going in the cavernous living room's fireplace. The house was chill, colder — if possible — than outdoors. Had Jerene and Duke fallen so far that they were struggling to heat this house?

And then there was Jerene coming forward to give her brother a hug. Dorrie heard her say, "Oh Gaston. You reek of bourbon. I'd hoped you'd given it a rest."

"I did give it a rest, Jerry. That's why you dry out, so you can soak up again, or didn't you know that about these so-called rest clinics."

"How was Paris?"

"Same old tourist trap it ever was, but with more Ay-rabs and Africans than Frenchmen these days." He turned to Dorrie, falteringly, and said, "No offense."

And then there was Duke Johnston, emerging from the shadows. Well, the smile was intact. Dorrie first went over to hug him; he was a skeleton under his cardigan and cotton shirt. He leaned on an old-fashioned walking stick with a glass knob.

"Dorrie, you look wonnerful," he said, not entirely able to rise to the harder consonants. "Gaston, old boy! D'you recognize this?" He meant the walking stick.

Gaston smiled. "A relic from our Arcadian evenings." He hugged his old friend, briefly.

"Nice to see you up and around. Recovered."

"I wun't say recovuhed."

Gaston held the Dunlap's Hundred aloft. "Perhaps you'll permit me to put this in the liquor cabinet where it belongs, since I know my sister has likely poured out all my fine collection, down some drainhole of temperance."

"There wasn't a bottle extant when I arrived," Jerene said, arms crossed. "You left no drop behind, I assure you."

Gaston left for the kitchen, leaving the others in the foyer. The three of them were quiet. What was there to say, with a drunken

Gaston Jarvis back in their lives for the first time in years? Jerene glanced knowingly at Duke and then sweetly at Dorrie. Dorrie began an explanation about his taxi ride to the ABC store, and Jerene waved it aside. "Of course, if he's determined to drink there is nothing to be done about it. Duke, I can't see how we can stay here if he is going back to his old ways."

"Certainly not, dear."

Dorrie saw Jerene's worry for her husband, and a weariness — to move again, to be like a vagabond, a charity case at her age. Dorrie looked away briefly, not wanting to see something private between them, but when she raised her head, Jerene Johnston was all serenity and extending her hand to gently take Dorrie by the arm. "Let's go into the kitchen, make some coffee, and let the boys catch up."

Gaston returned with a glass of bourbon with ice cubes in his hand. So much for retiring the bottle to the cabinet. "Hate to lose you, ladies, but Duke and I are going to get something straight. The big question is whether you both know it and have been faking it all these years, or whether it's something you really don't know."

Jerene's stare was a study of regal indifference. Dorrie would deplete her life savings never to have that aimed at her. "Gaston, I hear in your tone, you wish to argue about something and may I request that whatever it is be put off until tomorrow morning?"

"You don't want to hear my news? My revelation? Or *will* it be a revelation? Heh-heh."

"Oh, out with it. Get it over with."

Gaston took a fortifying sip. "I always thought it strange. Some of the Johnstons down east. I used to see them when they came to my readings, down at the Manteo Booksellers, I'd get a big crowd down there. And I'd see, what's her name, Mary Johnston? Maggie Johnston? Anyway, I'd always joke we were somehow connected, thanks to your marriage with Duke, but they never seemed to claim Duke. Very polite about it, considering. They never seemed to agree that he was really one of *their* Johnstons." He laughed to himself, looking into his glass, swirling the ice around. "So I did a little homework. Wrote a few letters and sure enough. This Joseph E. Johnston brother who went off to Tennessee in the mid-1800s . . . he has nothing to do with Duke's great-grandfather."

"Don't be ridiculous," said Jerene.

Dorrie noticed Duke wasn't saying anything.

"My theory is that Duke's great-grandfather moved to Charlotte and, with no internet or public records or library to refute him, he claimed to be related to General Joseph E.

Johnston since he had the same name, Joseph. Maybe even came to believe it over time. The grandfather went along with it, and Duke's own father, that ol' son of a bitch, Major Bo . . ." He nearly swayed enough to fall forward saying the word "Bo" with such relish. ". . . he really ran with it, made a whole military career out of the legacy. I wonder if he ever did his own research and found out it was a lie. That he wasn't Joseph E.'s hundredth cousin, and lived in fear that someone would expose him. Maybe that's why he'd get tight and flail away on his boys like he did."

Still Duke wasn't saying anything.

"Are you done with your theory?" Jerene said crisply.

"It's not a theory, sis. I got it here." He staggered to his lighter bag and opened the zipper on the side. He brought out some papers of different lengths and sizes, bound by a clip. "Here's your genealogy, for you. Read it and weep, oooold boy, oooold sport, heh-heh . . . You gotta feel for the real Johnston family. Every trailer-trash teeth-missing clodhopper named Johnston from every red-clay fork in the road claims descent from the general. They must tire of all you pretenders."

"What pains you take with your malice, brother."

"Oh it was no trouble at all!" Then Gaston got giddy with the next bit, almost unable to bring it out fast enough. "And it was so fucking obvious! I mean, right in front of all of our faces: Joseph *Beauregard* Johnston, Reverend *Bo* Johnston, Major *Bo . . .*" No one understood what he meant. "Who was General Joseph E.'s archnemesis, after Jefferson Davis, of course? Huh? You know the answer, Duke."

Duke took a deep breath and with effort brought out, "General Beauregard, I suppose you mean."

"The man who took Joseph E.'s credit for Bull Run, the man who was part of the wave of promotions that, in effect, demoted Johnston, did an end run around him."

Duke smiled, somehow. "I do not believe they were bitter enemies."

"But no one in the family, the *real* Johnston family, would have named a child for P.G.T. Beauregard!"

Jerene was tense. "What could any of this possibly matter to you?"

"I've come back from Switzerland and Paris a new man, Jerry. Devoted to honesty and transparency. Our families are a ragtag bunch held together by the glue of secrets, and I hate secrets now. Our family's secrets, Jerene — a mountain of them. And Duke's family's fraudulence. We've been tyrannized by these secrets."

Dorrie knew to keep out of it, but she flashed in her mind on Mr. Jarvis's recourse to prostitutes. He had some nerve.

"Better," Gaston continued, "that *I* found out than had you run for governor and some reporter found out. Not that you had it in you to run for governor. That dream was right up there with my winning the National Book Award for *Lookaway, Dixieland.*"

"The resort development that so offended you, Gaston," Jerene informed him, "never was built. Bob Boatwright and those men you thrust upon us are under indictment. The title reverts to you. When shall we expect the publishing date?"

"I think we both know my writing days are through. But we're off topic! Just tell me, satisfy my curiosity. Did you know you weren't related to Joseph E. or is this news to you? Oops, out of libation!"

Gaston returned to the kitchen for a refill.

"If you want me to go," Dorrie offered.

Jerene: "Absolutely not. I still want to talk to you." Then she stood by her husband, whose stamina was nearing its end, his eyes sunken and lost. "Don't give him the satisfaction of confirming this. I couldn't care less, but I'll be damned if —"

Gaston, refueled, was back. "Be damned if you what? I'm just here a final time to learn the truth from Duke. If he's been lying to all of us all these years. If when I sat there looking up at him worshipfully at university, like a little first-form British public school faggot at Eton, did he know he was running a scam on the state of North Carolina?"

Still Joseph Johnston didn't say anything.

"In other news that may interest you both, I've signed over this house to you. Pretended I sold it to you for one dollar. You'll get the papers soon — my lawyers did all the scut-work. The property taxes are your own affair, but you need a mansion and I don't." He sloshed another measure of bourbon into his glass of ice. "I don't want to be in this house or this ugly, pre-fab town anymore. I'm going back to Paris and play out what's left of my liver." He toasted everyone, one, two, three, then sipped lightly his brimming glass. "I've been assured that belabored organ doesn't have a year to go. So you stay here and play at being an old venerable family, in that old venerable Society in the old venerable South that doesn't exist anymore except in your mind, Jerene. You play with your Civil War toys, Duke, and she can go on presiding over her little collection of mediocre boring landscape art from two-bit American nobodies, until the trumpet blows up yonder —"

Jerene slapped his glass of whiskey out of his hand; the tumbler and its contents smashed against the wall.

"Oh hoo hoo," Gaston laughed, revived. "We're gonna act like that, are we? So what's the truth, old friend?" He braced himself against the table in the foyer, nearly knocking the oval mirror off its hook.

Duke took another deep breath. "There may be some'sing to wha' you say. I've had my suspicions, also. But I never wished to look too closely." Another deep breath. "I'm sorry it's important to you to take . . . take dis from me."

Dorrie couldn't look at Mr. Johnston's eyes. She was suddenly completely full of love and pity for him. Dorrie wondered if even Gaston saw the pathos within his triumph, the dwindling, ill man he had come to diminish further.

For another minute all was silent, then Duke spoke:

"I should have helped you, Gaston. You were right."

Gaston stared at his friend, unsure what he meant.

"*Lookaway, Dixieland.*" Duke took a small step so he might lean against Jerene who, with the slightest hand on his arm, steadied him. "It was my mission to see you through your book . . ." Duke Johnston struggled for breath and clarity. ". . . only you coul' have written it but it was always a project we both ha' a part of."

Dorrie saw a change come over Gaston, a weakening.

Duke added, "And I failed to report for duty."

Gaston and his old friend looked into each

other's eyes for a second, but it moved them both too much to continue. "There was dereliction," Gaston began, barely audible. Then he found his voice too, and it seemed astonished, as if he had only realized where he was and whom he was talking to. ". . . enough dereliction on my part to sink us both, old friend. To sink us all."

Jerene, quietly, knelt down to pick up the two pieces of broken glass and dropped them with a clang into the small foyer trash bin.

Gaston briefly turned to the oval mirror, then turned away. "My house. I'm . . . It's yours. Did I tell you? The paperwork's in the mail. You better get your tax guy on it. I'll get Norma . . . no, I mean, the lawyer . . ." And his mind wandered off again. "I never really moved in, did I? Never liked this big old place, never really felt like home. The Nineteenth Hole and Arcadia — the only places I felt at home, and neither of them *were* my home." He ran a finger along the foyer marble tabletop. "Oh well, this is the last time I'll see this place. And I suspect the last time we'll see each other, Duke."

"Having been stripped of my family his'ory, I'm not sure there is so much left to say."

Gaston now looked almost panicked. Dorrie wondered if he'd beg for a civil parting. "I think we're entitled to one last good conversation. A few last points of honor. Destiny, as

I think you will see, is not quite done with us yet."

Duke looked at his wife and nodded faintly; she turned his arm over to Gaston's care (his left side, his bad side) and Gaston escorted him to the long living room, sparsely filled with Duke and Jerene's refugee furniture from the old Johnston house. "I'll get us both a glass."

"Joseph," Jerene said calmly, "do not drink more than a wee dram. Your medicines will be interfered with."

"Of course, swee'heart."

After Gaston tore through the kitchen and retrieved two glasses of ice for the last splash of bourbon, Dorrie sat at the kitchen table and Jerene began to make coffee in the coffeemaker.

"Sorry you had to be part of such a gothic drama. We're becoming something out of Tennessee Williams around here."

Dorrie smiled. "I apologize for saying it to your face — I was raised better. But I've always thought he was a . . ." The serene countenance of her hostess made Dorrie soften her judgment further. ". . . very badly behaved, your brother."

"He's what our father made him, sad to say. Dillard and I rose above it, just barely." She made a noise close to a laugh. "He's been dead, Daddy, thirty years. Yet he perpetuates himself, in all of us, in his way."

Jerene was briefly distracted making the coffee. Then she went to look in on the boys sitting by the fire with the lights off. In the interim Dorrie looked around the kitchen. Perhaps Duke and Jerene would sell the place, become flush again, find something other than this big gloomy house of outsized rooms and shadows to live in. Dorrie wanted her back in action, back in the art acquisition game. Dorrie could be a help to Mrs. Johnston now; she relished the idea of working with Mrs. J. (Wow, it was really hard to convert to "Jerene.") What could Jerene want to talk to Dorrie about? The Trust. She suspected Jerene was going to ask her to join the Jarvis Trust for American Art. With Kate gone, and her sister Dillard passed on, there was an opening, after all.

"Okay," Jerene said, bringing two mugs of coffee, setting them before Dorrie and herself, taking a seat across from her. "The boys are back to playing nice, it seems. Perhaps the world won't end if Duke has a drink. It is a night for it, I think. Now, at long last, Dorrie." A thought flashed across her face, a small smile. "You know, I've never known, what is Dorrie short for?"

Dorcas was a little flirty. "Ah now, I try not to let that secret out."

"You heard my brother. We're all past secrets now."

"Dorcas, from the Bible. You can imagine

how much I dreaded roll call in school with that name sitting there: Dorcas the Dork." She laughed. "And I was a perfect little bookworm teacher's-pet nerd girl, too. My middle name is Jehosopha, so there was no place to run with that, either."

Mrs. Johnston's eyes were distant. "If you went by your middle name and had joined this family, you would have been Jehosopha Jourdain Johnston, wouldn't you have been? J-J-J. Isn't that something?"

Dorrie smiled pleasantly, not quite seeing the wonder of it.

Jerene pursued it. "Would you ever consider marrying my son?"

Dorrie must have appeared dumbstruck, so Jerene continued, meeting her gaze with level sincerity.

"I am thinking of an economic union, a tactical union, in the ways of earlier centuries. I know you both for the moment are homosexual, perhaps waiting to marry someone of your own gender under the law in North Carolina, which I don't think is very likely for some time. But there would be many advantages to such a marriage. Stability, money, which if Gaston is telling the truth for once, we may be seeing again soon."

"I don't think . . ."

"No, of course you don't. This is something you'll have to think about for some amount of time. But this is an option for you. You see, I would be honored if, once I'm in the cemetery, the Jarvis Trust for American Art passes on to you as chief trustee. You see, if you married Josh, you'd be family. Perhaps the line would end there. No one seems to be having any children; maybe it's time the Jarvises crawled to their collective graves." Another laugh. "You'll note my sordid old mother hangs on and on — she is the one who will outlive us all. But all I can ask is that you think about it. Josh would gain the most from it. I fear he's a bit adrift, following in his father's footsteps where career and ambition are concerned —"

There was an explosive sound — a loud *pop.*

They stared at each other.

Then they realized what they'd heard simultaneously.

Jerene sprang from the chair. "Not again!"

Dorrie came running after.

They rounded the corner of the living room: both men clutching the dueling pistols, both men lying on the carpet, the smell of burnt powder in the air.

Gaston was feeling himself. "Did you hit me? Good God, Duke, I don't think you fired — I'm not hit!"

Jerene ran to her husband on the far side of the room.

"Sorry, darling. It'll be quicker for both of us this way."

"What . . . what — Joseph Johnston? Are you shot? *A duel? A duel* in 2012? Are you both *insane* — well, yes, you are both insane!" Jerene looked with incredulity straight up at the ceiling. "That goes without saying! You could have been killed."

Dorrie screamed out, "Jerene!" She pointed down to Duke's side, redirecting Jerene's gaze: a pool of blood was soaking into the rug, under his waist. Jerene knelt and pulled up the cardigan. He was hit above his hip.

Jerene said faintly, "Call 911."

Gaston drunkenly from his position on the floor demanded, "Duke, take another shot . . . I don't think you hit me."

Dorrie fumbled with her cell phone, dropping it — it had become a piece of soap. She chased after it. She dialed 911. "Hello, we've had an accident here, with guns . . . Jerene, what's the address?"

Jerene bent farther down and surrounded her husband's face with both hands, pressing her own face into his, not so much a kiss as a futile gesture of closeness to breathe the same air, to live the same moment.

"Duke, old boy, you didn't hit me," uttered Gaston.

So Duke with his good arm raised the pistol as if he might take another shot.

But Jerene snatched it from him, hopping up. "For the love of God! How long is this Civil War nonsense . . ." She marched over to the fireplace. ". . . going to haunt this benighted family?" She threw the $11,500 antique 1854 French dueling pistol into the fireplace.

Gaston: "No, Jerry, I don't think it . . ."

And then the unfired gun still full of powder, roasting for a moment in the fireplace grill, exploded. This sent its chamber, its fractured handle, a spray of metal and a .22 caliber ball whizzing across the room. Dorrie ducked instinctively. The base of a lamp, struck with some piece of it, disintegrated. Dorrie, now from floor level, saw the ball roll across the room, having bounced off the far wall. It rolled past her to the heating vent and disappeared.

"Mrs. J.? The address here?"

Jerene was standing perfectly still.

"Jerene, what's . . . ." Dorrie looked up: Jerene pulled back her silk jacket to reveal her blouse. Upon her shoulder there was a small black tear . . . and Jerene's fingers came back from their exploration red.

"You've been hit," said Dorrie.

"This is a three-hundred-dollar blouse. Just bought it at Nordstrom, of all the . . ." Jerene nearly tripped making her way beside her husband to the nearby armchair, which she fell into. Duke groaned and she reached down to take his hand and hold it in her own. "It will be all right, Duke. Just stay still."

"Did Dorrie say you'd been hit?"

"Sssh, stay calm. Let me think."
"My only love."
"Sssh, now."
Gaston blurted out his Wendover Road address. Dorrie told the dispatch they would need a second ambulance, and as Gaston moaned away, unable to raise himself, saying his arm was broken, maybe they should send a third. And when the red flashing lights arrived, casting their patterns on the ceiling, Dorrie realized she had not stopped staring at Jerene.

Her face registered no pain, but in her eyes . . . Before this night was out, Mrs. Johnston would likely be a widow. Soon enough she would be at her brother's funeral, too. And this improbable gunplay would make for a risible scandal with ten times the publicity of what her daughter occasioned. So perhaps the art would have to be auctioned, and the Trust disbanded, and this house sold too, and maybe this was the long-feared ruin, the long-deferred sundering of family destiny, of legacy and repute, the work of years, the vainglorious work of years, slipping blithely from her tenuous purchase. Was that what was in her eyes? Defeat? At the very last — defeat?

Jerene Jarvis Johnston then looked at Dorrie squarely, her squint, her usual steel serenity returned, with just a touch of annoyance. Having seen all she cared to see of oblivion, she turned a resolute face to the difficult pathway ahead.

"My land," she said.

ACKNOWLEDGMENTS

To answer the reader's most burning question: yes — yes! — Colonel P. S. Cocke DID defend Balls Ford, in July of 1861. Valiantly defending Balls, Cocke was spent and soon withdrew from military life, unable to engage again.

There are a great many more books than I include here to which I am indebted, but most indispensable were *The Civil War in North Carolina* by John Gilchrist Barrett, *Joseph E. Johnston: A Civil War Biography* by Craig L. Symonds, *Storm in the Mountains: Thomas' Confederate Legion of Cherokee Indians and Mountaineers* by Vernon H. Crow, *When Whites Riot* by Sheila Smith McKoy, *The Free People of Color of New Orleans* by Mary Gehman, Thomas W. Hanchett's incomparable *Sorting Out the New South City,* and *The Destructive War: William Tecumseh Sherman, Stonewall Jackson, and the Americans* by the always splendid Charles Royster.

There are also too many friends and fellow

writers to list who fed, clothed, housed, laundered, and generally sustained me along the way, but for all administrative mercies shown by my department head Antony Harrison, for the collegiality and beneficial conspiracies of my MFA brothers- and sisters-in-arms — John Balaban, John Kessel, Dorianne Laux, and Jill McCorkle — at North Carolina State University, an immense and loving thanks. If you're going to the debutante ball, one could have no finer escort than Nora Shepard; Susan Langford earns thanks for a magnificent copyedit. I further celebrate my damn good fortune to have come to George Witte's attention, first at Picador then at St. Martin's Press, and I feel like thanking myself for my inspired inertia, staying happily put with my extraordinary literary agent, Henry Dunow, for twenty-four years and counting.

The employees of Thorndike Press hope you have enjoyed this Large Print book. All our Thorndike, Wheeler, and Kennebec Large Print titles are designed for easy reading, and all our books are made to last. Other Thorndike Press Large Print books are available at your library, through selected bookstores, or directly from us.

For information about titles, please call:

(800) 223-1244

or visit our Web site at:

http://gale.cengage.com/thorndike

To share your comments, please write:

Publisher
Thorndike Press
10 Water St., Suite 310
Waterville, ME 04901